WHERE DREAM FADES TO NIGHTMARE

Denise
Thank you for your
Constant support and friendship!

Adam Feindt

ISBN-13: 9798533513173

Cover design by: Ryan Bunting
Editing by: Sonia Fincke and Chad Meadows

To Leo,
Never be afraid to pursue your dreams, no matter how long it takes or how hard it might be.

To Sonia,
Thank you for your unwavering support in making this dream of mine a reality.

Chapter 1

A First Look at "Real Action"

Nothing quite screams "your shift's not over yet" like the giant, black mass of a creature I saw flying right at us from our window on the seventy-seventh floor. I was like a deer in the headlights, completely frozen in fear, unable to do anything but stare. It was hands down the most menacing thing I had seen in my life up until that point.

I couldn't believe its size. It was getting larger by the second as it continued to rocket towards us. How could it still look so big from here? It was on the outskirts of the city. Maybe it was some kind of optical illusion with the window, or maybe my eyes were just strained and tired from a long day. I rubbed them, desperately hoping when I opened them again, I'd see an empty skyline.

Nope. It was still there. The window was the entire length and height of the wall with no curvature to it. This thing wasn't being magnified. It wasn't some kind of trick or delusion. This thing was real and we had a handful of minutes at best before it bulldozed us into oblivion. My stomach started to nauseously churn.

This monster was a runaway train and we were a car stuck on the tracks. Its features were starting to become too visibly clear for comfort. Ibex-like horns protruded from its head. Its body was as dark and menacing as a black hole and made of nothing but muscle. Each of the claws on its hands and feet gleamed in the setting sunlight and nearly matched the length of its finger or toe counterpart. Its wings looked like a bat's and somehow managed to keep it flying like a bullet with just a few powerful flaps. The dragon-like creature let out a high-pitched, gritty shriek that we could easily hear through the four-inch thick, Artificer-made glass of the window. We could barely hear airplanes through that glass.

"Come on kid, let's go! We need ALR50s for those two now!"

Trevor, our squad leader and Duelist, yelled out to me with a stern look on his tanned, weathered face.

Duelists were a hybrid of what used to be law enforcement, soldiers, martial artists, and military minds. They studied law, combat methods, and military strategies. They could also materialize weaponry out of thin air. I had some Duelist training and abilities, but couldn't hold a candle to Trevor. I usually got too anxious or overwhelmed to use anything I knew.

I couldn't keep my eyes off the dragon. It was getting more massive and terrifying with each second. I imagined it crashing through the building and tossing my lifeless body like an old rag doll down the seventy-seven stories to the street below.

I shook off that thought. ALR50. Which one was that? I couldn't focus. My eyes kept looking back to that damn window. It kept getting closer, kept getting larger, kept getting louder. Thoughts of how we were going to die were bombarding me. When I did manage to rein my mind in all I could think of was handguns. The ALR50 wasn't a handgun though. Damn it! A handgun probably wouldn't even put a dent in that thing. I knew I had conjured an ALR50 before, but it was only a handful of times while at the academy. I squeezed my eyes shut as tightly as I could, hoping by some miracle I could block out what was going on around me and remember. ALR50. Automatic long-range rifle, 50 caliber. I let out a quick sigh of relief.

I took a glance around the room before materializing the guns for my other squadmates: Erica and Paxton. Paxton, our squad's Savior, had just finished tossing the chairs and flipping the coffee table aside to give us more room to materialize. Erica, our squad's Artificer, was finishing up conjuring jetpacks and headsets for the four of us. The jetpacks were about the size of a regular backpack with two thrusters and hand controls. They were kind of hand controls that extended out making it look like the user was constantly in position to do a set of squats. The headsets were basic, adjustable headphones with a small microphone sticking out from the right ear positioning itself in the corner of the mouth. The headphone on that same ear also had a dial to control the channel.

Paxton started pacing the room. With his eyebrows raised, eyes wide open, and an excited grin on his face he stared out the window. He had been badgering Trevor all week about wanting to see some "real action." Well, this was his chance. This was his, and our, first look at some "real action" since our squad had officially formed two weeks ago at the Academy for Conjierum Studies and Applications's Support Squad Draft.

"Graham Garnett, if your ass knows what's good for it, you'll get those two ALR50s now! There's no way in hell I'm lettin' that black bullet go all kamikaze on us!" Trevor yelled. A first and last name—he wasn't happy with me.

The ALR50s. My memory of them was starting to come back. I remembered one of my Duelist professors telling me that the ALR50 was "one of those guns you hope you never had to use," or something like that. I remembered its sheer power, tearing through almost anything we shot at on the practice range. It wasn't the standard rifle we had been trained to use. This thing was meant to do serious damage, meant to kill.

I focused on what I wanted, letting the conjierum inside me do the rest. Instantly an ALR50 materialized in each of my hands. Once I made sure the safety was on, I tossed one to Erica and the second to Paxton. The other three had their jetpacks and headsets on by now. My shaky hands struggled to strap mine on and adjust the headset to fit me.

"Channel seven," Erica called out. Her eyes were locked onto the dragon.

I didn't want to look out again, but some sick sense of curiosity made me. My heart skipped a beat. It was already halfway across the city now. It was even bigger than I imagined. This dragon wouldn't just take out our floor if it hit us, it'd take another five or more with it at least.

"Let's make this quick. I have plans tonight," Paxton remarked. I couldn't believe how calm and cocky he was, or at least how he was trying to fake it at a time like this. I was worried about waking up tomorrow and Paxton was worried about making a dinner reservation or something.

"Do you ever shut the hell up?" Trevor turned and scolded him. "Your skinny ass might not make it too tonight if we're not quick and careful."

My nausea started to intensify. A pit grew in my stomach. I could still feel my hands shaking a bit. My foot started tapping out of nowhere. Bile slowly creeped up my throat, but I immediately swallowed it back down. This was actually happening. We were really going to fight this brick house of a dragon. We just came up to the squad room to grab our things and go home. Our shift was over. Did we really have to do this?

"Alright, plan is we draw this thing out to the ocean. Last thing we need is it dyin' on us here and takin' out a whole block."

A whole block. A *whole city block*. The pit in my stomach grew even more.

"Here's how we're doin' it. Once I shoot out the window Graham and I'll fly in tight. Take a few shots at it. Get it all nice and riled up. You two keep your distance and take a few shots with those ALR50s. Wear it down, no kill shots. You all hear me? And keep ahold of those guns too. They got a bit of kick to them."

That pit in my stomach now felt like an abyss.

"Let me fly in with you!" Paxton exclaimed.

"I don't mind switching with him, Trevor, really," I said hoping he didn't hear my voice crack.

He looked at us like we were out of our minds. "Why the hell would I do that?" Trevor said in his agitated voice, which wasn't that much different from his regular voice. "How the hell does that make any sense? Really, think about that for a second. The both of you." Trevor was now looking at me as he spoke. "He's eight feet tall, a

Savior, and has basic combat training at best. *You. You've* got Duelist training and you're the Factotum. The jack of all trades. The secondary fighting force behind me in this squad. You forgotten your role here, kid? Why the hell would I let *him* trade tactical positions with *you*?"

He was right. It was stupid of me to even suggest, but I was scared out of my mind and Paxton was itching for this fight. The dragon let out another ear-piercing shriek. The glass did next to nothing to even muffle it now and the vibrations from the soundwaves shook the entire building slightly.

"Holy shit," I heard Paxton mumble under his breath.

"Now, if we're done talkin' stupid let's get to work. We don't have a lot of time; he's closin' in fast."

Trevor materialized two identical handguns that I had never seen before. He tossed them both to me. I was so anxious, and now embarrassed, that I nearly dropped them both. They looked like typical Uzis, but I knew they weren't. The guns had a bright silver metallic shine, and each had an extended magazine which made them much heavier than I expected.

Trevor noticed that I had no clue what I was holding. "The academy won't teach you how to conjure up anything like those. Really hold on to them. They've got even more kick than those ALRs."

"What are they?" I asked while he materialized a pair of the silver guns for himself.

"Custom creation of my own," Trevor said, while turning around to face the wall of glass. "They don't look like much, but they'll get the job done. All of you take a step back."

He took a shot at the window. The kickback from the gun almost flung his arm over his head; it looked like he wasn't quite ready for it himself. His "custom creation" was as strong as advertised. The slug struggled to break through the thick glass.

"Son of a bitch," he grumbled as he fired another round, which only gave the window a few cracks.

"You gotta be fu—" Trevor muttered under his breath before

unloading six more rounds into the glass.

I watched his shooting hand. The guns were fully automatic. Good to know.

Eight bullet holes later the glass finally shattered completely and rained down to the streets below. Shooting out the window wasn't our best option, especially for anyone using the sidewalk. It was our only option though if we wanted to stop this meteor of a dragon before he could potentially collide with DREAM Tower.

Trevor ignited his jetpack which prompted the rest of us to do the same. His voice came in through the headset, "Alright kids, remember the plan. No kill shots, just piss him off. Paxton, I better not see your skinny ass anywhere near that thing. You hear me?"

"I hear you, Trevor. I hear you."

Trevor was the first to fly out of our room. Both Paxton and Erica got a running start and leapt out into the open sky as effortlessly as birds. I, on the other hand, had a hard time getting my feet off the ground.

I was absolutely terrified of heights. I crept to the edge and stupidly looked down. My stomach felt like it dropped all the way to my shoes. I started feeling dizzy. My body was jittery and the slightest breezes began to feel like a F5 tornado. Looking down, dumbest thing I could have done.

The people below were nothing but moving specks from up here. The shorter, surrounding buildings looked like spikes ready to impale me. I had no clue how I was going to leave the ledge. It felt like I had two options: fall and die or take on the dragon and die.

"Everything okay with your pack, Graham?" I heard Erica ask over the headset, snapping me out of my death scenarios. She knew I was afraid of heights and knew how much I hated the window for reminding me how high our squad room was in DREAM Tower.

"Uh, yeah. Just need to adjust my straps real quick. I'm right behind you."

Trevor wasn't one to tolerate what he believed to be "trivial fears." He made that clear on one of our squad's first patrols together when Erica saw a clown on the street corner and nearly jumped out of her seat on her patrol bike. He gave her a hard time about it, and not in a joking way either. If he knew I was lagging behind because I was afraid of heights, who knows what he would do to me.

I took a deep breath, shut my eyes, flipped on the switches to ignite the jetpack, and took off. Once I was in the air, I opened my eyes and kept them fixed on my squadmates in front of me. It was the only way I could keep myself somewhat calm given the circumstances.

"Where the hell are you, Garnett?" Trevor nearly yelled. Calling me by my last name only; now I knew he was really pissed.

I picked up speed trying to catch up to him. Within a matter of seconds, he and I were flying side by side with Paxton and Erica not too far behind us. The dragon spotted us and we were now its center of its attention. Even with our squad being a few hundred feet away from it, all of its hellish features were on full display.

The dragon had to be close to 90 feet tall. Its black body was covered with rugged scales that were about the size of a trash can lid. Its horns were about a third of the length of its body. Each claw was about as long as Paxton, and easily weighed over one hundred pounds. I noticed its eyes were a neon green, which really stood out against all the black of its gigantic body.

It sprawled out its massive bat-like wings, snarled its jagged teeth, and flexed its muscular arms, while letting out a deep, deafening growl in an attempt to intimidate us. The vibrations shook through my body. I stopped dead in my tracks. Its fear tactic worked on me but didn't stop Trevor for a second.

He showed no signs of backing down as he flew full speed towards the girthy gut of the dragon and opened fire. The dragon's claws swatted at Trevor, but he was able to dodge each attack. He made it look effortless, like a boxer ducking and weaving past punches. Erica and Paxton kept their distance and began to open fire too. I found myself hovering in place totally mesmerized by what was going on around me. It was unreal.

"You weren't joking about the kickback on these things," I heard Paxton say over the headset.

"No kidding. I almost dropped mine after the first shot. I wasn't ready for it," Erica chimed in.

"Nobody asked for your two cents on the gun. Stop chattin' and keep shootin'," Trevor reprimanded. "And Garnett, I swear, if I don't see bullets flyin' out of those barrels in a matter of seconds I'll feed your ass to this thing, understood?"

I felt bad for Paxton and Erica. They were used to the lightweight handguns we used on our patrols. How did Trevor expect a Savior and Artificer to react to using such high-powered guns for the first time? They hadn't trained with heavier-duty weapons like we had. So he didn't like their chatter, but at least they weren't floating around idly like me.

Trevor continued to fly around the dragon like a fly around a piece of fruit, taking strategic shots when he could. Using him as a diversion, I flew in behind the dragon's neck and took my first shot. Between the kickback from my gun, which I should have seen coming, and the startling I got from the dragon's soprano-like shriek of pain, I nearly dropped the silver Uzi to the streets.

I was shocked by the size of the wound the round left in its scales. It had to be at least four times the diameter of my gun's barrel. I had no clue how that could be, but decided to just chalk it up to Trevor's Duelist expertise.

Dark red blood began to flow from its neck down its back. I must have struck a nerve, maybe both literally and figuratively, because the dragon instantly began to rotate its body to take a swing at me. My adrenaline kicked in. I only had a split second to plan an escape. I flipped the switch on my jetpack, shutting it off, putting me in freefall. Gravity yanked me down and my eyes grew wider as the buildings and streets below charged towards me. I got lucky though. The dragon's massive claws just missed me. The wind from its swipe whipped my hair to one side.

As soon as I could, I flipped the switch, and my jetpack reignited. I flew out of harm's way and took a moment to recompose myself. My stomach needed to settle. My body desperately wanted to vomit from the fear and the fall, but I kept it down.

My mind raced through everything that just had and could have happened. I could have *died*. I was an inch or two from it at best. An inch or two from decapitation. It shook me up pretty bad.

"Graham! Are you okay?" Erica asked, a bit panicked.

My mind was still racing and scrambling. I heard her, but didn't really register what she was saying right away. "Yeah. Yeah. I'm fine." I didn't know what else to say.

"What the hell are you doing, Garnett?" Trevor screamed over the headset. "Takin' a shot at that thing's neck. Were you not listenin' when I said no kill shots? I tell you what, son, you're lucky you didn't hit anything vital or you would've had more than just the blood of *that thing* on your hands."

Trevor was right. What was I thinking shooting at its neck? I wasn't, I guess. I saw what looked like the safest shot for me to take and took it. I was too afraid of Trevor in the moment to think of anything else to say. The magnitude of what I had done then hit me. How many innocent people below could I have killed if the dragon fell out of the sky? I felt even more unsettled just thinking about it.

I was hovering at the dragon's eye level, close enough to get a good shot in, but far enough to be out of its reach. Erica and Paxton kept lodging bullets into it, remembering the plan: no kill shots. The dragon winced and let out a small, shrill shriek with each shot that hit, but its eyes, its neon green eyes, were now locked onto me.

Suddenly, it flapped its wings like it was ready to charge at me. It knew I shot it in the neck, and it was beyond pissed. It snarled like a vicious junkyard dog, showing off its impressive set of teeth. My hands were shaking like crazy. I held up the guns but couldn't keep them steady. I tried to fire a few rounds and hit next to nothing. The best I managed was to hit a tooth but the bullet ricocheted down to the world below.

"You two take a few shots at those wings!" Trevor's voice sounded over the headset. "If it goes for Graham I don't want it gettin' a full head of steam. I'll fly around back and try to get its attention on me. Then let's pull this son of a bitch out to sea and finish this!"

Paxton and Erica did as they were told, taking shots strategically and sparingly. Trevor was soon out of our sight, but not the dragon's. The beast's eyes were still fixed onto me, but it knew exactly where he was.

SMACK!

The whack from the dragon's tail made Trevor a middle-aged meteorite plummeting to the ground.

"SHIT!" Paxton blurted out, then immediately darted after his falling body. I heard Erica let out a horrified gasp. I was stunned and speechless. This whole situation felt like a cruel nightmare. Trevor was surely dead and the rest of us couldn't be too far behind him.

Erica quickly flew to my side. She gave me a look and gesture that told me to take in a deep breath. Before I had that chance, the dragon finally made its move for me. Erica, being quicker on her feet than me, managed to get out of harm's way. I had to pull off another life-saving miracle.

Its claws came lunging at me. I managed to dodge the first set using the same kill-the-jetpack tactic as before. I got lucky, for the second time that day. I then saw the second set coming for me and frantically flipped the switch back on while simultaneously pushing the throttle as hard as I could. I pushed so hard I was surprised it didn't break off. I just out flew the claws which nearly caught the jetpack, barely winning the race for my life. My heart pumped harder than ever before.

Erica unloaded a few more rounds into its shoulder, trying to grab its attention. "Now, Graham!" We both turned and started pushing our jetpacks as hard as we could for the ocean.

The dragon was livid. It roared in both anger and agony. Erica twisted her body every now and then to fire a round to provoke it more. I wasn't doing that. My eyes were locked onto the horizon and I wasn't even entertaining the thought of turning around until we were well out at sea.

Then, out of nowhere, I heard the most ungodly noise. It was an ugly, high-pitched, furious wail, like the cry a little kid makes when in pain, upset, and angry all at the same time.

I turned my head and looked back at the dragon. It was doing all it could to keep up with us, but was really struggling. Erica and Paxton had really done a number on it; holes riddled the membrane of its wings. Blood was raining down to the city below from the punishment it had taken all over its body. I then noticed that its left eye wasn't neon green anymore; in fact, it wasn't much of anything anymore, except another slow waterfall of dark red.

"Did you shoot it in the *eye*?" I asked her in astonishment.

"Yes," she said casually, "and it wasn't too thrilled about it."

I let out a brief laugh and so did she. I had a ton of respect for Erica. She always seemed calm, cool, and collected no matter what the situation was. She reminded me a lot of my older sister, and in a way, Erica was sort of becoming one to me.

"Hey," Paxton's voice emerged, "I somehow managed to grab a hold of Trevor before he could crash into anything. The wind's been knocked out of him, but everything else looks fine for now. Bring that thing down you two!"

Erica stopped once she felt as if we were far enough out that its body would easily sink to the ocean floor. I followed her lead. We raised our weapons as the dying monster continued with what little it had left to pursue us.

"Alright, Graham, now—"

Before she could finish her statement, the dragon began taking a huge beating from behind. We heard the whistling of what sounded like missiles followed by the *thud* of whatever actually was hitting its back. Its body jerked forward with every hit it took. Blood started to cascade down its back and into the ocean. Eventually the dragon was too weak to keep itself in the sky and began its divebomb descent. For a few seconds it scratched and clawed at the air like it was trying to climb an invisible ladder back up to the clouds. Its hole-riddled wings gave it all they had to keep it airborne but it was no use. It eventually ran out of steam. The lifeless dragon was in freefall for what seemed like ages.

CRASH!

Its impact with the sea shot water and mist high enough to hit a colony of seagulls flying by. Massive waves began to make a break for the shore line. They effortlessly plowed past the beach's sand and smacked into the concrete barricade of the boardwalk. The water easily surged over the wall and continued to run across the boards towards town taking trash cans, loosely nailed down benches, and a few unlucky people with it into the nearby streets.

All the ocean water in the surrounding area began to turn dark red. The air had a strong scent of salt and iron. The waves started to bring the dragon's blood to the shore, staining most of the beach's sand to a faded maroon color.

"What that hell was that?" a very hoarse sounding Trevor called out.

"Something, or someone, just brought down the dragon," Erica replied.

Erica and I squinted into the setting sun, trying to see who, or what, just brought down the dragon.

Chapter 2

Not Bad for a Kaisiust

"It's kind of hard to see with the sun in our eyes, but it looks like there are five guys on jetpacks coming towards us," Erica reported to Trevor.

"Damn it!" he barked. "I bet that's Randy. Listen here you two, don't say anything until I get there. You hear me?"

Erica and I flew ourselves down to the shore. We both took off the jetpacks and stood in the muddy, pungent-smelling sand, taking a minute to unwind. We dematerialized all of our weapons and equipment and waited for Trevor, Paxton, and the mysterious group of five to join us.

Erica turned to me and asked, "Trevor said he thought it was Randy up there. You think he meant Randy McGregor? Like, Vice President Randy McGregor?"

I was exhausted, barely keeping myself upright, and honestly couldn't have cared less who was up there. I found the energy to answer her. "Maybe. He's also in charge of Militaristic Operations, right? It probably is him then."

"We've had some kind of day, haven't we? First, we fight off that dragon, and now we're about to meet the vice president. We've seen more action in one day than some squads see in a lifetime."

"I think I need a vacation already," I said, staring up into the orangey-blue sky.

Erica showed no signs of slowing down though. If anything, the fight with the dragon hyped her up. I was doing all I could to focus on what she was saying and not let the calm crashing of the waves behind me put me to sleep.

"Where do you think that thing even came from?"

"I don't know. I've never seen anything like that before. Have you?"

"I've seen animals get some weird mutations from conjierum poisoning. They drink it not realizing they shouldn't, and then they grow an extra toe or something, but nothing like *that*. That thing was no mutation. It had to have come from somewhere, and if there's one, I bet there's bound to be more of them."

The thought of there being more of those dragons was beyond horrifying to me. Her point, as dreadful as it made me feel, had some validity to it. If there was one, then there had to be at least two at some point. There was also no way that the dragon was a conjierum mutation. Right? What could have possibly mutated into *that thing* over time?

Paxton and Trevor floated down to the shore ending our conversation, with the group of five right behind them. "What the hell happened here?" he asked looking down at the blood-stained sand and up at the waterlogged boardwalk. "Never mind. Let me do all the talking," he stated before turning to address the men behind him.

Erica's suspicion was right. Standing in front of us was Vice President Randy McGregor joined by the Presidential Support Squad, or the PSS as most people called them. The PSS doubled as both the president and vice president's personal bodyguards as well as a support squad like ours. However, only the best of the best in their conjierum strand made it into the PSS. The two most important people in DREAM couldn't have a pack of scrubs protecting them. The four men were all wearing suits instead of the gray, janitor-esque squad uniforms like us. I guess they didn't plan on seeing any "real action" today.

The vice president took off his sunglasses, revealing his pale blue eyes. They were as light as a husky's. He had a slender build and a seriously unfortunate blonde bowl cut. He was baby-faced with very pale skin. Even though I could tell he was similar in age to Trevor, he looked a lot younger. The vice president smiled seeing Trevor, which put his slightly unaligned teeth on full display.

"Well, this was not what I was expecting. This is *your* squad, isn't it Trevor?" he remarked with a condescending tone.

"Why exactly does that surprise you, Randy?"

Paxton, Erica, and I picked up the vibe quickly. It didn't take long to see why Trevor wanted to do all the talking. The moment became so tense so fast that I had to remind myself to breathe.

"With your rather *questionable* draft selections this year, I figured I wouldn't be seeing, or hearing, much from this squad. I'm a bit shocked *you're* the ones here taking down a threat of this magnitude," he said looking at the three of us up and down. "And at your age, well, you're not exactly in your prime anymore."

"You've got room to talk," Trevor's tone was becoming increasingly annoyed, "From what I could see *your* squad was here supportin' *mine*."

Randy looked me over and continued on like he'd never heard Trevor. "Maybe I misjudged your group though, especially that Factotum of yours. He showed quite some skill up there. Oh, and *she* handled herself alright. Not bad for a Kaisiust."

"Excuse me?" Erica blurted out in disbelief.

"What the hell!" Paxton yelled while being held back by Trevor's arm. He then started yelling something at Randy in Kai: the Kaisiust language. I didn't speak it, and by the looks of it the only other person who did was Erica who quickly tried to calm him down.

How was I getting recognition in all this? I was a mess up there, arguably the worst and least helpful. Erica was the one that put the PSS in position to take that thing down. I thought Paxton was going to try to rip him to shreds. The veins bulged in his neck as he continued to angrily point and scream at Randy over his racist remark. Trevor joined Erica in trying to calm him down. The PSS even showed a slight tinge of concern. Their Duelist's hand twitched a little like he was ready to materialize something to put Paxton in his place, but Trevor and Erica finally got him to cool off a bit.

"*You* oughta know that rankings and race aren't everything,"

Trevor increased his own condescending tone. "Don't be mad 'cause the runners-up have stolen your spotlight again."

I had no clue what Trevor's last sentence meant, but it worked. It really rubbed Randy the wrong way and shut him down before the conversation could get too ugly. Erica still looked annoyed and Paxton couldn't hide his fuming face. As Kaisiusts they were, unfortunately, used to racism. They probably never imagined hearing it from someone like the vice president though. I know I didn't.

"Regardless, since *your* squad helped bring that dragon down, I have a new assignment for the four of you. Effective immediately."

"Our shift is over," Paxton spat at him.

"Your squad is now on a special assignment. Your regular shifts are suspended indefinitely until it's complete. Time is of the essence, and the expectation is that you work until your task is done."

"That's not—" Paxton started but was then cut off by Trevor. "What is it?"

"I want you to investigate the origins of that beast. Where exactly did it come from and how exactly did it come to be? I've been receiving reports from DREAM Tower that it was first sighted in Brexley, around City Hall."

I almost cringed at the word Brexley. It was the poorest and roughest city in DREAM. Brexley had a large Omitted population, people who weren't chosen by a strand of conjierum and subsequently didn't have the ability to materialize things like everyone here on the beach did. Omitteds typically didn't like conjierum users either. They all had their own reasons why: jealousy, fear, bad interactions or experiences, the list goes on. I can't say I'd blame them either. I'd feel some type of way too if a magic-like substance didn't choose me to be able to conjure up things from thin air at will. Needless to say, Brexley was probably the last place any of us wanted to be. It was arguably a close second for me anyway.

"You mean to tell me no one knows where *that thing* came from? That the best you've got is 'somewhere in Brexley around City

Hall?' How does a thing that size just show up out of nowhere in a place like Brexley? What happened? Did it come up from the sewers to pay its taxes over at City Hall, got pissed 'cause they were too high for its liking, and then decided to come down here and take it out on us? You know how incredibly stupid you sound right now?"

Randy's face looked incredibly frustrated. I could tell he wanted to lash back at Trevor but was desperately holding his tongue. "You have your assignment. Once again, effective immediately. I look forward to hearing about your findings. Oh, and Trevor," Randy said before he and his men flew off, "that window's coming out of your paycheck."

Once Randy and the PSS were out of earshot, Paxton angrily said something to Erica in Kai. Erica tried to cool him off again, but Paxton didn't want to let it go, which wasn't abnormal for him. It was one of the reasons why he earned the nickname Spitfire from Trevor after only two weeks of knowing him. There was no way Paxton was going to let it go until he got whatever he needed to get out, out.

"Can you believe that asshole! 'Not bad for a Kaisiust,' what the hell was that shit? That dick's the vice president of DREAM and he's going to say shit like that to us?"

I was used to Trevor cursing by now, but not so much Paxton.

"Don't let him get to you Paxton, you're better than that. *We're* better than that," Erica tried again. She was flustered too, but was at least trying to take the high road.

"He's the vice president! If he can talk to us that way then that sets a precedent for everyone else in DREAM to talk to us like that too!"

Kaisiusts were different, which made some people, too many people, in DREAM uncomfortable. Paxton was about eight feet tall and Erica was a few inches shorter. They both had very slim builds, which was typical for a Kaisiust. I would guess neither one of them weighed much more than 200 pounds and their skin was a bluish-gray color. Yeah, they stood out, but they were just as human as me or

Trevor.

To racists, Kaisiusts were just a nasty byproduct of an accident in a conjierum and silver processing plant many years ago. To the rest of us, they were just another part of DREAM, like anyone else.

"And the whole 'questionable draft selections?' What the hell does that even mean? She was the best damn Artificer in her class and I wasn't too far from the top of mine either. What, because Erica and I are Kaisiusts we're 'questionable draft selections?'" Paxton defensively half-asked, half-told him.

The answer to his question was yes. We all knew it. One Kaisiust in a support squad was pretty uncommon, but two was unheard of, until our squad formed at least. Paxton was fishing for some type of reaction or defensive stance from Trevor. He needed some type of affirmation or validation.

"Don't let him get into your heads," Trevor tried to assure all three of us. "I wouldn't have drafted any of you if I didn't think you weren't the strongest candidates available to me."

It was a rare look at Trevor the diplomat, and in true diplomatic fashion, he was lying. Only two of us were the "strongest candidates available" to him and they were Paxton and Erica.

Erica was unanimously projected to be the first overall pick from the School of Artificers. Like Paxton said, she really was the best in her class. Artificers were what used to be engineers, contractors, and in some cases even scientists, bundled into one. I had heard of her around campus even before draft night. Once I overheard a professor call her a "once in a generation talent." I never heard anything about her personally, just that she was a crazy hard worker. It was extremely rare to have a female Artificer in the top of a class, let alone a Kaisiust one. For one reason or another she wasn't selected in the first, second, or third round, and ended up being Trevor's pick in the fourth.

Paxton was projected to be a top three pick from the School of Saviors, but also slipped down to four. Saviors were what used to be doctors, nurses, surgeons, and medical researchers. I didn't recognize his name immediately, but had certainly seen and heard him around campus. He was very loud and at times, combative, and abrasive. Paxton would get into arguments over just about anything. He was quick to get angry and frustrated, but always stood up for what he believed in.

"What was with his comment about Graham? It was like he was completely shocked to see him dodge some claws and fire a gun," Paxton asked. It was a moment where he was too intuitive for his own good.

Unlike my squadmates, I was projected to be picked anywhere between the twelfth and sixteenth round. The middle of the pack that year. I hadn't gotten any requests from Trevor, or any other squad leader, for any academic records, interviews, or physical evaluations which was normal for draftees projected to be picked in the top five rounds or so. I wasn't invited to the campus-wide televised selection ceremony either. This was where newly formed squads had a chance to meet with their new leader and squadmates for the first time. The draft was made up of new graduates from that year's class as well as any graduates from previous years who hadn't been selected before. With that in mind I was terrified of graduating from the academy without a job. Not only were there a dozen people from my class that were better than me, but all the ones who had missed the cut from years past that wanted another crack at landing a spot in a support squad.

When I heard my name being called over my dorm's TV as the Factotum pick in the fourth round, I was totally shocked. I remember hearing the crowd mumble and gasp as our squad's picture was taken on stage. It was definitely a sight to see: a mid-forties Duelist leader in the middle, a top female Kaisiust Artificer to his right, a top Kaisiust Savior to his left, and not pictured: the no name Factotum who was projected way too low to even get an invite to the show.

Erica made a statement before Trevor could, "Trevor picked us all in the fourth round, because he knew we were more than capable of getting any job done. We proved that to him and the rest of DREAM today."

"Couldn't have said it better myself," Trevor the diplomat returned. "That assclown Randy was never a good judge of talent. Only lasted a year and a half as a squad leader, you know. In this job it doesn't matter what you look like; it matters how hard you work and how hard you're willin' to work. And I can tell already you three are gonna to be something special to work with."

His little speech appeased Paxton and gave me some needed reassurance. Trevor had to have had his reasons for picking me over so many other better people. What they were though, I couldn't tell you.

We made our way off the beach and onto the boardwalk. Our shoes flinging and splashing the water that was still sitting on the boards with each step. The surrounding streetlights began to flicker on. Trevor paused for a moment and shook his head. It looked like he had just remembered something important and was disappointed he hadn't thought of it sooner, a how-could-I-have-been-so-dumb moment.

"Any of you been to Brexley before?" he asked.

The three of us shook our heads.

"Good, Lord," he said with a bit of exasperation. "Well then, there's some things I should get you up to speed on before we head out."

Chapter 3

The Road to Brexley and the Detour at Lynch

Trevor didn't tell us much about Brexley that we didn't already know. It got very little funding and attention from the government, which had made it a cesspool for crime.

"The fact that we're a support squad only makes the people up there hate us more. In fact," he said mulling over an idea to himself, "we need to get out of these uniforms, get into something more comfortable. More civilian, you know what I mean? You all live close enough to meet at DREAM Tower in a half hour?"

The three of us nodded our heads.

"Alright then. Erica, SB3s for everyone. Make them black, we don't need to be drawin' any type of attention to ourselves."

She materialized a sports bike for each of us. I remembered learning about the SB line of motorcycles at the academy. As a Factotum I learned how to materialize a little bit from the other three strands of conjierum, emphasis on 'a little bit.' Anything beyond a bicycle was past what the conjierum would let me do.

The SB3s were similar-looking to your average crotch rocket. Three was a pretty old model and most people were riding SB7s or newer by now. Trevor's reasoning for that specific bike was solid. Nobody would look twice at us riding those. The bikes could seat two adults, but not very comfortably. Erica modified the bikes for her and Paxton to be taller to accommodate their size.

"Thanks, Erica," Paxton said, noticing this. "I remember learning to ride these at the academy. They never made the bikes any bigger for me. Those things were tiny! I felt like a clown riding a kid's tricycle."

"I would've paid to see that!" she replied.

Erica and I laughed picturing Paxton on a tricycle.

"You all can laugh at Spitfire once we're out of Brexley." Our laughter quickly died down. "DREAM Tower. Half an hour. Get out of here. Go get changed."

The ride to my apartment was only about ten minutes. I took a few backstreets home to avoid some of the early stages of the nightlife scene and congestion that comes with it. I lived in a small apartment building between the shore and DREAM Tower. The building was four floors high with an apartment on each floor. I lived on the third. I unlocked the door to the building and began the walk up the stairs. My place was nothing special—one bed, one bath. It was all I needed.

I headed straight for my bedroom to change. The last thing I wanted was to be late and get another earful from Trevor. I had enough of that for one day, enough for a while. I tore through my dresser looking for something comfortable and easy to move around in. I pulled out a plain purple long-sleeved shirt and a pair of black shorts. I left my uniform on the bed, the dresser drawers open, and headed out the door.

I was the last one to make it to DREAM Tower, but had time to spare. Our squad's SB3s lined the curb near the front entrance. I got off the bike and made my way towards the front door where the other three were standing. I nearly tripped over the raised lettering from the plaque embedded in the pavement in front of the entrance. It read. "DREAM Tower. Epicenter of DREAM: Desired Reality Established And Materialized."

Paxton and Erica held back their laughter as they watched me stumble over the plaque. It was weird to see everyone in real clothes and not our uniforms. I tried to get the focus off me by pointing out that Paxton's blonde hair had become a bit windblown. I pointed at him and gestured for him to fix it. He did and then returned the same point and gesture. Erica chuckled at both of us trying to fix the mess on our heads. Her long black hair was perfectly fine, and Trevor didn't have enough hair to have a problem.

"Alright you divas let's get goin'," Trevor said, refocusing us.

"Remember, don't draw any attention to yourselves. You hear me, Garnett? We don't need anything else chargin' at you today." A wave of embarrassment rushed over me. "I'll lead. Erica and Spitfire next, then Graham. We oughta have some type of Duelist in the front and rear."

"Wait!" Erica jumped in before we walked over to the bikes. "Everybody take one of these."

She materialized headsets for each of us. They were just like the ones we had earlier in the day during our dragon duel. We each turned them on, agreed on a channel, and tested to make sure they worked properly.

"Good call," Trevor said, giving her a look of approval.

The four of us then started walking back to the curb to get moving. Paxton took an unnecessarily exaggerated step over the plaque ahead of me. I went out of my way to avoid it entirely, not wanting to give him anything else to laugh at. Trip me once, shame on you. Trip me twice, shame on me. Paxton turned around and got one last shot in.

"Watch out for that plaque, Graham! If you're not careful it'll getcha."

Admittedly, it was funny. I passed that thing every day getting to work and never had any issues with it until now.

Once we all started our bikes Trevor's voice came in over the headset, "The ride should take us about an hour and a half if traffic's good. Stay close. I don't need any of you getting lost, especially once we get close. Don't go fallin' asleep on me either. If you start dozin' off say something. I'll keep you awake, trust me."

The night started growing darker and darker. The further north we drove the smaller and less impressive DREAM Tower looked. It went from a one-hundred-plus story juggernaut of modern architecture when we left to a glowing toothpick by the time we were on the outskirts of Brexley. Like Trevor predicted, it took us about an hour and a half to get there. The metal "Welcome To Brexley" sign was bent like it had been bashed with a bat several times and only had one of its two posts still in the ground. It swayed back and forth in the breeze like one of those old Western saloon doors. Not a great first impression for me, Erica, or Paxton.

I was surprised that all of the streetlights we drove passed were working. I hadn't decided whether that was good or bad though. To be seen or not to be seen, that was the question. I guessed it worked in our favor. The SB3s weren't terribly loud, but people would still hear us coming. At least with the streetlights on we had a shot at seeing anyone who might try to pay us a visit.

Brexley's streets were cracked and worn-down. I almost got motion sick from having to dodge all of the potholes. Many of the buildings were in desperate need of repair. Dilapidated row houses lined the streets. Windows were cracked, shattered, or boarded-up. Shingles from surrounding roofs had found their way to the sidewalk, which was uneven and crumbling. Siding on the houses not made of brick was peeling off like petals on a flower. Paint was either chipping away or sun-bleached beyond recognition. The only paint that had retained its color was the graffiti decorating the fronts and sides of many of the buildings. Trash was everywhere and blew around like tumbleweeds.

DREAM was supposed to be a near perfect place for everyone, hence 'Desired Reality' in the name. That clearly wasn't the case for the people here. How could a city in DREAM come to this? I knew all the different cities and towns in DREAM weren't as well off as Center City was, but this was a whole new level of disparity.

"Oh my god," Erica said. "This is so sad. This whole place is just so sad. I learned a little about Brexley in my architecture class at the academy. You guys probably already know that each city in DREAM has a different architectural flair based on the Artificers' taste and abilities when they founded it. Center City has a modern design like New York, Tokyo, and Dubai had. Sterling is more gothic. Mylo is more Tudor."

Mylo. The name gave me a chill when it came out of her mouth.

My hometown. Bad memories from my time there came crashing into my mind. I fought them back and pushed them aside as fast as I could. I couldn't and wouldn't think about them now.

"Anyway," she continued on, "Brexley was supposed to have a more Federal vibe. The Artificers who founded it wanted to keep it simpler, nothing too crazy or fancy. This place is so run-down you can hardly recognize it."

"Let me tell you a little somethin' you won't find in your textbook. The Artificers that built this place were *told* to do it that way. It wasn't based on their *taste* or *abilities*. It wasn't supposed to be pretty or grand, it was built to be a blue-collar town. It's Center City's overflow, its cheap alternative, its shadow, its…its ugly stepsister," Trevor said rather heavy-heartedly. It was weird to hear him talk like that.

"How do you know that?" she asked.

It was quiet for a second.

"I'm from here. My whole family is. And let me tell you something, people from Brexley hardly ever get the chance to leave Brexley. My family helped build this town, literally. The Artificers conjured the materials and we built it. It was meant to be simple and efficient, like its people," his voice was somber. "Wasn't ever supposed to look like *this* either though. Times got tough around here, and they only got tougher. So did the people. Brexley never got the help it needed, and now it's this. I knew things up here were bad. I haven't been back in a while, but I didn't know shit had gotten this bad."

His story ended as we rolled to a stop at a red light. I had just noticed how quiet the streets were. It felt odd to me. I was used to my life in Center City, where something was always going on, even late at night. I thought to myself how I wouldn't want to be walking around here at this hour if I lived here, and that helped shake the feeling off.

The three in front of me kept their faces forward and waited for the light to change. I tried to do the same until I saw something moving a little less than two blocks away. Two or three shadowy figures suspiciously scampered outside the glow of the streetlight and into what must have been a nearby alley.

Anxiety started throwing all kinds of worst-case-scenario thoughts at me. It was probably people just screwing around or at worst a drug deal, but something about it felt off to me. I thought about saying something but didn't. I was sure that Trevor wouldn't want any more of my paranoia at this point. My fear had already earned me multiple verbal lashings from him today. I didn't need another.

By the time I looked back up at the light it was green. The group had gotten a pretty big head start on me. I must have been stuck in my head longer than I thought. I turned on the throttle pretty hard, harder than I should have, trying to catch up. There was no way I was going to fall behind and get lost here.

CRACK! POP!

Before I could even react, the front tire of my SB3 started hissing and wobbling. Someone had shot my tire out. I was going way too fast to keep control of the bike. The handlebars twisted back and forth too wildly for me to control for long. I went down, bashing my head into the pavement. The pounding pain was immediate. The rough road chewed up the skin on my leg. I was pinned between the unforgiving street and the hundreds of pounds of motorcycle. I could feel my vocal cords cry out in pain, but I couldn't hear myself. My vision blurred to black as my squadmates drove away.

* * *

When I opened my eyes, I found myself tied to a cheap plastic chair with my hands bound behind my back. My head was still throbbing. It took me a second to get my bearings. My leg burned. I didn't need to see it to know I had a nice chunk of road rash. I could feel the dampness drying blood in spots from my knee down to my ankle.

The room was dark, only lit by a few lightbulbs dangling from exposed wires in the ceiling. There was a thin layer of dust on the scratched-up hardwood floor. The white walls of the room were scuffed up, dirty, and in some spots even moldy.

The three men with old jeans and dirty t-shirts stood in front of me. It was hard to make them out at first, but they eventually came into focus. They were older, probably close to fifty, and pretty out of shape. Each had a handgun pointed straight at my face, so close I could smell that distinct sweaty-hand-on-metal scent. I was scared out of my mind. I could feel a cold sweat starting to pour down my back and armpits. The pain in my head only amplified with the fear of eating one of their bullets.

I saw a man sitting in the right-hand corner of the room get up. His features became clearer to me as he left the shady spot and came closer to me. He looked fairly young, older than me but younger than Trevor—maybe in his early thirties. He wore a red bandana over his jet-black hair along with a black eye patch over his right eye. He sported dark stubble on his face, and his tan made it clear he spent a lot of time out in the sun. The guy was actually very handsome and had a unique smile. The kind of smile that was infectious, manipulative, and slightly psychotic all at once. He wore a red button-down shirt, similar in color to his bandana, and black jeans that weren't nearly as beaten up as his co-conspirators were.

"Look, boys," he said smiling to the others around me, "our friend here is waking up."

He patted me on the shoulder. I was super jittery and flinched a little after he touched me. He began to pace around my chair. I could tell he was strategically planning his next question. I decided then and there that this guy, whoever he was, was creepy and way off his rocker. He told the three to put their weapons down. It put me at ease ever so slightly. The leader made his way back around the chair to face me and bent down to stare me square in the eye.

His smile and tone quickly turned sour and his body tensed, "Don't even think about trying to materialize anything. If you so much as twitch, you die."

I froze for a second. A shot of nervous adrenaline pulsed through my body. He went from eccentric to lethal instantly. "Understood," I somehow managed to muster out.

"Good!" he said, flipping the happy-go-lucky switch back on. My heart felt like it was in my throat.

He retreated to the corner of the room where he was originally sitting, grabbed his folding metal chair, and dragged into the light a few feet away from me. He sat down in it backwards and rested his folded arms on the back. He then motioned for the other men to pull up chairs around me too.

"So, what's your name, kid?" he asked me.

I knew nothing good could possibly come from answering him, but nothing good could come from not answering him either.

"Graham," I replied while wincing. The pain in my head and leg was flaring up.

The man's face took on a pleasantly surprised look. His eye widened and his weird smile returned.

"Graham, eh? Like the cracker?" he said, nodding with approval. His men laughed and he prompted, "You got a last name, Graham?"

Everything inside me screamed not to tell him, but there was nothing stopping this guy from shooting me on the spot if I didn't. "Garnett."

"Graham Garnett," he reiterated to himself. "It's got a superhero ring to it, doesn't it boys?"

The three others either grunted or nodded half-heartedly.

"So, Graham," he began, getting out of his chair. I watched over my shoulder as he made his way towards a large, double window in the back left corner of the room and looked down at, what I assumed to be, the street. "What are you?"

"I'm...I'm sorry?" I stuttered.

"What are you in your support squad? What's your role? Are

you the Artificer? I could see that. You look like a more-brains-than-brawn kind of guy," he asked as he continued looking out the window.

"What makes you think I am part of a support squad?" I slowly worked up the courage to reply. I instantly regretted it. Why did I test him?

"Don't play dumb with me, kid," he said with a chuckle which was followed by an edge in his tone. "How many people do you think drive around here in packs of four on SBs? Doesn't take a genius to know what a support squad looks like."

A jolt of panic surged through me. The cold sweat was intensifying. My torso felt drenched. I could faintly hear my heart beating in my ears now. He knew who I was. He knew what I did. I thought about what Trevor said about how people felt about support squads here. I'd be lucky to die a quick death.

"So, Graham," he said this time a little bit louder and with a bit of impatience. "I'll ask you one more time. What are you?"

"I'm the Factotum," I quickly answered, not pressing my luck in potentially irritating him anymore.

"The Factotum, huh," he said now looking straight out the window instead of down at the street. "You're the Factotum? The squad sidekick? Damn it! Sorry boys, we won't get as much for Graham here as we thought."

The men let out a few sighs to themselves. I could hear one or two of the men swear under their breath. The leader now made his way back to his chair, sitting down the same way he had before.

"No matter, we can still get something for you," he said as he looked me in the eye. "Cut him loose. Graham here is a Factotum. He should have some Duelist in him; I want to see what he can do. Maybe he has more value than we thought. If he's any good we can demand more for him."

He smiled. The other three didn't. They looked exhausted. "We just tied him up," I heard one of the men mumble to himself as he reluctantly came and started to cut me loose.

CRASH!

The window that the leader had just been standing at only a minute or two ago had shattered. The man cutting my ties instantly stopped and scampered back across the room. A walkie-talkie came flying in through the newly opened window. The leader walked over to pick the brick of a thing up and held down the button to speak.

"Hello, members of the DREAM support squad down below. How are we all doing tonight?"

"I'm not here to play games," Trevor's voice resonated over the walkie-talkie. "What do you need in return for our man up there?"

The leader looked at me and smiled as he spoke into the walkie again, "Before we get into that conversation, whom do I have the pleasure of speaking with?"

"This is Trevor," he replied, pretty annoyed.

"Trevor," the leader repeated to himself. He thought about the name for a moment. I could tell it meant something to him. When he figured it out, he looked at me with that uncomfortable smile, his one eye widening again, and said, "Trevor. Trevor Donaldson?"

"…Yes. How do you know—"

"Trevor, this *man* of yours here tells me that his name is Graham Garnett and that he's a Factotum. Is that true?"

Trevor was getting even more annoyed, "Yes."

"Excellent," the leader said, still looking at me with that smile, which was now taking more of a psychotic turn. He also had an eerie gleam in his eye. "Is Graham the Factotum of *your* squad, Trevor?"

Trevor was at his limit, "Yes. Now it's my turn to ask the questions. Who the hell are you and what the hell do you want?"

If the eyes are the windows to the soul, there was no doubt in my mind this guy's deranged soul was already in hell. He was visibly excited now. His sickening grin was as big as ever and that eerie gleam was in full force. He held the walkie-talkie close to his mouth to be sure Trevor heard him clearly. Nausea started to sweep over me. I knew this wasn't going to end well for me. This lunatic was going to kill me. Not even Trevor could save me now.

"Well, Trevor, you may remember me from a while back. This is Jay Lynch. How have you been?" His voice became more serious, and borderline angry, as he spoke.

I could tell Trevor pulled the walkie away from his mouth to swear. However, he didn't pull it far enough. I was screwed. I was dead. Trevor knew it. Jay was as amped up as ever. He knew he had Trevor and me right where he wanted us.

Chapter 4

Sunshine

"You know what, Trevor, maybe it's time you call it quits. You seem to have a chronic issue with protecting the people you're supposed to be watching over. Getting a hold of Graham here was incredibly easy. How the hell are you going to look out for DREAM if you can't even look out for your own squad?" He took his eye off the walkie and focused on me. "Graham here doesn't look like much to me, Trevor. Not very toned. Pretty pale, too. You get your squad out much?" Jay said as he paced around the room.

"What do you want, Jay?" Trevor asked again.

"You know what I want."

"Listen, Jay," Trevor answered with a bit of remorse in his tone, "I'm sorry about your eye, I really am, but I can't change what happened. There's nothing I can do for you. You know the academy's—"

"SHUT UP!" Jay yelled.

His smile was gone. He stopped pacing and stood still with a serious look on his face for a moment. I could sense what he was thinking, and it wasn't good for me. An evil smirk began to curl from the side of his mouth.

"Well then Trevor, I'll just have to show you, and the rest of DREAM, what I'm *still* capable of," Jay dropped the walkie to the floor. He stared me down like a lion ready to take down a wounded gazelle.

"Don't be stupid, Jay," I heard Trevor plea from the walkie.

I desperately tried to snap the ties keeping my hands together. I jerked my upper body around frantically trying to get free. The feet of my chair danced around the dusty floor. Every movement hurt but I had no other choice.

"Watch the window and door, boys," Jay commanded, still giving me his undivided attention. "I have a feeling we're about to have some company." He then materialized a handgun. Jay was a Duelist, or at least a Factotum like me!

Within moments of his order, what glass that was left in the window crashed to the floor. Jay's men scurried to his side as Trevor somehow swung in through the window. He then took a few steps forward to give Erica and Paxton room to swoop in too.

I looked over my left shoulder again and saw that the three were wearing bullet proof vests over their shirts. They had a standard-issue handgun in one hand and a clear, military-grade riot shield in the other. Jay and his men were in front of me pointing their guns at my squadmates. Paxton and Erica aimed for his men, while Trevor kept his focus on Jay. The tension in the room became so thick you could almost choke on it. Three guns behind me and three guns in front of me. I was just a sitting duck in the middle of the room waiting to be shot by someone. No one moved. No one spoke. I'm not sure anyone even took a breath. I was too afraid to.

"Now we finally have someone of value, boys. And how lucky is this! Of all the squads that could have strolled by tonight it just happened to be Trevor Donaldson's, one of DREAM's finest."

"Let him go, Jay," Trevor's voice was firm. "We'll handle this off the record. Forget it ever happened. Get out of your way."

Jay chuckled, "That's easy for you to say Trevor. 'Forget it ever happened.'" Jay started shouting. His gun started to angrily shake a bit in his hand. "You think this will be as easy as taking Graham back and shrugging this whole thing off! Just like how you shrugged me off after you royally screwed me over! After *you* did this—"

He pulled up his eye patch. It was hard to see the green color in his right eye. It was really cloudy; he had to be blind in it. A scar ran down from about the middle of his forehead, through his eyebrow, and stopped at the top of his cheek. His patch did a nice job of covering most of it up, but something clearly horrendous had happened to him.

Jay pulled the patch back over his eye.

"There's no honor in killing a defenseless man. Go finish cutting him loose," he directed the man who started the job earlier. He locked in on me as my ties were being cut and said, "I'm at least going to give you a fighting chance. Once you're dead, your blue friends are next. Then Trevor, if he's lucky."

I stood up slowly from the chair. I felt a bit woozy. I didn't know if it was vertigo or maybe something more serious with my head. I was scared out of my mind and unarmed. What was stopping him from just shooting me down now? That's when it hit me. Code. There's no honor in killing a defenseless man. That was a Duelist code. He wouldn't shoot me, not until I had a weapon in my hand at least. That didn't mean his lackeys wouldn't though.

I inched my way back towards my squad. Each step on my right road-rashed leg stung. I thought having a gun pointed in my face was horrifying enough, but walking backwards into a handful of guns ready to fire while facing a handful of guns that were also ready to fire was almost as nerve-racking. I had never seen Trevor's face more intent and stone cold. This was serious. People in this room were probably going to die. Trevor, or Paxton, or Erica could die. I could die.

Once I passed Trevor, who was standing a few steps ahead of Paxton and Erica on either of his sides, I helplessly scampered to hide behind Erica. I needed cover to arm myself. I didn't want to fight, but it was looking like I wasn't going to have a choice if I wanted a shot of getting out of here alive.

Jay was ready for whatever revenge he so desperately wanted from Trevor. He materialized a similar riot shield to the ones our squad was using. "Graham and the bean poles are all yours gentlemen," he instructed, not breaking his gaze with Trevor. "Good luck. You may or may not need it." The men exchanged confused looks at each other for a split second. They were the only ones in the room without shields. These three men were destined to die unless we took pity on them or

Jay materialized some kind of protection for them. It didn't look like the latter was happening. Their faces began to panic, but before they could think too long and hard about their potential death sentence Jay opened fire.

The room exploded with gunshots, louder and more chaotic than even the craziest finale to a fireworks show. I materialized a shield and gun of my own now being forced to fight. Holes began to pop in the walls from all the missed shots by Jay's lackeys. Some made a loud pinging sound as they flew through Jay's metal chair while one wild shot took out one of the ceiling lights. Tiny shards of glass rained down to the floor making the already dim room even dimmer. Chunks of drywall crumbled to the ground, dust filled the air, and it got harder to breathe.

The men managed to get off a few shots at our shields, but ultimately were no match for us. They were really good at holding and pointing the guns, but when it came to actually using them, not so much. Paxton shot and killed the man who untied me while Erica brought down the other two. I was once again too overwhelmed to fight, just hiding behind my shield and blocking the few shots that came my way.

Trevor and Jay were still fixated on each other. Jay had stopped firing once he realized he was alone.

"Hold your fire!" Trevor commanded us.

"Damn it, Trevor! It's four on one. Let's just end this!" Paxton pleaded with him.

"Hold your fire," he reiterated.

"Now what fun is this? Anyone can point a gun and pull the trigger," Jay said with his shield still up and the gun still pointed at Trevor.

"Why don't you put the gun down then, Jay," Trevor advised.

"Good idea. Let's settle this like *real* Duelists," He dematerialized the shield and gun and replaced them with a katana-like sword in each hand. "I'll slice you up a little first. Then I'll let you watch as I take out those three. Ooh, maybe I'll give you a matching scar before you completely bleed out." His sick smile came back. "What a hell of a story that'll be, huh? Jay Lynch single handedly eliminates a whole support squad, Trevor Donaldson's nonetheless."

"What the hell are you waiting for? SHOOT HIM!" Paxton nearly screamed.

"Jay feels like he has something to prove here so let's see if he can do it," Trevor calmly stated, still keeping his eyes on his opponent.

"What the hell? Quit playing macho man and put a cap in his ass!" Paxton barked back.

"SHUT UP! I can't just shoot him. He's a Duelist. We have a code. If he challenges me with a sword, I have to fight with a sword."

"Code? You know how stupid that sounds right now! Screw the code, just shoot him! Hell, if you're not going to let me shoot him!"

"BACK DOWN, SPITFIRE!" he yelled. Trevor caught a quick breath and cooled down his tone. "This is between us now. He's all yours if he kills me." He dematerialized his old weaponry, and conjured up a sword and a new type of shield for himself. I wasn't exactly a weapons expert, but Trevor's looked like a knightly sword. The shield in his left hand was dark, metallic, and oval-shaped. It was just large enough to cover most of his torso.

"Now we're talking," Jay's voice raised confidently.

"Trevor, you can't be serious!" Paxton's was starting to sound hoarse.

Trevor turned around just long enough to look me in the eye and say, "Be ready. Just in case."

A horrible thought suddenly entered my mind. If something were to go wrong, if something were to happen to Trevor, I'd have to lead this fight for my squad. I had Duelist training. The same nasty feeling I got while looking down at the street from our window reared its ugly head back and landed like a pit in my stomach.

"You don't want to do this, Jay," Trevor warned him. "This doesn't end well for anyone if you do."

"This doesn't end well for *you*, Trevor. You've broken one of the cardinal rules for Duelists now, haven't you? Never fight a man with nothing to lose!"

Jay lunged at Trevor first. His blades crashed into Trevor's shield, then again, and again. His assault was relentless. Trevor did all he could to keep blocking blow after blow after blow. Jay's strikes were so hard and fast that Trevor couldn't do anything but stay defensive.

Jay showed no signs of slowing down. His face was a sick combination of enjoyment and rage. Trevor managed to get a few swings in but Jay easily blocked them. It went on like that for what felt like hours. Trevor's breathing started to become heavy. Jay noticed. He stopped his barrage, took a few steps back, and took a quick breath himself.

Trevor went down to one knee, but kept watching Jay like a hawk. His shirt was drenched with sweat and his head was gleaming with it. I wasn't sure how much longer he could keep it up. Paxton, Erica, and I were getting antsy.

"Is that all you've got, Trevor?" Jay taunted him. "You're getting too old for this."

"Come on, Trevor! Get up!" Paxton urged him.

"You can do this, Trevor," Erica added in.

Jay made another rush at Trevor. His left arm was pulled back, ready for a backhand swing. His right was positioned for a big forehanded slash. Trevor was too slow to get back on both feet but just managed to hold his shield up over his head to protect himself.

BANG!

CLANG! CLANG!

The first sound wasn't the familiar sound of metal on metal. It sounded like a gunshot. Trevor let out a cry of pain. He managed to block the blow of the swords, but fell over, grabbing his lower shin. Blood started running down his ankle, over his shoe, and onto the floor. Paxton and Erica rushed over to Trevor while Jay backed away admiring what he had done, again the predator watching his prey. The enjoyment he was getting from this was sickening.

A small puff of smoke came out of the pommel of his left blade. He brought it up towards his mouth and blew it away. A confident smirk overtook his face. It wasn't until then that I figured out what we were really up against. His swords were really gunblades: swords with the ability to fire live rounds.

Jay was no ordinary Duelist. Being able to materialize gunblades was a very advanced skill. A skill I guess Trevor didn't anticipate Jay having, or maybe it just didn't cross his mind. With Trevor now injured and Jay showing us just how deadly he could be, I knew we were in some serious shit.

Before I had too much time to get caught up on that, Jay charged again. Trevor was sitting on the floor while Paxton and Erica knelt down to evaluate his wound. They looked up and saw Jay getting ready to deal them a blow. I knew they wouldn't have time to defend themselves, dropping their weapons to help Trevor wasn't the smartest idea, but none of us could have seen what happened to Trevor coming. I had to do something about Jay.

My mind wanted to seize up with fear, but my body, oddly enough, wouldn't allow it. A coursing wave of adrenaline rushed over me. I materialized my weapon, leapt over my three squadmates, and did a baseball slide into a defensive position.

CLANG! CLANG!

I managed to block his strikes, but it came at a price. I slid into the pile of lightbulb shards. Both my legs were now injured and a bit bloody. The sudden rush to stop Jay's attack turned out to be a bit too much for my head. I stood up a bit woozy.

All eyes were now on me. Jay took a few steps back, lowering his swords. It was like he was evaluating what had just happened. There was a pleasantly surprised look on his face. I took a split second to try and wipe off what glass shards I could from my left leg. After that I broke out of my defensive stance and clicked the button on my weapon which retracted its shield components. It was now in what I called its "normal state," where it looked like a slightly smaller version of a fighting staff. The upper two-thirds of it was made up of sixteen black metal plates that formed and retracted the shield. It basically looked, and worked, like a killer umbrella.

"What the hell is that, kid?" he asked me almost in disbelief at what he was seeing. "You think you're gonna beat me with some umbrella, sunshine?"

I didn't respond. I had nothing to say and no time to say it. I knew I had to somehow end this fast. I needed a plan. I couldn't keep up with Jay, not like Trevor did. I took a quick glance back at Paxton and Erica. They were dragging Trevor out of harm's way, back towards their weapons on the other end of the room. Paxton materialized a bandage and gave it to Erica to start wrapping his wound. While she did that, he conjured up equipment to check Trevor's vitals. Their guns were in arms reach, if need be, which gave me an ounce of relief.

Erica's face caught my attention. She smiled and winked at me. Why? Then it hit me. I knew what to do.

I focused my attention back on Jay, firmly standing my ground now. He came running at me again. I could tell his plan was to wear me down like he did Trevor. Just as Jay's blades were about to come down on me, I pressed the button opening up my shield. Then, without hesitation, I pressed the second button below it which unsheathed a hidden blade on either end of the staff.

The blade on the tip of the "umbrella" shield pierced through Jay's right shoulder as he ran at me. The shield kept his body from sliding any further down the staff towards me. He screamed. I swept my leg behind his. Jay fell to the floor where I pinned him down. Erica, knowing this was coming, was right behind me with freshly conjured handcuffs and her handgun.

I pressed the buttons retracting my shield and blades. After she cuffed him, Paxton walked over to help pick up Jay. They led him over to the chair that he had tied me to earlier, picked it up, and sat him down. Paxton treated his shoulder while Erica pulled out her cell phone and called for a CLES, civil law enforcement squad, to escort Jay and Trevor to the hospital. Paxton did a nice job patching them up but recommended they go. His reasoning was that there was only so much he could do out here in the field. He wasn't comfortable stitching up Jay and trying to remove the bullet in Trevor's leg here in this room.

I sat down next to Trevor to see how he was doing. I could tell he was still in pain but sounded a bit more like himself. Paxton knelt down next to me and started tweezing out the glass shards I had missed on my quick brushing.

"So, what the hell's that thing anyway?" Trevor asked as he looked at the weapon still in my hand.

I let out a chuckle, "I don't know. Something Erica and I have been working on this past week. She saw some of your old Duelist books lying around in the common room, and got inspired, I guess. She drew up this design and told me what materials would work best. Luckily the conjierum let me materialize everything she suggested in the way she suggested and we got this."

"Well, you certainly didn't learn *that* from any book. I've never seen anything like it before. Looks tricky. You must have more Duelist in you than you thought. What do you call it?"

"Huh?"

"That thing in your hand. Your weapon. What do you call it? Does it got a name or something?"

I mulled it over briefly. "I guess Jay was right—it does sort of look like an umbrella. I'll call it Sunshine."

"Sunshine?" Trevor questioned, totally confused.

It was a bit out of character for me, but I was feeling good and confident for once. "Yeah. 'You think you're gonna beat me with some umbrella, sunshine?'" I said doing my best Jay impression.

A few minutes later the CLES arrived with two ambulances. "You three better come and get me first thing in the morning. I'm not trying to drag out this bullshit assignment any longer than I have to.

You hear me?" Trevor irritably said as they loaded him in. The CLES recommended a nearby hotel for us. They said it was the politicians and celebrities used when they rarely came to town. I hopped on Trevor's SB3 and we headed out.

Chapter 5

False Savior Lynch and Squad Leader Paxton

"Graham...Garnett." The Savior read my name off her clipboard and then scanned the room for me. I stood up out of my chair and she immediately stated, "Come on back."

She led me to a room that looked like a padded solitary confinement cell. I was here to take my CAA, Conjierum Acceptance Assessment, not get locked up in a psych ward. The room was nearly empty. There was a small, sleek desk that looked more like an end table, a wheeled office chair sitting beneath it, and the seat for me that looked like a dental chair.

"My name is Savior Corbin. How are you today, Graham?"

"I'm fine."

"That's good to hear. Why don't you have a seat right over there and we'll get started in just a minute," she instructed me, gesturing to my seat.

I was nervous. The room felt cold to me and I couldn't get my hands and feet to stop fidgeting. Savior Corbin sat down in the office chair, looked over the syringes of conjierum sitting in a tray on the desk, and then read over my paperwork on her clipboard again.

"Oh wow," she said, looking down at her papers. An anxious panic struck me. My feet started tapping faster. "Today is your birthday! Happy eighteenth birthday, Graham!" She gave me a warm smile. She had gotten me all worried for nothing.

"Thank you," I squeaked out.

"March fourteenth. That was my grandmother's birthday. She would have been ninety-one this year. Anyway, this is a big day for you, huh? Your birthday and your CAA. Have you gotten your driver's license yet?" She picked up one of the syringes, a sterilizing wipe, and started to wheel her chair the few feet away over to me.

"I have my test after this," I replied, doing my best to relax.

"We see a lot of people here that do that. First day you can do both so you might as well, right? Get a head start on your adult life."

"Right," I answered, only half listening. I was having a hard time focusing.

"Let's get right to it then. This is your Conjierum Acceptance Assessment. It's a test to see if any of the four strands of conjierum have chosen you, and if so, how skilled in that particular area we project you potentially become based on a set of tasks I'm going to ask you to do. The more tasks the conjierum allows you to do without any formal training the higher your projection will be. Make sense so far?"

I nodded.

"Do you mind me asking if either of your parents are conjierum users?"

"My mom is an Omitted and my dad is an Artificer, but he's pretty limited."

"Okay, so there does tend to be a correlation between conjierum acceptance and genetics. However, that doesn't mean you're going to be an Omitted or an Artificer, but statistically you are more likely to fall into one of those categories. Studies have also shown correlations between certain strands and gender. The Savior and Factotum strands tend to favor females more while the Duelist and Artificer strands tend to favor males." That didn't seem very progressive for a magic-like substance. "Again, those are just correlations. Does that make sense?"

"Yes."

"Great. Let's get started." There was a perk in her voice as she pulled up the sleeve on my left arm and wiped down a patch of my skin with the sterilizing wipe. "We're going to start with the Factotum strand first," she told me, getting the syringe of light brown liquid ready. "The jack-of-all-trades strand as some like to call it. We start with this one first to see which strand to move onto next, if any at all. If you're unable to materialize any basic things from one of the other strands we don't bother testing them and if you can't materialize anything at all the result is non-conjierum user, or Omitted. Any questions?"

I shook my head.

"Alright. You might feel a weird sensation as the conjierum starts running through your body," she said as she stuck the needle in my arm and started to slowly inject the fluid. "That's completely normal. We'll give the conjierum a few minutes to get familiar with you and then get on with the tests."

It could almost pinpoint how the conjierum traveled through my body. There was a warm, almost burning feeling as it reached a new location and then it left that spot feeling icy cold once it was gone. I thought I had a heat stroke and hypothermia all at the same time.

A few minutes passed and then she asked me, "How are you feeling, Graham?"

"Okay."

"Great. As you probably already know, conjierum limits what its users can and cannot learn to materialize. You could go to the academy and be taught how to conjure up a stethoscope for example, but you may find that no matter how much you try and practice you can't do it. That's just the limit the conjierum has set for you. You most likely wouldn't be able to materialize anything equally or more complex than that stethoscope. As of right now we don't know why the conjierum chooses its users or why it limits them the way it does. Like I said, there are some correlations in play but it's mostly the luck of the draw, Graham. Any questions about any of that?"

I shook my head again.

"Alright, let's get started then. We've found that some items need little to no training or study to materialize, just focus and the power of the conjierum itself will do it for you. I'm going to ask you to try and conjure up a few of those things now. What I'd like for you to do for me first is try to materialize a basic steel nail. Really focus on that nail in your mind and then will it into existence right in your hand."

I tightly shut my eyes and poured all of my mind's energy into that nail. I had never wanted anything more badly in my life than for a stupid little nail to pop into my hand. After a few seconds I felt a weight in my hand; something cool and smooth was resting in my palm. My jaw almost dropped to the floor when I opened my eyes and saw the nail in my hand. I was speechless.

"Very good, Graham!" Savior Corbin said encouragingly. "Let's see about conjuring up something from the Savior and Duelist strands before diving deeper into the Artificer, what do you say?"

"Sounds great!" My heart was pounding with excitement. If nothing else, I was an Artificer like my dad!

"I want you now to try to materialize a pair of plastic forceps for me. They're the medical tweezers that look kind of like scissors."

I shut my eyes and focused again, hoping the same process from before would get me the same result. A few seconds passed again and I felt the plastic in my hand. There they were! I did it!

"Very nice! Now we'll test the Duelist strand. Since you were able to materialize items using the first two strands it's very likely you will be able to do it for the Duelist strand as well, but we still need to check. It's rare, but there are Factotums who only have abilities in two strands."

Factotum. My new reality set in once she said that word. I was a Factotum! My parents were going to be so proud! I was going to be able to materialize anything! I started to think about all the things I was going to help my friends and family back home. Mylo was a town with a pretty big Omitted population. I'd be a star, a hero.

"Now, Graham, I want you to try to materialize a simple pocket knife. The simplest one you can imagine."

I kept my same routine, desperately wanting this. It was hard to keep my focus in all of the excitement, but I did my best. It was there. I had done it! Before I could open my eyes, it was gone. I opened my eyes to see what had happened. In Savior Corbin's chair was sitting Jay

Lynch. His sick, twisted smile overtook his face. His eyes were wild and crazy. The pocket knife was his hand. He flicked it open and started laughing maniacally as he drove the blade as deep as it could go into my right shoulder.

* * *

"Graham," Paxton called my name as he tapped my shoulder trying to wake me up.

I nearly jolted out of bed, letting out some kind of scared grunt with it. Paxton jumped back a few steps, nearly dropping a plate of food he had in his other hand.

"Whoa! You okay, man?"

My heart was racing. My breathing was short and frantic. I did a quick scan of the room. No Jay, just Paxton and a groggy Erica. I must have woken her up. I took in a deep breath and answered him.

"Yeah. Just a bad dream."

"You almost made me drop breakfast," he said, handing me the plate of food. "Eat up. I've got a feeling we've got a long day ahead of us." There was another plate of food sitting on a nearby dresser which he walked over to Erica.

Mass-produced scrambled eggs, a freezer waffle with a pad of butter, a pair of thin, wrinkly sausage links, and a packet of syrup were all on the plate, along with plastic utensils. Erica and I looked at each other. I could tell she had the same expression on her face that I did on mine. Who was this Paxton? Who died and left him in charge? Because unless he knew something we didn't, it definitely wasn't Trevor's decision. Paxton was typically the guy fighting and questioning leadership, not the one actually doing the leading.

"Where did you get this?" Erica asked as she took a bite of her breakfast, which was exactly the same as mine.

"Continental breakfast downstairs. Not a huge spread, and most of it is pretty old, but it's better than nothing. Once you guys are done we should head out."

"We still need to check out," Erica added.

"Already took care of it," he countered.

"You've already taken care of it?"

"Yeah. I checked us out while I was down there getting breakfast."

"Have you eaten? Word is we might 'have a long day ahead of us,'" she asked with a playful smirk.

"Funny, real funny. And yes, I did. I actually got the last jelly-filled donut, too. I know how much you like them so I asked the guy restocking the pastries if there were more. There weren't and he said that they only order so many from their supplier each week. I left a huge complaint in the what-can-we-do-to-improve-your-stay box at the front desk. However many they're ordering is clearly not enough."

There was the Paxton we knew!

Erica and I finished our breakfast, freshened ourselves up, and made our way to the lobby. We placed our dirty plates with the rest of the pile that was growing near the food line. Erica checked to see if Paxton was telling the truth about the donuts. She was disappointed to see that he was.

"You could have shared, you know," she disappointingly mumbled to Paxton on the way out.

"You know what they say Erica, early bird gets the donut."

Outside the sun was just high enough in the sky to be right in our eyes. I materialized a cheap pair of sunglasses for myself. Eyewear was not my forte when it came to my Artificer skills. Erica has conjured herself a stylish pair while Paxton, who was a few steps ahead of us, just blocked out the rays with his arm.

We got on our bikes as Erica materialized and handed out the familiar headsets.

"You mind giving me a pair of those before we get going?" he asked, not directing his question at either of us in particular. "This sun is brutal." He was squinting hard and still shielding his eyes with his arm.

I still wasn't super comfortable joking with Paxton yet, definitely not like Erica was, but I decided to give it a shot. I conjured up a pair of butterfly sunglasses and tossed them over to him. The lenses were shaped like wings, the bridge had little antennas sticking up from it, and they were a bright pink which really stood out against his bluish-gray skin. They were also too small for his face. Again, eyewear wasn't my strong suit.

Erica started cracking up and Paxton laughed a bit too, but played it off when he responded, "What? You've never seen a man wear sunglasses before?"

Erica started laughing even harder. I couldn't help it now either. They looked ridiculous on him. I conjured a pair like mine and tossed those to him. He gave the butterfly pair a little underhanded flip back to me. I dematerialized them and we started up the bikes.

"I have the directions to the hospital. Just follow me," Paxton said over the headset.

Erica gave me the same look from breakfast and this time I couldn't help but laugh. Squad leader Paxton was back. He didn't turn around to look at us but heard me laugh.

"You guys alright?" he asked.

"Yeah. Everything's good. Let's go," Erica responded.

A few minutes later we pulled into the parking lot. "This is it my friends. Arthur Brexley Memorial Hospital. Let's go see a Savior about a Duelist," Paxton said as we walked to the front of the building. The sliding entry doors opened for us, and we proceeded into the lobby. Lo and behold a wheelchair bound Trevor was already there waiting for us. He sat there alone with a freshly bandaged lower leg.

"What the hell took you three so long?" he barked. "I've been waiting here all morning for you."

"All morning? What are you talking about? It's not even 8:30 yet!" Paxton fired back at him. Those two were back to normal pretty quickly.

Trevor looked at the wall clock to confirm. "Alright. Alright. Sorry I got snippy. Let's get out of here. I hate hospitals." He started to wheel himself out the door.

"Do you need help—" a nurse from around the corner saw and started to ask.

"No," he interjected proudly, "I'm fine."

"Let me at least walk you out," she countered.

"What did your Savior say about your leg?" Paxton asked as we walked through the parking lot back to the SB3s.

He was reluctant to answer. "She said I should keep off it for another day or two at least. I got lucky. The bullet didn't hit anything important. Still hurts a whole hell of a lot though. Too bad I don't have the bullet. I'd love to shove that thing up Jay's—"

"Why don't you ride with Graham today, Trevor," Erica cut him off before he could finish.

Just the thought of it irked him, I could see it in his face. He didn't lash out though; he actually started to entertain the idea.

"Fine, only for today though. I'm not ridin' in a sidecar or any shit like that either. Just make sure I get up alright."

The nurse didn't bother to fight him on it even though her face and body language told us she thought it was a terrible idea. She took the wheelchair back towards the hospital and didn't look back. Erica conjured up an extra headset for Trevor, walked it over to him, and thanked him for complying, like a mother would do when her kid makes a good decision. We got on the SB3s and started them up. Trevor gingerly hoisted his leg over the bike and sat down.

Trevor's voice came over the headset, "I want you two to follow our lead. City Hall's not too far from here."

I pulled out of the parking lot and took directions from him over the headset. Like he said, the drive over wasn't very long, maybe fifteen blocks. I noticed the streets were pretty barren, even during the day. Hardly anyone was on the sidewalks and there was even less traffic on the roads. There were plenty of cars parked along the curb, but they were just sitting there. Was Brexley a ghost town, or did people just not come outside?

Erica noticed this too, "It's pretty quiet out here."

"Is that normal?" Paxton's voice came through.

"Wasn't when I lived here. Times are different now, though. It should be this building on the corner here, Graham."

I parked along the curb in front of the building; it was one of the few curbs I had seen that was completely vacant. There was enough room for Erica and Paxton to pull up and park behind us.

"Is this *really* it?" Paxton asked in disbelief as he swung his leg over his SB3.

Chapter 6

City Hall Investigation

City Hall looked like a three-story mansion. It was closed off from the rest of the block by high brick walls, except for an opening to enter through. Like most of the other buildings we had seen in town, it was also pretty badly sun-bleached. Only a few pieces of its white siding were either missing or had fallen off and there were a variety of differently sized claw marks on the pieces that were still attached. Glass shards from all the broken windows on the front of the first floor sat in their frames like jagged teeth.

We moved past the brick walls and set our sights on the front door. The surrounding grass and plants were unkempt and starting to grow longer and more wildly than they probably should have. It was crystal clear to me that no government employee had been here in a while, and hopefully no wild animals or sketchy people were here either.

"What the hell happened to this place?" Paxton asked in astonishment.

We all looked to Trevor, our resident expert, for some kind of explanation. He was just as shocked as we were. "Like I said, I knew Brexley was in rough shape, but didn't know it was *this* bad."

"You sure this is the place? They haven't moved to somewhere else?" Erica added.

"This is it," Trevor stated. He was starting to look a little concerned.

"Let's just do what we came here to do, and get the hell out of here," Paxton blurted out. "I'm more than ready to head back home."

We cautiously walked up to the porch, partially because we didn't know what to expect from this place and also because Trevor couldn't move much faster than a slow, nervous walk anyway. Once we got there Erica materialized a folding chair for Trevor.

"In case you want it," she told him.

"You think I'm just gonna park my ass here while you three go on a scavenger hunt?" I would have happily traded places with him. I didn't like the looks of this place at all.

"You better," Paxton interjected. "You're supposed to be taking it easy on that leg."

"You better watch your tone with me, Spitfire." He paused for a moment. "Fine. But if any of you find anything even remotely suspicious you report it back to me. You hear me?"

We all nodded in agreement, as Paxton reached for the handle to pull the door open.

"Where the hell do you think you're going? I haven't given you any intel on our assignment here yet."

"Sounded pretty straightforward to me yesterday. Anything relating to the dragon gets reported back to Randy."

"Slow down, Spitfire. You're no detective. Randy wants us lookin' for specifics. How about I tell you what those are before you go around parading in this shit hole?" His tone was unmistakably condescending now. He hated when Paxton challenged him.

Paxton begrudgingly let go of the handle and gave Trevor his attention.

"We're lookin' for any evidence that the dragon originated from here. That much you know," he said directing his attention from Paxton to the group as a whole now. "Randy also wants us bringin' in anyone we see here on the property for questioning. Wants pictures and molds of any footprints or unordinary claw marks. You got all that? That a bit more straightforward for you?" He directed the last sentence at Paxton.

We all nodded.

"Good. Be careful while you're all in there. Keep an eye out. Take these." He materialized a SRHG6 for each of us after taking a seat in his chair. They were the standard, short-range handguns that support squads typically used. They looked like any other gun you'd see in a secret agent movie: black, sort of boxy, boring. "Hopefully you won't need 'em."

I looked at the gun in my hand and started to have a bad feeling about this whole thing. I hesitated for a second, wanting to keep the question to myself but it squeaked out, "Keep an eye out for what?"

He sighed, lowered his head, and ran his hand down his face. "Anything that could land your ass in Brexley General or a six-foot hole, kid! Dealers. Gangbangers. Squatters. Rabid dogs. More dragon things. Who the hell knows what's in there?" I thought he was joking about the dragons, but his face stayed dead serious. "You want me to keep goin' or you get the point?"

"No, I got it," I replied, feeling incredibly stupid and embarrassed for asking.

"Can we get going now or are we not done wasting more time?" Paxton nearly whined.

"Get movin'," Trevor said, visibly agitated. He then conjured up an SRHG6 and loaded it. "Find something useful in there. And lose that shitty attitude while you're at it, Agton!"

It was the first time in a while I heard him call Paxton just 'Agton.' Normally he stuck with Spitfire and that was usually enough of a sign to let Paxton know to back off or cool down. Just 'Agton' meant he was genuinely pissed at him. Yesterday was the first time I remember him calling me Garnett in a while too. I'm not sure I ever heard him call Erica by just her last name, Towson. Maybe he did the day she freaked out about the clown, but I can't remember for sure.

"I'll keep an eye out for anything suspicious out here. If you hear me hollering get your asses down here ASAP."

Paxton, not acknowledging Trevor at all at this point, opened the door with his gun drawn and walked in first. Erica followed him next and I brought up the rear.

The SRHG6 shook a bit in my hands as we walked into a grand

foyer. It was dark, only getting limited light from the windows along the front wall and the open entry door. There were even more scratches and claw marks inside on what appeared to be a marble floor along with a thin layer of dust in spots that weren't as creature-traveled. It reminded me of the room Jay had me in. Dark. Dusty. Deteriorated. I started having flashbacks of being tied down to that chair, how I desperately tried to get myself free when I thought Jay was going to kill me. That smile. I thought about that deranged smile. I didn't like what this place reminded me of or how it made me feel.

A massive chandelier was mounted to the ceiling on the third floor and stretched all the way down to the first. It was gorgeous and elegant, clearly designed to be a focal point in the building. Brexley City Hall had an interesting layout. It almost resembled a large, U-shaped apartment building. The left and right-hand sides of the building each had large, meticulously crafted, spiral wooden staircases leading to the second and third floors above. Straight ahead of us was an archway, which took the place of what would have been more rooms in the middle of the first floor. It led to a space that we couldn't see from our spot in the doorway.

"Ten bucks says there's nothing here," Paxton mumbled to himself but loud enough for us to hear. "Alright, I'll take all the rooms on the left side. Erica, you take the middle rooms above the arch. Graham, you take the rooms on the right. Why don't we start from the top and make our way down? Meet back here once your sweep is done, and we'll see where this archway leads together. Sound good?"

He didn't even wait for a response and headed toward the staircase on the left. Erica and I decided to use the one on the right; it felt like it was best to give Paxton some space. The steps were wide enough that Erica and I could walk side by side.

"Weird there's not an elevator in here," I whispered, trying to keep my nerves calm.

"Yeah. Legally, there should be. But let's be honest, it probably wouldn't be working anyway if there were one. I'm guessing there's plenty of other things here that aren't up to code either."

We slowly climbed the winding stairs. Every now and then one would squeak and I'd jerk my gun up into position, ready to fire. There were animal droppings on the stairs and we could hear scampering in the distance. Some noises sounded like they came from something too big for my liking. The stench from the poop and the sour scent of urine started to really hit us.

The higher we got the darker and more ominous we got. With each step the light from the first-floor door and windows seemed significantly further and further away. It was like the night we first rode here driving away from DREAM Tower and watching its light fade away. By the time we made it up to the third floor it felt like all I had was the flickering of a candle inside of a deep, underground cave.

"Stay safe, Graham." Erica kept her voice low as we went our separate ways. I watched her shadow of a body painstakingly step down the hall towards her assigned rooms. Her gun was locked and loaded, ready for anything that might come her way.

I was on edge and really didn't want to be alone in this place. I took the same approach as her, almost creeping through the building. I heard more knocks and scratching sounds occasionally but never saw what was making them. It really started to mess with my head. Was I being watched? Was there something here or just the creaks and noises of an old building? I had to psych myself up before going into every room. Each one terrified me. What if something was inside? I took in a deep breath, made sure my gun was loaded, then went in ready to fire if needed. I checked my gun every single time as irrational as that was. If something was going to get me, I was at least going down with a fight, I hoped.

I meticulously searched all of my rooms, looking back at the door every minute or two to make sure I didn't have any guests. All the spaces had similar layouts and designs. Rummaging through desks and filing cabinets, I found out each room was a different office for the various departments of the city. Something about this place was odd though. It was as if the workers just decided to suddenly leave one day and never come back. Sensitive documents were just sitting on top of desks. Coats and hats were still hanging on racks.

I heard noises coming from the second to last room I had to check. Light shuffling. Tapping. Some kind of crumpling, like something being moved around in a plastic bag. The door was cracked. I stood with my back to the wall next to the door and just listened. The sounds weren't going away. My heartrate started picking up. My mind immediately went to a hostile squatter.

A rancid odor hit me after a few horrible thoughts of being attacked by whoever was in this room passed. I nearly gagged. The smell of spoiled meat was coming from the room.

It took me a minute but I finally worked up the courage to investigate. I gripped my gun tight. I could feel my pulse in my fingers wrapped around the handle. I kicked the door the rest of the way in and aimed. As soon as it hit the wall all kinds of chirping and fluttering erupted. I was totally caught off guard and flinched.

Birds, just birds. They must have flown in from the broken window in the office. They were pecking at a half-eaten turkey and cheese sandwich sitting on the desk, still partially packed in its bag. Those birds were my sounds and that sandwich was definitely my smell. I held my breath as much as I could, did my search, and got out of there.

I didn't find anything useful on the third floor. I did find out that one of my offices on the second floor was assigned to the department of public works. There was letter after letter complaining about potholes in the roads, trash not being collected weekly, and playground equipment needing desperate repair, among other things.

One woman wrote that if the massive pothole in front of her apartment building on Wedgewood Avenue wasn't filled soon, she was going to fill it with water and start charging local kids admission to swim in it. That gave me a bit of a laugh, which helped ease some of my tension for a little while.

"Find anything?" I asked as I saw Erica walking towards the staircase. I still kept my voice pretty low. She was still alert, but seemed a bit more relaxed than when I last saw her.

"Something's been in here, Graham," she said, stopping me before we went down the stairs. "Something big. I saw a few chewed-up rat corpses and figured it was just a cat or something. I thought that at least until I found a mauled feral cat. Something ripped that thing apart. It was so bad that it took me a few minutes to figure out what the thing was, Graham. I materialized a camera and took some pictures. Here."

I was already freaked out and looking at her pictures was only going to make it worse, but I did it anyway. Blood and fur were scattered all over the floor. The poor thing really had been torn limb from limb. Its entrails were lacerated and oozing juices.

"This looks fresh," I barely choked out.

"I thought so too." Her voice was somber. "Hopefully he's found something that can get us out of here." We both looked across the building and saw Paxton's figure enter one of the offices on the first floor. "I'm going to check on Trevor and give him an update. Show him these." She held up the camera. "Be careful."

She quietly hurried down the stairs. I stood there for a moment in shock. What animal in a city like this would be able to do that? None that I could think of, unless it was one sick and perverted person. The thought of that only made me feel worse.

I found nothing on the first floor. My mind was still wrapped in Erica's cat, my near heart attack with the birds, and just how creepy and disgusting this place was. When I walked out of my last room, I saw Paxton chatting low with Erica. He had a newspaper in his hand.

"Find something?" I called out to him.

He took a second to choose his words, "I found *something*. Not a shredded cat and not exactly what we were looking for, but something still interesting regardless."

As I reached where they were standing, he handed me the

paper. It was only an insert and had no sign of a publication date. The title read, *Jay Lynch: From Hometown Hero to Hoodlum.* Before I had a chance to read it any further, Paxton spoiled it for me.

"Turns out our buddy Jay is from the area and was a Duelist at the academy. He got kicked out after a dueling accident left him blind in that right eye of his."

I skipped the obvious question of why he was kicked out, already having the answer. The academy wouldn't let him become a Duelist without having vision in both eyes.

"I'm surprised we didn't hear about this at the academy," I said to Paxton.

"I'm sure it's not something they're proud of and wouldn't want publicized, especially since it's their fault. The article says that he was pretty talented, projected to be a top Duelist pick in his class. It could just be hometown bias, but either way it's a shame."

I handed the paper back, figuring he would just keep telling me the story anyway, "How was it the academy's fault?"

"Faulty eyewear. Protective glasses for practice duels are supposed to be regularly checked by instructors for weak points or damage. Those instructors are supposed to be logging any glasses needing repair and then sending them to some civil Artificer agency to repair them. Well, Jay took a blow to the face in a practice duel and his glasses didn't hold up. The hit not only destroyed the glasses, but blinded him in that eye.

"Academy Artificers analyzed his glasses to see if it was just a freak accident or if there was prior damage to them," he paused to take a breath, or maybe just for dramatic effect. "His pair hadn't logged as inspected in weeks. The Artificers concluded that there had to have been prior damage done for them not to withstand the hit they took."

"How negligent is that? Who was the instructor?" I asked intently.

Paxton looked at me like I was an idiot. "Trevor! Did you not hear Jay ranting and raving about how his eye was Trevor's fault?"

He was probably right, but I felt like I had to defend myself. "That doesn't necessarily mean he was the instructor. He could have been someone's supervisor or something. Do we even know what Trevor was doing before he became our squad leader?"

"Believe what you want, Graham. Trevor had to have been Jay's instructor and the reason why he's so screwed up now. After Trevor destroyed his future, the article says Jay came back here and that's when things really went downhill for him."

"Anyway, let's wrap this up before whatever got a hold of Erica's cat gets a hold of us," Paxton prodded.

The three of us passed through the archway leading to an open lounge space with our guns drawn. To the left was a kitchen with a wraparound bar for people to sit at. To the right was a sitting area with torn-up couches and chairs. A large TV was mounted above a brick fireplace. Large sliding glass doors stood ahead of us leading to the back of the property, which looked like some sort of courtyard. The whole back wall where the glass doors stood was made of floor-to-ceiling windows. The lounge was spacious, but only one story high.

"Let's split up and get this done faster," Paxton suggested. "I'll take the kitchen. Graham, you check over by the couches. Erica, you go see what's out back."

We all agreed with his plan and went our separate ways. I pulled the ripped-up cushions off couches, nothing under them. I hesitantly checked inside the fireplace too. Nothing. Towards the corner of the room, near the fireplace, I found a door that we couldn't see on our way in. I was anxious about where it would lead or what was inside. I readied my handgun and then opened the door. I was relieved that it was just a bathroom with a single toilet and a stand-alone sink.

"Any luck?" I called over to Paxton after an exhale.

"Nothing yet," he said as he opened another cabinet.

Erica slid the doors open, drawing our attention, and motioned for us to come with her.

"Guys, I think I found something."

Chapter 7

The Green Substance

Paxton and I trotted over to the door and followed her outside. The grass out here was just as long and unruly as the stuff out front, growing through the stone paver patio near the door. The courtyard was probably half the size of a tennis court and pretty secluded thanks to those brick walls surrounding the property. There were a few towering trees as well as weather-worn and splintering wooden picnic tables.

Erica led us off the patio and into the grass. She found her spot and bent down to take another look at what she called us out here to see. Paxton and I also bent down to get a better view.

"So, about that ten bucks?" she asked Paxton jokingly, but he didn't react to her at all.

He reached down and carefully picked up a vial of neon green liquid. The top of it was cracked slightly, and not knowing what was inside, he was careful with it. He slowly swirled it around, like a fine wine. It was viscous and wasn't swishing around at the same speed a normal liquid would. The look on their faces told me that we all had the same idea of what this stuff was.

Both of them were so enthralled and dumbfounded that I was left yet again to ask the obvious question at hand. "This can't be conjierum...can it? *Green* conjierum?"

The four strands of conjierum had their own distinct color. Duelist was a bright red. Savior, bright yellow. Artificer, bright blue. And Factotum was light brown. So what conjierum, if this actually was conjierum, would be green, neon green?

"It definitely looks like conjierum," Paxton said, examining the vial closely, bringing it closer to his eyes, "but I wouldn't be injecting this stuff into my arm. Who knows what it would do to you?"

We all stood there for a second pondering. All our lives we had been taught that there were only three distinct strands of conjierum and a fourth hybrid strand: the Factotum. Could this have really been a fifth? I almost couldn't fathom it. It couldn't be. It had to be something else. Something that just looked like conjierum, moved like conjierum, and just happened to be vialed like conjierum would be.

"Let's see what Trevor thinks," Paxton suggested.

We started walking back through the house to the porch where we hoped to find a resting Trevor. He was still there, but no longer sitting, claiming he was trying to stretch out his leg.

"Find anything else besides animal carcasses?"

"Erica found this out back," Paxton said, handing him the vial.

"What the…" he said, pulling it close to his face while squinting at it. "This looks a hell of a lot like conjierum to me. You found this out back?" he addressed Erica.

"Yeah."

"You find any more?"

"No. Just the one vial."

"Any syringes with it?"

"No."

"Interesting. Can you seal it for me? Last thing we need is this stuff leakin' out of here."

Erica materialized what looked like some kind of plastic wrap. Paxton handed her the vial, and she loosely wrapped the top. It somehow, almost magically, tightened itself into a vacuum tight seal; no green stuff was going to be leaking out of there. I stopped my mouth from gaping as I was the only one who looked even remotely impressed by this. Trevor then immediately reached for the vial.

"We gotta get this back to DREAM Tower. The labs are gonna want a look at this. I need to make a quick call, then we'll head back."

Trevor stepped away to get some privacy. Paxton and Erica looked tired. Erica was doing her best to hide it, while Paxton, on the other hand, wasn't. Letting out a deep breath, he plopped down into

Trevor's chair and locked his fingers behind his head.

"Between that dragon, Jay, and now this vial, I think we've earned *at least* one day off."

"That'd be great," Erica added.

Before anyone else could get a word in, Trevor hobbled back over to us. "Alright. Let's get out of here."

Walking back to the bikes, Erica conjured up a brown, leather satchel to carry the vial in. Paxton became the designated "Sultan of the Satchel," a title she gave him as he took it from her offering hands. Trevor handed him the small glass of green goop, and he tucked it away, positioning the bag over his shoulder and across his body.

"Back to DREAM Tower," Trevor called out as he carefully swung his leg over the SB3 behind me.

We put our headsets back on, got the bikes started, and began the trek back. The first ten to fifteen minutes of the ride were quiet besides Trevor giving directions. We were leading the pack again. Eventually a different voice came through over the headset. It was Erica.

"Trevor, I know you said things have been bad here, but what's really going on?"

He took a second to respond, and it became clear pretty quickly that she was onto something. "What do you mean 'what's really going on?'" The tone in his voice was weird: unnecessarily and suspiciously defensive, like a little kid trying to keep a playground secret.

"Why is City Hall abandoned and in such bad shape? Why isn't there anyone out here on the streets? Even if Brexley is a rough town that doesn't add up. People would still have to leave their houses at some point, to go to work, go out for food, run errands, do something. Where is everybody? Something weird is going on here."

"She's right," Paxton hopped in. His voice was getting excited. "I didn't really think about it until now, but something is really off about this place."

Trevor paused again. Erica was too perceptive for her own good, and Paxton was now a shark smelling blood in the water. He hated not being in on a secret or not having as much information as possible. This looked like a shot to get in on something, and he was going to take it.

"Nothing gets by the two of you, does it? You're puttin' me in a tough spot here. I can't say anything about it."

"The hell you can't!" Paxton had now stolen the conversation from Erica. "If we're in some kind of serious danger by being out here, we have a right to know!"

Trevor let out a quick chuckle. "Can't argue with that logic now can I, Spitfire? It'd be irresponsible of me to keep that kind of information from you when you put it that way. Just the loophole I needed. I'll tell you what's going on up here, but you need to keep your mouths shut on this. We clear? I already have Randy on my ass about figurin' this dragon out, I don't need him bitchin' to me about how my squad leaked information that put DREAM in a full-on frenzy."

"We're clear," Paxton confirmed for the three of us.

"About a week or two before the draft strange shit started happenin' up here. People claimed they saw weird things runnin' down the streets, possessions and property being damaged, their pets being attacked, the whole nine yards. Reason why you don't see anyone out on the streets is, one, because they're too afraid to come out and, two, they're not supposed to. The big wigs in DREAM Tower don't want everyone gettin' all hysterical about it, so they've been sendin' trucks with food and medical supplies every few days and promised to cover the town's utilities costs until they can get rid of the problem. Whole city's on unofficial lockdown. They're gettin' food and a handful of their bills paid; that's why no one's said a peep."

"How could Hornsby let this happen? How could he just hide that, *this*, from DREAM?" Erica asked, a bit distraught. She was a huge fan of President Vincent Hornsby.

"He doesn't know it's going on. Randy's been handlin' it all behind his back while Vincent's been on vacation."

"Let's cut to the chase, what sort of 'weird things' are we talking about?" Paxton chimed back in as we turned a corner and down a new street.

"Things like *that*?" I said slowing my bike down to a complete stop.

In the middle of the street, maybe forty feet from us, were five giant, mutant-looking raccoons feasting on a large dog. Its collar had been tossed aside by its killers and it didn't have a leash attached, which led me to believe the poor thing had escaped from its home and ran into the wrong crowd. We all, slowly and quietly, got off the SB3s, realizing we couldn't go any further until the five fiends moved on out.

"Whoa," Erica whispered.

"Those things have to be like fifty, maybe sixty, pounds each," Paxton added in a low tone. "I have a guess at what killed your cat."

"We can take a different street, can't we?" she half-asked, half-suggested.

"Too late now," Paxton said with a nervous tinge to his voice.

One of them looked up and saw us watching it. It stood up on its hind legs and growled at us. Paxton was right. It had to be close to sixty pounds and almost four feet tall when standing upright. Even with a chunky frame, it still looked pretty muscular. Blood and cream-colored foam dripped down from its teeth.

Once the first one started hissing at us the other four decided to stand up in a defensive position too. They took a few steps towards us, walking upright rather naturally, which made them that much more disturbing, the muscles in their legs flexing with every step. Those legs were strong despite their size, and I had a gut feeling these guys were probably deceptively quick. I noticed they all had the same neon green eyes that the dragon had. Their stares looked angry but empty, almost like it was being possessed by something.

"They've got the same weird green eyes like the dragon," I nervously pointed out.

"Admire their eyes when they're dead, Garnett," Trevor said, shoving one of his custom handguns into my gut. "Get ready." He then motioned for us to slowly get off of our bikes.

It was the same gun I had used to fight the dragon. If this gun had done so much damage to that huge dragon, I could only imagine what it would do to these raccoons. He conjured two more, one went to Paxton on his left and the other to me to pass to Erica on my right.

The raccoons continued to make their way towards us but stopped when they saw the guns. It seemed like they knew what the guns were as all five went down on all fours and into a pouncing stance. Their growling and hissing became louder and fiercer. Drool from their mouths splashed onto the street, instantly corroding it.

"Oh, shit!" Paxton exclaimed seeing the pavement dissolve away.

"Don't let these bastards get ahold of you!" Trevor called out, not minding his volume anymore. "Hold your ground. Don't make any sudden movements. We don't want these things chargin' at us. Especially with that spit. On my count, we'll all fire. Take them all out at once."

We had our guns aimed and ready waiting for Trevor's command. My hand was shaking and my arm felt ridiculously heavy. I could feel my heartbeat pounding in my trigger finger. Their growls and hissing continued as they slowly crept toward us again. I started breaking into a nervous sweat. All of the worst-case scenarios started playing in my head.

I desperately hoped they would just turn around and go back to the dog, totally forgetting and ignoring us. We could hop back on the SB3s and get out of here, turn around, take a different street. Fat chance. They were over their snack and now looking forward to a four-course meal.

They were maybe twenty feet from us now; why hadn't Trevor told us to fire yet? The one I was aimed at let out a loud growl and quickly stood up again. I was jumpy and accidentally pulled the trigger.

My round hit it in the neck.

The raccoon fell flat on its back. Blood poured out of its wound, staining its fur red, and started to pool in the street. The skin around the bullet wound was burning away like it did with the dragon. Trevor's bullets must have had some kind of corrosiveness of their own. That was it. I had done it. It was on now. The other four charged at us. It only took them two or three swift strides to get within striking distance. They were even faster and more powerful than I thought.

"FIRE!"

The popping of successive gunshots filled the air. We didn't hesitate to unload our rounds on them knowing what they could do if they reached us. Luckily everyone hit their target before it could hit them. Shell casings, raccoon innards, and sticky, dark red blood now littered the street. Each raccoon fell only a few feet from us. What saliva that was left in their mouths began to eat away at the street.

When all was said and done Trevor hit me hard on the shoulder. "WHAT THE HELL WAS THAT?" he yelled at me.

"It...I..." I couldn't get my words together.

"His target moved, and he reacted," Erica came to my rescue.

"You stay out of this!" he reprimanded her with an angry, pointed index finger.

She bought me enough time to put a few words together, "It caught me off guard. I didn't expect it—"

"You're lucky we were just a hair quicker than those bastards! You could've gotten us all killed!"

"I know. I'm sorry."

"You wanna stay in this squad, Garnett?" He only gave me a split second to respond before following up with, "Well, do you?"

"Yes, sir," I said, ashamed and defeated.

"Then you better learn to get your shit together and keep it together!" He took a few seconds to cool off. It was dead silent, no one dared to speak. "Alright, let's go. We've wasted enough time."

We got back on the SB3s and went on our way. It was only

Trevor's directions over the headsets for a while, until I heard Erica's voice again.

She must have been able to talk to me directly somehow. "Hey, don't beat yourself over what happened back there. It could've happened to any of us. What matters is that no one got hurt."

I didn't want to respond with Trevor behind me. Even with the engine running, I felt like somehow, someway, he'd be able to hear whatever I said. I appreciated Erica trying to console me, but I still felt miserable.

I was ready for this day to end. I was ready for this assignment to end. I was ready to go back to our mundane daily patrols and relaxing evenings. No more nine story dragons, psychotic, Duelist kidnappers, or oversized, acid-spitting raccoons. I was tired of fighting, tired of screwing up, tired of being scared, tired of being yelled at, and most of all tired of feeling like shit over all of it. It was such a relief to pull up to DREAM Tower and know that my two-day nightmare was finally about to end.

Chapter 8

The Vial and the Vision

I never thought I'd be so excited to see only one broken window. The wall of glass in our common room still hadn't been replaced, but man was it good to see DREAM Tower again and be back in Center City. The closer we got the more relaxed I felt myself becoming. Our hellish time in Brexley was finally over and I was more than ready to put everything that happened behind me. Paxton, Erica, and I parked the SB3s on the curb in front of the building, cashing in on some delivery truck pulling out. It was just big enough to squeeze all three bikes. As we walked up to the main entrance, I made sure to avoid the plaque that I tripped over the last time we were here.

I was hoping the other three would have forgotten about that by now, but Paxton didn't, "Hey, guys, watch out for the plaque."

I didn't know if I should make some kind of funny remark back. After the butterfly shades I was feeling a little more comfortable joking with Paxton so I decided to go for it.

"Thanks for the heads up. How embarrassing would it be to trip over that thing, right?" I was finding that a little self-deprecation went a long way with him. Both he and Erica smiled.

Trevor led us to reception. The woman sitting there, Connie, according to her nametag, looked up at Trevor as he planted his forearm on her desk. I imagined he was probably trying to focus his weight on that arm instead of his leg.

"Hello, Trevor," she said warmly, "How are you feeling?"

Word of our escapade with Jay Lynch must have made its way around. Trevor gave her a half smile. It was clear that he wasn't expecting that question.

"I'm alright," he replied. "We're here to see Dr. Ryken. He knows we're comin'."

"Okay. Let me give his lab a call real quick and see if he's ready for you."

Trevor turned to us as Connie dialed down to the lab. "Alright, while we're down there, mind your own business. Don't be tryin' to snoop around either, you hear me, Spitfire?"

"Wait, you're letting us come with you?" Paxton asked.

"Yeah. You all found it, not me. If he's got questions, I can't answer them. But don't say anything unless you're spoken to, got it?"

The three of us were fine with that. Support squads typically weren't allowed in the labs. They were kept pretty confidential.

"Dr. Ryken's ready for you. His lab is on minus four," Connie informed us.

"Thanks, Connie," Trevor said as he half-limped, half-walked to the elevator.

In addition to the one hundred seven stories DREAM Tower had above ground, it also went five floors underground. Those floors were where all the labs were housed. Keeping labs in a glorified basement with limited ventilation and specialized Artificers playing with chemicals, conjierum, and who knows what else on a regular basis, didn't seem like the smartest floor plan to me. But, hey, what did I know? I'm only part Artificer and architecture wasn't my forte there either.

When the elevator door opened to let us out, Trevor once again hobbled ahead of us, leading the way. The place was buzzing with activity. Men and women in white lab coats were performing all kinds of experiments and recording observations on tablets. This one lab took up the entire floor and had dozens of different things going on at once. There were groups testing out different pieces of machinery that I'm sure they had created themselves. Some of it looked like robots, others like engines, and I think one group was even working on some type of fancy traffic light. There were other groups stretching and compressing materials I wasn't familiar with, probably to gauge their durability.

What really caught my eye was a group near us examining each strand of conjierum in its own petri dish. Ever since the first person injected themselves with the liquid and discovered what we could do through it, Artificers have been trying to understand how and why conjierum works. Why it chose to work for some people and not others. Why it chose to let certain people conjure a wider variety of things than others. I just figured if it wasn't magic, it was the next closest thing, and was plenty satisfied with that.

Anyway, the lab was certainly impressive, and definitely sterile looking. I felt bad standing there in my dirty, sweaty clothes. A man with the smile and swagger of a used car salesman started to approach us. It was Dr. Ryken, I knew because his name was embroidered on his lab coat. He was younger than I imagined, maybe in his late thirties. His skin was dark, his body was pretty lean, and his short afro was perfectly kept. Once he saw Trevor his smile grew bigger and brighter than a full moon.

"Trevor, old friend! Good to see you again," he exclaimed. "Where is this vial you wanted to show me?"

"Hey, Dante. It's good to see you too." Trevor gestured for Paxton to hand Dr. Ryken the satchel. "My squad and I were sent on assignment by Randy to do an investigation. These three found this on location. We thought you might be able to tell us what we've got here."

He opened the satchel and pulled out the vial, holding it up towards the light. He squinted at it for a moment, as if he were trying to read some really small print on the glass, then gave it a swirl. He seemed as perplexed as we were when we first saw it.

"Call me crazy, but it looks like conjierum to me. However, I've never known conjierum to be green in color."

"We were thinkin' conjierum too, but like you said, I've never seen green conjierum before either."

"My team and I will have to run a full series of diagnostic assessments on it to find out exactly what it is. Come by my workstation for a second and I'll give you at least an educated guess at what we have here," he said as he started walking towards a lab table, waving us along to follow him.

Dr. Ryken removed the wrapping and cap off of the vial. He pulled out a fresh syringe from one of the table's drawers, put a small sample of the liquid into a petri dish, and took a look at it under a microscope.

"Interesting," he stated as he looked up at us from the lens. "It definitely looks like conjierum, at the structural level at least. Again, I won't know for sure until we run some tests on it. Hopefully by tomorrow, the following day at the latest, I'll be able to tell you exactly what this is. I'll send my findings to Randy and we'll go from there. Sound good?"

"Yes, sir," Trevor replied.

"Alright then, if you'll excuse me. I have one or two other things I need to take care of before I get to this."

"Of course. It was good seein' you, Dante," Trevor said, giving him a friendly tap on the shoulder. He then turned to us as Dr. Ryken scurried across the lab. "Let's go."

We filed into the elevator and started our ascent.

"I want the three of you to get off at the ground floor and wait for me there," Trevor instructed. "I need to file a formal report with Randy on that vial. I'll try to convince him to give us the day off tomorrow while Ryken's runnin' his tests. I think we could all use it. Heard Spitfire over here could use *at least* one." He said using the same inflection Paxton did back in Brexley. I guess he heard Paxton over his phone call.

Paxton wasn't embarrassed in the slightest, where I would have been. Trevor wasn't typically one to make jokes or poke fun. I think it caught Paxton off guard, but he just owned it and reiterated, "*At least* one."

Everyone laughed. Trevor even let out a few chuckles, before shaking his head in joking disbelief. The three of us got off at the ground floor, as directed. We each found a seat in the lobby and geared up for what would most likely become a marathon of a wait for Trevor's return.

"So, if Trevor manages to get us all the day off tomorrow, any ideas on what you might do?" Erica asked.

Paxton answered first, sounding pretty tired, "I might just stay home and take it easy."

I thought about what I would do for a moment. Part of me wanted to just take the day to lounge around and relax, like Paxton was planning, but something else inside of me wanted to stay busy. I wanted something in the middle; something to keep me occupied but didn't require too much energy or effort. That's when the idea popped into my head.

"I might go to the boardwalk. Get a bite to eat, play some games, ride some rides, do some people watching," I answered, getting more excited about it the more I spoke.

"That sounds like fun!" Erica said as her face lit up. "Mind if I joined you? I haven't been to the boardwalk in ages!"

"Sure. Paxton, you're more than welcome to come too if you want."

"Thanks, but no thanks," he said disinterested. "I wouldn't want to be a third wheel on your little date."

"It's not a date," she said before I could. "We're just hanging out."

Erica and I planned out our trip, granted we would get the day off, while Paxton fell asleep in his chair. Trevor finally made his way back into the lobby after what felt like hours.

"I convinced Randy to give us tomorrow off. Go home, relax, enjoy yourselves, and I'll see you all later."

We were happy, and relieved, to have the day off. Trevor started heading back to the elevator instead of the door.

"Aren't you going home too, Trevor?" Erica asked, a bit surprised.

"Not just yet. I've got a few things to take care of upstairs."

He continued on before we could ask any follow up questions. It didn't stop Paxton from calling out to him, "Careful not to fall out that window. Don't forget, it's coming out of your paycheck."

"Go home, smartass," he sassed back, not even bothering to turn around.

"Anybody else find it weird that he's not leaving too?" Erica asked as we stepped out onto the sidewalk.

"He's probably got squad leader stuff to take care of." Paxton remarked.

"'Squad leader stuff?'" Erica asked. I wasn't sure if she was mocking him or genuinely asking. It was probably a bit of both.

"Yeah, like backed up paperwork, catching up on emails, finding an Artificer to replace our window."

We couldn't help but laugh out loud. I'm not sure if it was because it was actually funny or we were just really tired. It didn't really matter though. We said goodbye to each other and went our separate ways. When I got home, I immediately plopped down on the couch, picked up the remote, and turned on the TV. I was tired, but wanted to get caught up on the world of sports. I was usually on top of what was going on in baseball, at least, with the exception of these last few days.

To my disappointment, all professional sports in DREAM had been suspended indefinitely. The majority of the sports writers and reporters on TV took "indefinitely" to mean until the dragon situation was completely figured out and the public could be reassured they wouldn't see another dragon flying over their stadiums. I was bummed, but understood why it was happening. So instead of watching the Mylo Otters, my favorite baseball team, take on the Carmine Comets tonight like I was hoping to, I settled for the mind-numbing infomercials.

* * *

I was paralyzed in place. There was Jay Lynch, right in front of me. The space around him was empty, just different shades of red and black nothingness swirling and flowing around us. His clothes torn and dirty, his good eye bloodshot, his teeth tightly clenched, and his body noticeably twitching in agitation. The look of pure rage on his face turned into one of sick pleasure once he reached into his pocket and pulled out a syringe filled with what looked like the green liquid we found at Brexley City Hall. He held it up, showing it to me, laughing menacingly like a lunatic. I tried to materialize something. Anything. Anything to defend myself. Anything to stop him. I couldn't. Nothing was happening. I was petrified.

Jay slowly raised the syringe to his neck, shoved the needle in, and injected the fluid into himself. His eyes began to change colors. The whites turned black while his irises and pupils turned white. His muscles and veins began to bulge, nearly bursting out of his skin. His fingernails became long, jagged, and disgustingly discolored.

Jay's voice had grown eerily deep and terrifying, almost demonic, as he cried out to me, "Goodnight, Sunshine!"

Just then he materialized the same dragon our squad killed hours before unfortunately running into him. The beast was furious. It looked like Jay had brought it back from the dead. Thick clumps of blood oozed from its wounds. Its body had started to decay. This zombie of a dragon was even more nightmarish than when it was alive.

How did he do that? Jay materialized a dead dragon back to life. Impossible. People couldn't materialize beings—living or dead. The beast let out a deep, deafening roar followed by a glass-shattering shriek. I covered my ears as fast as I could but they still rang like never-ending church bells.

Jay continued to laugh hysterically. As he did, he became less and less human. He began to grow fur all over his body, which was becoming larger and even more muscular. His clothes ripped and ripped until they couldn't hold him anymore. Jay had become a larger, more savage version of the raccoons we saw in Brexley. The thing that was once Jay was now on all fours, hissing at me. It had the same god-forsaken stare the other ones did. The foam and toxic drool started leaking from its mouth.

My mind was racing in fear, completely overwhelmed. This was it. I was going to die. Even worse, I knew between these two that it would be excruciating. What was to stop them from tearing me limb from limb?

Out of nowhere both of them began to charge at me. The dragon flying at full speed and what used to be Jay pounding the invisible ground with the force and speed of a cheetah. My mind went blank but my adrenaline went into overdrive. This really was the end now!

The raccoon reached me first. It leapt at me, knocking me flat on my back. My head smacked against and bounced off of whatever was below me. I gasped for breath; the wind was knocked out of me. It pinned me down by the shoulders. Its sharp claws slowly dug deep into my skin. Drool fell from its mouth onto my cheek. I could feel my skin burning away like it had been dipped in a vat of acid. All of the pain was brutal but I couldn't scream. It gave me one last wicked smirk before yanking its claws out of my right shoulder, raising its arm, and taking a vicious swipe at my face...

Chapter 9

Erica's Roller Coaster Day

"Hey, Graham!" Erica called to me as she made her way up the ramp to the boardwalk.

"Hey, Erica. You ready?"

"Yeah. Let's get going."

The boardwalk was buzzing with action. Familiar smells of greasy, junky boardwalk food drifted through the air. Burgers, pizza, fries and cotton candy all pounded my nostrils at once. Every now and then the scent of the salty breeze would beat the other scents out.

Chatter from people, roars from game hosts, and electronic music from rides and arcade machines came from every direction. People flooded in and out of the different shops, games, and attractions.

I looked down in the direction of where we landed after defeating the dragon. It was way down towards the end of the boardwalk where all of this hullabaloo didn't exist. There was definitely something to be said for that section of the walk. Much calmer and more relaxing, especially in the evenings. It was a great place to kick back on a bench and take in more of the natural sights and sounds of the shore. Oh, and it was the best place to catch the fireworks shows.

"What do you want to do first?" I asked.

"Hmm. Want to head to one of the piers and ride some rides?"

"Sounds good to me."

We set our sights on the pier closest to us. The boardwalk had three different piers with different amusement and water rides. I personally didn't prefer one pier over the other, but some people did.

I noticed a lot of people making weird faces as we passed by. They ranged from annoyed to disgusted, even angry. I couldn't hear what they were saying but I could see people mumbling things under their breath either to themselves or whoever they were with. Nobody looked directly at me or Erica which made me wonder if something was going on behind us.

I turned my head to check, paranoia getting the better of me. Nothing out of the ordinary. That's when the self-consciousness kicked in. Were these people making looks and whispering about me? I casually looked down to my shirt, pants, and shoes. No stains on my shirt or pants. Zipper was zippered. Both shoes were tied. I hadn't stepped in anything. I may not be the most attractive guy in the world, but I definitely wasn't hideous enough to be drawing the weird attention we were getting.

I looked over to Erica, hoping she had picked up on it. Whatever *it* was. The excitement she had only a few minutes ago was now totally gone. Her face was completely stoic. I felt stupid, like everyone we passed was in on some big secret that I wasn't. What was going on?

We finally arrived at the pier. A small, forced grin made its way back on Erica's face. I could tell she was really trying to push aside whatever it was that had sucked the joy out of her.

"What do you want to ride first?" she asked.

I scanned the pier looking for a fun ride with a small line. I found one, and it seemed like the perfect ride to start the day. "How about The Hydra?"

The line for it was surprisingly short. Typically, it was one of the more popular rides on this pier. Maybe it had just opened for the day. This would get her spirits back up for sure.

The Hydra was a one-of-a-kind roller coaster. It had a bunch of corkscrews and loops as well as one of the biggest initial drops of all the rides across the piers. It was known for this one section where it went down into the ocean for a bit. A clear covering came up from the sides of each car, meeting each other at a point to keep the water out and the rider and air in. It was like riding in your own personal submarine. The very last car acted as the propeller for the underwater portion, pushing all of the other cars along. The sea blue structures and dark green cars with painted scales really made it look like you were riding a sea serpent through the air and sea.

Her eyes widened as she took in the ride from a distance. I had never seen her like this. She looked like a kid in a candy store.

She turned to me and enthusiastically said, "Let's go!"

We first stopped at a kiosk to get the tickets we needed for the ride. The line for The Hydra was a little bit longer now, but still reasonable. Erica couldn't have cared less; she was mesmerized. I was starting to wonder if she would get more enjoyment out of just staring at it instead of getting on.

"The last time I came to the boardwalk I was a little girl," she told me while admiring the different structural supports. "Most of the rides here now are new to me."

"Like this one?" I asked even though I was already pretty confident I knew the answer.

"Yeah. It would be amazing to build and design rides like this. When I was a younger, I would spend hours building things out of rocks, blocks, sticks, tape, glue, whatever I could get my hands on. I remember my parents would always put my creations up on display all over our house. When I took my CAA, I desperately hoped the Artificer strand would choose me. When it did and I saw just how high my potential in it was, I ran around the house screaming in excitement for literally hours once I got home, Graham. My parents would have been proud. At least *they* always supported me."

"What do you mean? Other people didn't support you going to the academy? Like friends and family?"

She shook her head.

"Why not?" I questioned having an answer in my mind already but wanting to see what she would say.

"I was a Kaisiust woman trying to get drafted as an Artificer in a support squad. You know how rare that is. Everybody thought I was wasting my time. I thought things at the academy would be different.

That people would be more, what's the word I want—accepting maybe."

I didn't really want to get wrapped up in a deep, potentially sensitive conversation. Today was supposed to be a relaxing, easygoing day. But I felt like trying to change the subject when she was sharing something personal with me would be beyond rude, so the only choice I had was to keep it going, find out more. "So what did they suggest you do instead?"

"The civil Artificer track. You know, work for a company building and designing whatever, make a decent living, and maybe work my way up the corporate ladder eventually. Don't get me wrong, there's nothing wrong with that lifestyle, but it's just not me. I wanted something more than that, something where I felt like I was making more of a difference. Something where I was helping people.

"Get this, I remember a guy in a class of mine at the academy called me out in the middle of one of the courtyards one day. He said that even if I made it through the courses, tests, interviews, and physical evaluations, no one would draft me because I'm a slim. And that 'slims don't belong in support squads—especially female ones.'"

"He really said all that to you?"

I was shocked. Slim was a really derogatory term for a Kaisiust.

"Yeah. It really hurt and wore on me for a long time. I know it shouldn't have, but it did. There were nights where I would cry myself to sleep. Between what people would say to me along with the stress of all the work we had to do, it was hard to keep it all together sometimes.

"Things were just as bad when I went back to my aunt's for the holidays too. You would think I would be able to just put all of the stress and negativity aside and relax for a few days, but no. I couldn't. My family would always try to talk me out of trying to get drafted or urge me to quit the academy altogether.

"I remember my grandma pulled me aside once and said, 'Are you sure you want to go through all of that studying and training, sweetie? I'd hate to see all of your hard work go to waste. Why don't you just come and find a place where you can actually get a job.' My grandmother. My own grandmother said that to me."

The conversation had finally gotten to a place I feared. Her eyes were starting to get misty, but she held back her tears. I wasn't sure what to do, what to say, or how to help.

"I'm sorry to hear that." That was the best I could think of.

"I'm sorry; I didn't mean to dump all of that on you. Thanks for listening though. Sometimes it's good to just let some of it out, you know?" she said, trying to regain her composure. "Anyway, have you ridden this one before?" She changed the subject, trying to get herself excited about the ride again.

"Yeah, it's great," I said. "The best part, hands down, is going underwater. It's really cool to see that first splash against your car and then all the fish off in the distance."

That perked her up a bit. "That sounds awesome!"

The handful of people in front of us were seated and we were next in line. There was a teenaged employee mindlessly directing people onto the ride. When he caught sight of us his eyebrows raised and he was broken from his trance.

"Uh, hold on a second, please," his shaky voice requested.

He walked down the long platform to the other employee who was operating the ride's controls. The operator went back and forth with him from her stand. She looked at him and then glanced at us every now and then. I was starting to get a little worried. What was this all about? People behind us were starting to grumble under their breath. Our man made his way back to us with a troubled look on his face and an anxiousness in his voice.

"Uh, I'm sorry ma'am. We think you might be too tall for the ride. We're not sure if the overhead covering for the underwater section is tall enough to accommodate you. I'm sorry."

I looked over at her. I could tell she was secretly devastated by the news, especially after the conversation we just had in line, but she put on a good face. I felt like such an idiot. It never crossed my mind that she would be *too tall* for a ride; usually it's the other way around. A huge wave of embarrassment came over me.

"It's okay," she said calmly. "Thanks for checking on that for me. It's not worth losing my head over, right? I appreciate it."

The young man awkwardly smiled, nodded to us, and then got back to work. Erica and I, uncomfortably, turned around and started walking back to the end of the line, towards the rest of the pier. What was a stretch of about forty feet to get to the front of the line felt like forty miles to get to the end.

When we were just about to reach the end of the line when I heard a guy say to his friends, "Dumbass slim. Wasting everybody's time, making us wait even longer."

I stopped dead in my tracks once I heard that. Sadly, it took that douchebag's comments for everything to start clicking for me. The looks, the mumbles, it all made sense. It had nothing to do with me. They were judging her, ridiculing *her*. How could I not have put any of it together until now? Erica, one of the nicest and most genuine people I had ever met, was being judged by these ignorant assholes for no reason other than looking different from them.

Erica continued a few steps until she noticed I was behind her now, not moving. I wondered if she heard him. Normally I would try to let comments like this roll off my back. Normally I would try to be the bigger person. I just couldn't do it this time. The guilt for putting her through all of this was too much. The judgement, the sad memories, the embarrassment, and now the shit coming out of this guy's mouth, it was all too much. He was the cherry on top; the straw that broke the camel's back. I was pissed. Pissed in a way that I'm not sure I'd ever been before.

"Shut up you, prick!" I yelled at him. "Who the hell are you anyway, talking about her like that!"

He wasn't very intimidated by me, which wasn't surprising. He snickered to himself, as he lifted the rope leaving his spot in line to come deal with me. This loser had at least four inches and forty pounds on me. But if I had to guess based on his white tank top, jean shorts, overpriced shoes, and a few poorly done tribal tattoos, there wasn't much going for him upstairs. This guy nailed the tool stereotype to a T.

"Oh yeah? What're you gonna do about it, tough guy?"

Out of the corner of my eye, I could see Erica approaching nervously. His patronizing tone only pissed me off even more. I materialized a pair of brass knuckles in each hand and was ready to swing. My body tensed. My eyes locked onto him. One wrong word, one wrong move, and I was going to knock his ass out cold. I didn't even care about the repercussions. I couldn't. All of my negative emotions had completely taken over.

His tough guy demeanor vanished once he saw the knuckles. He was legitimately terrified. I could only think of one reason why he would be; he was an Omitted.

"Whoa, whoa, now. Take it easy, buddy. I'm sorry, alright." He said, backing down. "I'm sorry miss, okay," he called over to Erica. He didn't materialize anything to defend himself, nothing at all. I was confident I was right.

"You're seriously going to stand there and talk shit about Kaisiusts when you're an Omitted? She's a top tier Artificer. At least she has skill! She can actually do something! What the hell are you good for, jackass? What the hell can you do besides talk shit?"

The others in line oohed at what I said. His friends didn't even try to back him up, in fact they turned around and pretended they didn't know him. What I said to him was wrong. It was out of line. It wasn't even true. Omitteds played a huge role in our society. I was no better than him after saying all of that, but I couldn't take back what I said now. And there was no way in hell I was going to apologize for it.

The pent-up pressure from the situation was beginning to die down. The guy sheepishly got back into his place in line. He and his friends were silent, while the people around them began to murmur and stare like they did at us earlier. I dematerialized the knuckles, then Erica tapped me on the arm.

"Hey, let's go," she said softly.

She led me to a bench and decided to sit. It was quiet for a minute or two. My mind couldn't get past what had just happened. Part of me was proud for having the guts to call that guy out, but the majority was disgusted that it had even gotten to that point.

"I'm…I'm sorry for what happened back there. I just—"

She cut me off, "I know. "

"I just feel so bad. Today was supposed to be fun. I feel so ignorant. People have been rude to you since we got here and I didn't even realize it. I'm so sorry."

She let a moment pass and then said, "It's not your fault, Graham. You're not the one staring, and laughing, and saying mean things under your breath. This is just how life is sometimes for someone like me."

"Well, it shouldn't be."

"I know," she smiled and assured me. "As bad as that whole situation could have been, I'm glad you stood up for me. I'm really lucky to have a friend like you. Just don't pull out the brass knuckles next time, okay? I don't have the time, or energy, to write up that incident report."

We both laughed a little and then the sad truth sank into me. *Just don't pull out brass knuckles next time.* She already knew there would be a next time. How many *next times* had there already been? The thought of it was heartbreaking.

Erica pulled her vibrating phone out of her pocket and looked at who was calling. "It's Trevor," she said, a bit surprised. She put it on speaker and held it between us. "Hey, Trevor. I have you on speaker with Graham. What's up?"

"Good, saves me a call. I need you both at DREAM Tower pronto. Ryken's results are in and Randy wants to share them with us immediately. Got a feeling it's not a good sign if he's callin' us in like this."

"I thought he gave us the day off—" he cut me off before I

could go any further.

"You and me both, kid. I wouldn't have polished off half a six pack already if I knew I'd be goin' in today."

"Trevor, it's not even noon yet," Erica said astounded.

"Just get your asses to DREAM Tower!"

Chapter 10

Dr. Ryken's Findings

"We've got *the pleasure* of meetin' with Dr. Ryken and Randy up in the Presidential Suite," Trevor said, as he shuffled us into the elevator. He wasn't limping nearly as badly today, which was good. "Ryken's got intel on that vial and Randy's givin' us our next assignment."

Our next assignment. That wasn't what I wanted to hear. Ugh. My mind drifted back to the first part of his sentence. The vial. Ryken already had information about the vial. I thought about my dream, nightmare, from last night. Could the liquid in the vial really be conjierum? Like the conjierum from my dream?

"I'm warnin' you now." Trevor's voice regained my attention. We started to ascend up to the top floor. "Don't ask any questions about anything either of them tell you. They'll give us what they want and nothing more." Paxton opened his mouth to speak, "You heard me, Spitfire. Not a word."

Erica broke the silence after ten or so floors of awkwardness. "So, Trevor, how's your leg doing?"

"Better. Movin' around's a lot easier today."

"You don't look like you're in much pain anymore."

"Let's hope it stays that way."

The Presidential Suite was on the one hundred seventh floor. Between stopping to let people on and off and having to switch elevators every thirty floors or so, our trip to the top felt like it took ages. It might have been quicker to take the stairs. My legs burned just thinking about it. When we finally arrived, Trevor led us out.

We were met by a large meeting room with double doors made of thick privacy glass. A placard on the wall next to each door read: DREAM Tower: Presidential Suite. This suite made up the entire floor.

I looked back to the double doors and saw Trevor grabbing one of the handles, ready to show us in.

"Remember what I told you," he said pulling the door open.

A strange wave of nervous excitement came over me. I was about to see the Presidential Suite, the very place where the president ran all of DREAM. This was a once in a lifetime experience. I should have been more excited, but I remembered why I was here. Something told me that I wasn't going to like what I was going to hear in there and that I probably wasn't going to like where we were going once we left.

A fancy, cream-colored carpet covered the floor. It was pristine, like it had just been put in, even though I was almost certain it was older than it looked. There was a set of three huge, elegantly-crafted wooden tables shaped in a U in the middle of the space. At the top of the U stood a marble pedestal, just as delicately crafted as the tables, with some sort of audiovisual technology built into its top surface. Way beyond my Artificer skill to recognize. Past the pedestal sat a grand, elevated desk, similar to a judge's in a courtroom. On the front of the desk was the official seal of DREAM and above that was a nameplate with the engraving: President Vincent C. Hornsby.

The suite's walls were lined with large rooms with signs on the doors that read: Official Quarters. I had heard about those before. They were apartments for visitors, fellow politicians, or other guests to stay in while meeting with the president. I'm sure one of those apartments belonged to President Hornsby himself. I didn't get a chance to take in any more of this elegant and elaborate place before we were down to business.

"Trevor," Randy said with Dr. Ryken standing to his side. "Thank you for having your squad meet us here on such short notice."

"Dante." Trevor greeted Dr. Ryken with a slight nod, which Dr. Ryken then returned. "This better be important, Randy. My squad and I aren't too pleased about losing our day off here, especially after all the shit you've put us through these past few days." His tone towards Randy was bitter and annoyed.

Oddly enough, Randy didn't invite us to have a seat anywhere. I guessed that meant this meeting wouldn't be too long. Trevor didn't look like he would have taken a seat even if he'd been offered one. He kept his agitated eyes on Randy.

"You were assigned to investigative Brexley City Hall and its surrounding area. As much as I would have liked for you to have expanded your search beyond the building, I realize that Trevor was recovering from a minor gunshot wound. Regardless, your search of the premises proved to unearth something of significance."

He paused after that for a moment. Almost as if he was trying to create some kind of grand moment of suspense in a campfire story. He took the time to look at each one of us individually before moving on. Way more creepy than climactic.

"I asked Dr. Ryken to join us here today to give you some insight as to what it is you found. Doctor."

"Good morning," Dr. Ryken stated rather timidly. "I'll keep this brief and to the point. You've discovered a new strand of conjierum."

Our suspicions were right, but now hearing that they were true was unreal. I could feel my eyebrows climbing up my forehead and could see Erica and Paxton's doing the same. Trevor though, he looked like he couldn't care less, like it was old news or something.

"Congratulations," Randy said as he gave our squad a weak golf clap. I don't think he meant it to look condescending but it did.

For a man who had just finished analyzing something as rare and potentially life-changing as a new strand of conjierum, Dr. Ryken didn't seem, or look, overly excited. This could very well have been the highlight of his career but something was off. He looked incredibly apprehensive. Every now and then, he glanced over his shoulder at Randy, almost as if he were looking for some kind of approval or reassurance, like a guilty puppy or something.

An awkward silence filled the air. By the looks on their faces I could tell Erica and Paxton were wanting more information—Paxton especially: he always did. He wasn't even trying to hide the anticipation on his face.

"Well," Dr. Ryken tried to start.

He wiped his forehead then looked at us again. It was like he was stuck. His mouth was open but words weren't coming out.

"I…I suppose we can't really congratulate you on *discovering* the conjierum. It's been vialed so someone else has obviously discovered it first. I imagine that person has also probably injected him or herself with it too, and probably others as well."

He paused again. Randy was watching him closely now. The vice president was trying to look calm and casual, but I could sense if Dr. Ryken gave us too much he'd be in hot water.

"When I say 'new' I mean it's a strand that we currently don't recognize or know the properties of. I believe this green conjierum is a fourth, distinct strand."

Randy quickly stepped in. "Thank you for your time Dr. Ryken. I'm sure you have plenty of work to do in your lab figuring that out for us. I'll take it from here." Ryken definitely had more to share. His mouth was ready to form his next sentence before being cut off and dismissed by Randy. He gave us a weak smile and quietly left, looking majorly relieved. Randy waited until the suite's doors closed behind Ryken before continuing.

"Since your squad located this vial of new conjierum, I have decided to have the four of you continue your investigation," Randy stated.

And just like that, he knocked all the wind from my sails. My heart sank. I felt my shoulders shrug a bit. Damn it! This was exactly what I didn't want to happen!

"Your new assignment is to find the source of this conjierum, plain and simple. Once you do, you are to report back to me and the PSS and we will take over from there. Be advised, this assignment is strictly confidential. You're not to share any of this information with your families, friends, or other squads. Doing so will result in immediate termination and legal ramifications. Understood?"

Erica, Paxton, and I were caught pretty off guard. This conversation got intense fast. Outside of driving around and patrolling DREAM, almost any assignment a support squad was given was confidential. It wasn't every day we were reminded that breaking confidentiality had serious consequences.

"If word of this conjierum were to leak before we had a chance to figure out where it came from and what it allows its users to do, there's no doubt in my mind that DREAM would fall into pandemonium. Many people are already afraid as it is after the dragon attack on Center City."

"I hear what you're sayin' and I get where you're comin' from, Randy. But what do you really expect from us here? You want the four of us to scour all of DREAM? 'Cause there's no guarantee there's more of this stuff up in Brexley. If the guy vialin' this stuff up has any sense, I bet you there won't be a drop of it left up there. And what the hell are we *actually* lookin' for? A dealer? A stash? A conjierum deposit? This ain't as *'plain and simple'* as *'find the source.'*" Trevor delivered his last sentence mockingly. I think he wanted to be done with this assignment as badly as I did.

"Here's what I'll tell you, Trevor." Randy was as angry as I ever heard him. He still managed to sound professional, but Trevor was clearly under his skin. "I would imagine finding a dealer would, in turn, help us find a stash, which would then help us find a deposit. You find me any one of those things and we'll take over from there, how's that?" His professionalism was fading and his irritability growing. "If you want to go back to Brexley, go back to Brexley. If you want to grab a pickaxe and start hacking away at the mines in Dunnesburg, go for it. You're the leader of this support squad, aren't you? Your job is to take on special assignments that endanger DREAM when we have them. I don't care how you do it, just do your job. Figure it out, or resign now." He paused to collect himself. "That goes for all of you."

This was our cue to leave, at least according to Trevor. I could almost feel the angry heat radiating from his face. He turned around and started walking out of the suite, signaling for us to follow.

"Oh, Trevor," Randy called as our leader was opening the door for us. His voice was more relaxed now. Probably reveling in the fact that he had gotten the better of Trevor this time. "I am expecting frequent updates on your squad's progress."

He gave Randy a nasty look and replied, "Of course."

The elevator door opened and we filed in. "Does he really expect us to find this conjierum with basically nothing to go on?" Paxton asked after letting Trevor cool off for a few floors.

Not a question I would have asked a guy who was ready to explode over the topic just a few minutes ago.

"Yeah. Yeah, he does," Trevor replied.

"Trevor," Erica began, "what got you so worked up there? I mean, he's right. As much as it sucks, an assignment like this, with next to nothing to go on, is our job. What's really going on?"

Paxton didn't give him a chance to answer Erica's question before posing his own, "Yeah. What isn't he telling us? There has to be something. You saw Ryken up there. He was definitely holding back." Paxton's voice was so demanding. I knew it wasn't going to sit well with Trevor.

Trevor didn't say anything; he just tensed up angrily again. Whatever progress he made cooling off had been erased, Paxton was fueling his fire. Paxton started grumbling under his breath to me and Erica.

"Get over here, now! All three of you," he spoke in a soft yet pissed off voice. It seemed odd but we did it anyway and he pulled us all into a huddle. "I can't tell you anything about this conjierum, but I can tell you this. You can bet your asses Randy will be watchin' us this entire assignment. And you watch, as soon as we find something the PSS'll show up out of nowhere and *relieve* us. You can also bet your asses we'll see more mutated animal bullshit out there too." He closed

90

his eyes tightly for a second, like he was trying to muster the strength to say something, then looked over at Erica.

"You wanna know why I'm so pissed off? This assignment's a suicide mission for just one squad. If those freaks of nature don't kill us, some kind of conjierum cartel will. Randy knows it. That's why he's makin' us, makin' me, do it."

Our three pairs of eyes lit up. Before any of us could even ask what that meant he kept going. "Careful what you say and what you do while we're out there lookin', 'cause big brother Randy has eyes and ears everywhere. And he's always watchin'. And he's always listenin'. The three of you better take what he said seriously and don't say, or do, anything stupid, you hear me?"

"Damn it, Trevor! What aren't they telling us?" Paxton demanded again.

Trevor yanked Paxton by the shirt and stared him dead in the eye. "Shut. The hell. Up." He pushed his fist full of Paxton's shirt away and broke our little huddle. "We're goin' back to Brexley City Hall to cover our asses. We'll make our way into the rest city from there. If we can't find anything maybe somebody's at least seen something that can point us in the right direction. It's a long shot, but I think it's the best one we got at this point."

Paxton made a disappointed and disgusted face. I could feel the muscles in my face starting to contort to make one too.

"Save your bitchin', boys," Trevor told us. "I'm just as excited about it as you are, trust me."

Chapter 11

The Boy and the Bird in Brexley

"As fun as it was rummaging through this god-forsaken place the first time," Paxton snarkily began as he swung his leg over his SB3 to get off, "is there anything in particular we should be looking for?"

Frustration started to grow in Trevor's voice. "Randy not clear enough for you? You know what we're lookin' for, Spitfire. Just do your job."

"We were just here, what, two days ago? What could have possibly changed since then?" Paxton asked, almost whining.

"Damn it, Agton! We're doin' a sweep of this place one more time! If you can't handle that, you can take your ass home!" We had been here for less than five minutes and Paxton had already managed to piss him off. That had to be some kind of record. Our leader turned his back to us and began to scan the outside of the building.

"Spitfire, take the third floor. Erica, take the second. I'll take the first and Graham, the grounds outside. Meet back in the foyer when you're done. Understand?"

We all gave a nod in agreement.

"Careful in there," he warned, materializing SRHG6s for everyone. "You see anything weird in there, shoot to kill. We don't need a repeat of the raccoon escapade."

I was a bit relieved to be outside. If something was going to attack me it wouldn't be able to surprise me by jumping out of a doorway or sneaking up behind me down a dark hall. I was worried about my squadmates though. Trevor still wasn't a hundred percent and if something were to happen to Paxton or Erica there wasn't anyone around to quickly back them up.

I decided to start out front, carefully sifting through the long grass and patches of brush. Pushing back branches, leaves, and long strands of grass only to find nothing. I was being as thorough as I could. I didn't want our squad to miss something because of me. Besides, the sooner we found something the sooner we could put this new conjierum assignment to bed, get ourselves out of Brexley, and get things back to normal.

After combing through the front and both sides of City Hall I still had nothing to show for my efforts; well, except for a t-shirt drenched in sweat, a pair of dirty, tired hands, and an attitude growing worse by the second. I saved the back of the property for last, figuring if I was going to find anything at all it would be out there. I sat on the back patio of pavers catching one more breath before I got back to it.

Erica opened the sliding glass door and walked outside. I turned around and caught the look of shock on her face. She looked a bit tired and sweaty herself, but it was nothing compared to me.

"Whoa, looks like you're taking the '*grounds outside*' order pretty seriously." Her Trevor impression was less than impressive, which made it funny.

"Yeah, well," I said, trying to think of something witty to shoot back at her. My mind was fried. I had nothing. "You know me." I wasn't even sure what that meant.

"I can help you if you want," she offered. "Trevor and Paxton are just about done and I know neither one of them wants to be here any longer than they have to."

"Thanks."

We began rooting through the backyard, which proved to be just as exciting as the other three. Then, out of nowhere, I saw one of the bricks in the wall move. The grinding sound of brick on brick also caught Erica's attention. Another loose brick fell, then another. Erica motioned for me to hide with her behind a nearby tree. She stood while I took a crouching position.

"Did you notice those bricks last time we were here?" I whispered to her.

"No, but I wasn't exactly looking at them either."

Our guns were locked and loaded. My mind instantly overloaded with terrible thoughts of what was moving those bricks. Trevor's voice was playing on repeat in my mind: 'You can bet your asses we'll see more mutated animal bullshit out there too.' Those giant raccoons could definitely move bricks like that. What if this was something even bigger and worse though?

"Easy, Graham."

My leg had started shaking. The bouncing of my heel on the ground made a rustling sound against the grass and some fallen leaves. I was so lost in my thoughts I hadn't even heard it.

"Breathe," she told me. "We got this."

One final brick fell and then it was nerve-rackingly quiet for a few seconds, a few seconds that felt like several minutes. A shuffling noise came from the hole. Whatever it was, it was struggling to fit through. An arm came through first, a bluish-gray arm. Then another as it tried to pull itself through the opening. It wasn't a monster, it was a boy, a Kaisiust boy. He was about my height and weight but definitely not my age. You could see it in his face; he was maybe ten or eleven years old.

After he managed to squeeze through the hole his messy mop of brown hair flew with every nervous motion his head made. It was like he was looking for something, but what? Erica and I began to shift around the tree as he made his way closer to us, trying to avoid his sightline.

Snap.

I accidentally backed up and stepped on a twig. The boy's eyes and face lit up, like a deer who had just spotted its hunter.

"Shoot!" his pre-adolescent voice cracked as he made a break for the hole in the wall.

Before I could even react, I heard Erica yell to me, "Walkie!" She was off like a bolt of lightning.

That quickly she had materialized a walkie talkie for each of us and was in pursuit of the kid. My reflexes were just sharp enough to catch her toss and avoid taking the radio right to the chest. She had already made it through the hole in the wall by the time I had stopped bobbling it. I sprinted back inside to find Paxton and Trevor waiting in the foyer.

"Erica's onto something. We need to move now!" I said, sucking in wind.

I thought about hopping on the SB3s, but there was no way we would hear her over the walkie while riding. I led them way through the hole and out to the sidewalk. I materialized bicycles for the three of us as fast as I could. To my left I saw nothing but a barren street, but to my right was Erica in the distance chasing the boy. They had maybe a block and a half lead on us. We pounded the pedals as hard as we could trying to catch up.

"Erica, we have you in our sights," I huffed and puffed into the radio.

"Copy that," she replied, breathing heavily too.

"It had to be a Kaisiust, didn't it? Couldn't have been anyone with shorter legs. That guy can probably run for days!" Paxton blurted out over the sounds of our gears turning.

My mind took over while my body went on autopilot. What was this kid's deal? Erica must have sensed something was up to go after him like that. What was he doing in the yard? Drugs? He was too young for drugs. Well, maybe not. Was he waiting for someone? Maybe. Why would he run off like that? Then it hit me. Maybe he was the dealer we were looking for. I desperately hoped that he wasn't for his own sake.

"Right on Spruce," Erica's voice brought me back.

We made the turn and were finally starting to gain some serious ground on them.

"Left on Gordon."

She didn't have much left in the tank. We were close enough at this point that we didn't need her directions anymore. They were both slowing down. How long could the boy keep it up? At this point he had to be running on pure adrenaline. The three of us passed Erica and the boy, cutting him off.

The boy flailed himself to a stop like a sprinter who had just finished a race. He hunched over with his hands on his knees and gasped for air like a fish out of water. Trevor, Paxton, and I had him surrounded in front, while Erica caught her breath behind him. Without hesitation, Trevor conjured one of his silver handguns and aimed it at him.

"What are you runnin' for, boy?" Trevor asked, still working on catching his breath. He was wincing a bit too. All the pedaling must have been hard on his leg.

"What. Are *you*. Chasing *me* for?" he replied in between deep breaths.

"What were you doing in that yard?" Erica added.

"Nothing. Why do you care anyway?"

"You sellin' drugs kid?" Trevor turned up the aggression, no longer needing to frantically inhale.

"No! Who are you anyway? Leave me alone!" he fired back.

Without realizing it, the boy's hand hovered over his right front pocket.

"What's in that pocket, boy?" Trevor asked, gradually approaching the boy.

He pulled out a syringe, uncapped it, and held it like he was ready to stab Trevor with it. His face had a nervous furiousness to it.

"Back up!" the boy cried out, making motions like he would stab any one of us, "BACK UP!"

The syringe was full of a neon green substance. It had to be that conjierum. The four of us did our best to keep our calm and not give the boy the upper hand here. Trevor started to take charge of the situation.

He kept his ground and his gun pointed, as he said, "What're you doin' with that syringe, boy? You sellin' it? Deliverin' it for someone?"

The kid didn't respond. His eyes fixed on Trevor and his body tensed. I could see his grip on the syringe getting tighter but shakier. He was starting to panic.

"You know what's in that syringe, boy?" Trevor asked.

He stayed quiet as his shaking intensified.

"Who you workin' for, kid?" Trevor kept bombarding him with questions.

The boy then erupted. "SHUT UP! Or I'll stab you with this!"

Trevor smirked, "Let me tell you something, kid. I know what's in that syringe of yours. That stuff's not gonna hurt me. You stick me with that and all you'll get is one hell of a beating from your boss when you come back empty-handed. Not to mention the ass whoopin' you'll get from me first."

He lowered his arm and his body relaxed, realizing that he couldn't win. The boy opened his mouth, prepared to speak, until something in the sky caught his eye. The look on his face was genuine terror. This was no acting job or attempt to throw us off. I turned around to see what was freaking him out, knowing that Trevor would keep him in place.

"Holy shit," I mumbled to myself.

Overhead flew what looked like a massive bald eagle. It let out an ear-shattering screech, which caused us all to immediately cover our ears. The bird swooped down, nearly knocking us all to the ground in the process, and landed within a hundred feet of us.

It was close to twenty feet tall. It stretched out its wings to intimidate us. Each one had to be close to ten feet long. I glanced down at its talons, which were broad and dug into the pavement effortlessly, like it was sand on the beach. There was no doubt those talons could easily slice us up like platter cheese.

The bird screeched again causing the white feathers around its head to stand and stretch out, like one of those frilled lizards from the desert. I scrambled to cover my ears again, so did the others. It took to the air and hovered overhead. The boy was behind me and called out something, but I couldn't make out what it was over the powerful flapping.

"What?" I yelled out to him.

"She shoots!" he cried out, absolutely mortified.

I noticed I was the only one who hadn't heard him the first time. Everyone had now shifted and was ready for the fight. Trevor must have already materialized shields for himself, Paxton, and Erica in anticipation of whatever it was the bird would shoot. We stood in a diamond shape with Trevor up front. Paxton was behind him on his right. Erica, holding onto the boy with her other arm, was behind Trevor on the left. And I, the only one not protected at this point, stood behind all four of them.

I looked up and saw the bird winding its wings back, like how a person would pull their arms back to splash someone in a pool. Without thinking, I materialized Sunshine, pressed the button deploying the shield, and braced myself for whatever was to come. Not a moment later a strong surge of wind plowed into us. I heard something clashing against our shields, plunging into the pavement, and shattering nearby windows.

"Hurry, we need to go before her feathers regrow!" the boy yelled out. It sounded like a weird thing for him to say at first.

I lowered Sunshine, getting my first look at what had pierced my shield. Feathers. Ridiculously strong feathers. They were lodged not only in Sunshine, but in the street, sidewalks, surrounding buildings, and my squadmates' shields. It looked like a maze of giant, killer, feather missiles all around us.

The bird returned to the ground. Her feathers were already regrowing. She slowly started to walk towards us. We all retreated cautiously, not knowing what else she had up her wing.

"If we're takin' this thing out we need to do it now!" Trevor called out while materializing some type of assault rifle.

"NO!" the boy screamed.

With one arm Trevor took aim and shot at the eagle's face. She anticipated the rounds perfectly and flexed the white feathers near her head, looking like a frilled lizard again. All of Trevor's bullets ricocheted off of the feathers and beak. His attack pissed her off even more, causing another terrible screech to pound our eardrums.

"Damn it! Where's her weak point, kid?"

The feathers on its wings were almost completely grown back when the boy frantically yelled out, "I don't know. I've never actually seen her before."

I couldn't fathom what was going on. I felt like I was having an out-of-body experience, like I was about to watch my own death. Something was different this time though. Maybe I'd already had so many close calls that finally running out of luck just didn't feel scary to me anymore. Maybe I was just ready to accept my own demise.

The bird took to the sky. We needed to think fast. We couldn't just keep playing defense. The hurricane force gusts from her wings began to pick up. We all braced ourselves again. At any moment more of her feathers would rain down on us.

The wind was getting too hard to fight against. Staying in place and holding up Sunshine to protect me was near impossible. Then it dawned on me. She was trying to blow us out of place, blow the protection out of our hands, leave us totally open and helpless.

I began to lose my footing, my shoes scraping against the pavement as I began to slide and step backward. It was taking everything I had to keep Sunshine in place. The muscles in my arms looked ready to burst out of my skin. I kept losing ground, losing footing, losing strength. Sunshine began to quiver in my hands. It was only a matter of time before something would give, either my footing or my grip.

I grunted and yelled trying to keep everything still but couldn't take any more. Sunshine violently flew over my head, pulling me slightly off the ground with it. I fell flat on my back, my head hitting the street.

I sat up as fast as I could. My vision was blurry. I squinted into the wind trying to get a look at the bird's next move now that I was down. It raised its wings back in preparation to let another onslaught of its feathers go. Panic struck me. Adrenaline took over. Reality sunk in. This was really it for me. I was going to die at the wings of a giant, freakishly-feathered eagle.

My drive to survive kicked in. I pulled my knees tightly into my chest. I had just enough wherewithal to materialize a riot shield large enough to cover my huddled, curled up body.

The bird's missiles connected with the shield just as I got it into place. The force of the impact knocked my grip on the shield loose. I couldn't keep it in my hands. It fell to the ground. I was defenseless again.

I was spent. I had nothing left. My vision was giving out. I could only see the silhouettes of my squadmates in front of me. I heard voices but couldn't make out anything that was being said. All the sound around me was muffled. Was I just losing consciousness or was I dying? The last thing I heard was a very faint shrill of pain coming from the eagle as my body slowly collapsed back on the road. The hazy blue sky and white clouds faded to black.

Chapter 12

The Biotect Strand

"Graham! Graham!" she desperately cried out.

I couldn't find her. The rain was coming down in buckets and the thunder banged directly overhead. Waves were thrashing against our small fishing boat so hard it was a miracle that it hadn't capsized yet.

"Graham! Help me!" Her words were strained and frantic.

I panicked. I still couldn't find her. It was taking almost everything I had just to keep myself from falling overboard. I had to find her. I had to get her out of the water. These waves were too strong. If I didn't pull her in soon, they'd pull her under for sure.

"Graham!" I heard her gurgling, choking voice yell.

Lightning lit up the dark sky and my eyes finally caught a glimpse of her. I scrambled port side and clutched on to the crane that pulled up the nets for stability, nearly falling over the edge myself. I wiped the rain and seawater from my eyes to try to get a clear look at her.

"Graham! Help me!" she pleaded, trying to keep her head above the violently surging waves. She spat out the salty water that relentlessly tried forcing its way down her throat and into her lungs. Her arms flailed to keep herself afloat and keep the water as well as her long black hair out of her face. Her eyes were wider than I had ever seen, full of terror and desperation.

There was nothing I could do. I couldn't throw a life preserver that far. The wind or waves would just knock it off course anyway. A paralyzing and alarming rush of energy pulsed through me. There she was. I could see her; I just couldn't reach her. I had to though, I just had to. I couldn't just watch her drown in front of me.

"Graham." It was a different voice calling me. "Graham."

I opened my eyes and saw it was Paxton.

"Whoa, you alright buddy?"

I was hyperventilating. I glanced around at my surroundings and recognized where I was, the medical ward of DREAM Tower. The lights in the room were off. Only the ones in the hallway were keeping the space dimly lit. I did a quick scan down my body and saw that I wasn't hooked up to any monitors or anything. In fact, none of the medical machinery was even on.

"What happened?"

"You hit your head. Hard enough to knock you out. I wouldn't be surprised if you had a pretty bad concussion."

"No, I meant what happened with the eagle?" I asked with a small headache now starting to settle in.

"Erica had the idea of aiming for its eyes, it was definitely risky considering the ricochet from those feathers around its head, but it worked. Once we blinded it, it didn't know where to fire those feathers. Trevor and Erica split up to find its soft spot. I had to watch you and the kid. Anyway, a few shots in the back of the head ultimately did her in."

I was becoming more coherent, "Man, Erica really has a thing for shooting out the eyes. What happened to the kid?"

"The PSS showed up right after we took down that eagle, just like Trevor said they would, and *escorted* the five of us back here. The boy was pretty shaken up. They're questioning him now. Enough of all that for a minute. How are you feeling? I'm surprised you have the wherewithal to have a conversation with me right now."

I sat up straight; a dull pain took over my head, but it was manageable. "A little headache, but besides that I feel fine."

"A little headache. That's it?" I could see him making a mental note for himself. His tone told me that he was a bit surprised. "No dizziness, nausea, blurry vision?"

I waited a second to answer him to see if any of those things would set it. "Nope."

"Your speech sounds good. No slurring." More mental note taking. "Are you having a hard time focusing while we're talking right now?"

"No. Just the headache."

"I'll tell you what, you're one lucky man. I was thinking you'd wake up a mess and be out of commission for at least a few weeks. Concussion symptoms could still sneak up on you a little later though. Be mindful of that, but it looks like you're going to be alright."

"Where are Erica and Trevor?" I asked while holding the back of my head.

"The PSS is questioning them too. Everyone in DREAM is going nuts now over these crazy, destructive monsters that pop up out of nowhere. I guess one giant dragon can be overlooked, but a feather-missile firing eagle is the icing on society's cake of concern. I don't even think they know about those raccoons. My guess is they're talking about these monsters and how to pipe down the public's hysteria," he stated rather matter-of-factly. "Oh, and the conjierum the kid had too. They're definitely talking about that."

"Why didn't you go with them?"

"Look around, Graham," he told me. "All the other Saviors went home for the day. Trust me, I'd love to be in that room trying to dig up some of the dirt on this, but someone's gotta take care of our sidekick."

After his last sentence he flashed me a playful smile, knowing I wouldn't take offense to what he said. Sidekick was a slang, and usually crude, term for a Factotum. A lot of people found it offensive, but it didn't bother me.

"Besides, Trevor and Erica will give us the details once it's over," he assured me even though I didn't need it. "Maybe not all the details I'd like, but I gotta take what I can get, I guess. Something's better than nothing."

"Did the boy say anything?"

"What do you mean?"

"About the conjierum. How he got it. Where he got it. Who he is."

Part of me felt bad for him, whatever his story was. He was now caught up in this mess with us.

"Nope. He was dead silent the whole way back here. He did know about the eagle's feathers, so he definitely knows something."

I was starting to feel tired. Whether it was from just another crazy day or a possible concussion I wasn't sure. Paxton caught me yawning and said, "You should be okay to nap if you want. Rest up. It'll be good for you. I'll wake you up when I hear from Trevor and Erica."

* * *

I looked around and recognized where I was. It was the same block where Lynch's guys shot out my tire and kidnapped me. It was dark and desolate, just like that night was. All of the sudden I heard a cry from up the street. It was the boy from Brexley. I could've sworn he wasn't there a minute ago, but that didn't matter now.

Slowly approaching him was another mutated, hybrid, messed-up animal. Instead of a dragon or eagle, this thing looked like a saber-toothed tiger. It certainly had the head and teeth of a saber-toothed, but the rest of its body was built like a bear. With every step it took, muscles bulged against its skin. It had few black stripes along its body which really stood out against its thick white fur.

The boy was screaming his lungs out as he stumbled backward towards the wall of a brick building. The bear-tiger was in no rush to attack; it knew it would have no problem taking down its prey. I materialized Sunshine and yelled to get the creature's attention.

Its savage, neon green eyes widened with anticipation at the sight of me. The boy was a snack; I was a meal. The creature burst into a sprint, charging at me with everything it had, digging up broken pavement with its powerful claws and long strides.

I had just enough time to crouch and brace myself before it made its lunge at me. Without thinking, I deployed Sunshine's shield and hidden blade, hoping the same move I used on Jay would work again. The bear-tiger's massive body collided with the shield, and the distinct sound of metal tearing through skin filled the air. Somehow, I managed to stay on my feet as I caught the bear-tiger in midair, despite it being even heavier than it looked.

It screamed out in agony. Its paws reached over the shield and halfheartedly swatted at me. I could see the light leaving its eyes. The screams turned to whimpers and the whimpers turned to silence. I mustered up some kind of superhuman strength and flung its dying body over top of me, like a wrestler suplexing his opponent.

The creature smacked down hard on the street. I retracted the shield and blade, pulling Sunshine away from its body. It was dead. I turned to see if the boy was alright. He wasn't.

A blurry figure of a man held him. One arm was locked around his neck holding him in a headlock while the other pointed a gun to his head. I couldn't make out any of the gunman's features. Before I could move, or speak, or even breathe, he pulled the trigger.

* * *

"Graham." It was Paxton again. "Trevor and Erica just called from upstairs. They want us to meet them in the squad room to talk."

I nodded my head slightly, which wasn't hurting as much now. The medical ward was on floors two and three, designed that way with the thought of ever having to evacuate in mind. One of the better ideas they had when it came to building this place. That being said, it made the elevator ride up to the seventy seventh floor a long one.

Trevor and Erica were sitting around the coffee table in the common room when we finally made it upstairs. Trevor motioned for us to come over and have a seat. I noticed Erica was very still and looked really uneasy.

"We've got a lead," Trevor said.

"What happened in there?" Paxton asked.

"We've got a lead," Trevor reiterated.

"I'm sure we do," Paxton blurted out. "You were in there for over two damn hours! What the hell is going on? Don't just skip over the details and tell me what our next death project for Randy is!"

Erica said something softly to him in Kai. Trevor reached across the table, grabbed a fist full of Paxton's shirt again, and with clenched teeth, furiously whispered to him, "Remember what I told you in that damn elevator!"

Paxton immediately sank back in his chair. I guess our squad room wasn't even safe from Randy's prying eyes and ears.

"As I was saying," Trevor said, beginning to cool off. "We've got a lead. Turns out the boy is a dealer for someone who's been sellin' and experimentin' with the conjierum."

"What's the conjierum do?" Paxton cut him off before he could continue.

Trevor paused, his face turning red. It was easy to see he was pissed off by the interjection, but he kept his cool. I could see he was conflicted on whether he wanted to actually tell us or not, but he did, "It creates life. Non-human life. Plants, animals, shit like that."

Paxton and I, now hearing this for the first time, started to put the pieces together.

"So somebody's materializing these things? These monsters. The dragon, the raccoons, the eagle." Paxton asked.

"Yes." Trevor simply stated.

But before Paxton could follow up, Erica picked up where Trevor had been cut off, "Our job now is to find the head dealer Kent's been working for."

"Kent?" I asked.

"Sorry, Kent's the boy's name."

"Why?" Paxton asked, beginning to get aggravated. "Kent's a dealer, right? Shouldn't that be enough for Randy? Wasn't that the deal? Once we found a dealer Randy and the PSS would take over from there?"

It was finally a question that didn't piss Trevor off, and a good question at that.

"Randy's scared to have the PSS take over the assignment because it would '*compromise his own safety*' or some shit like that. Can't have another monster take a shot at DREAM and have the vice president unprotected."

"So this whole thing is now our problem permanently?" Paxton asked in disbelief.

"I told you it was a suicide mission, Spitfire. Randy said we can start fresh in the morning. It's been a long enough day, and he wants to make sure *his* head is alright before we start another investigation," Trevor said, pointing at me.

"What about Kent? Where is he going to stay tonight?" Erica inquired.

"Randy's lettin' him stay in one of the apartments in the Presidential Suite until this whole thing gets figured out. He said they're viewin' Kent as more of a victim than a perp. They're hopin' he can be a witness or asset or something in catching whoever's causing these attacks. Anyway, I'll tell you more about our lead in the morning, I guess. Get out of here. Go get some rest. Especially you, Graham."

Everyone got up to leave except for Trevor. He said he had a few more pieces of paperwork to fill out for Randy and the PSS about the day's events, but would be leaving soon. During our elevator ride down to the ground floor Paxton asked Erica and me if we wanted to go out for dinner. It was a bit odd considering Paxton usually kept to himself after work hours. I couldn't quite tell if he was turning over a new leaf or up to something. I stopped questioning his motives and said I'd join. Shortly after I answered Erica decided to come too.

He took us down the street to a pub he said he really liked: *The Prestigious Pony*. The dark and smokey dining area was nearly packed but we managed to get a table. A man sitting behind Erica exhaled whatever it was he was smoking, which gave her a bit of a coughing fit.

"So, what's Trevor not telling us?"

I could tell by her body language that she didn't want to answer Paxton's question. "Is that what this was all about? Seriously, Paxton?" she replied rather discouragingly. "Trevor told you everything that Randy and the PSS wanted us to know."

I picked up on her word choice. "Does that mean you know something you shouldn't?"

She left out a short, nervous laugh and put her head down for a moment. Paxton's face lit up. I was right.

She looked around to make sure no one else was listening in and then lowered her voice, "Okay, fine. Towards the end of the questioning, they dismissed me and asked Trevor to stay for 'further questioning and instruction.' Something about that seemed a little weird to me so I listened through the door. Long story short, the government has secretly known about this conjierum for ages. In fact, finding the source of this conjierum has been a hush-hush, side priority for years and years now. Randy told Trevor that DREAM used to have attacks like this pretty frequently back in the day. They figured once the attacks stopped that the Biotect, or Biotects, that were causing them had died."

"So the conjierum creates life, like those freakish animal monstrosities. And the people chosen by the strand are called Biotects?" Paxton asked, looking for confirmation.

"Yeah. He told Trevor that our squad needs to find the Biotect, or Biotects, behind the attacks before things get worse and DREAM becomes even more freaked out. Randy also doesn't want any additional squads working with us. He figures that the more people who know about it, the more likely it is to leak to the public."

"So this strand isn't new at all. These Biotects have been a dirty little government secret for years, and they still haven't been found," Paxton said with a smirk to himself.

"Basically, but they haven't exactly been on DREAM's most wanted list. Think about it. The Biotects had been dormant for so long until earlier this week."

"So why a resurgence now? What do they want?"

She shrugged her shoulders.

"So what's the plan?" I asked. "What exactly are we supposed to do?"

"Same as last time I'm sure," Paxton butted in. "We go in, do the dirty work for Randy, and then the PSS swoops in and '*takes it from there.*'"

Erica let out a chuckle and said, "More or less. That lead Trevor was talking about is a house in Brexley where Kent's boss has been keeping some of her conjierum."

"*Her* conjierum?" Paxton asked, a bit surprised.

"Yes, *her*. What? You've never seen a woman be anything other than a Savior or an Omitted before?" she replied with some semi-serious snark trying to keep a straight face.

"You know I didn't mean it like that," he said, letting out a nervous laugh.

"I can't believe we have to go back to Brexley, *again*," I said. I didn't mean for it to sound whiny but it definitely did.

Paxton made an exacerbated face and let out a deep sigh. His eyes rolled back just thinking about Brexley.

"Believe it, boys," Erica's voice stole back the attention.

He groaned before looking over at me and jokingly saying, "Hey, let's try to get in and out of Brexley unscathed this time." He gave me a playful pat on the shoulder. "No kidnappings, no killing giant raccoons prematurely, no getting knocked out by a few puffs of wind. What do you say?"

I couldn't help but smile and let out a little laugh. "No promises."

Chapter 13
Hello, Natalia

I was the last one to arrive at DREAM Tower the next morning, again. Everyone was waiting for me on the curb next to four SB3s. Kent was standing there with them doing his best to fight off the morning sun. He looked tired, having some pretty big bags under his eyes. I could tell his clothes had been washed and he had showered, but he still looked really unsettled. His right leg had quite a jitter to it and every passing car seemed to startle him. When he wasn't using his hand to block the sun, he was chewing on his finger nails. I couldn't blame him. The poor guy got snatched up by us and was expected to give up the person, or persons, that had probably been giving him a means to survive for who knows how long. It was a tough spot to be in.

"It's about time," Paxton said with sarcasm as he tossed me a headset.

"I'm on time, aren't I?" I replied as I put it on.

Looking at his watch, he countered, "I suppose so."

"Enough chit chat." Trevor broke up the banter. "We're headed back to Brexley where we had our run in with that bird yesterday. Kid says there's a house not too far from there where they deal the conjierum out of. Bunch of kid dealers live there too."

"Alabaster," Kent said, almost quivering.

"What was that?" Erica asked.

"*That bird.* Her name is Alabaster. I had never seen her before yesterday. I wasn't even sure if she was really real or not, but I've heard scary stories about what she does to people who cheated the boss. Please don't make me go back there. She'll have her people hurt me even more now that you've got me."

An eerie silence came over the five of us. I'm sure we were all curious about what this poor kid had been through, but I definitely wasn't pushing him to talk anymore right now. Last thing I needed was for him to have a meltdown here on the sidewalk. Or worse, have Trevor lash out at one of us for causing him to have a meltdown on the sidewalk.

Trevor tried to comfort him; the keyword being tried. "Well son, that bird's long gone and we won't let anyone hurt you. You're safe with us. But we need you to show us where that house is. We'll get your friends out too, just like we promised. Don't you worry."

It didn't exactly come across as the most sincere thing Trevor had ever said, and Kent sensed that. He didn't loosen up at all. If anything, his leg started to twitch even faster.

"Please," his eyes were wide and misty with tears as he pleaded with Erica. "Don't take me back there. Please. If they find me—"

"Kid rides with you, Graham," Trevor called out right before starting his engine, not even giving Kent a chance to finish.

All five of us got on the bikes and were ready to ride off to the block where we had faced Alabaster. I figured if Kent and I would be riding together we might as well have a bit of conversation to make it less awkward and calm both of our nerves. I was anxious about going back to Brexley again too. I kept thinking about what Paxton had said last night, about how both times we had gone there didn't turn out so well for me. I set his headset so the two of us could talk to each other privately. It took me a minute to figure out how to do it, but I got it. After that, we were off.

The first fifteen minutes were quiet, almost painfully so. I felt like I should say something, but didn't know what. Would he even want to talk to me? I didn't want to say or ask him anything that would upset him, or worse, trigger bad memories.

I asked him the safest question I could think of. "So, Kent, what's uh, your favorite food?" It didn't sound so forced in my head. He didn't respond. Maybe I shouldn't have asked him anything at all and just left him alone.

He eventually answered and it dragged me out of my whirlpool of negative thoughts, "I bought myself pizza a few times. It was *really* good." His voice was still a bit shaky, but he sounded slightly more relaxed than before we left.

"Do you have a favorite kind?"

"I tried Hawaiian pizza once. I thought it would be gross, but I liked it."

His tone was becoming more relaxed. This was good for me too. I didn't want to think about what was to come, not until I had too anyway.

"Well, hey, we could go out for pizza after we're done here today. Would you be into that?"

There was a pause but then he replied with some cheer in his voice, "Yeah. I'd like that."

"Awesome!"

It was quiet for a few seconds until he asked, "What are you guys gonna do if you find the boss?" He sounded nervous again.

I wasn't expecting a question like that. I didn't know how to answer it. And I definitely didn't want to think about it either. The last thing I wanted was to come across someone who could materialize some kind of freak of nature that could kill me on the spot. I had seen enough of those already for one lifetime.

"I don't know exactly." I didn't know what else to say but felt like I owed him more. "But I do know that Vice President McGregor and the PSS want to stop the boss from using creatures like Alabaster to hurt people and cause destruction across DREAM. I imagine she would go to court and then most likely jail, but like I said, I don't know for sure." It felt risky, but I decided to ask. "Can you tell me what her name is? The boss." As soon as the words left my mouth, I regretted it. Completely afraid he was going to shut down.

"I don't know it. Everyone I know just calls her the boss."

"Okay," I thought I'd press my luck just a little further. "Is there anything you can tell me about her? Maybe, what she looks like. Is she young? Old? Tall? Short?"

"I've only seen her a couple times, and it wasn't for very long." At that point I was sure I had gotten all I could out of him. "But," he said, causing my attention to perk up a bit. "She looked kind of short, shorter than me. And I think she might be Asian. At least that's what the other kids that have seen her said."

Female, short, and Asian, it wasn't much to go off of but was at least something. If nothing else it seemed like I was gaining his trust. DREAM was a massively diverse place and that his description wouldn't do a whole lot for us.

"Thanks Kent," I decided to change topics again, not wanting to get any deeper in the heavy stuff. "Hey, you like any sports?"

"I like baseball."

"Me too! I'm a huge baseball fan!"

Baseball was the one sport in DREAM that didn't have a separate Kaisiust-only league. It wasn't a sport overly populated with Kaisiust players or fans either, so his answer caught me a bit off guard.

"You know I read a book about the history of baseball once. Turns out, back in the day they had human umpires who called the balls and strikes and the outs too."

"Really?" he asked me.

"Yeah, weird right?"

"Yeah. Were the umpires ever wrong?"

"A lot. So much that they kept changing the rules and incorporating more and more tech into the game to help fix their mistakes."

Artificer technology eventually reached a point where umpires were no longer needed. Balls and strikes were decided by a strike zone that was projected above home plate. Gloves were infused with sensors that flashed if a player caught the ball, if they were touching the base with the ball, or if they tagged the runner. Bases lit up either green for safe or red for out. Even with some Artificer background, I couldn't begin to explain how all of it worked. But it did, and that was good enough for me.

"So, who's your team?"

"The Greyhounds."

The Sterling Greyhounds. With Sterling being the city with DREAM's largest Kaisiust population, and the team with the most Kaisiusts on it, I wasn't too shocked by that answer.

"Not a Blue Collars fan?" I asked, referring to Brexley's team.

"No. I'm not from Brexley. The Collars aren't good anyway. Who's your team?"

The question instantly sent chills up my spine. *Mylo*. Memories flooded my mind, more bad than good. I shoved as many of them as I could aside to answer him, "Well, I grew up in Mylo so I'm an Otters fan even though I live in Center City now." The Otters were one of the only things in Mylo that I still had a positive connection with.

We kept talking about baseball for a while. I was impressed how much he knew. "You really know your stuff for only being, what? Ten? Eleven? You must watch a lot of games."

"I'm ten, and we don't have TV at the house. We do jobs for the boss, come home, and wait for the next job. If we're out too long, her people find us, drag us back home, and beat us. They're always at the house and they always find us if we're gone too long. A lot of times while I'm out I'll steal the sports section out of someone's paper if I see it on the street.

"A few times I haven't gone home right away and snuck into a pizza place or deli to watch a few innings of a game. Sometimes I tell the people I sell to that the boss raised the price a few dollars so I can buy something to eat and not get kicked out of the stores. They don't usually like having people just sit there not buying anything."

I was speechless for a second. I felt so incredibly bad for him.

"You said they beat you if you're out too long?"

"Yeah." He paused for a little bit, probably debating on whether or not he wanted to say any more. "I have a few different scars from when they caught me. It really hurts, but I think it's worth it. It's nice to actually have some real food, watch TV, and do what I want, even if it's not that long and they hurt me later."

What the hell was wrong with these people? Using and abusing kids like that. I could feel a fire starting to burn inside me. I was scared to come back here at first, but now, after hearing everything Kent had been through, I wanted to find this woman. I wanted her to pay for what she had done to him and those other kids.

We parked a block away from the section of street that nearly killed us all yesterday. There were still feathers speared into the pavement and nearby buildings. The sight of it gave me an ominous feeling, like I was staring at some kind of gruesome battlefield. I could feel the flame in me starting to die out. The boss, whoever she was, could probably make another Alabaster. An Alabaster even stronger than the one before. An Alabaster that could skewer this whole town to a wasteland maze of feathers.

Kent stayed by the bike while I walked over to Trevor, who already had Paxton and Erica standing near him. I kept my voice down, not wanting Kent to hear me, "Kent told me a little about the woman we're looking for."

Trevor looked at me a bit funny, which stopped me in my tracks. "Kid, I know *exactly* who we're lookin' for. I just don't know where to find her."

I was shocked. I didn't know that. I glanced over at Paxton and Erica. She looked just as surprised as me while he was about ready to blow a gasket.

"Then who *exactly* are we looking for?" Paxton asked, majorly irked.

Trevor gave him a "watch it" type of glare. "Woman goes by the name Dune. Asian. Mid-thirties. Average build. About five one. One arm's got a tiger tattoo. Other arm's got a ring of bright green pigmentation around the bicep. Side effect of the conjierum."

"Why didn't you tell us that before?"

"I'm tellin' you what you need to know now. Leave it at that if you know what's best for you, Spitfire!"

Paxton did, but by the look on his face it pained him to do so. My attention turned from Paxton to Kent. He looked super uncomfortable again, even worse than he did at DREAM Tower. My squadmates noticed him too.

"Do we really have to put him through this Trevor?" Erica almost pleaded. "Just look at him."

I was torn, wanting to speak up but afraid to. The words somehow found their way out of my mouth though. "Whoever this Dune is has put him and those other kids through hell. He was telling me that she has people who find them, drag them back to the house, and beat them if they're out too long. Says he has the scars to prove it."

Erica's eyes widened and she covered her mouth in shock. "Oh my god! Trevor, we can't make him do this."

"Wouldn't have to if he knew the damn address of the house. He knows it's in this area but doesn't know where exactly," he said coldly amongst us. "Come on kid," he called out and waved to Kent. "Let's get movin'."

Kent begrudgingly started walking towards us on the verge of tears. Trevor handed us each a SRHG6 as we waited for Kent. "You see anything out of the ordinary shoot to kill. I'm done with this place's bullshit."

A very upset Kent led the way with the rest of us close behind. Brexley was as creepy and quiet as ever. This time I did manage to see a few peeping eyes through the blinds of a few windows. Every little noise had us drawing our guns, rats scurrying, trash rolling down the street, the occasional bird chirping anything and everything. We were all on edge.

We walked for another twenty minutes or so. Kent stopped us at an old, rundown building. It was only five stories high and made of brick, much of which was losing its color, cracking, or crumbling. Kent looked a bit unsure at first. A lot of places around here fit that bill. He peered around the side of the building and down a narrow alley, then turned to us and said, "This is it." He looked uneasy. "The door to the basement's in back. That's where they keep the conjierum."

"Erica, you keep him close," Trevor commanded as he took the lead down the alleyway.

At the end of the alley was a back porch area. It was made of concrete tiles and had one of those glass patio tables with the umbrella sticking through the middle of it. The umbrella was closed and sun bleached. The table was gross, covered in dust and mold. The back of the house had a few steps led down to a white, rickety storm door.

"Graham, you follow me in second. Then Spitfire. Then Erica with the boy."

He slowly went down the stairs and quietly pushed down the door handle. It was locked.

"There used to be a spare key underneath one of the tiles," Kent uttered.

Paxton and I started picking up loose patio tiles until he found the key. He gave it to me and I gave it to Trevor as we got into formation. My heart was pounding. Who knew what was on the other side of that door? More raccoons? Massive killer bees? A firing squad just waiting shoot down whoever was stupid enough to come through.

Trevor wouldn't let me think about it any longer. He unlocked the door, swung it open, and led the charge in. My adrenaline kicked in. Now was the time to act, not over analyze. Our guns were raised and ready for whatever we encountered. The room was dark and silent. I heard someone hit a switch. The lights flickered on. The basement was completely empty of equipment, furniture, you name it. Just a concrete slab. Whatever had been here before was long gone now.

The only thing in the room was a woman, who looked roughly around Trevor's age, sitting upright in a wooden chair with her legs crossed and her hands neatly placed on her lap. Her eyes were brown, like her hair, which came down to her shoulders. Bangs draped her forehead. She wore a bright red formal dress. Her heels were so high they would probably give the average person altitude sickness.

She stood up from her chair and said, "It's good to see you

again, Trevor."

I quickly scanned the woman again. She wasn't Asian. Wasn't five one—more like five six, before her skyscraper heels. No tiger tattoo. No ring around the bicep. If this wasn't Dune, who was it? And how did she know Trevor?

His eyes widened when he saw her, almost as if he'd seen a ghost. That didn't make the rest of us feel any better about the situation. I'd never seen his face puzzled before. Erica made sure to keep Kent behind her, sensing something was off here.

Trevor lowered his gun and said, "Hello, Natalia."

Chapter 14

Two Sad Stories

"It's been a long time," Natalia began. "It looks like you're doing well for yourself."

"You know I'm not one for small talk," he replied curtly. "What're *you* doing here?"

"I could ask you the same thing," she countered rather smugly. Trevor was growing impatient. "You haven't seen me in how many years and the first thing you ask is what I'm doing here?"

"Quit dickin' around. Why the hell are you here?"

"I see much hasn't changed with you. Work still comes before everything else." She let out a small sigh. "I'm here on behalf of Dune. Once she heard your squad had captured one of her carriers, she knew the boy would bring you back here. All the conjierum, all of the kids, have been cleared out. It's just the six of us."

There was a brief lull in the conversation. Her heels clicked loudly against the floor as she took a few steps towards us. Even though Trevor said we had nothing to worry about, that Natalia couldn't hurt us, some kind of mama bear instinct took over Erica. She clutched Kent's arm even tighter and made sure he was behind her.

"Did you seriously think it would be that easy? Just walking in here and finding everything you were supposed to be looking for?" she confronted him in a bit of a condescending tone.

"Why are you really here, Natalia? Why the hell are you caught up with Dune?"

"For a better and brighter tomorrow." Before Trevor could even ask what that meant, she cut to the chase, "Dune is well aware that you, along with the PSS, are looking for her and the Biotect conjierum. You've seen firsthand what the strand can do."

She paced the room a bit, her heels clicking and clacking even more, her eyes fixed on Trevor. It was like the rest of us were not even there. Erica loosened her grip on Kent, sensing that whatever was going on was bigger than us and that Natalia was more interested in Trevor than anyone else in the room.

"So what's she want?" Trevor asked.

"You. She wants to speak with you privately."

"How the hell am I supposed to do that, Natalia? You know damn well that Randy would lose his shit over that! That asshole wants his nose in everything! You know what meetin' with her, alone, would look like to him? I'm not risking my job, or…or, hell, potential treason charges for her."

"She wants to speak to *you*, so find a way," she said sternly. "If you and the big wigs in DREAM Tower value DREAM as we currently know it, you'll find a way." Her next sentences sounded like they came from Natalia, the person, versus Natalia, Dune's messenger. "Dune and the Biotects are on a mission. Meeting with her could potentially stop future attacks and calm a lot of the chaos down. Unless you'd rather keep fighting off all the monsters they come up with?"

"Damn it, Natalia!" He sounded defeated. "You know what kind of shitty situation you're putting me in?"

"Doesn't sound like too hard of a choice to me, Trevor. Better to ask for forgiveness than permission this time."

"Shit." He thought about it for a few more seconds. "Fine, I'll do it." Then he started mumbling to himself.

"Good. Meet me at midnight by our fountain. I'll take you to Dune from there."

He turned around to face us and signaled for us to leave. I guess he figured there was nothing more we could do there. He was torn, you could see it on his face. Paxton looked as puzzled as ever. His dam of pent-up questions was about to burst, I could feel it.

"We're just leaving? We're not taking her with us? We're not investigating the building? Just leaving?" Paxton asked in disbelief.

"We take her, Dune finds out, we risk another attack. We go

snoopin' around this place, she reports it back to Dune, we risk another attack. Unless your ass is lookin' for another fight, I'd suggest we leave and let me take care of this tonight."

"You should listen to your squad leader," Natalia finally acknowledged someone in the room other than Trevor. "Dune currently isn't in the best of moods and you wouldn't want to test her limits any further."

Paxton didn't like it, but we left. The hike back to the SB3s would give him plenty of time to try to grill Trevor for whatever information he could get. I wasn't touching this ordeal with a ten-foot pole. As far as I was concerned, the less I knew about this the better.

Paxton at least had the generosity of giving Trevor a block of peace before starting his barrage of questions. "So, are you going to fill us in on what that whole awkward thing was about? Who exactly are Dune and Natalia?"

Trevor, to my surprise, didn't lash out at him but kept his cool. "Dune ain't just a high-profile dealer, she's the leader of the Biotects. Natalia. She's…an old friend."

Paxton wasn't satisfied. "The hell she is. Just like your *old friend* Jay Lynch, right?"

Trevor turned, looked him square in the eye, and yelled, "Watch it!"

Paxton eased up realizing he hit a nerve.

Trevor took a breath. "She's my wife."

It was a statement none of us saw coming. All of our eyes widened, including Kent's. Paxton had a huge look of guilt on his face.

"She's your wife? Like, present tense, your wife?" he asked.

"I wouldn't have said it if she wasn't," he said snarkily.

Trevor tried to continue walking but the rest of us stood there in shock. None of us knew how to process all of the new information that had just been dumped on us. He turned around noticing we weren't following, then reluctantly came back to where we were.

"The hell you all standin' around for?" he said, "Keep movin'."

"What happened between you two?" Erica asked. "You never mentioned you had a wife, and, and from the look on your face, it seemed like you hadn't seen her in a really long time."

His usually hardened facial features softened. It became crystal clear that this was a really touchy topic for him. "Is that what you want? Is that what it's gonna take to get our asses out of here?" His voice was walking the line between sad and annoyed.

"Yes," Paxton said, a bit too bluntly for everyone else's liking.

"Alright, Spitfire. I'll tell you, but we keep movin'. You understand?"

We all agreed.

"I met her at the academy. She was trainin' to be a Savior's assistant. Couldn't be a Savior herself, because she's an Omitted," he took a breath and recollected himself. "She spent her time outside of class by this one fountain. That's where I first noticed her. She was an artsy type, always workin' on something by that fountain. She caught my eye, so I started spendin' a lot of my time there too."

There was another break in his story. I took my eyes off him for a second and glanced over at the Kaisiusts. The three of them were totally enthralled, even Kent who barely knew him. Trevor had never shared anything like this with us before. The only thing he ever really shared with us was criticism and a collection of cuss words.

"We got to know each other, started datin', blah, blah, blah. I proposed to her at that fountain after graduation. I'd never seen her face so excited. She said yes, and we got married the next year. After the wedding we bought a condo near DREAM Tower. Problem was we both had different work schedules. She was at Center City General during the day and I was in a support squad overnight. Lived like that for two years."

He stopped again. He was trying even harder now to hide his sadness as his eyes began to swell up.

"It's okay, Trevor," Erica said, placing her hand on his shoulder. "You don't have to tell us anything else if you don't want to."

"No," he replied with a bit of certainty. "I've already started. Might as well give you the whole damn story. Spitfire'll just give me more shit if I don't anyway." He composed himself and kept going. "Natalia got burned out at the hospital. Told me she wanted a simpler, less stressful life. 'Let's both leave our jobs,' she said. 'We can open up a business together.' I…I didn't want to quit my job, but she wanted to quit hers, and did. I should've too. I should've listened to her and left when she did. Instead, I told her I'd request to be transferred to a day squad so we'd at least see each other at night.

"She wasn't thrilled about it, but workin' days was better than nights. They granted my transfer request and we rented out a space near the condo for her to open up an art studio. She sold her own drawings and paintings and did contracted work for companies designin' logos, billboard ads, shit like that. She was doin' well for herself and seemed happy. Things were gettin' better between us, but she still tried everything she could to get me into that damn studio."

A tear rolled down his cheek. Trevor, our rugged, fearless, foul-mouthed leader, was standing in front of us beginning to cry. It was a sight I never thought I'd actually see.

He wiped the tear from his face and continued. "Things started fallin' apart when I got promoted to squad leader. Shifts got longer and I had to work on my off days every now and then. She begged me to quit and kept sayin' shit like, 'Trevor look what this is doing to you. You have no time for *us* anymore. I've never seen you so angry and miserable. Please, come work with me in the studio.' I…I just couldn't do it. I loved her, but I just couldn't quit the squad.

"I remember I had a rough day and was really angry that night. She desperately pleaded with me, 'Trevor, please! You're not the same person I married. You've become so angry, so tired, so cold. Leave the squad, please! I won't even beg you to come to the studio anymore. If you won't do it for me then at least do it for yourself.' That's when I lost it. I blew up. Screamin' about how I was doin' what was best for us. That I was in the squad for her, so she could live the life she wanted to. 'The life I want is with you!' she yelled back, 'You don't have to do this! We earn enough money at the studio for us to live off of! Please, Trevor! The squad has changed you...' That was the last straw. I was pissed, beyond pissed. I picked up one of the stools from under the kitchen counter and threw it at the balcony door. Totally shattered the thing. Natalia ran to the bedroom and locked the door, cryin' like crazy.

"I didn't go after her. I didn't apologize. I should've. I know that now. I fell asleep on the couch, like any asshole after a fight with his wife. When I woke up in the morning she was gone. I thought she just went into the studio early, not thinkin' too much else of it. When I got home from work, she wasn't there either.

"I was worried. Wasn't like her to leave early and stay out late. I went down to the studio to see if she was still there. The door was locked. All of the lights were off, even the light-up sign above the door. I cupped my hands and looked inside. Place was empty, completely empty. She left a sign taped to the window: *Closed Indefinitely. Thank You For All Of Your Support.*

"I was scared. I walked home and tried to relax, hopin' she'd be there when I got back. She wasn't. She never came back. I filled out a missing person report and everything, but she never turned up. She never even filed for divorce. I thought I might never see her again. Hell, at one point I thought she might even be dead. And now we're here."

It wasn't the most poetic way to end his story, but that's how he did it. When we got back to the SB3s Trevor hopped on his and said, "Why don't you all call it a day. Nothing left for the three of you to do at this point. I'll take Kent back to DREAM Tower and I'll see you all tomorrow. Meet in the common room. Regular time. We'll go from there."

"I can take Kent back, Trevor," I stated. "I actually promised him we would get pizza after we finished today."

He looked a bit unsure at first. "Just be careful. Randy's already gonna chew my ass out if this shit with Dune goes south. I don't need any more shit from him if something happens to the kid," he said before speeding off without so much as a goodbye.

"Do you guys want to come too?" Kent asked Paxton and Erica once the roar of the SB3 died down.

"I'd love to," Erica replied and then looked to Paxton for his response.

He was a bit more hesitant but said, "Sure."

We decided to ride back to Center City for pizza. Erica recommended a place a few blocks from DREAM Tower called *A Little Slice of Heaven*. I knew with a name like that it had to be good, or at least hoped it would be. The place had a cool vibe to it. I don't know how I had never heard of it before. Sports memorabilia littered the walls. I was drawn to all of the baseball stuff they had, and there was a lot of it. There were a few jerseys that had been signed by some of Center City's greats like Kris Belt and Johnny Boiler that had been framed. There was a picture of two guys, who I assumed were the owners, alongside current Titans all-stars Derek Paulson and Karl Finne. Pennants, pictures, rally towels, scorecards, from every major sport everywhere.

"I thought you might like it here," Erica said as she walked over.

"This stuff is amazing," I said, still taking everything in. "You know Kent's a baseball fan too."

"I kind of got that by the way he's been making googly eyes at everything with you. You two look like two kids in a candy store right now," she said trying to hold back a laugh. "What team do you like, Kent?" she called over to him.

"The Greyhounds," he replied with his eyes glued to one of the team pictures on the wall.

"Me too!" It wasn't a shocker to me. I knew she grew up in Sterling. "We should go to a Greyhounds game once this is all over. What do you think?"

He turned around after hearing that. "Really? That'd be great!

I've never been to one before."

"Pizza's here," Paxton called over from our table. He hadn't gotten up from his seat since we got here. Not being a huge sports guy, he didn't feel the urge to do anything other than sit and wait for the food. We started inhaling the pizza, well, me, Paxton, and Kent at least.

"It's not worth burning your mouth guys. Take it easy," Erica said, mothering us. "It's not going anywhere. Neither are we. Take your time."

"It's so good," I could barely understand Paxton through his bites. "And I'm so hungry."

We didn't say anything for the first few minutes, focused on shoveling pizza down.

"I lived in that building you know," Kent said as he bit into a slice of meat lover's. "On the second floor." This certainly wasn't the topic I would have thought Kent would want to talk about, especially here and now.

Paxton couldn't help himself. "How long were you there?"

"I don't remember for sure. I think three years if I counted right. I used to live in Sterling with my parents. It's getting harder to remember that though. One night they broke into our house and took me away. They gagged and blindfolded me. I was really scared. We drove for a long time and then when they took the gag and blindfold off, I was in that house."

Erica, now intrigued, joined in. "Who took you away?"

"The boss's people. They said if I didn't do what they wanted they would hurt me and my parents. This one's really good," he said, putting another slice of meat lover's on his plate. "It was hard to sleep at night sometimes because the people working downstairs could get pretty loud. I heard scratching and growling noises sometimes too. I always wished that my room was on one of the higher floors. Those kids were lucky."

"What was the inside of the house like? Was it nice?" I could tell Erica's heart was breaking more and more with each answer, but I imagine she just had to know.

"Not really," he said, trying to replicate the cheese pull from his last bite. "It was pretty dirty. There was a family of rats living on my floor. They pooped everywhere. We tried to catch them so they'd stop pooping all over our stuff, but they were too quick. The water and lights didn't always turn on either." He took another big bite.

"Oh my god!" I heard Erica mumble to herself. "Did you all have beds, or clean clothes?"

"We got new clothes sometimes, but it was only when what we had was ripping too bad or we outgrew them."

"What about beds? You didn't sleep on the floor, did you?"

"No, we slept on these wooden things. I forget what they're called. I see them coming out of the back of trucks sometimes. I think they're meant to help carry heavy things."

"A pallet?" Paxton chimed in.

"Yeah. I think that's what they're called. The bed back at DREAM Tower is much more comfortable."

Erica was in utter disbelief. From across the table it looked like she was starting to get a little teary-eyed. "Then why didn't you sleep well last night?" I guess he shared that with her before I got to DREAM Tower this morning.

"I was scared."

"Of what?"

"Scared that they would find me and hurt me for not coming back."

Kent continued to casually eat his pizza while the rest of us sat there utterly horrified at everything we had just heard come out of his mouth. We looked at each other dumbfounded. How could something like this happen? Kids being stolen from their families and being forced to deal a dangerous strand of conjierum.

"Well, once we catch the boss we'll find your parents and get you back home. How does that sound?"

"I'd like that," he said nonchalantly, almost as if he didn't really believe it.

Paxton whispered over to her, "And what if you can't find his parents, or any of his family?"

"Then he can stay with me," she snapped at his pessimism. "No kid should have to go through the hell he has."

"I'm going back to DREAM Tower tonight, right?" the boy asked.

"Yes," Erica answered him. "Just until we find the boss. Then we'll take you home. To your real home."

It was quiet for a while until I decided to strike up what I thought would be a lighter conversation.

"So, Kent, why do you like baseball so much?"

"It reminds me of my dad."

That's all he offered up at first. "What do you mean?"

"We used to play together. He would pitch and I would hit. I always tried to hit a homerun over our fence. Sometimes I would hit the ball right back at him and he would dance around like it really hurt. Or we would play catch. I always tried to throw it as hard as I could. I thought it was funny when he would catch it and then take his glove off to shake his hand. He said I threw it so hard it stung. I miss that. It's been getting harder for me to remember things before they took me away so I think about baseball and my mom and dad a lot."

I felt bad for asking. I wasn't expecting anything like that. That was the last straw for Erica. She started crying at the table and quickly tried to cover it up so Kent wouldn't notice. Even Paxton had a somber look on his face. His mouth moved a few different times like he wanted to say something, but couldn't figure out what.

"It's okay, Erica," he tried to comfort her. "You guys are gonna find the boss and then take me home, remember?" He seemed to have more faith in the idea this time.

She wiped up her last tear, let out one of those you-caught-me-off guard laughs, and said, "Absolutely."

Chapter 15

The First Steps of the Fade

The news rang through the radio on my dresser while I got myself ready for work in the bathroom. I couldn't help wondering how Trevor was doing today after his meeting with his long-lost wife and how Kent was adjusting to life outside of the dealer house in Brexley. Once I finished putting on my uniform, I stepped out of the bathroom and reached to turn off the radio. Before my hand could kill the power, an interesting story stopped me.

"Breaking news this morning. We have gotten word that the leader of a Center City support squad is missing. Vice President Randy McGregor has just released a statement stating that Trevor Donaldson, the Duelist leader of the Center City-based squad, was attacked and abducted early this morning by a group of three individuals."

The cut of Randy's statement started to play. "At approximately one-thirty this morning we received information from an anonymous citizen who reported seeing Mr. Donaldson being viciously attacked, and subsequently abducted, by three individuals several blocks from the Academy for Conjierum Studies and Applications.

"It was reported that each of the assailants had a neon green ring of pigmentation around one of their biceps. This ring is a physical marker of the newly discovered Biotect strand of conjierum. Recent investigations have pointed to the Biotects as being the group responsible for conjuring the monsters that have been terrorizing DREAM, as their strand grants them the ability to materialize nonhuman life. We have chosen to release this information about the Biotects to the public at this time not to cause panic and fear but to raise vigilance and begin the implementation of more protective measures across DREAM. If you see anyone with this marker please alert your local authorities immediately. Biotects are considered to be armed and dangerous. We are currently investigating Mr. Donaldson's disappearance further and have no additional comments about him or the Biotects at this time. Thank you."

"Additionally," the news anchor's voice returned, "President Hornsby released a brief statement of his own this morning saying that he will be returning to DREAM Tower early from his scheduled vacation in light of these recent events."

Shit! Natalia set him up! If Dune was as savage as her monsters, he could be as good as dead by now. I stood there motionless for a minute not knowing what to do, then pulled myself together; Trevor or not, I still had to go to work. Hopefully Randy was holding back and would give us more information than he gave the media.

Unlike my typical, uneventful walks to DREAM Tower in the morning, the streets were buzzing today. It was fear—total and complete fear. I overheard some people talking about how the Biotects needed to be stopped before things got even more out of hand. Some people were afraid of Center City becoming as desolate as Brexley. I guess word about what was going on up there had finally gotten out. Some people were even bold enough to lay on their horns and yell vulgar threats and curses to Biotects out their windows. I had never seen the city so on edge.

Nobody met me at the front door, so I figured Paxton and Erica were up in our squad room. When I opened the squad room door, I saw Erica sitting in the common room looking anxious, almost to the point where she looked sick. Paxton was pacing back and forth between her and the window, livid. His arms were folded and his fists clenched tight. This wasn't a good sign.

"We need to talk, Graham," Erica said before Paxton could get a word in; and trust me, he tried.

"I know, I heard about Trevor this morning. Can you believe Natalia set him up like that?"

Paxton started bouncing on the balls of his feet. "Randy's lying. Trevor *is* missing but he wasn't jumped and captured last night. Randy's trying to get the public to not only help him get Trevor back, but find Dune."

"How do you know that?" I asked him.

"Because I'm the 'anonymous citizen' that reported him missing!"

A pool of questions flooded my mind but only one managed to escape, "So what actually happened?"

He began to ease up as he told his story. "So...this whole thing with Natalia felt really sketchy to me. I knew Trevor wouldn't give us the whole story once everything was said and done so I wanted to see if I could see or hear any of it for myself. I hid in the lobby, waited for Trevor to leave, and then followed him to his meeting with Natalia."

"He was here that late?"

"Yeah, I thought it was weird too. Anyway, he met her at this weird little park tucked away in one of the corners of campus. I didn't even know the place existed. Sure enough, there was a fountain right in the middle of the park. I only saw Trevor and Natalia, no Biotects, nobody else. I was keeping my distance, trying not to get caught, so I didn't hear a ton of what they said. But what I did hear seemed fine, nothing alarming. They talked about themselves and their marriage. Nothing about Dune or Biotects. When all was said and done Trevor left with her *willingly*. He wasn't attacked or forced to go.

"After they left, I contacted Randy. That's where I screwed up. I wasn't sure what to do. Even though everything looked and seemed alright, something told me it wasn't, or wouldn't be soon. I had a bad feeling something was going to happen between him and Dune, so I reported it. I don't think Natalia would hurt him, but who knows? Besides, there was no way I could have fought off anything a Biotect would have thrown at me. I wasn't armed or anything. I should've kept my mouth shut and waited to see if he would be here this morning. There's nothing I can do about it now. What's done is done," he said remorsefully.

"So, nobody's seen him since?" I asked both of them.

The two shook their heads.

"Then maybe you were right. Maybe something did go wrong. Trevor's always here on time."

"Randy told you that he wanted to meet with us once we all got in this morning, right?" Erica looked over and confirmed with Paxton.

"Yeah."

"So, what does he want from us? He knows we know that he lied to everyone. Does he think we were in on this?" I spewed out, afraid that we were caught up in something way over our heads.

"We play it cool," Paxton said. "We keep quiet, hear what he has to say, and go about our business."

Both Erica and I nodded in agreement. After another long elevator ride, we made it to the Presidential Suite.

"Remember," Paxton said, putting his hands in his pockets as the elevator door opened, "play it cool." He sauntered out with a weird, confident bounce in his step. He didn't normally walk like that.

"If that's his idea of playing it cool, we're screwed," Erica whispered in my ear as we exited the elevator after him. We both laughed, which caused Paxton to turn around.

"What?"

"Nothing," Erica said, suppressing her last laugh.

I held the door open for Erica and Paxton and pulled it shut behind me. Randy stood in the middle of the U-shape configuration of tables. Paxton stopped before reaching them and Erica took her place to his right. I filed in at his left.

Randy looked eager to see us, but I couldn't make out what type of eagerness it was. I wasn't sure if he was pleased, nervous, or upset, but he was definitely alert.

Paxton decided to take the lead, "You wanted to see the three of us." His tone was almost smug. Why?

Out of the corner of my eye I could see the door to one of the apartments crack open. Kent's brown eyes peered through, eavesdropping on the conversation that was about to take place. From what little I could see of his face he looked nervous. I didn't want to draw attention to him so I quickly switched my gaze back to Randy.

"Yes." He was irritated. It was an upset eagerness—not the kind I was hoping for. "I appreciate you stepping forward and informing me of Trevor's rendezvous with his wife, but you have thirty seconds to tell me where the hell he is and what the four of you are up to!"

Paxton exploded. So much for playing it cool. "Whoa! Whoa! Whoa! We're not up to anything! If we were, why would I report Trevor to you in the first place?" He paused for a moment and his tone became smug again, "However, Mr. Vice President, why don't *you enlighten us* on what *you* are really up to behind your blatant lie to DREAM about what happened to Trevor!"

Randy's eyes widened and he became even more testy. "Listen you loudmouth slim, if you want any chance of keeping your job and not going back to one of the god-forsaken factories you were born in, you'll speak up. That goes for your little friend here too," he said, directing his attention to Erica.

His words flashed me back to the comment he made about Erica on the beach, and then what that asshole had said about her on the boardwalk. At this moment Randy was no longer the vice president. He was just another racist prick. A tense surge of anger ran through me. Vice president or not, I wasn't going to let him talk to Paxton and Erica like they were lesser people. Not again. "Who the hell do you think you are talking to them like that?" I exclaimed.

"If *you* don't speak up your ass will join them too, sidekick." He was nearly screaming now.

Paxton smirked and suddenly decided to go back to keeping his cool, "We're not up to anything. We're just three squadmates concerned about the well-being of our leader, that's all." Why was he acting and talking so weird?

Randy didn't believe Paxton for a second, despite the fact that he was actually telling the truth, "You three halfwits have until noon to come clean about whatever the hell it is you're plotting. And if you don't, I personally assure you that your lives will become a living hell! You hear me?"

"Always a pleasure to speak with you Mr. Vice President, but it looks like my squadmates and I have a new assignment: finding our leader. You know what they say, the first forty-eight hours are the most crucial." Paxton turned to leave with a huge smirk on his face.

"Noon. You hear me, jackass? Noon. Or I'll have every civil Duelist in this damn city hunting your asses down!"

The sliver of Kent's face that I could see was now terrified. He gently pulled the door closed and retreated back into his apartment. Erica and I followed Paxton out of the suite. His hands were still in his pockets like they were when we walked in. No one spoke until we got in the elevator.

"Did you hear him in there?" Erica asked. Her face had a baffled and concerned expression. "What the hell is going on?"

"I'm not sure what Randy is up to, but I'm ready to expose him for the fraud he really is," he said, pulling a voice recorder out of his pocket.

"You recorded that whole conversation?" I asked.

"Absolutely!" he said with his smile bigger than ever. All of his odd behavior now made sense.

Erica chimed in, "Are you sure you want to do that? We can't really prove that he did anything else besides lie about Trevor, and politicians lie all the time. He's probably just trying to avoid more hysteria."

"Avoid more hysteria? Have you seen the news? Did you not hear anyone out on the streets this morning? The hysteria is already here. A good leader doesn't avoid hysteria by trying to sweep things under the rug. He, or she, acknowledges and addresses what's going on. Why hasn't he said anything about Brexley or made a real effort to get rid of all the crazy shit running around up there instead of covering it up? Why hasn't he mentioned anything about the Biotects until now if he's known about them all along? Why is he lying about Trevor? And, what I think are the two most damning questions of all, why has he been hiding all of this from President Hornsby and how in the world has he been doing it? None of that seems shady to you?"

I could tell by the look on Erica's face that she was in the same boat as me. Neither of us had thought that deeply about what had been going on. He was right. Something about all of this did seem really off.

"You're right, Erica. I can't prove anything just yet, but I know he's up to something. Did you see how defensive and paranoid he got? People with nothing to hide don't act like that."

"Put yourself in his shoes for a minute. DREAM hasn't had a Biotect problem in ages. The man is clearly stressed and isn't sure how to handle everything that's going on. It doesn't give him a right to talk to us the way he did, but I get that he's got a lot on his plate."

"I understand he's in a tough spot. But Erica, you gotta admit, something about the way he's gone about everything is odd. Why would he withhold information from the president?"

I wasn't sure if she believed what she said or was just playing devil's advocate, "He's in charge of militaristic operations. It's his problem to worry about."

"Come on, Erica. Wouldn't a group of dangerous conjierum users be something you'd share with the president even if they have been quiet for ages?"

"Think about this for a second. Has Randy known about the Biotects? Yes. And I agree that withholding that information from everyone else isn't the best look or idea. Now, I'm just playing devil's advocate for a minute here, but look at who our president is."

"What's wrong with Hornsby?"

"Wow, for once you're not the cynic. Again, I'm not saying that I think this way, but I know there are too many people out there who do." She stopped for a second, probably trying to carefully phrase what she wanted to say. "President Hornsby is an Omitted, right?"

He was the first Omitted president DREAM ever actually had.

"Your point?" Paxton asked.

"We have an Omitted president facing what could potentially become one of the biggest conjierum crises in DREAM's history. You don't think people won't notice that and think he's not fit to run DREAM? There's already a ton of people who think that way. A non-user making choices and decisions for users. You don't think Randy could be taking all this on himself to protect Hornsby? And if we go to war with the Biotects, a conjierum-based war, do you realistically see DREAM rallying behind an Omitted man, no matter how great he is, to get us through it? Or are they going to rally behind the Duelist vice president and toss the Omitted man aside? Maybe Randy thinks if he keeps Hornsby in the dark the public will go easier on him if something does become of all of this.

"We know that Randy and Trevor have some kind of past. Maybe Randy could be doing all this work trying to save face and now thinks that Trevor is undermining and sabotaging him. We're Trevor's squad, of course Randy thinks we're in on something.

"I'm not saying Randy has been handling everything well. I agree we all should have known about the Biotects a long time ago, the people in Brexley shouldn't be prisoners in their own homes, and he shouldn't be lying to the public about what has or hasn't happened. But I would like to believe—I'm hoping—he's doing it for something other than his own, possibly suspect agenda."

I was torn between the two sides.

Paxton held up his audio recorder, gently waving it back and forth. "I say we take a trip to the news stations and provide them with some breaking news of our own."

"Did you hear anything I just said? What would that solve?" she asked him.

"We know he's lying, about Trevor at least. The people have a right to know that. And you heard the way he talked to the three of us in there. Stressed or not, you can't talk to people like that, especially as the vice president."

"What's this about, Paxton? Is this really about the people having a right to know or your personal spite for Randy over this whole Trevor fiasco and what he said about me on the beach?" she asked, giving him a stare that a mother would give her son catching him in a lie.

"Ooh. I almost forgot about what he said on the beach," he mumbled to himself.

"Which is it Paxton?" she asked, getting a bit short tempered.

"Yes."

"Yes to which?"

"Exactly. Now let's go!

Chapter 16

Graham the Duelist

Erica was reluctant, but agreed to go along with Paxton's plan. "Fine, I mean, I can't stop you, but let the record show that I don't approve of this." Her gaze shifted to Paxon, "And, you need to promise me that after you finish your slander campaign you'll take us to that park so we can look for any clues as to where those two could have gone."

"Slander campaign? Really?"

"I call 'em as I see 'em."

"Let's just go."

Once we made it outside, Erica materialized SB3s for us and we rode around the city from news station to news station. Randy said we had until noon to come clean about whatever we were plotting with Trevor. Well, by noon Paxton's recording was spreading like wildfire across not only Center City, but all of DREAM.

Whether Erica was right about Randy or not, she was definitely right in not wanting to release the recording to the public. Paxton was hoping for honesty, clarity, and probably an apology from Randy. What he got was far from it.

I thought the streets were loud, tense, and even hostile when I walked to DREAM Tower earlier in the morning, but Paxton's recording had opened up a whole new can of worms. This was no longer just about the Biotects. Shouting matches and a handful of fist fights nearly broke out on the sidewalks of Center City. People yelled all sorts of nasty things about Randy, the government in general, Trevor, our squad, and even Kaisiusts. It turned out that his recording was just what closet crazies and racists needed for a coming out party.

I overheard some people say things like "those slims got what they deserved." There were people calling for Trevor's head, believing that he wasn't really captured but betraying DREAM. Others were upset at the three of us for not stopping him. A whole different group blamed only the Biotects for putting DREAM in this position. Then I heard some conversations out-of-left field that pointed the finger at conjierum itself, claiming that none of this would be happening if it weren't for "that vile substance." I doubted that their pun was intended, but I still found it kind of funny. A few in that same group shook off the idea of everything being the conjierum's fault and pointed the blame at the Kaisiusts for the most mind-boggling and nonsensical reasons. Some even thought that the Kaisiusts had somehow provoked the Biotects and brought this upon us. Everything I heard on the airways and on the streets was insane.

The only thing we had going for us was that Paxton's clip was only audio. Nobody would be able to recognize us as the ones in it, hopefully. I had never seen Center City like this before, everyone so divided and in an uproar. It scared me to death. And with even more Kaisiust hate growing and spreading, my fear for Paxton and Erica was at an all-time high.

The drive to the park was a bit longer than I expected, but we made it. It was just as Paxton described. The fountain was beautiful, one structure with four levels and multiple jets firing water at different heights every few seconds. It was almost like a layered cake, each level representing a different strand of conjierum with its jets shooting water of that conjierum's color. The layers had the different mottos and creeds of the various strands as well as busts of famous members of each strand. It didn't take me long to find one Duelist line embossed from its tier that really stood out: *Never fight a man with nothing to lose.* I thought back to Jay Lynch, how he said that to Trevor right before he started going at him, and everything we had gone through in such a short amount of time since then.

"Let's split up," Paxton advised. "Try not to look weird or suspicious or anything."

We did, and after a few minutes of searching for familiar

footprints, pieces of torn clothing, anything that could lead us to them, an odd noise coming from the sky caught our attention. The few people that were in the park screamed bloody murder. I could hear, and almost feel, the strain in their panicked voices. With wide, terror-filled eyes they sprinted for nearby buildings nearly tripping over fallen branches and their own feet as they went. You would have thought everyone was being chased by something straight out of a horror film. I looked to see what all the commotion was about and couldn't believe my own eyes.

"Son of a bitch!" I heard Paxton exclaim from across the park. Three ape-like creatures, bulky yet somehow agile, flew overhead with broad wings. The three of us regrouped to get a better look.

"A dragon, raccoons, an eagle, and now flying monkeys. What the hell is wrong with these people?" Paxton said to himself, but loud enough for us to hear.

They dove down to the ground after seeing us, kicking up dirt and small pebbles. Their force and weight drove each of them an inch or two into the ground after impact. In the blink of an eye, they went from skyward to earthbound. All three let out a menacing, throaty roar.

"Shit." It wasn't a we're-in-a-tough-spot-here type of shit. It was an I'm-genuinely-scared-about-this-situation type of shit, and it came from Erica. I was dumbstruck for a second. I don't think I ever heard her say that. What was worse was, Erica, the person I believed to be the most optimistic, quietly confident, and even-keeled in our squad, was afraid. Her fear only amped up my own.

The Biotects' newest creations most resembled gorillas, each one standing about a foot taller than Paxton and Erica, which was intimidating enough on its own. Their wings were long, thin, and fleshy like a bat's—similar to the dragon's too. They had dark, tired, irate eyes that stared at us and through us at the same time. Muscles bulged from their short-haired bodies. The most horrifying thing about them was their faces, which looked eerily more human than ape-like. Their facial expressions were angry and violent, yet somehow tormented, like they needed to hurt us to stop their own pain somehow.

I heard Paxton mumble something vulgar under his breath, wishing that Trevor was here. I wished that too, but without him it was my job to be the squad's Duelist. My hands started shaking. My stomach dropped. Reality set in. *I* was the Duelist now. It was my job to lead the charge in taking out these apes.

Their lives were in my hands now, like hers was. I couldn't let them down like I did her. I couldn't handle any more guilt, regret, or fear. I didn't need any more nightmares. I couldn't afford to fail anyone else again.

"Graham!" Paxton yelled over, snapping me out of my mental paralysis. "We need something here! These things don't look overly friendly to me."

I had no clue what to materialize to fight these things off. We didn't exactly cover savage, flying, man-faced apes at the academy. ALR50s. It was the first thing I could think of that would probably do some heavy damage to these guys if we were good and quick enough shots to catch them. The thought of that opened up a whole other door of anxiety. What if we couldn't catch them and were just spraying stray bullets everywhere? This park was surrounded by off-campus apartments and stores.

"Here," my voice almost cracked. I didn't even look at Paxton or Erica. I just held out my arms with an ALR50 in each for them to take. Once they took their weapon I materialized one for myself, quickly loaded it, and aimed.

"Let's keep our distance," Erica said. "They're quick, and look strong, but who knows what they can actually do."

Paxton and Erica cautiously aimed their guns at the creatures. For a second I didn't see flying apes; I was back in Brexley aiming my unsteady gun at an acid-spitting raccoon. I was holding up Sunshine against a crazed Jay Lynch. I was captaining the boat. I snapped myself out of it. I didn't want to endanger my squadmates again, I couldn't. I needed to focus. It felt nearly impossible to keep the barrel of my gun steady. The ALR50 suddenly felt like it weighed a ton. My finger quivered on the trigger, tapping it a few times, but never pulling it, thankfully. Not yet at least.

"You're okay," I heard Erica say. I knew she was talking to me. "We'll be okay. Just try to stay relaxed. We've been through worse."

The three, growling, took a few short steps towards us. Hard to stay relaxed at that.

"NOW!" Paxton yelled, catching all of us off guard. His bullet connected with the shoulder of the ape in front of him. It screeched out in pain, but before we could get any more shots in, all three re-took to the sky and began to circle above us.

"Damn, those things are fast!" Paxton said before beginning to shoot wildly into the sky hoping to bring one of them down. They dodged each shot with ease, looking like they were performing some acrobatic routine for fun. I stood there petrified. This had to be it. This had to be how we died, at the hands of massive, flying man-apes. Not exactly how I pictured it, but I was starting to accept it, slowly realizing we were completely outmatched on our own.

I felt this way every time we were in some kind of fight, but this time really did feel different. Before it seemed like we always had the tiniest sliver of a chance of survival with Trevor being there. At least we had a real Duelist against that dragon, Jay, those raccoons, and Alabaster the eagle. Now we had me. Me, Paxton who was spraying the sky with bullets like a little kid playing with a water gun on a hot summer day, and Erica who was trying to keep everything in check.

"Stop!" Erica called out as she slapped Paxton on the back. "This isn't going to work! We need to think of something else! And you," she was calling out to me, "we're not done here. I know what you're thinking. We're not dead yet, and we're not dying here. Wipe that look off your face. We've tackled things just as dangerous as these three in the past week alone. We need you to be Graham the Duelist now. The brave fighter. The quick-thinking tactician. If you can find that Graham we'll get through this."

"If you can't, we're dead for sure," Paxton reassured me.

She smacked him again for saying that. I don't know if she really believed that or was just telling me what I needed to hear, but she was right. I was the Duelist here. I was our best shot of getting out of this situation alive.

The three let out more shrieks from the sky. I was too distracted and overwhelmed by them to think of a plan. I looked around hoping to see other squads come to our aid, or rescue for that matter. No one was in sight. No alarms sounded nearby or in the distance. This was our fight and our fight alone. I desperately hoped it wouldn't be though.

"Anyone else find it weird that there aren't any other squads here since stopping these things is now a government priority?" I could hear the nervousness in my own voice.

"We can't worry about that, Graham," Erica said, sounding almost a bit annoyed. I could tell she was locked in now. Too determined to be afraid anymore. I needed to follow her lead. "We need to find a way to slow them down. They move way too quickly for us to shoot them out of the sky."

I looked around, hopelessly trying to come up with a plan, pushing back my nerves and negative thoughts along the way. The park was a relatively open space outside of a few trees here and there. There wasn't much that could help us slow them down or force them back to land.

Paxton stated what was fairly obvious, "Well, whatever we do, we can't stay here. We're sitting ducks."

Even if we took cover behind the few trees that were here it wouldn't be enough to protect us. The trees. That gave me an idea.

"I think we might be able to beat them if we use some guerrilla warfare, no pun intended." It sort of was though. I was just a bit too jittery to enjoy it.

"Yes!" Erica said excitedly. "But where? We can't fight them here. There's not enough coverage."

Paxton had it. "We're at the edge of the academy. The old Duelist dorm! It should still be in decent enough shape. We could definitely make it work."

The apes in the sky were ready to make their next move. They broke from their circle formation and swooped down towards us, rapidly weaving from side to side to make themselves harder to shoot down. Their arms were extended like they were trying to grab us. We didn't even have time to take aim, just barely diving out of the reach of their outstretched arms. Erica managed to roll herself into a shooting position from her dive. She unloaded a few rounds into the base of one of the ape's wings as it flew past us.

For a moment it started to fall to the ground, like a plane with a failed engine, but then managed to recollect itself. The three then regrouped back in the sky again.

"Aim for the base of the wings!" she exclaimed. "I doubt they're as fast on land as they are in the air."

The three circled around and took another pass at us, exactly as before. Paxton and I dodged their reach and rolled into a shooting stance, doing our best to mimic what Erica had done. I hit my target. Paxton missed his but was relieved when he saw Erica hit it for him. The three retreated back to the sky, screeching in pain. Drops of blood started to sprinkle down like the first few drops of rain from an incoming storm.

"This is our chance!" Erica called out as we slung the ALR50s across our backs and made a break for the SB3s. "Split up. That way all three aren't on us. The dorm can't be more than a few blocks from here. We'll regroup from there."

"Wait!" I yelled over the roar of the SB3s.

I conjured two SRHG6s, one in each hand, and tossed them to Paxton and Erica. There was no way we could defend ourselves with the rifles while riding the bikes. Hopefully the handguns would have enough oomph to do some damage if we had to shoot while on the move.

"Good call, Graham," Paxton assured me as I materialized one for myself.

We mounted our bikes and peeled out in different directions. It looked like Paxton was making a beeline for the academy. That meant Erica and I now had to be more creative and less direct with our routes. The apes also split up, each choosing one of us to follow. The one Paxton originally shot picked me. Even with an injured wing, the thing wasn't slowing down much. If anything, it was more driven and fiercer than ever.

It looked, and felt, like I was back in Brexley again. People must have ditched their cars while they were still driving in order to hide from the apes. The street had its fair share of vehicles lodged into each other as well as streetlights and even nearby buildings. I caught a break; the middle of the street was mostly clear.

The growling of my bike's engine wasn't enough to drown out the furious cries from my ape. My attention was split between the maze that was the road ahead of me and the pissed off flying monkey that wanted my head. I tried throwing it off by turning down random side streets and alleyways, but I couldn't lose it.

I finally made my way onto a street that was completely clear. I told myself that now was the time to try to get some separation from this thing. I went full throttle, but couldn't outrun it. It was now flapping its wings with everything it had, and was gaining on me. I made sure the stretch of road ahead of me was still clear before twisting my body to take a shot at it. With my left hand I aimed for its chest hitting its right shoulder instead. The sound was nauseating. A popping noise mixed this gushy, fleshy splat. The ape let out a cry, slowed down for a split second, but then kept coming for me.

I was starting to panic. The ape's face looked more human-like than ever. It was a deadly cocktail of emotion: torment, sadness, anger, and determination. I twisted again and fired a few more shots, putting a few holes in its right wing. I couldn't keep myself still enough to hit something vital. Blood began to drizzle down to the street as it flew. I had two rounds left and wasn't exactly in the best position to materialize more.

I veered down another street and was relieved when I realized where I was. My convoluted path brought me within two blocks of the old Duelist dorm. The only problem was that the road was cluttered with a slew of cars all over the place.

My focus shifted to avoiding all the obstacles around me, which forced me to slow down. I didn't dare look back; I knew it was gaining on me. I was hoping I had put just enough distance between us that it wouldn't be able to catch up with me in time.

I wasn't so lucky. Out of nowhere it grabbed me by the shoulders and pulled me off my bike, like a bird using its talons to snag its prey. Its grip was so strong that I couldn't help but scream. It had me pinched so tight that I thought its thumbs could be touching its other fingers through my flesh. It felt like one jerk, one good yank, would rip the tops of my shoulders right off, that my body would break and fall to the ground. The SB3 stayed upright for a few seconds before wobbling its way onto the pavement. I had to think fast. I couldn't let this thing take me away. And if I could get myself free, I wouldn't survive the fall if it took me much higher.

I raised my left arm as much as I could, my gun almost perpendicular to its body. I aimed a desperation shot at the ape's gut, hoping it would let go. My plan worked. My eardrums nearly exploded from the bang of the shot and the ape's shriek as I fell.

There was a split second of celebration in my mind, until I realized I was heading right for the rear windshield of a car below. I tried to twist my body, hoping to take the impact on my back. Barely making the spin, my spine smashed through the glass, landing me in the back seat of the car. An excruciating pain jolted through my body.

As much as I wanted to stay down, I had to get up. I had to be sure the ape was dead. I was covered in blood, hoping it was just the ape's and not my own. It took nearly everything I had to pull myself out of the back seat of the car and onto the trunk. I flopped onto the street, doing the best I could to stay on my feet. The pain was taking over, but I was doing everything I could to push it aside. I couldn't let myself feel anything until I knew that thing was dead.

I used the trunk to steady myself then hobbled out into the street. The ape had collapsed in the middle of the road, a pool of blood beginning to form around it. I sighed in relief. I was almost there; I just needed to pass the ape and I was in the homestretch. I stumbled along as fast as my body would let me. After only a few steps the unimaginable happened. It started getting up. I stood there stupefied. How was this thing still alive?

It wobbled to its feet, like a baby trying to get up. Its face was grimacing, and almost looked like it was on the verge of tears. I could tell it had next to nothing left. Blood was pouring through the fingers covering what I thought was my kill shot. The ape clinched its teeth and put everything it had into one final aerial charge, launching itself right at me.

I was in shock, but something took over. Instincts, the will to live, my conjierum, I don't know what. But I held out my right hand, materialized a new SRHG6, and fired. The bullet hit the ape square in the forehead. Its lifeless body skidded to a halt with only a few feet separating us. I fell to my knees. My body wanted to quit, but I knew I couldn't. I had to get up. I had to get to the dorm. I had to find Erica and Paxton.

Chapter 17

Veronica and the Apes

A bunch of blurry figures had gathered around me, not doing anything other than standing and staring. My senses were a bit shaky and the more they slowly came back to me the more I understood what was going on. These figures were people hovering over me in the middle of the street asking me all types of questions. Who I was. What was going on. What I was doing there.

I felt bombarded and I didn't have the wherewithal to really process and answer their questions. The sound of their voices kept getting louder and louder to me. The words began to jumble and fight over each other. It was becoming overbearing. All the noise became a strong buzzing in my mind.

One woman in particular broke through the crowd, quieting them down. She crouched down next to me, putting her hand on my shoulder. "It's okay," she said with a bit of an accent. "I'm a Savior on an overnight support squad." She showed me her ID, but flashed it so fast I couldn't make out anything it said. "Here. This should help until we can get you to a hospital."

She materialized two small bottles of liquid. One was maroon and the other a deep purple. She handed them to me one by one.

"That should help numb the pain," she explained as I drank the maroon one. "And this should help keep you conscious." She extended the next bottle to me.

Once I finished swigging down the purple liquid I could feel my mental fog starting to lift. The woman asked a few of the guys in the small crowd to help me to the sidewalk. I felt bad. The wet blood from my clothes had seeped over to theirs. They didn't look overly pleased about it either.

"Thanks everyone. I'll take it from here," she said, causing the crowd to head back to their homes. Once it was just the two of us she introduced herself. "I'm Veronica."

"Graham."

She gave me a warm smile. Veronica was probably only a year or two older than me; my guess put her at twenty-five or twenty-six. Her olive skin and accent led me to believe she was Latina. Her green eyes were a pretty contrast to her dyed red hair, which was cut in a stylish bob. Veronica had an average build and height, but as someone who spent a lot of his time around Kaisiusts, she seemed small to me. The worst part was Veronica was one of the most attractive women I had ever seen, which made me extremely nervous.

"Are you on duty right now, Graham?" she asked.

"Yes," I managed to spit out.

"Why don't you let me give you a ride to the ER."

"That'd be great. Thank you." I was so mesmerized by her that I wasn't thinking straight. Veronica led me down an alleyway behind what I assumed was her house. Then, with two fistfuls of my shirt, she pinned me up against the siding of the house next to the back door.

"Alright, what's really going on? Who are you?" I definitely wasn't ready for that.

"My name really is Graham."

Her stern look was somehow both terrifying and breathtaking. I felt like it could make me totally freeze up or completely melt at any second. I had to keep my cool here, not say anything stupid. Not say anything that could get me into more trouble.

"Graham Garnett, and my squadmates and I are looking for our leader." Damn it! So much for not saying anything stupid. I probably couldn't have lied to her anyway, even if I wanted to. She must have believed me. I guess if my bloody squad uniform wasn't enough to buy into my story then Trevor's disappearance and Paxton's recording probably were. I couldn't believe I just gave myself away.

"Are you...are you part of Trevor Donaldson's squad?"

I broke eye contact. It was the only thing I could think of. Her grip was too strong on me mentally and physically. I had already said way too much. She took my lack of answer as a yes.

"You guys are all over the news right now." She eased up and let go of me.

"I know." As soon as those words left my mouth Paxton and Erica popped back into my head. I must have made some kind of face or gesture that she picked up on.

"What's wrong?"

"I…I need to get to the old Duelist dorm. My squadmates are there fighting off more of those apes."

"You're not exactly in the best shape to do that. Let me call in backup."

"No! There's no time. I'm the Factotum, and with Trevor gone they're just sitting ducks up there." A dark thought crossed my mind. "If they're even still alive."

Her face went from shocked to serious almost instantly. "Let's go then."

Not far from where we were standing was a tarp covering some kind of motorcycle. Veronica tore it off and underneath was a CLES patrol cruiser. Not sure why she had one, but she did. This one had been modified to sit two, and did so much more comfortably than the SB3s did. She drove as quickly and carefully as she could.

I couldn't help but worry about Paxton and Erica. What if they had run out of rounds by now? All they had were a SRHG6 and ALR50 each, and Paxton wasn't exactly a conservative shot. I couldn't shake the thought of them not making it. It made my stomach churn.

The dorm was seven stories high. The sky had become increasingly overcast since we arrived at the park, and now it looked like it could burst at any second. Despite being built by some of the best Artificers at the time, many of the windows in the dorm were now missing or broken. I heard an all too familiar scream and saw one of the apes circle around the top of the building. One. Only one. Hopefully that meant this was the only one left. I put some of the other pieces of logic together. If the ape was here, that meant someone else had to be too. As weird as it was, the ape gave me hope that Paxton and Erica were still alive.

Veronica inconspicuously parked the bike behind some bushes in a courtyard not too far from the building. There was no way the ape didn't hear us coming, but it must have been too preoccupied to care. I sprung off the bike and materialized both of us an ALR50, realizing that I must have lost mine along with my SRHG6 in the backseat of that car.

"In case you need it out here." I gently tossed it to her. She gave me an are-you-serious type of look.

"Oh, no. I'm coming with you."

That caught me off guard. "You sure you want to do that?"

"Stop wasting time. Let's move," she said, running towards the building.

I followed close behind her, feeling nearly one hundred percent now. The ape was so fixed on whoever was inside that it didn't notice Veronica and I charging into the dorm. We entered a lounge area that was filled with dust and long forgotten furniture. It reminded me of Brexley City Hall, like everyone had just up and left one day and never came back. I stopped her before she found the staircase.

"We need to be careful. I only saw the one, but there could be another one of those things lurking around here somewhere, maybe more."

"You got it." She let out a confident smirk that nearly took my breath away.

I chased after her as she flew up flight after flight of stairs. Once she made it to the fourth floor she stopped. Not because she was tired, not at all, but because I had fallen behind and she was waiting for me to catch up. At that point I figured we were high enough to get some good shots at the ape. I also didn't want to embarrass myself any further by huffing and puffing my way up more stairs.

"Let's split up," I suggested, trying to catch my breath. "Search each room for a good spot to pick that thing off. My squadmates' names are Erica and Paxton; they're both Kaisiusts. If you find them, tell them you're with me."

She nodded, and we headed in opposite directions. The floor looked like a tornado had plowed through it. The walls were cracked and missing chunks in certain spots. It was hard to tell what color the carpet was because it was caked in so much dust, trash, and debris. The dust was thick in the air, too, making some rooms harder to see in than others. Much of the furniture was either in shambles or scattered across the floor and into the hall.

I cautiously peered into each room I came across. Knowing that almost all of the glass in each window was gone, I didn't need to make myself an easy target by standing right in its sightline. I couldn't see my squadmates or the ape, but could hear them. Gunshots rang from what sounded like down the hall. The further I went, the closer they sounded.

As I stood outside the next room I was about to investigate, I heard shots being fired and nearly jumped. I pulled myself away from the door and, inadvertently, slammed my back pretty hard against the wall. It took me a second to recollect myself.

"It's Graham," I called out, competing over the screams of the ape.

"Graham!" I recognized Erica's voice. "You finally made it! Are you okay?"

I peeked into the room, seeing that the view of the window was clear first. The window faced the doorway, so I quickly scurried up against the far wall, not wanting to give the ape a chance of spotting me. I huddled up against the wall on the side opposite of Erica, who had done the same thing. The window was in the middle of the space so we were able to hide on either side of it.

Her body was covered in dust, sweat, and bits of who knows what, but she was in one piece. I materialized a fresh box of ammunition and pushed it across the dirty tile floor for her. She took one look at me and was mortified.

"Don't worry. It's not mine, well most of it isn't, I think," I made a gesture referencing the blood slowly drying over me. "Where's Paxton?"

"He's above us somewhere, maybe the top floor, but I'm not entirely sure. We've been alternating shots and then changing rooms and floors to keep it guessing. Your plan's been working. We managed to take the other one down already."

Through the glassless window I could hear rain begin to fall.

"How cliché is that?" Erica said, trying to keep things lighthearted. "Raining in the middle of a fight like this. It's like a scene from a bad action movie or something."

I let out a chuckle and so did she. Her words calmed my nerves and gave me a small shot of confidence that we could do this. Four of us versus one ape. I liked our odds. I couldn't stay here with her though, we both knew that.

I crawled out of the room and then spoke to her from the doorway. "A woman named Veronica brought me here. She's a Savior in a night squad. Keep an eye out for her. She should still be on this floor. I owe her one. I'm going to head up towards Paxton and see if I can help. He's gotta be low on rounds too."

"I wouldn't doubt it the way he shoots. Stay smart. Stay safe."

I could see the ape flying by in the distance just as she finished speaking. It was dodging Paxton's shots. He was being more selective than usual, which told me he was most likely low on ammo.

I ran back to the staircase and went up to the next floor, looking for Veronica on the way but not seeing her. I was getting anxious. One, because I dragged her into this mess and wanted to know she was okay, and two, because I really didn't want to hike it up to Paxton alone.

I stopped on the next floor just to make sure Paxton wasn't there before going any higher. I took a few steps into the hall to be sure he would hear me calling for him.

"Paxton!"

I didn't realize how far down the hall I had gone. To my left was a dorm room that had lost both its door and the glass from its window. The room to the right at least had a door that was shut. I felt exposed but wanted to hold on for a few seconds to give Paxton a chance to answer if he was here. I couldn't help but keep looking to my left, making sure there was nothing in the window.

I heard an ape cry. It sounded close, much closer than I would have liked. My eyes darted left. The window was empty. I let out a quick sigh, closed my eyes, and took half a second to try to relax before climbing the stairs to the sixth floor.

My eyes flung open when I heard what sounded like a huge gust of wind rushing toward me. The ape. Flying full speed. Towards the window. Right at me.

I couldn't move. It was like a terrible nightmare where you ask yourself if this is really happening. It was reaching for me, like they had been had earlier in the park. There was no way it would fit through the window, but that probably didn't matter. It was so massive and strong that driving through the wall was probably like snapping a dry strand of spaghetti to it.

"SHIT!"

My adrenaline finally kicked in after what felt like hours of watching this thing fly at me in slow motion. I collapsed onto the floor, like I was back at the academy doing a burpee. It came crashing through the window, taking the frame and a large chunk of the surrounding wall with it. Its momentum carried it straight through the door opening, through the hallway, and into the room across the hall.

Pieces of the wall, door frame, ceiling, and dust all crashed down on me like a strong wave on the shore. I was half buried in it. I rolled over and sat up slowly, trying to push the rubble off my body as quietly as I could. I needed to cough desperately. I had inhaled so much dust, and who knows what else, but couldn't let the ape hear. If it was still alive, I didn't want it to know that I was too.

The room where the ape crash-landed was dead silent. And with everything in the air still churning, I couldn't see into it clearly. I very cautiously started to stand, pointing my rifle in the direction of where I thought the ape would be. My mind raced back and forth between whether it was dead or not. I was nervous, knowing firsthand that these things didn't die easily. My grip on the gun was tight. My trigger finger, and the rest of my body, began to shake a little. I had just gotten myself standing soundly when I saw a giant black mass rush at me.

I gasped for breath, but wasn't getting any. It felt like I had just been leveled by a linebacker. Not only had it knocked the wind out of me, but there was an insane amount of pressure on my ribcage, so tight that I thought my ribs might be broken.

Rain started pelting my body as the ape flew us out of the building and over the courtyard. I started panicking. I tried to squirm my way free, but could barely move. If anything, it was only making the pain worse. I punched at its hands and arms but it didn't even flinch. My torso was on fire. I could barely breathe. I couldn't even scream to let my squad know what was happening. I wasn't sure what was worse, the possibility of suffocating to death or whatever it was this giant monkey had in store for me.

My instincts started scrambling to figure out a way to get out of this mess. I felt trapped. Any sort of physical resistance would only hurt me more. How was I going to get out of this alive? I materialized a handgun. I wasn't sure how I did it or what kind it was, but it was there in my hand. I had to do something fast. I couldn't let the ape get any higher and I couldn't let it take me away. I took a gamble and aimed the gun at its right wing. If I killed it now the drop would kill me. If it took out its wings I had a shot at surviving a crash-landing. I was lucky that it somehow hadn't managed to pin my arms against my body.

It saw my gun and began to scream like I had never heard before. I was so loud and terrifying that I nearly dropped the gun and covered my ears, but I managed to hold on and take my shot. Blood began to stream from its wing. I hit my mark, or close enough to it. We were falling from the sky. It squeezed me even tighter. Pain exploded from my ribs and poured into all the nooks and crannies of my body. I gasped for breath, not getting much in return. The intensity of it was too much; I dropped the handgun to the ground below.

After a swift and gut-wrenching drop, the ape found the strength to level us out, gliding about twenty feet or so from the ground. A fall from this height wasn't ideal, but twenty feet definitely beat fifty or more. And a grass landing definitely beat a building top, pavement, or the backseat of a car. This had to be it. Now or never.

I materialized a new handgun in my left hand. I mustered every ounce of strength I had left. The surge of pain kept erupting through my upper body, especially as I raised my arm higher and higher. I did everything I could to keep my aim steady and desperately hoped to hit something vital.

The shot connected with its left wing. Not my first choice, but with both wings now injured we began dive-bombing to the ground. Damaging the wings to this point was a small victory until I realized how dangerous the ape still was on the ground. It could still walk. It still had arms and legs that were ridiculously strong. If I survived our crash-landing, and that was a big if, the ape would still be able to get up and beat me to a pulp.

I couldn't give it that chance. With my adrenaline pumping harder than ever, I raised my arm again and took my best shot at its head. Before I could see where my bullet hit, we plowed into the grass of the courtyard and skidded to a halt.

My back took the brunt of the fall again, but the pain there was nothing in comparison to my ribs and chest. The ape's body was lying on top of me. It wasn't moving. It wasn't breathing. It was literal dead weight crushing me. The smell of iron from its spilled blood was growing stronger by the second. I frantically squirmed to get free. Every movement was excruciating, but I had to get out from underneath it.

After pushing, twisting, and turning, cringing with each shot of pain, I was free. I managed to drag myself a few feet away from the corpse before giving up. I laid in the grass flat on my back. The rain was coming down steadily and was cool on my face. I breathed in and out slowly, wincing with every breath. I had nothing left.

"Graham! Graham!" I heard a voice call from a distance.

I couldn't tell who it was. I could barely make out that it was my name. I was done. I had nothing left. I decided not to fight it any longer and just give in, let the world around me fade to black. My body relaxed and my eyes closed.

Chapter 18

President Hornsby's Exciting Return

I was alive. My vision was blurry and my ribs hurt like hell, but I was alive. As my vision cleared up, I saw three relieved faces hovering over me: Erica, Paxton, and Veronica. I had a small hospital room to myself. Sharp pains jolted through my chest as I tried to find a comfortable—more like less miserable—sitting position. After a good amount of wincing and gasping, I was up.

"So what's my diagnosis?" I asked, still shifting around a tad to see if I could find any more relief. I wasn't having much luck.

"Broken ribs," Paxton answered. "A few on each side. That thing must have had some kind of grip, huh?"

"You're telling me," I said breathily. I was doing all I could to keep a straight face. I didn't want Veronica to see me hurt. I knew how dumb that was, but I didn't want to look weak around her.

"Your Savior prescribed some meds to help with the pain and speed the healing process. She said you should be able to return to work in two weeks if you take them like you're supposed to," Mama Bear Erica told me.

"I couldn't have said it any better myself," the Savior said walking in. "Hello, Graham, my name is Savior Melling. How are you feeling?"

"As good as expected, I guess," I replied. My torso was on fire. I would've given a finger to be able to sit or lie down and not hurt—a pinky finger maybe, nothing too important. I felt the need to pretend that flying ape didn't just crack my rib cage like a peanut shell at a baseball game.

She looked pretty young for a civil Savior. I would have been shocked if she were a day over twenty-seven or twenty-eight, definitely not thirty yet. Her dark hair was pulled back into a tight, short ponytail.

Her skin was fair, and she stood a few inches taller than Veronica.

"Like your friends already told you, you have a few broken ribs. Two on each side actually. Over the next couple of weeks you'll probably experience some discomfort on both your right and left side. Our ribs naturally heal on their own in about six weeks, but since you're a support squad member, especially at a time like this, I'm prescribing you medication that will accelerate the healing process. It typically isn't covered by your insurance, and is pretty expensive out of pocket, but President Hornsby insisted that you have it. If taken as directed you should be fully healed in about two weeks. I'm also prescribing you something to help manage any soreness you may experience.

"That being said, I want to see you back here in two weeks for an x-ray to be sure those ribs have healed properly, or are at least very close to it. Until then I recommend that you take some time off work and rest. If that's not a possibility, then I would strongly advise you to only do desk work until you've fully recovered. Do you have any questions for me?"

"The president is paying for my medication?" I asked, almost in disbelief. Vincent Hornsby, the president of DREAM, was paying for my medication. Why would he do that? I didn't know him. He didn't know me. I was surprised, grateful, and honored but more than anything confused.

"Yes. He called and insisted on it while you were resting. He was adamant about getting you healthy as quickly as possible. Any other questions about your treatment?" It took me a minute to finally shake my head no. I was still wrapped up in why the president was doing this for me. "Alright. I'll go get your discharge paperwork."

The room became quiet causing me to sink into my own thoughts. How could I just sit around for two weeks? We still had to find Trevor. We had to find Dune. We had to find those kids and get Kent back home. Then a totally different thought crossed my mind.

"What do you think she meant by me 'being a support squad

member, especially at a time like this?'"

Odd looks came over their faces. It was like they all knew something but none of them wanted to be the one to tell me. They stared and glared at each other trying to decide who was going to fill me in on whatever it was. Erica eventually gave in.

"Why don't we just show you," she said as she turned on the wall-mounted TV.

It was tuned to a local news station which was airing an address that President Hornsby had given earlier that evening. It must have happened while I was out. We caught it right at the beginning. President Hornsby took to the podium, with Randy by his side.

His skin was dark and a bit worn. If I remembered correctly his sixtieth birthday was coming up later in the year, and a big celebration was already being planned for it outside of DREAM Tower. You could tell the job was wearing on him. His short, curly, black hair was now starting to fade to gray. Bags of stress, sleep deprivation, and aging were noticeable under his eyes, in addition to the wrinkles. Whatever R & R he had gotten while on vacation was now long gone. He typically had a very warm smile, but today he was serious and somber.

"Citizens of DREAM: it is with a very heavy heart that I speak to you tonight. I have returned to assist Vice President McGregor and our support squads in a joint effort to get to the bottom of the heinous attacks that have taken place in DREAM over the past week. We will continue to work together to restore normalcy into your lives once more."

The president paused to an outbreak of applause. I was always a Hornsby fan. He won my vote two years ago when running for office. One of the things I liked about him was that he always tried to practice what he preached. If he said he would be working to get to the bottom of this, I knew he actually would.

"Additionally, I would like to address the recent audio recording that has surfaced of what appears to be the voice of Vice President McGregor making inappropriate remarks and racial slurs towards members of one of our support squads. We are currently looking into the authenticity of the recording. However, I want to make it clear that the type of speech heard on that recording is certainly not condoned no matter who it is coming from. Until our investigation is complete Vice President McGregor will be taking a mandated leave of absence. His day-to-day duties will be delegated to Maya Varma, the current headmistress of the School of Factotums at the Academy for Conjierum Studies and Applications. Thank you and good evening."

The camera focused on Randy's face. He was doing everything in his power to stay poised, but it was apparent that nobody had told him he'd be taking mandatory time off beforehand. The reporters in the room began badgering him to make some form of statement. He blew them off and followed President Hornsby off stage doing his best to mask the stunned look on his face. Paxton smiled and turned off the TV.

"That part gets me every time," he said to himself.

"Whoa," I commented.

Before I could get anything else out Savior Melling returned with the discharge papers. I filled them out and the four of us left the hospital. I wanted to talk more about the president's address, but waited to get out of there first. A Savior's assistant wheeled me to the front of the building. Outside it was dark out and the street lights were on full display. She and Erica helped me out of the wheelchair.

"Well, I guess this means our squad is on its own leave of absence?" Erica half-asked, half-stated once the Savior's assistant made her way back inside.

"About that," a man from outside our circle interjected. I could've sworn he wasn't there a second ago, or his friends either. "President Hornsby would like to speak with the three of you privately."

He showed us identification. A member of the PSS, but I had never seen him before, or the other three with him. This definitely wasn't the crew we had seen with Randy. All four of them looked to be in their mid-thirties and wore black suits. The man speaking to us was probably six-foot-one or -two, just a little taller than me. He was pretty plain looking, average build, short, brown hair that he spiked in the front. The rest of the squad wasn't nearly as bland as him. There was a huge, dark-skinned man with a short, neatly groomed mohawk. He had to be close to six-foot-five wearing a suit that could barely contain his muscles. There was a woman with very fair skin, red hair, and freckles that was about Veronica's size. Last, was a man with brown skin and an impressive head of thick black hair—the kind of hair that you would see in a shampoo commercial. He was shorter than me, very thin, and had this aura of suaveness to him.

"You're not the same squad I've seen with the vice president," I said skeptically.

"The vice president has his own squad," he explained. "We're President Hornsby's. Like I said, he'd like to speak with you as soon as possible."

"Like, right now?" Paxton asked.

"Yes, if Mr. Garnett is well enough."

I was initially shocked that he knew my name, but that soon became an afterthought. All eyes were on me for an answer. "We can go now."

"Alright." The man now turned to Veronica. "The President has requested that you rejoin your squad tonight for your shift. He also asks that you not share anything with anyone regarding your involvement with Mr. Donaldson's squad today."

She agreed. We said our goodbyes, each of us personally thanking Veronica for all of her help. She told us her shift started in two hours and she needed to go home and get ready. As she hopped her cruiser, a weird sadness came over me. The kind of sadness someone gets watching a friend leave and not knowing if, or when, they'll ever see them again.

The PSS herded the three of us into the back of a dark, unmarked van. I kept my eyes on Veronica driving away until the doors shut. Once she was gone I started taking in my surroundings. There were no individual seats, only padded benches along the perimeter of the walls. Within minutes of leaving the hospital I started feeling sleepy, still exhausted and drained from our crazy day. The limited light in the back of the van didn't help either.

"Graham, you sure you wanna do that?" Paxton called over from the bench across from me. I must have started dozing off. My body was starting to slouch to the right and I didn't even realize that my eyes had shut. "There's no way sleeping on this bench will feel good on those ribs, especially if we hit a few bumps along the way."

I grunted at him, hearing what he was saying but not comprehending it. I must have fallen asleep because before I knew it Erica was waking me up. We were back at DREAM Tower. The seven of us squeezed into an elevator, gearing up for a long trip to the top.

It was incredibly awkward. The PSS just stood there in the middle like freshly pressed, pristine, government statues. Paxton, Erica, and I slouched against the walls in our disgustingly sweaty and dirty uniforms doing everything we could to keep ourselves upright. The three of us were beat.

After what felt like years, we finally made it to the top. The PSS motioned for us to enter the suite, but didn't follow us in. In fact, they went back to the elevator and left. It seemed a bit weird to me, but if they had somewhere else to be, who was I to stop them. As we passed through the set of double doors, President Hornsby rose up from his seat. He had arranged four upholstered armchairs in front of his desk, all facing each other in a circle-as much of a circle as you can make with only four chairs. We were greeted by his wide smile as we walked in.

"Ahh, here they are! Trevor Donaldson's squad. It's a pleasure! I've heard you've been extraordinarily busy recently."

We all took turns shaking his hand and sharing greetings. I was starstruck. I had never met anyone famous before, let alone the president. I knew we would be meeting him on the way here, but it didn't really sink in until he stood there right in front of me.

Once we said our hellos and introduced ourselves, he asked us each to have a seat. We were a bit reluctant at first considering how gross we were, but he told us not to worry about it. It was like he didn't even notice how bad we looked, and most likely smelled. President Hornsby sat facing the double doors and me. Paxton sat to his left and Erica to his right.

"I want to start by making sure I have all of my facts straight. Is it true that none of you know where Trevor is?"

Paxton decided to speak on behalf of the group, shocker. "We don't. We were out searching for him today when we were attacked."

After hearing what Paxton said he switched his attention over to me, "I'm sorry, I should have asked this first. How are you feeling, Graham?"

"I'm alright, sir," I said, trying not to wince as I answered him. My heart pounded. "Thank you for paying for the medicine. You didn't have to do that."

"It was the least I could do. We're going to need your help figuring out what exactly is going on with these Biotects. I can't believe Randy kept information about them from me, and the whole situation in Brexley too." He tilted his head down and pinched the bridge of his nose. "We need to get this under control ASAP. Your squad has been so instrumental in not only getting us information about the Biotects, but fighting off their monstrosities, that I didn't want those ribs holding you back longer than they had to. Was that the extent of your injuries? I mean outside of any cuts, bumps, or bruises, just the ribs?"

"Yes, sir."

"Please, call me Vincent. I'm not a big fan of formalities," he said with a grin. "Well, I'm glad to hear that you and your squadmates didn't have any other serious injuries. I apologize that Randy didn't send you three any backup. Despite your proven ability to take them down, I'm sure a little help would've gone a long way. Maybe you wouldn't be in the situation you are now." He directed his last sentence at me.

"As soon as I had gotten word of what had happened with you four out by the academy, I had my PSS and a few other choice support squads investigate where they may have come from. They've been interviewing witnesses and checking security cameras of different buildings around the city and near the academy. The good news is we believe we know where the apes were materialized from. The bad news is that it was somewhere here in DREAM Tower."

Our three pairs of eyebrows immediately shot up. There was a Biotect here, in DREAM Tower. Right under our noses this whole time.

"That would mean that someone working here is a Biotect. Or, I guess, that maybe there was a visitor today who is," Erica half-asked, half-stated again.

"Our secretaries downstairs haven't reported any unusual visitors to the tower today. With the recent attacks, Randy has been asking them to check everyone coming into the building for the Biotect mark. They haven't reported anything. Now that doesn't mean someone couldn't have snuck in through a side door, but I personally don't believe this was some random person who just found their way in here. I suspect it was an inside job."

Paxton blurted out before anyone else even had a chance to think. "Ryken! We brought him a vial of Biotect conjierum from Brexley to research."

Vincent cut him off before he could go on. "Dr. Ryken was our first suspect. He, and his staff, have been interviewed. Everyone's alibis checked out, and no one has the Biotect mark. The odd thing is the vial is missing from the lab, but no one knows how it disappeared."

"Can't you check the security footage from the lab to see if someone snuck out with it?"

"I wish I could, Ms. Towson, but the labs currently don't have security cameras in them to protect the confidentiality of their studies and research. However, you can bet that first thing tomorrow I'm going to have a team of Artificers down there installing them, whether those researchers like it or not. With all due respect to what Dr. Ryken and his colleagues have done, and are doing, there is no way we can let something like this ever happen again."

I was hesitant at first, not wanting to sound stupid for even suggesting it, but worked up the nerve to throw my hat into the suspect ring. "What about Randy, I mean, Vice President McGregor?"

He turned his attention to me. "Randy was our next suspect, just because of all of his knowledge on what's been going on. No mark. Randy and I received the information that the apes came from DREAM Tower shortly after I finished my address. He was there with me, so he couldn't have stolen the vial personally. He was immediately questioned though, and once everything checked out for him; he was sent home to begin his leave of absence. The tower has been in lockdown ever since, well with the exception of letting you three in. I now have my PSS and a few different CLESs sweeping the building, including the labs, looking for anyone with the Biotect mark or any information. Any DREAM Tower employee who left prior to my address will have a CLES knocking on their door soon enough to interview them as well, but nothing's come up yet."

We digested what he said and tried to think of any other potential suspects. Erica glanced around the room. Her eyes zeroed in on the apartment Kent had been staying in. The door was wide open and from what we could see the place looked vacant.

A worried look swept over her face. "Where's Kent?"

"Kent?" Vincent asked, "Who's—"

Before he could finish, the front wall of the apartment closest to Vincent exploded inward towards him. Dust and debris shot into the room like it had been fired from a cannon, creating a fog near the new gaping hole through the apartment into the rest of the suite. We all reacted as quickly as we could, rolling out of our chairs and trying to hide behind them. I did everything I could not to scream. Having to move that fast along with all of the thick air I was now inhaling made breathing even more hellish than it already was.

Something was in the room with us. It was quiet, almost whimpering, but I recognized it. The same whimpering from only a few hours ago. A dying ape.

I materialized SRHG6s, realizing what we were up against. If there was one, there were bound to be more soon. I waved to get Paxton and Erica's attention and slid the guns across the floor to them. I had to get out of there. I was in no shape to fight. With guns in hand, Paxton and Erica sprang into action, leaping up from behind their chairs.

"Get yourself and Vincent out of here," Paxton yelled out as he and Erica opened fire on the ape.

It didn't take much; the thing was nearly dead already. I guess launching yourself through an Artificer-made wall used to protect the president and then the entryway of an apartment would do that to you. I was a bit surprised it even made it that far. It reminded me just how strong these things were. That ape torpedoed itself through two heavy-duty walls and still nearly hit its mark.

For whatever reason, Paxton unloaded his magazine into the thing. I could hear its blood splattering onto the surrounding chairs and carpet. The PSS plowed through the double doors with guns drawn. Better late than never, I guess.

"I wouldn't be surprised if there were more of them on the way," Paxton warned them. "Looks like this guy was just the battering ram."

"Are you okay, sir?" the red-haired woman asked, rushing over to help Vincent up.

"I'm fine, Carrie. I'm fine." Vincent was extremely lucky; if that ape would have made it a few more feet it would have hit him dead on.

"Amir, Code 14," the bland man called out after he and the muscular man finished a quick sweep of the area. "Emmett, help me get Graham up."

"I'll take his right side, Dave. You get his left," Emmett said as he and his squadmate swooped over and got me to my feet. I saw Amir type in a code at the intercom box by the double doors. A siren blared and a woman's voice came over the speaker instructing everyone to evacuate the building. Just as Vincent and I had gotten to our feet we heard a howl coming from the direction of the two gaping holes leading into the suite.

"Shit!" Emmett spat. "Get them out of here, now!" he ordered. He sprinted from my side to face the opening.

"Down the stairs, move!" Amir shouted to us all, flinging the double doors open. Everyone shuffled out with Dave and I bringing up the rear. I was moving as fast as I could but was hurting with each step.

The howling was unsettlingly loud now, like an ape was in the room with us. I turned my head, needing to see what was going on behind me. Emmett had materialized some type of Uzi and began unloading it into the wall openings. Fading cries of death followed the string of gunshots.

"Come on, Graham," Dave urged me as we approached the double doors.

Amir led our escape down the stairs. He was followed by Vincent, who was being watched carefully by Carrie. Erica and Paxton were next followed by me and Dave. Emmett brought up the rear. I could hear him slamming every door shut behind him. Not that it really mattered. Those apes hadn't been ones to let doors stop them yet.

"You realize there's no way in hell we can run down all these flights of stairs," Paxton called out to Amir.

"Once we get to a vacant floor we'll shoot out a squad room window and fly out of here," Emmett instructed from behind. "Should be old hat for you guys."

"And what if they see us and follow," Paxton asked, not buying into his plan.

"We'll take care of it. Just keep moving."

The thought of having to jump out another window was terrifying. I nearly had a panic attack the first time from seventy-seven floors up. Having to jump from over a hundred stories up would surely put me into cardiac arrest.

We stopped on the one hundred fourth floor and kicked in the first squad room door we could find, knowing it would have the window wall we needed. I started to feel sick to my stomach. Bile creeped up my throat. I could hear the screeches from a handful of apes above us. Who knew how far behind us they actually were?

Vincent and I both sat down to catch our breath. This common room was nearly identical to the one in our squad room. Erica and Amir, who turned out to be their Artificer, worked on jetpacks and headsets for everyone. Emmett, their Duelist, watched the squad room door. Carrie, their Savior, and Dave, their Factotum, took what little time we had to evaluate Vincent, making sure he hadn't sustained injuries he might not have realized. Vincent insisted that he was fine, but they continued to question and examine him. Paxton moved all the surrounding furniture away except for the chairs Vincent and I were sitting on.

"Graham, I need something to shoot out the window."

I sat up in my seat and materialized an ALR50 for him, hoping it would be powerful enough to shatter the glass. He scurried over, took it from my hand, and without hesitation unloaded the magazine, in true Paxton form.

"Damn it!" he yelled. "I need another clip!"

I materialized it for him and gave it my best toss. Man, did that hurt. The apes above us were getting louder and more excited. Hearing the gunshots, they must have known we were close.

"Break! Damn it!" Paxton screamed as he fired all of the rounds at the window again. Finally, the glass gave in. Shards of all shapes and sizes rained down to the street. Flashbacks of Trevor, the dragon, and the fear of plummeting to the ground below flooded my mind.

Erica called our attention, "Here we go!"

Amir passed out the equipment to Vincent's squad. Erica

tossed a jetpack and headset to Paxton and then readied herself. She only materialized two of each.

"They're closing in!" Emmett was firing some kind of rifle now from the doorway. "Get moving!" I could hear the dying shrieks of the apes as they took on his bullets.

"Put this on, you're coming with me," Erica said urgently, handing me a harness.

I didn't fight her on it; there wasn't time. I worked as fast as I could to put it on, flinching with every move. She latched me onto her and we were ready to go, like tandem skydivers waiting to make their jump.

"Dave first," Emmett directed in between shots, "then the rest of you. I'll bring up the rear. Meet at Center City Suites. NOW GO!"

Dave materialized a rifle I didn't recognize and took to the sky first. Carrie and Amir flew alongside Vincent next. Paxton followed. Emmett was firing even more shots at an even quicker pace. There were more angry and dying ape screams than ever before. Erica and I needed to act fast. I looked down at the tips of my shoes on the very edge of the building. More bile started coming up, but I forced it back down.

"Are you sure about this, Erica?"

"As sure as I'm going to be."

She started up the jetpack pulling my attention away from the ground.

"JUMP!"

We leapt in unison; somehow, I got the nerve to do it and not screw it up. My stomach dropped. We were moving fast but in the wrong direction. My worst fears were becoming reality. We were free falling. I was too much extra weight.

It felt like we had been falling to our doom for years. Out of the corner of my eye I caught Emmett's figure against the scattered lights of nearby skyscrapers. There wasn't much he could do. Even if he were to have grabbed a hold of us, I highly doubted the two jetpacks would've supported all three of us.

"HOLD ON!" Erica warned me.

About halfway down the side of DREAM Tower she maxed out the propulsion on the pack. It roared like it was in miserable pain. We were still falling, but pushing it to the max was slowing us down. It was like we were parachuting down to the street.

Emmett, now seeing that we would land safely, spoke over the headset. "I need to stay with Vincent. We'll see you at the hotel."

Paxton's worried voice came through next. "What's going on? Where are you two? What happened?"

Erica, wanting to keep him calm, phrased her words carefully, "We're fine. Just running a bit behind. We'll see you soon."

We landed in the middle of the street, hoping that if there were any apes left we could make our escape by blending in with the mob of people frantically evacuating DREAM Tower. Erica unlatched me and dematerialized all the equipment. She helped me over to the sidewalk to give herself space to materialize a ride for us.

"Sorry about that," she said, making a CLES patrol cruiser with a sidecar appear. "I know this can carry both of us."

She helped me into the sidecar and then started for the hotel, dodging people and other vehicles along the way. Both civil and support squad vehicles rushed past us towards DREAM Tower. A symphony of sirens rang down all the different streets leading to the building.

We were met outside the hotel by a very anxious Paxton. His arms were crossed and he was pacing nervously. "What the hell happened to you guys?

Erica answered for us. "We, uh, had a few technical issues. We're fine though. Is everyone else here?"

He took a breath of relief. "You had me scared to death, you know that." His tense body was starting to relax. "Yeah, everyone's here. They're waiting inside." Paxton must have felt good enough to take a playful jab at her as we all walked in. "What kind of Artificer has 'technical issues?'"

She chuckled and shrugged, "You know what they say. Even monkeys fall out of trees."

"Little too soon for a monkey reference," I commented. The two of them started cracking up and I did my best to suppress my laughter.

Inside the lobby Vincent promptly started a conversation about where to go from here. "I don't think it's safe for us to stay in the city right now."

"Especially you three," Emmett added, looking at me, Paxton, and Erica.

"What're you trying to say? That this is our fault? That we're some kind of Biotect creature magnets?" It was Paxton being Paxton, the captain of controversy.

"I'm just giving you the facts. The eagle, now these two different sets of apes. They seem to have some kind of interest in you. I agree with Vincent. We all need to get out of here. If the Biotects are after you three, or the president, we can't stay. We can't have Center City becoming a battleground."

"So what are you suggesting?" Erica asked.

"There is a presidential safe house hidden out in the woods a few miles west of Mylo. We should stay there and lay low for a while until we can figure out what's really going on here."

The word Mylo shot goosebumps down my body. Luckily Paxton responded before my mind could recall too many of the bad memories.

"You just want us to run away from this? Leave the city? Hide? I don't know if you've heard, but they've tried that up in Brexley. It hasn't been working out so well for them."

He had a point; it felt wrong to leave the city like this. Although if we really were a Biotect target Emmett was right; we really didn't have a choice. There's no way we could stay here and risk the lives of everyone in the city.

"Give it a few days. I'll bring in some other support squads and try to gather more intel," Vincent tried to reason with Paxton. "We'll put a plan together, get this whole thing sorted out, and it'll be business as usual in no time."

It was quiet for a few seconds until Erica joined the conversation. "Let's give it a shot, Paxton. Maybe they're right. Everywhere we go these things have been finding us: Brexley, the park, now DREAM Tower. If we are the target of some Biotect operation we shouldn't be putting the city, or the rest of DREAM for that matter, in harm's way."

Paxton took a second to really choose his words. "I don't like this. I think it's cowardly and I'm not convinced it's going to solve anything. But. I'll go along with it." He glanced over at Vincent. "I'm holding you to your word. Only a few days."

Chapter 19

Another One Goes Missing

The otters were out in full force, chasing alongside our boat hoping we would drop a fish their way. I was captaining the small, commercial fishing boat while she worked the crane, pulling up one of the nets. I looked around to see who else was on board, but it was just the two of us.

It was early evening. A storm was rolling its way inland, but I wasn't worried. We'd make it back home before it could catch up with us. The smell of salt filled the air, and the cool ocean breeze felt great. Some of the otters squeaked in excitement. This was their shot at an easy dinner before we made port.

I heard the crane pull the net up on board. It plopped down onto the boards causing our catch to flop around even more. It was full of fish, all different shapes and sizes. I watched her get to work, throwing back the fish that weren't edible or that weren't large enough to be keepers yet. The otters were going nuts chasing after our rejects.

"Another nice haul, Graham," she called to me.

I left the bridge to go help her sort the fish. She was a bit taller than average—around five-foot-seven. Her body was lean from her daily work on the boat, her hair was long and black, and her skin was as pale as mine.

"Look at this one!" she said in excitement. A super cheesy smile overtook her face as she hoisted the huge fish close to her chest, pinning it against her bright orange fishing waders. It was no small feat. That fish had to be close to fifty pounds.

"Nice!" I replied as she began to carry it over to the hold.

"You can head back. I'll be done by the time we get to the next one. I want to try and get back home before dark."

Seeing that she didn't want or need the help, I started back towards the bridge to get us moving again.

POP! THUMP!

Hearing a thump wasn't uncommon on the boat. Fish thumped around all the time. The popping sound though, that was odd. The more I thought about it though the thump wasn't an ordinary one either. It had to have come from something larger than a fish, something that shouldn't be making that kind of noise.

I turned around and found her face down on the deck. A strange dart was sticking out of the left side of her neck. She wasn't moving. I couldn't see her breathing. Everything inside screamed that she was dead. I started freaking out.

I turned my head toward the bow, the direction where the dart logically would have come from. Before I could even get a good look at what was there, I heard the pop again and felt a needle pierce my neck. I winced. It stung pretty badly. I could feel something hot immediately coursing through my body. My vision instantly blurred and started to fade.

I was in a full-on panic. Not only was she dead, but now I was dying. My knees started to buckle. I was losing control of my body. Everything was getting dark. I touched my neck trying to feel what was going to kill me too. Another dart.

* * *

"Graham," a muffled voice called me. "Graham!"

I sat up and saw Paxton. He was sitting with Erica on a couch adjacent to me. I was lying down on a couch all to myself, not recognizing where I was. Then it hit me, this was the safe house.

"You alright, buddy?" Paxton asked me as he grabbed the TV remote and turned it on. I'm guessing he wasn't expecting me to actually answer.

He flipped through one or two channels until he landed on one where Maya Varma was just starting to make an address. Her black hair was pulled back into a tight bun. She wore an aqua colored pant suit which nicely complimented her brown skin. She was similar in age to Trevor, maybe a few years younger, but hid her age well. I could see why Vincent chose her to temporarily replace Randy. She had a great reputation at the academy and got things done when she said she would—like Vincent.

"Good morning." Her voice was strong and confident. "Many of you are already aware that last night the Presidential Suite of DREAM Tower was attacked by a multitude of flying ape-like creatures. I received word early this morning that the president is indeed okay and is currently seeking refuge in a secure location. I am pleased to inform you that there were no fatalities in the incident; however, a Kaisiust boy who was residing in the tower as part of an ongoing investigation is now missing."

"Kent!" Erica blurted out, shooting some oatmeal she was chewing across the room towards the TV.

"Citizens who witnessed the attack last night, or were in the proximity around the time it occurred, are encouraged to share any information they may have regarding the whereabouts of this boy with their local authorities. Thank you."

Cameras snapped and questions erupted from antsy reporters. Maya ignored it all and gracefully stepped down from the podium, exiting the room. By this point Erica had gotten up from her seat to wipe up the oatmeal from the floor while Paxton turned off the TV.

"That has to be Kent!" she continued.

He and I were quiet. I guess neither of us wanted to say anything that might upset her. Kent had proven to be a sensitive topic.

"Would he just up and leave like that?" Erica asked, somewhat rhetorically.

"I don't think so," Paxton responded. "I mean, where would he even go? He's not familiar with Center City, and it's a long way back to Brexley or Sterling. I don't think he'd be able to make that trek on his own." He paused for a second, thinking about what he had said.

"You never know though. He's pretty resourceful."

Paxton's words didn't do much for her, in fact they might have made things worse. By the look on his face, I think he thought that what he said was helpful. Erica's expression said otherwise.

I decided to take a stab at it, hoping I wouldn't pull a Paxton. "He's right. Kent's pretty resourceful. But maybe he just wasn't in the apartment while we were there. He could have been on some other floor, or maybe someone took him somewhere. He probably just hasn't come back to DREAM Tower yet. I can't say I blame him either. I'd be scared to go back there if I were him. Wherever he is though, I'm sure he's fine. He's a strong, smart kid."

Paxton jumped back into the discussion, "I think something happened to him. Why else would he have left and not been back by now?" Damn it, Paxton!

His conspiracy theory was the last thing Erica needed, or wanted, to hear right now. I shot him a what-the-hell kind of look. He didn't even see it, focusing on her and not me. It was one thing to think that, and Paxton very well could have been right, but now didn't seem like the time to bring it up. Erica was upset enough.

"How could that have happened?" she contemplated. "He wasn't in his apartment when we were attacked. He was already gone."

Before Erica could come to her own conclusion Paxton offered his. "Which means this had to be an inside job. Who else in DREAM Tower would have an interest in Kent other than the Biotects?"

"But Vincent said the support squads didn't find any evidence of Biotects in the building."

"Then maybe it wasn't a Biotect; maybe it was a Biotect supporter."

Vincent had now entered the room from the hallway behind us. We straightened ourselves up and tried to look as presentable as we could. Part of me still couldn't believe that we were staying here with him. He casually asked what we were talking about, and we got him up to speed.

"So this Kaisiust boy, Kent, is a Biotect conjierum dealer?"

"Well…" Erica started her defense. "Yes, but it sounds worse than it really is. He was kidnapped from his family when he was younger by a group of Biotects and was forced to deal for them."

"So if you think the Biotects kidnapped him what do you think they would want with him now?" the president asked. "Are they just looking to get their traitor of a dealer back? Not to be rude, but why go through all the trouble to kidnap a kid dealer from the top of DREAM Tower?"

"…I don't know," Erica discouragingly answered, looking to see if Paxton or I had any input.

"He must have some sort of value to them, or whoever took him," Paxton stated. "If not, why not just let him be?" There was a break in the conversation. "Maybe just to make an example out of him?"

"Or," I said, trying desperately to keep optimism alive. "Or he was just out of the apartment and hasn't come back to DREAM Tower yet. Maybe he got caught up in the evacuation pandemonium and got lost."

"You're probably right, Graham. It's pretty hard to look up and find the one hundred seven story building you've been staying in."

"Then maybe he left and just doesn't want to come back. Maybe he's already back. That recording is how many hours old now? We don't have any evidence proving anything bad has happened to him!"

Erica was visibly upset and stressed out. She slumped down on the couch and raked her hand through her hair. A few audible exhales later, she slowly stood up, catching everyone's attention, and said, "I'm going for a walk."

"Do you want some company?" I asked.

She needed to get out of the house and process everything that had been going on. I got that. We hadn't had much time recently to just think and decompress. She hesitated to answer my question at first, but gave me a slight nod. The other two didn't try to stop us or tag along. Vincent just suggested that we didn't stray too far from the house.

Before we left, Vincent and Erica headed down the hall together. He placed his hand on her back, which looked awkward with the big differences in their heights, and tilted his head up to say something to her that was too soft for me to hear. Halfway down the hall Vincent opened a door and headed down to some kind of basement. I could also see a step or two of another staircase next to that door which led to a second story. Erica went all the way down the hall towards a large back window and then turned right. Soon she was out of sight and I could hear the water from the sink running. She must have been washing out her oatmeal bowl in the kitchen.

I stood up from the couch and tried to stretch, wanting to shake off the last bit of grogginess in me. I instantly regretted it. Some part of me had forgotten that I had four broken ribs.

"She's taking this pretty hard," Paxton said low enough for only the two of us to hear.

"Yeah. She really liked him."

He gave me an are-you-that-stupid kind of look.

"What?"

"I mean, yeah, she likes him, but it's more than that." He started to speak even lower, "I think she sees a lot of herself in him. You know she was only a few years older than him when her parents died, right?"

The water from the sink stopped and so did our conversation. I could tell Paxton had more to say but wasn't going to risk her hearing it. Erica had made her way back into the room.

"You ready?" she asked rather unenthused.

I nodded. She grabbed the doorknob, twisted it, and ducked through the doorway. I painstakingly followed behind, not needing to duck, and shut the door behind me.

The house had a covered wooden porch. It was nothing

extravagant, but had plenty of space along the width of the front of the house for people to sit. To my left, towards the end of the porch, was a peaceful-looking, wooden swing for two. All of the wood here had lost its finish but was still in great shape.

I didn't have too much of a hard time getting outside from the couch, but each of the porch's three steps down to the ground were killer. I could feel my jaw clenching and eyes twitching as I tried not to make noise sucking in air. Erica, who was standing in the grass by now, heard me.

She turned around. "Are you okay?"

My feet had just reached the ground. "Yeah. I'm fine."

"You sure you don't want to go back in and rest."

I took a few steps towards her, which was easier now on flat ground. "I'm sure. As long as we keep this a walk and not a race."

"I wouldn't embarrass you like that. You know I'd beat you in a race whether you were hurt or not. It wouldn't even be fun for me," she said, trying to put on a good face. Her look, her tone, this was the same Erica from the boardwalk. She was trying to be strong, trying to keep everything as normal as possible, but she was hurting.

"Hey, if I had beanstalks for legs like you I'd at least have a fighting chance!"

She laughed. I did too, but with the discomfort it caused me, it didn't last long.

"You would never guess this place is what it is," she said, looking at the house.

I turned around to get a view of the place. It was an old, two-story log cabin. The outside was worn and sun-bleached, with some of the logs starting to splinter. Leaves and sticks had collected on the roof of both the porch and second floor. Erica was right. From the outside you would have no idea that this was a safe house. I probably would have guessed that it was abandoned if I didn't know any better.

Woods surrounded us except for the rugged dirt driveway leading to the home and a field off to the cabin's left. The field looked like it was once prime real estate for crops but those days were long gone. Erica kept her head down as she walked towards the produce graveyard. I gingerly picked up my pace to catch up with her, which didn't please my ribs. We silently strolled through the dead soil together for a few minutes until I broke the ice.

"Do you want to talk? About what's going on? About...anything?"

She let out a sigh. "I don't know, Graham. There's just so much going on right now. Trevor's missing, now Kent's missing, Randy's on a leave of absence, and now we're out here hiding in the woods with the president because weird mutant animals keep trying to kill us.

"Center City's beyond crazy which means the rest of DREAM isn't far behind. We're still next to nowhere with any information on the Biotects. It just feels like no matter what we do, no matter how many monsters we fight, no matter how many pieces we try to put together, this puzzle doesn't seem any closer to being solved, you know? It feels like every time we're on the verge of figuring one thing out another bombshell gets dropped on us."

"I hadn't really put a lot of thought into it until now, but you're right."

"We definitely have our work cut out for us," she said as a smile slowly returned to her face. "But life wouldn't be fun if it were easy, right?"

I gave her an are-you-serious type of look. "I think I'm gonna have to disagree with you on that one. As great as all of this has been so far, the near-death experiences, the injuries I've had, and this weird game of detective we've been playing, I think I could still find some fun in going back to our normal lives."

We both started laughing.

"Where did you hear that from, anyway?" I asked.

"My dad used to say it," she said. "I mean, sure, you can have fun in an easy life, and not to sound cliché, but think about how all of the terrible stuff we've gone through so far has pushed us. How all the craziness has brought our squad together. Think about how many support squads just punch in, ride around all day, then punch out. Then they go sit at home and wake up the next day to do the same thing all over again. Yeah, in the moment a lot of what we've done has been overwhelmingly stressful, but looking back, we've been growing from it.

"I get what you mean now. I could've done without broken ribs, though."

A mischievous smile came over her face, "Think about it, if we didn't run into those apes you never would have met Veronica."

I could feel my face flush. "What do you mean?"

"Come on, Graham," her smile became bigger and her voice more excited. "I saw you staring her down while she drove away last night. Like a sad puppy watching its human leave for work."

I wasn't sure if my face could turn any redder, but my cheeks were on fire.

"I've got good news for you. We talked a bit at the hospital while you were sleeping. You know, just some get-to-know-you small talk. Turns out she's single!" She gave me an exaggerated wink and poked me gently with her elbow a few times. I wanted to curl up in a ball right there, the embarrassment was too much.

"You've got good taste. She's gorgeous. Extremely smart too," she continued on until finally noticing how red I had turned. "Okay, okay. I'll stop. Let's go."

She started walking back to the house. After a few steps I stopped feeling my heart pounding in my throat. My face started to cool off.

"Is it that obvious?"

"Oh yeah."

I nervously laughed.

"You think she'd be interested in someone like me?" I asked after getting myself together.

She stopped dead in her tracks which immediately gave me anxiety. Her face looked really serious, like she was about to deliver bad news. She bent her head down to look me square in the eye, which made me even more nervous, and said, "I think so." Her mischievous smile returned. "It might take some time, but maybe, just maybe, you could *eventually* win her over." She looked back up towards the house. "Life wouldn't be fun if it were easy, right?"

I felt ten pounds lighter after those words left her mouth. My body relaxed, and I exhaled.

"Don't worry," she said. "I'll put in a good word for you."

"Geez, Erica," I said, continuing to calm myself down. "Did you really need all the theatrics for that? The dramatic pause, the stone-cold face, that look in your eyes, I nearly had a heart attack." I chuckled a little.

"Did I lay it on a little too thick?"

"Not if you were looking for an award for that performance."

"You think I have a shot at winning this year?"

I stopped in my tracks, which caused her to stop too. I looked her dead in the eye and said, "I think so. But don't worry, I'll put in a good word for you."

We both started busting a gut. Erica was laughing so hard she was nearly bent in half. My ribs were raging, but I couldn't stop myself and didn't want to. Then Erica snorted which only made it worse. I started to tear up and she did too.

We eventually settled and made it to the front door where Paxton met us. "Vincent wants to talk down in the bunker," he said.

The bunker? Erica followed him, and I followed her. I hadn't explored the house yet, so I had no idea what or where the bunker was. We walked through the living room down the hall where I had seen Erica and Vincent earlier this morning. The hallway seemed to be the main vein to much of the house. I remembered the big back window and the kitchen on the right.

Paxton opened the door to the stairs that Vincent went down

this morning. This had to be the bunker. The walls were white and appeared to be made of some kind of stone or cement. The space had an open area with enough tables to hold forty people or so. It had apartments too, similar to the ones in the Presidential Suite of DREAM Tower, that lined the walls. At the very end of the bunker were two larger rooms. The room to the left had its door shut, and the room to the right looked like a conference room. Vincent spotted us from a built-in kitchenette to the left of the stairs.

We sat at a picnic-style table that was made from the same material as the walls and was built into the floor. The kitchenette was completely open, with all of the appliances and cabinets lining up in a row. Vincent walked from the counter to the table, a few mugs clustered in one hand and a coffee pot in the other.

He passed us each a mug and poured us a cup. "Have you eaten yet, Graham?"

"No, no I haven't."

"You should. We still have some oatmeal here. It's not good to take those pills on an empty stomach."

He got up from the table and headed over to the stove to get me some oatmeal. I felt around in my pockets, looking for the medicine. I placed the bottles on the table as he arrived back. I took a few bites of the oatmeal, popped the pills into my mouth, and washed them down with a swig of coffee.

Vincent didn't sound tired, but he certainly looked it. His eyes were glossy and had more bags than an airport baggage claim. He slumped back into his seat and wrapped both his hands around his mug on the table.

"I just spoke with Maya Varma; in fact, the PSS might still be talking with her back in the control room. Anyway, we agreed to arrange for a select few support squads to do some further investigation while you three are here. I recommended that Veronica Tavares's squad be chosen since she already has some insight and experience in dealing with the Biotect creatures. Her squad will report directly here with any pertinent information they gather. From there, I'll inform Maya of anything she needs to know."

My face flushed again. I desperately hoped that no one noticed.

"I'll keep you posted with any news I get. Enjoy your day."

He got up from the table and headed down the length of the bunker to the room with the sealed door. That was the control room.

"What do you think they're doing in there?" I asked.

"Running DREAM remotely," Paxton said with a bit of snark. "The door was open when I was getting breakfast, and I peeked in before they saw me."

"Of course you did," Erica sighed. "Come on, Graham. I'll show you the rest of the house."

Chapter 20

"Squad Bonding" and More Bad News

"Pick one," Erica instructed me. She stood in front of Paxton and me on the couch. The bowl she extended to me was filled with folded slips of paper.

"Go on. They're not going to bite you or anything." I must have had a wary look on my face or something.

I pulled a slip from the bowl while Paxton asked, "What's this?"

"Squad bonding," she began.

"Squad bonding?" he replied with an are-you-serious look on his face and tone in his voice.

"Come on, it'll be fun. Besides, the academy recommends all new squads do an activity like this to get to know each other better."

"Trevor wouldn't make us do this," he countered.

"Trevor's not here. And this'll be good for us. Think about it, we've spent all this time together and how much do we really know about each other?"

She had a point. It wasn't like we had anything better to do anyway. I thought for sure Paxton would think up some kind of rebuttal or comeback, but he didn't.

"Graham has the first question. We'll go around and take turns answering it. Go ahead, Graham."

"What would you do if you weren't in a support squad?" I read aloud.

"Couldn't have picked something easier, Graham? Like what's your favorite color?"

"Sorry."

"Shut up, Paxton," Erica said, giving him a playful hit as she took a seat on the other couch and sat the bowl down next to her.

"You first, Graham."

I thought about my answer for a second. "I'd love to work in baseball somewhere."

"Somewhere? You wouldn't go back to Mylo and work for the Otters? Aren't they your team?"

I would've loved to work for the Otters. They were my team. But that meant going back to Mylo. "They are, but I live in Center City now," I told her, hoping that would be a good enough answer to end my turn. It looked like both Paxton and Erica were still a bit skeptical but left it alone.

"My turn, I guess. I think I'd be a politician," Paxton began. "Start small and then work my way up to the Presidential Suite. DREAM's got some serious problems and I think I could be someone who could fix them."

That answer didn't surprise me at all. I could see him doing it too. He'd have to learn to control his temper a bit more, but he was smart and charismatic enough for the job.

"Should I go warn Vincent that you're gunning for his job?" Erica teased.

"Very funny," he said, making a mocking face at her.

"Okay, my turn. I would love to design roller coasters for amusement parks."

"Really?" Paxton asked, surprised. "That's pretty cool. Well, as long as we get to ride them for free. Right, Graham?"

"Absolutely."

She laughed.

Paxton followed up with her. "Why didn't you then? You're crazy smart and were the top of your class. You probably could've gotten any job you wanted."

It didn't take long for us to see that this was a touchy topic.

"My parents. They always said if the Artificer strand chose me that I'd be a great fit for a support squad. Don't get me wrong, I do this because I want to, but it's also for them. To prove them right, to prove to everyone else in my family that doubted me wrong. To prove to myself that I could get this far." She paused for a second. Her gaze fell to the floor and I could tell this was starting to make her emotional. "Um." Her voice was getting shaky. "This job, weirdly enough, makes me feel close to them." Her finger reached behind the curtain of hair hiding most of her face to wipe away a tear.

We heard the door to the bunker open and turned our heads to see who was coming up. It was Vincent.

"You okay?" he asked Erica, who had just finished recomposing herself.

"Yeah, everything's fine."

Vincent didn't look so good. Bags drooped under his overworked, bloodshot eyes. He was struggling to keep them open. He leaned against the wall, which was the only thing keeping him on his feet.

"I've got some more bad news to share with you, but let's discuss it over breakfast. I desperately need another cup of coffee."

The president led us to the built-in table beside the kitchenette. A pot of coffee had just finished brewing as we reached the bottom of the stairs. Vincent headed straight for the pot, poured himself a cup, and then offered a pour to the rest of us.

By now I had definitely decided that I didn't like the bunker. It felt cold and bleak, almost like an abandoned prison. It gave me the creeps, I guess, if I had to pinpoint an exact feeling to it. How bright it was for being underground between the white walls and strong, artificial lighting, how large and empty it was, and how quiet it was outside of the humming of anything sucking up electricity all gave me weird vibes.

"Go on. Have a seat," he instructed the three of us.

Vincent placed his mug at his spot at the table and then went back to the counter to bring over the food.

"Vincent, we can get it. Why don't you have a seat? You look exhausted," Erica offered.

"No, no, I insist," he replied, forcing a smile.

"Then at least promise us that's not decaf in that pot," Paxton said. I wasn't entirely sure if he was making a joke or being serious.

Vincent's eyebrows rose and his face lit up as he started walking to the table with food in hand. "Trust me," he chuckled, "you don't have to worry about that."

With one hand he brought over a big plate of prepared powdered eggs and in the other a large, red bowl filled with canned fruit cocktail. This was our standard breakfast now that the expired oatmeal was gone. We all dished ourselves some fruit and eggs, took a few bites, and waited for Vincent to say what he wanted to tell us. I made sure to take my pills after a few bites of eggs and nearly burnt myself on my coffee. Not only was it hot, but man, it was strong.

"I don't think there's an easy or elegant way to say this so I'll just come out with it." Our eyes were glued to him. "In addition to Trevor and Kent, Randy is now also missing." I could feel my eyebrows rise and a soft whoa escape my mouth.

"Not only Randy but his PSS as well. Maya and I, along with my PSS, spent all night discussing what actions to take moving forward. We're hesitant to release the news to the media as things are chaotic enough as it is. The state of DREAM is very fragile right now."

He took a second to swig down another gulp of coffee.

"You all remember Veronica Taveras, don't you?"

"I don't think she ever told us her last name, but yeah. Of course," Paxton said, deciding to play squad leader again. He shot me a quick look after answering Vincent and out of the corner of my eye I caught Erica doing the same.

Either Vincent didn't pick up on it or he didn't care. "Veronica's squad was assigned to check up on Randy at his condo in the city last night," he began. "No one has seen or heard from him since my address. All I know so far is that they found one piece of evidence: a note on his dining room table that read '4 of 14.' The PSS and I did a bit of investigating ourselves. We've contacted his family, they haven't seen or heard from him. We checked with his building's security feed and personnel. He hasn't been there since the day the dragon attacked. Similar story for his PSS members. Everyone we've reached out to has no clue what happened to them either. Randy has his own suite in the Presidential Suite like I do, and he'll switch back and forth between staying there and his condo. I haven't seen him around DREAM Tower since I came back from vacation, but that doesn't necessarily mean he wasn't there."

"Weird," Erica said to no one in particular.

"So what's the theory so far?" Paxton asked. He was in business mode for sure.

"It's really hard to say with the lack of evidence we have. However, we're leaning towards kidnapping by the Biotects."

"What makes you think that?"

"The note on the table. We aren't entirely sure what it means, but our best guess right now is that it's a warning. There's been four major Biotect attacks on DREAM so far: the dragon, the eagle, and the two sets of flying apes."

"So even though there was no evidence of a kidnapping you believe the Biotects somehow nabbed Randy and left that note? And based on that extremely vague note, you think there's going to be ten more attacks on DREAM at some point?" Paxton asked, sounding more like a lawyer than a Savior.

"As of right now, based on what little information we have, yes. I've asked Veronica's squad to join us here later today so we can directly discuss with them in further detail what they saw in that condo and what they think the note might mean. Call me old school, but I'd like for the twelve of us to be able to sit down face to face, go over their investigation, and try to figure this out. They somehow forgot that they were to report straight to me and bypass Maya. As soon as they finished speaking with Maya, she discreetly and securely passed the information along to me and the PSS and now we're here."

Vincent took another sip from his mug as he got up from the

table. "That's all I have for you at this point, but I'll keep you up to date if I hear anything else. If you'll excuse me, I need to get back to work. I'm sure the PSS is waiting on me. I'll see you all once Veronica's squad arrives."

Chapter 21

The Squad's Report

"You know, every time I run into you you're sleeping." A familiar voice woke me from my nap.

I rubbed my eyes and a nervous jolt surged through my body. Veronica was leaning against the doorframe. Her arms were crossed as she smirked. I froze. My heart pounded in nervous excitement. She was even prettier than I remembered, even in the drab squad uniforms we had to wear. I instantly became self-conscious. I could feel my hair sticking up in certain spots from how I slept on the pillow and felt dried up drool on the left side of my mouth.

"How are you feeling?"

I slowly sat myself up, trying to avoid aggravating my ribs. I was sure the effects of my pain meds would be wearing off by now, if they hadn't already. "I'm getting there."

"Well, I'm glad to hear it. Erica told me I could find you up here. President Hornsby wants us all to meet down in the bunker. Whatever that means."

As she turned and began to leave the room I called out, "Vincent."

She stopped and turned back around with a confused look on her face. "Yeah, Vincent Hornsby, the president."

"No, no, I mean, he prefers just Vincent. He's not a huge fan of formalities. He made it a point to tell us so."

"Ahh," she said with a grin. "Good to know. Thanks."

I heard her footsteps as she walked down the stairs to the floor below. I took a second to relax and shake off my nervous energy. Literally. I heard somewhere that physically shaking it off helped. It sounded like a good idea at the time, until my brain got over Veronica and remembered that I had four broken ribs. I took in another big, calming breath, tried to fix the guest bed, and waited for my ribs to recover from the one poorly thought-out, upper body shake before heading downstairs to the bunker.

I was the last one to arrive and Vincent motioned for me to take the only open seat left. The conference room was a large open space with a bunch of folding chairs, a wooden podium, and another marble pedestal, like the one in the Presidential Suite, equipped with technology for presentations and whatever else. Vincent must have had everyone arrange their chairs in a circle, similar to how we first met with him a few days ago.

"Hello, everyone," he said, standing at his seat as if he were in front of a crowd of thousands. He still looked exhausted but much better than he did at breakfast. "I want to thank Ms. Taveras's squad for joining us here to talk about their investigation of Randy's condo. But first, I'd like to have everyone introduce themselves. I don't believe we all already know each other. So, who would like to begin?"

A man stood up first. He looked a few years older than his squadmates. I pegged him to be in his early thirties. His skin was light while his eyes and crew cut were dark. This guy was fairly muscular and probably three or four inches taller than me. He was a pretty good-looking guy with well-defined features and a small bit of stubble on his face. There was no doubt in my mind that he could've been on the cover of every men's health magazine in DREAM.

"Toby Andrews." His voice was deeper than I expected. "Duelist." That didn't surprise me.

He sat down, which led the other man in their squad to stand up. This second guy was baby-faced and looked closer to twenty than thirty. His moppy hair was slicked back and to the left, like he could have been in a boy band or one of those really old movies where the guys always worked their hair with the comb they kept in their black, leather jackets. His eyes were also dark and his skin was tanned from the sun. He was shorter than Toby and not nearly as muscular. "Stephen Hall. Artificer."

Veronica was next. A small rush of excitement hit me. She was the one person in the room that needed no introduction.

"Veronica Taveras. Squad leader and Savior."

Squad leader? I know Vincent had mentioned it being Veronica's squad a few times now, but my mind didn't piece together that she was the leader. I just thought he called it that because we all knew Veronica. She was young for a squad leader, and arguably the youngest member of her own squad. It was a toss-up between her and Stephen.

I tried to use the draft rotation cycle to see how old she could be. Each year a different strand took leadership of the drafted squads. Our year was a Duelist year, which started a new cycle, and was why we were all drafted by Trevor. I mapped it out in my mind. The last Savior year would have been two years ago since the cycle went: Duelist, Artificer, Savior, then Factotum. Unless she hid her age really well, or started at the academy at a weird age, she really couldn't be that much older than me, three years max. If my theory was right, Veronica most likely became a squad leader right out of the academy, which was unheard of.

The last member of their squad stood up. She was maybe an inch or two taller than Veronica and very thin, with next to no muscle mass at all. Her dirty blonde hair was collected in a ponytail that reached down to the base of her neck. Her skin was fair with a few freckles on her face and she was probably the second oldest in their group behind Toby.

"Tristine Vogelsong," she said. "Factotum." Her voice was interesting to me. It was a mix of anxious, annoyed, and confident at the same time. Her facial expression matched her voice: anxious, annoyed, yet confident.

Once she finished Vincent gestured for our squad to begin.

"Paxton Agton. Savior."

"Erica Towson. Artificer."

"Graham Garnett." I made sure to enunciate my last name. I

wasn't a fan of being called Graham Garnet, which was a common occurrence when I met new people. Trust me, I'm no jewel.

"Factotum." I scanned the faces of the other squad as I finished introducing myself, but found that I landed on Veronica's and my eyes were now stuck there. Realizing that I was now borderline staring at her, I shot my gaze over to Vincent.

"Trevor Donaldson is the Duelist leader of Paxton, Erica, and Graham's squad. My name's Vincent Hornsby, president of DREAM. Back there against the wall is my PSS. David, my Factotum. Carrie, my Savior. Emmett, my Duelist. And Amir, my Artificer." Each raised their hand as Vincent introduced them. "Alright, now that we know who's who, we'd like to hear about your investigation of Randy's condo."

Toby sat forward in his seat, forearms on his quads and hands folded. "Before entering the vice president's condo, we identified ourselves as a support squad and stated that we were on assignment to check in with him. I noticed that the door was cracked open and immediately armed our squad. We did a sweep of the condo. When it was all clear we searched for anything that might lead us to his whereabouts. The place was pristine. No significant fingerprints or hairs, nothing to work off of. There weren't any signs of forced entry, robbery, or foul play either.

"The only peculiar thing we found was a note on his table that said: 4 of 14. We collected it as evidence and had a lab back at DREAM Tower run it for DNA and fingerprints. Nothing. We interviewed surrounding neighbors, building management, reviewed all nearby security footage—still nothing. We reached out to his family and friends; no one has seen or heard from him since the day of your address. We tried reaching out to his PSS and couldn't find them either. It's like all five of them just vanished out of thin air."

Something beeped. We all turned around to see David holding his phone. "Excuse us," David said, leading the PSS out of the room.

"Do you need me?" Vincent asked.

"No. We can take care of it. We'll talk once you're finished here." The four of them left and turned the corner to the control room.

"Randy's PSS is a separate issue. I want to focus on Randy for the time being. So, do you have any ideas about what that note might mean?" Vincent asked. "It's not looking like we have much to go off of here."

Stephen decided to take a turn in the conversation, "We're not sure. Since the note read 4 of 14, we spent some time carefully rummaging through the condo to see if we could find any other notes, but didn't find any. I didn't notice anything unique about the type of paper it was written on or the ink it was written with either. We honestly didn't spend much time dissecting its meaning. We were focused on finding more evidence."

Vincent took the lead in the conversation again. "Fair enough. Then let's give it some thought now."

The room fell silent for a minute.

"I mean, it could mean anything or nothing," Stephen said.

"Okay then, let me tell you what my PSS and I think about the note then," Vincent began. "We do think it has meaning. Feel free to share your thoughts in a moment, but we think the note is a piece of Biotect foreshadowing. Our current thought is that the Biotects have somehow kidnapped Randy and left the note as a forthcoming threat. We've had four, large-scale Biotect attacks on DREAM so far and fear that ten more could be coming."

Veronica seemed to be open to Vincent's theory and reasoning. Her squadmates, especially Toby, seemed a bit more skeptical.

"We could barely find evidence that Randy had been in his own condo, let alone that any Biotects had ever been there," Toby respectfully pointed out.

"I understand," Vincent replied. He couldn't get any more out before Tristine jumped in.

"So you really think, based on this note, that the Biotects are planning ten more attacks?" Tristine questioned.

"As of right now, yes."

"Why? *If* your theory is true, what are they ultimately after? And why would they need ten more attacks to get whatever it is they want, especially if they already have the vice president hostage?"

They were valid questions.

"I don't know," Vincent responded half-heartedly. "The four in the note and the four Biotect attacks are the only correlation we have so far."

Veronica spoke up, "Unless we find something telling us otherwise, it could be possible. One of their creatures could have gotten to him like those flying apes did to these guys. Maybe they took Randy as some kind of bargaining chip."

"I could maybe buy into this if we had some kind of evidence to support it, but we don't. In all honesty, and with all due respect, it sounds like you're pinning it on the Biotects just to have someone to blame," Toby said. He was annoyed and trying his best to hide it. "But, let's just say for a minute that this theory is correct. That only leads to more pretty serious questions and problems. How do we even get Randy and his PSS back? What about Trevor, who's also allegedly been taken by the Biotects? Which there also doesn't seem to be any proof of if you believe his recording." He pointed at Paxton. "Are we blaming the Biotects for taking that Kaisiust kid from DREAM Tower, too?" He was beginning to get heated now. "Hell, why not. We'll add him in 'cause there's just as much proof that they took him as there is that they did Randy, or Trevor. So now how do we get back seven pretty important people from a helluva dangerous group we know next to nothing about?

"You know what, forget about them for just a minute. How do we prepare for ten more Biotect attacks? You've seen the shit they can materialize! It's crazy! Those three are beyond lucky to be sitting here today. We have no clue when, where, or who they could attack next. And we certainly have no clue what they'd be throwing at us. Hell, everything they've conjured so far could just be basic shit for them to get a feel for what we can do. And like Tristine mentioned earlier, we have no idea what their motive is. We don't know where they are. We don't know what they want. We couldn't contemplate negotiating with them even if we wanted to. Poking that bear is suicide until we get all of our facts straight."

"I disagree," Paxton jumped in. "Whether Dune and the Biotects are behind these missing people or not we need to find her before she gets a chance to strike again. I personally think she does have Trevor and if she doesn't have the other six maybe she can lead us to them. We should designate a handful of squads to investigate these missing people and see if they all lead back to her. If we think the Biotects are really behind their disappearances, finding any or all of them should give us some clues on what they're up to. Then, we need to have additional squads just searching DREAM for any general clues on where to find Dune or any other Biotects. We know there's been a lot of Biotect activity in Brexley. Go back and search there. We think there's been at least one Biotect in DREAM Tower. Sweep through Center City and the building again. Check Mylo, Sterling, Dunnesburg, Overton, Carmine too—just because nothing's happened there yet doesn't mean it won't. Doesn't mean the Biotects aren't there now."

I thought it was a brilliant idea. I was almost shocked, not because I thought Paxton was dumb or anything, but because it was the most well-thought-out thing anyone had contributed all conversation. He must have come up with that during Toby's rant.

"Paxton is right," Vincent responded after a beat. "This really should have been done right after that dragon showed up. The PSS and I will reach out to different support squads around DREAM and designate assignments."

"Mr. President," Stephen said.

"Please, call me Vincent."

"Vincent, I think it makes sense for our squad to be assigned to Randy."

"I agree. I want you four to just focus on finding him. Don't worry about his PSS. That'll be a task for a different squad at this point. However, I ask from here on out that any leads you find be brought directly to me. This is sensitive information and I want to keep it as secure as possible. I'll give Maya and the media all the information they need.

"Well, it looks like we have a plan in place. Any other questions, comments, or concerns?" No one spoke up. "Well, I want to thank Ms. Taveras's squad for making the trip down here to meet with us. I know the hike to Center City is long and your squad's sleep schedule is now a bit thrown off. The four of you are more than welcome to spend the night here with us if you'd like. Feel free to begin your assignment in the morning. I want to make sure you're well rested tonight, whether it's here or back home. We've got our work cut out for us here."

Chapter 22
Veronica

Vincent stood up from his seat at the end of two common area tables pushed together to make one long table. Each place setting had a bowl of canned chili, a side of canned vegetables as well as a glass of red wine and water. Veronica's squad had decided to stay and all three squads sat together for the most part.

With his wine glass raised he said, "I know this isn't a five-star meal by any means, and I know that DREAM is going through a lot right now. But I think even in hard times like these it's important to try and put on a good face. It's important to keep moving and working no matter how hard things get. It's important to celebrate the little things, even if it's just having a few extra guests for dinner, or somehow managing to find a few bottles of wine tucked away in a place like this.

"I am glad to have you all here tonight and truly appreciate all the work you've already done, and will continue to do, to put the Desired Reality back into DREAM. We will find Trevor. We will find Kent. We will find Randy and his PSS. We will bring the Biotects to justice for these attacks. And we will wake DREAM from this chaotic nightmare. To DREAM."

"To DREAM," everyone raised their glasses and said in unison.

Once Veronica's squad settled in after dinner, they came down to catch the news. There wasn't enough space between the two couches for everyone to sit so I got up.

"You don't have to get up, Graham. I can pull in a chair," Toby offered.

"No, it's alright," I replied as I started gingerly walking across the room. "I wanted to get up and go for a walk."

"Do you mind if I come with you, Graham?" Veronica asked.

"I could use a little fresh air before going to bed."

I froze for a split second. My heart rate skyrocketed. Of course I wanted her to come, but I didn't know how to say that without sounding like an idiot.

"Uh, sure."

I was so jittery I couldn't even turn around and mutter those two words to her face. I started feeling a bit paranoid about how this looked. Paxton and Erica knew I had a bit of a crush on her, but I hoped everyone else didn't, especially her. Had I just made it obvious by my response. Or worse, did it seem like I was disinterested and cold? I didn't want it to seem like I was just shrugging her off or just letting her come along for the ride.

I must have made some kind of queasy looking face that caught Stephen's eye. "You alright, Graham?" he asked.

Veronica was right behind me waiting for me to open the door.

"Yeah," I said, trying to sound and look as relaxed as possible. "See you all in a bit."

I opened the door and gestured for Veronica to go on first. She smiled and thanked me. I wasn't sure how I hadn't melted on the spot right then and there.

The porch light lit up as she stepped outside. I pulled the door shut behind me, materialized a flashlight, clicked it on, and began to meander towards the field where Erica and I had our little talk a few days ago.

The walk to the field was silent, awkwardly silent. My mind was bursting at the seams with all kinds of thoughts of what she would say to me. I did my best to keep myself loose, but I was just waiting for her to begin the conversation I knew had to be coming. I racked my brain, trying to come up with responses to any question or remark she could make.

We had just stepped onto the field when she began a conversation, "I liked Vincent's theory about the note and number of attacks on the DREAM. I think there definitely could be something to it."

My heartbeat slowed a few beats. We weren't talking about me, which was good. Unless this was just the icebreaker, the calm before the storm, her way of letting me down easier.

"Do you think the Biotects have it out for your squad?" she asked. "Their monsters seem to show up wherever you guys are."

It took me a few seconds to get the words out. "I don't know. Maybe. Now that I think about it, we are wrapped up with a lot of people who have Biotect connections. Trevor's wife, Natalia, works for Dune. The Kaisiust boy from DREAM Tower, Kent, was dealing conjierum for Dune when we found him in Brexley. And Randy's the one who assigned our squad to this whole Biotect mess in the first place. I don't know if they're out for us specifically or if we just keep getting in the way of whatever it is they're trying to do."

It was quiet between us again. I wanted to keep talking to her, but didn't know what to say next. I was feeling a little more confident. Talking to her wasn't so hard. I just needed to keep this momentum going. I thought about our past interactions together, and tried to think of anything I could strike up a conversation about. That's when it came to me. "Thank you."

"Thank you? For what?"

"I don't think I ever thanked you for helping us with those apes. Who knows what would have happened if you weren't around to scrape me up off the street? Seriously, we couldn't have done it without you."

I couldn't see her face in the dark, and certainly didn't want to shoot the flashlight on her, but I knew she wasn't expecting to hear that.

"You're welcome," she said softly. "That's really sweet of you."

"Well, it's definitely overdue," I added. "I'm sorry your squad's been dragged into this mess with us though."

"Don't apologize. I think we needed something like this."

"What do you mean?"

I heard her sigh. "I would love to be in a squad like yours. The three of you are actually friends. You guys joke; you care about each other; you're a real team. My squad, we all just meet up, complete our assignments, and go home. Toby and Tristine are friends outside of work, but aren't overly friendly with me or Stephen. And Stephen keeps to himself most of the time. It's nice to feel like part of something for once, you know?"

"I'm really sorry to hear that."

"It's fine."

"Too bad you aren't a Duelist," I said, adding some pep to my voice, trying to boost her spirit. "We're in the market for one right now."

She was quiet. I was really hoping she would find that funny. Did I hit a nerve? I scrambled to think of something different to talk about.

"Can I trust you, Graham?"

"Of course."

"I don't know what I am," she responded, sounding discouraged.

"What do you mean?"

"I'm not really a Savior."

"You seem pretty legit to me. That medicine you gave me worked. You graduated from the academy. How are you not a Savior?"

"I'm…I'm not *just* a Savior. Look."

I pointed my flashlight at her hands. She was holding a pair of sai. They were different from typical sai; these tips and shafts were double-edged. The two guards were rounded, like they would be traditionally, but the tops were sharpened to a point. They were also uncharacteristically long. I would have guessed each one was about two feet in total length. I was shocked. How did she do that? Sai weren't common for Duelists or Factotums to materialize, especially a pair this complex and unusual.

Before I could analyze that thought any further, she

dematerialized the weapons and a new object appeared in her hands. An oval piece of powder blue metal now rested in her palm. It sort of looked like a smooth stone. She squeezed it and it oozed through her fingers like it was some kind of gel. She opened up her hand again and the metal retook its original shape. Veronica then made it levitate above her hand. It floated there for a few seconds, fell back into her palm, and then was dematerialized. I thought I had to be dreaming at this point. I had never seen anything like that.

It took me a minute to come back to my senses and figure out what I had just seen. Veronica was right. She wasn't *just* a Savior. She was a Factotum, like me. The only difference being, she was unlike any Factotum I had ever seen.

"You weren't kidding. That was amazing!"

"You won't tell anyone will you?"

"Of course not."

Everything I had ever seen her materialize was complicated and complex: the sai, the weird metal, the super potent medication she gave me in the street. I couldn't wrap my head around the fact that she could conjure things that advanced as a Factotum. That's when I figured out what she really was.

"You're a Prime Factotum, aren't you?"

She answered my question almost somberly, "I'm not formally recognized, but yeah. I think so."

Being Prime in a certain strand meant that the conjierum put virtually no restrictions on its user. He or she could learn to materialize anything they wanted within their strand. She was a Prime Factotum, the best of all three worlds.

Being formally recognized as Prime was extremely rare and required passing a test to prove one's prime-ness, which was no easy feat. Twenty or thirty years ago the academy gathered up the handful of recognized Primes there were and ran a study on them to see if they had any specific traits or qualities in common. They were trying to figure out why the conjierum let these people have so much power and ability while other people only had some or none at all. They didn't find anything. We still had no clue why Primes were Primes, why Omitteds were Omitteds, or why certain strands picked certain people and limited what they can do.

"That's amazing!" I exclaimed. I remembered the tone of her voice. It wasn't amazing to her. "But you don't see it that way."

"There aren't any formally recognized Prime Factotums anymore. I'm torn. I feel like I'm living a lie by hiding it and pretending to just be a Savior. But I know my life would drastically change if I took the test for my recognition, got it, and people found out. Prime Factotums scare people, Graham. They're afraid of what we could do. Afraid of all the power we have. I can understand why. I don't know if one person should have that much power, but I can't help that I do. I didn't choose this. I don't want people to be afraid of me, and I don't want to live in fear of   other people."

"Well, your secret's safe with me. I know I haven't known you all that long, but from what I've seen so far, I can see why our conjierum picked you to be Prime. You're smart, caring, and brave. Not only did you potentially save my life, but then also risked yours to help me, Paxton, and Erica with those apes, no questions asked. I don't know how many people would have done that for a friend let alone a stranger."

Her voice perked up a bit, "Thanks, Graham. I definitely didn't save your life though, maybe just some more badgering from my neighbors." She laughed a little at her own joke. I did too.

I noticed that I wasn't feeling so tight anymore. I couldn't feel my pulse in my ears and my cheeks weren't burning up. It didn't feel like I was talking to the woman I was interested in. It felt like I was talking to an old friend.

"The key word was *potentially*. Who knows what would've actually happened if you hadn't showed up? And your neighbors weren't exactly helpful. They just kept staring at me like *I* was the ape or something."

"What can I say? I live on a street with some older, more skeptical, people. They see a young guy, bruised and bloodied, who had just fought off some weird monster now lying in the middle of their street. What do you expect them to think?" It was the most carefree and light-hearted she had sounded all night.

I paused for effect before replying, "Touché."

She laughed and so did I. Her laugh was so infectious that I couldn't help it. It eventually died down and the only sound left was the crunching of the dead leaves underneath our feet.

"If you don't mind me asking, how did you become a Prime so young? You can't even be thirty yet."

"Twenty-six," she clarified for me, "and just hard work and a bit of luck I guess."

"So how did you become a Savior if you're actually a Factotum? Did they mess up your CAA scores or something?"

"My family didn't even think I should take the CAA because they're all Omitteds. I eventually wore my mom down and she let me take it. When my results came back Factotum, we were shocked. And then when we saw that all three strands had well above average potential we couldn't believe it."

I was instantly blown away. The scoring for CAAs went: well above average, above average, slightly above average, average, slightly below average, below average, and well below average potential. My CAA results were slightly above average Duelist potential, average Savior potential, and slightly below average Artificer potential. It was rare enough for a Factotum to have a well above average potential in one strand, let alone all three.

"We thought it was a mistake at first. Some of my relatives went to the academy to be Savior or Artificer assistants, but I was the first to go as a conjierum user. My mom and I found out that Factotums with a well above average potential in any particular strand could technically apply to that school. A weird loophole in the system. I really wanted to be a Factotum and loved the idea of getting to learn all three strands even if that meant I wouldn't be able to master just one.

"My mom had her own ideas on what I should be doing, especially after I told her that I wanted to be in a support squad: 'You'll never get into a support squad as a Factotum, Veronica,' she told me. 'Those squad leaders don't draft women Factotums. Women only get drafted as Saviors.' She wasn't totally wrong. You know that female Factotums exist, but they're not as common. Anyway, I wasn't crazy about it at first, but I took her advice not knowing any better. When we went to the academy to formally apply it was at the School of Saviors.

"I remember meeting with a man from the school's admissions department. 'It says here you're a Factotum,' he said after glancing at my CAA results and trying to hand them back to us. But my mom didn't move: 'Please, have a look at her scores, sir.' He humored her and was blown away. 'I don't know if I've ever seen scores like this. You want to be a Savior?' he asked me. I remember nodding at him. 'Your paperwork says Factotum, but your scores are technically high enough to get you in here. Are you sure you want to be a Savior? With Factotum scores this high I'm sure you'll be able to learn most of what our top Saviors do *as well as* what the top Duelists and Artificers do.'

"I remember nodding at him again, too shy and insecure to talk. 'I don't know if we've ever done this before, but there's a first time for everything, I guess. Congratulations Miss,' he had to pause to find my name on the papers, 'Tavares. Welcome to the School of Saviors.'

"I got into the other strands just for fun. One day I was studying in the library and decided to take a break. I got up to stretch and found myself wandering through the Artificer sections. I took pictures of some of the lessons on my phone. I'm not even sure they used those books anymore; I'm pretty sure everything was digital. Anyway, that night I taught myself in my dorm room. It was fun doing more than just medicine. I eventually started teaching myself Duelist stuff too.

"The work was hard, but I was doing it. I was hooked. I started spending as much time on my Artificer and Duelist lessons as my regular Savior ones. It was miserably exhausting. I can't tell you how many all-nighters and gallons of coffee I went through, but I couldn't get enough. I was getting really good at all three and loved it.

"I made friends with some Duelists and Artificers who were in the top of their class to pick their brains. My Savior friends thought it was weird, but I would always use some kind of excuse to justify it like, 'We should get to know them because we might work with them one day.' I asked them to show me what they were doing in class and how they did it. Like what I needed to focus my mind on. If needed a certain posture or stance. How much energy and strain different things took to materialize. I played the smart-yet-ditzy Savior routine, but was really taking in and mastering everything they showed me.

"I just kept learning and working all three strands and the conjierum never stopped me. I never came across anything I couldn't materialize. Then I even started trying to combine all three." Just like Erica and I had done with Sunshine, minus the Savior aspect of it.

"I'm sorry you just didn't go to the School of Factotums. It probably would've made your life a lot easier, but how you taught yourself the other two strands is beyond cool. I don't think I know anyone who could have done that. You should be really proud of yourself."

"Thanks, Graham." Her voice was soft, warm, and soothing, like a blanket I just wanted to wrap myself up in.

"So how did you become a squad leader then? If you don't mind me asking."

"Well, my final year at the academy was a Savior year and I didn't think I would get a job right away because all the squad leaders would be more experienced or previously undrafted Saviors. And you know that people coming right out of the academy are almost never picked to be squad leaders. Halfway through the year the headmaster of the school pulled me aside after class one day. He told me this didn't typically happen, but he wanted me to be a squad leader in the upcoming draft. I went from losing sleep over wondering if I would have a job to basically being offered one on the spot.

"I couldn't say no, but the work leading up to the draft was killing me. Not only did I have to finish my work to graduate, but I had to prepare for the draft. Trying to schedule interviews, looking over transcripts and scores, attending physical evaluation showcases, on top of my school work—it was just too much. I went to the headmaster and apologized and told him I just couldn't find the time to prepare for the draft. I was devastated because I thought he would take the squad leader job away from me.

"He offered me a deal with me instead. Toby and Tristine's original squad had recently been disbanded. He didn't say why, but I would love to know. He told me he would make some phone calls and see if the two of them could just be assigned to me, instead of re-entering the draft, then I would only have to draft an Artificer."

"So you only drafted Stephen?"

"Yeah, and I did my due diligence on him. He might not have been the best pick for me on paper, but I thought we'd get along and work well together." She sounded sad now.

"Everything okay?"

"Talking about the draft just brought up some bad memories is all."

"You wanna talk about it, or no?"

"It's fine. I've already rambled on enough to you. I hope I answered your question. I don't even remember what it was now."

"You did. And if you think talking it out might help, I'm more than happy to listen."

"You sure? I don't want you to feel obligated or anything."

"No, I don't feel obligated, just want to help if I can."

She took a second to collect herself. I heard her take a breath in and then exhale slowly.

"It's my family. I remember seeing my mom's face light up in the crowd when we took our squad picture on draft night. Things really started to spiral down from there though. First of all, my family started bragging to everyone and their mother about my new job as a squad leader. I hated it.

"Being a squad leader made it really hard to see them. I was working a lot—too much. Then, when I wasn't working, I was too exhausted to do anything else really. We became pretty distant. I think they started to resent me for it. I stopped being invited to family dinners and holiday parties. I mean, in their defense, I did miss a lot of family gatherings I was invited to because of work, or oversleeping, or just losing track of days and time.

"Then one of my aunts brainwashed the rest of the family into thinking that I didn't want to come to things because I thought I was better than everyone else. I had this great new job as a squad leader. I was a Savior and they were all Omitteds. I was too busy and important for them.

"She must have been pretty persuasive because I hardly hear from anyone in my family anymore, even my own parents. I try to reach out and make plans with them, but somehow they always manage to fall through. The only time they reach out to me now is when someone dies, someone needs money, or if someone's sick and they want me to help them. It breaks my heart."

She stopped. Her breathing was becoming heavier. It sounded like she was choking up. She took in another deep breath and let out another, even longer, exhale.

"I'm sorry to hear about your family," I said once I was sure she was finished. "I have some family issues of my own. For the record, I think your family is really missing out by cutting you out of their lives. I realize that talking through it wasn't easy for you, especially since you haven't known me all that long, but I hope it helped. And it means a lot that you shared it with me."

"Well, thanks for listening. I know it was a lot to take in. I don't typically dump my life story and family problems on people I've just met."

"Hey, it was an interesting and inspiring story. You've worked really hard to get where you are today and that hard work has paid off, even if it doesn't always feel that way."

"Thanks, Graham. I'm glad that ape beat you up in front of my house."

We both laughed. "I'm glad it did too."

"We should probably head back."

I opened the door for her when we reached the house. Everyone had gone to bed. Paxton had too technically, since his bed was the couch tonight to make room for the others, but he was sitting there wide awake.

"There they are!" He quietly proclaimed. "Hey, Grahammy, make sure to lock up on your way in." Grahammy? What was that? He never called me that.

Veronica and I said our goodnights, and I eased my way down onto the opposite couch, which was my bed for the night.

Once we couldn't hear her footsteps anymore Paxton started prodding me. "So, how'd it go?"

"What do you mean, *how'd it go*?"

"You know," he said, trying to be cryptic but realized it wasn't working, "with *Veronica*." He said her name in a teasing voice.

I figured that's where he was going. "We just went for a walk. That's it."

"Alright, buddy. Whatever you say. Just a walk."

I flipped over, no longer facing his direction, and fell asleep.

I woke up the next morning to a note on my pillow. The only other person in the room was Paxton, who was still sound asleep and snoring pretty obnoxiously.

It was a sheet of plain, loose-leaf paper folded in half. I flipped it open and read it:

Graham,

Thank you for being a good listener and even better friend last night. I hope to see you, and the rest of your squad, again soon.

-V

Veronica. I guessed their squad had already left. I didn't even hear them leave. I hadn't heard Erica enter the room either.

"What's that?" she asked, startling me.

I folded the note to fit in my pocket and put it away, "Nothing." I felt like a little kid trying to hide something from his mom.

She smiled at me, that same teasing smile she gave me before. She whispered to me to come have breakfast with her, not wanting to wake Paxton. I gingerly stepped past Snoring Beauty, who continued his peaceful slumber on the couch.

"I thought it was sweet of her to leave that for you," she said on our way down into the bunker.

"What are you talking about?" I asked, trying to play coy and also not wanting to show pain in my voice. The morning hike downstairs was always that hardest on my ribs; that, and getting out of bed.

"The note that Veronica left you."

"How do you know that's what it is?"

"I guess I can't say for sure that's what it is. I haven't read it," she clarified. "I just assumed that's what it was after our talk last night."

I was now intrigued and she knew it. "Oh?"

"Yeah, she saw me reading on her way to bed last night and decided to stop by for a few minutes for some girl talk," she said, trying to reel me in. It worked.

"So what from your girl talk last night leads you to believe that the note I have is from her?"

"Ooh," she said with eyebrows raising and a grin taking over her face. "A very interesting question. Well played."

I gave her my own version of her mischievous smile realizing that I was now getting somewhere in this weird, chess match of a conversation.

"Alright, alright. It was girl talk, so I can't give you all of the details."

I didn't know how to feel. Scared, excited, happy, worried, all at the same time.

"She asked me about you and the rest of our squad."

"And…" I pressed her.

"And it was quite nice to have another woman to talk to around here for a change. I mean there is Carrie, but she isn't around much. Veronica seems very nice. I can see us becoming good friends."

I could tell she was pleased with herself, beating around the bush even more. We reached the bottom of the stairs, and I gave her an unamused glare.

"Alright, alright. She was asking what you were like. You know, as a person, a coworker, a friend. I talked you up, of course. She mentioned that she really enjoyed her walk and conversation with you last night. We talked about a few other things too, but it seems like you made quite the impression on her."

She gave me a wink, an overdramatic smile, and that elbow poking again.

"You're like an embarrassing, older sister, you know that?" I said trying to hide my face so she couldn't see me blush.

The words felt funny coming out of my mouth. They were true, but hit a little too close to home. Her hysterical laughter distracted me from thinking about it any further. She started snorting which caught Vincent's attention from the kitchenette. He stood by the coffee maker with a steamy cup of joe in hand. The mug was about halfway to his mouth when it suddenly came to a stop. His overworked eyes found their way to us.

"Did I miss something?"

Chapter 23

7

The three of us sat out on the front porch soaking in the morning sun and a cool, gentle breeze. Paxton and I sat on the porch's edge, his feet easily reaching the ground and mine barely making it. Erica was on the swing. It sat pretty deep, but her feet were still able to reach the floor planks. We were quiet; the only sounds around us were the birds chirping and the squeaky creak of Erica rocking herself back and forth in the chair. It was our seventh day at the cabin and Paxton was starting to go stir crazy. Erica thought some fresh air and relaxation might do us all some good.

The front door flung open, stealing our attention and breaking the tranquility around us. It was Vincent with a pretty serious look on his face.

"They found another note. Come on down for a debriefing."

He stepped out of the doorway, onto the porch, and held the door open for us. Paxton had a weird look on his face, a mix between intense and excited. He was the first through the door, moving kind of fast but trying to play it off like he wasn't—like a kid at the pool would do after a lifeguard says not to run.

Erica, who looked a bit bleaker, thanked Vincent for holding the door and followed next. I caught a good glance at Vincent. His head was down and his eyes were fixed on some random spot on the porch boards.

"You okay, Vincent?" I asked, breaking him out of his trance.

"Yeah, yeah. Sorry about that. Just zoned out for a minute," he said, flashing a politician's smile.

That's when I knew something was up. He never smiled like that. A fake, I'm-pretending-everything's-okay smile.

Down in the conference room, the chairs had been arranged

into a circle, just how Vincent seemed to like them. The four of us took a seat while the PSS stayed in the control room.

"So, we've found another note," Vincent began. "Maya stumbled upon it earlier this morning in the Presidential Suite. This one read: '7 of 14.' She said she found it sitting on the podium and immediately called me and then Veronica Taveras's squad to investigate."

"Why'd she call them?" Paxton asked, a bit confused.

"She thought since the first note was found in Randy's condo maybe this one had a connection to him too. They should be here to share their findings with us later this afternoon," Vincent explained. Despite the tension and uncertainty in the room, my heart leapt a little when I realized I'd be seeing Veronica again today.

"So, does Maya think that Randy has something to do with these notes?" Paxton jumped in.

"That I don't know."

"Wait," Erica interjected. "There haven't been any more attacks since the first note, have there?"

"No," Vincent replied as he ran his hand through his hair. "That's part of the reason why this new note has thrown us all for a loop. We're back to square one."

"So what's the new theory then?" Paxton wanted to cut to the chase.

"There isn't one, not just yet anyway, not until we hear from Veronica's squad. I called the three of you down as soon as I got the news to give you a head's up." he said, a bit disheartened. "We'll see what Veronica's squad has to say and hopefully we can all put our heads together and figure this out."

"Anything on Trevor or Kent?" Erica added.

"Not yet. I haven't heard from either of the squads assigned to their cases," Vincent said in the same sad tone.

"So you're telling me we're even more clueless than we were before," Paxton said with frustration increasing in his tone.

Vincent didn't acknowledge his statement. "I'm sorry, but that's all I have for you now. We'll meet here again once Veronica and her squad arrive."

The four of us got up and left. My squadmates started leaving the bunker and Vincent went next door to the control room. He ran his hand down his face before turning the knob to rejoin the PSS. I hadn't seen him like this before, so anxious, so stressed. He carried himself like he was in a fight he knew he couldn't win, but had to keep fighting.

Paxton and Erica were walking up the steps as I shot Vincent another glance and debated if I should say anything. "Vincent." I caught his attention just as the door to the control room began to open.

He turned around and painted on a weaker version of that fake grin he had upstairs. "What can I do for you, Graham?"

I worked up the nerve to flag him down, but now that I had his attention, I didn't know what to say. I wanted to know if he was really okay. If I could help him. What his gut reaction on this new note was—and not that sugar coated, surface-level, ambiguous garbage he had to tell us as a politician. I wanted to know if he was losing hope, and if we should be too.

"I, uh, is there anything we can do to help right now?" That was the question that won the race out of my mind and into the open.

"I appreciate the offer, but I don't think there's anything you could realistically do at this point."

I paused for a second. "How about a cup of decaf?"

"Actually, if you don't mind, that would be great right about now."

"Not a problem."

"Thanks, Graham."

"Cream? Sugar?"

"Black is fine. Thanks again."

"You got it."

He walked into the control room, closing the door behind him. I went straight to the kitchenette and got a pot of decaf going. I brewed enough for the PSS too. I figured even if they didn't want any Vincent would probably drink another cup at least.

I found a serving tray in one of the cabinets and then poured the four cups. It would be hard to tell whose was whose; all the mugs here were stark white. They definitely fit the apocalyptic bunker theme to me. I carefully knocked on the door, doing my best to balance the tray in one hand.

"Ah, great, you brought a cup for all of us! You're the man, Graham. We really appreciate it." There was some perk in his voice and a genuine smile on his face.

He took a mug in each hand and walked them into the room. I stood in the doorway, not wanting to intrude. I saw a laptop sitting on a desk messy with stacks of papers, highlighters, pens, and other office supplies in front of me. Above the desk were screens, panels, circuitry, and other technology I couldn't even fathom. Out of all of that, what really caught my attention was the laptop's wallpaper.

It was a picture of a younger Vincent with a boy who looked a lot like him. They were outside sitting at a picnic table with cake on their faces. The boy was wearing one of those pointy party hats and was belly laughing. Vincent wore a smile from ear to ear and was wrapping his right arm around the boy's shoulder.

"Is that your son?" I asked as Vincent came back for the other two cups.

He turned around to see what I was looking at and then grabbed the last two mugs. "No, my nephew Sid. Closest thing I have to a son, though. That was his fifth birthday party. He just turned eighteen this year. I love him to death, but don't get to see him nearly as much as I'd like anymore."

My question seemed to damper some of the excitement the coffee had brought him.

"Thanks again for the coffee. We'll see you and the others in a bit."

I didn't know what to do with myself after that. My mind was overloaded with thoughts of the note, a stressed-out Vincent, and the excitement of seeing Veronica later. I eventually began to feel tired and found myself lounging on top of the bed in one of the guest rooms.

"You know, we really have to stop meeting like this. It's like every time I see you you're either getting hurt or getting some shut eye."

Veronica. I sat up and saw her in the doorway again. She appeared more relaxed than the first time she found me asleep here. I rubbed my eyes and sat up on the bed.

I let out a yawn and joked, "Well, you know how hard they work me around here."

I couldn't believe how easily the words came out of my mouth. Sure, I still had a little bit of nervous energy, the butterflies, whatever you call it, but it was leaps and bounds better than a few days ago when we had almost this exact same moment.

I locked onto her green eyes, something I was too intimidated to do before, and asked, "How've you been?"

She didn't break eye contact. "I've been well. Thanks for asking. How about you?"

"Glad to hear it. I've been alright. I'm guessing Erica sent you up here because they're waiting for me to start the meeting again, huh?"

She let out a short chuckle, "No, Erica didn't send me. I came up here on my own figuring I'd find you here. But yeah, we are waiting on you again."

It was déjà vu down in the bunker, everyone was in the same exact seats as last time. Vincent got started once Veronica and I both sat down.

"First of all, I want to thank Ms. Taveras's squad for getting here on such short notice. I know it would be much more convenient to have these discussions over the phone or a video call, but I worry about how secure those lines can be. In fact, we only communicate with Maya through a private network based in DREAM Tower. I prefer to speak with you all this way anyway. I find it leads to a better and more open talk. Enough of that, let's get right to it. Do you have any new information on Randy or the note found in the Presidential Suite earlier today?"

Toby spoke first. "I wish we had more to tell you. We've had a few new leads on Randy but they haven't gotten us anywhere. We've been digging and digging, but we keep coming up empty. We've rechecked with friends. Rechecked with family. Rechecked places he frequented in the past. We've checked his personal suite in the Presidential Suite twice now. Nothing. Have you guys heard anything about his PSS?"

"I can't say that we have," Vincent replied. "We also haven't gotten any word on Trevor or Kent." It was quiet for a minute while everyone took the unfortunate news in. "What can you tell us about the note?"

Tristine took the lead on this one. "Maya claims she went to the Presidential Suite to check on the Artificers' progress on the wall and apartment repairs, found the note, and then started making calls."

"Progress on the wall and apartment repairs?" Paxton blurted out. "I saw on the news that the Artificers started working on that the day after the attack. That was like a week ago. How long does it take to fix two holes?"

Tristine ignored him and kept going. "She said that when she passed by the podium she noticed the note sitting there. She said she contacted you and PSS immediately, then us. We got there as fast as we could."

Paxton hopped back in the conversation. "I'm guessing there aren't any cameras in the Presidential Suite, are there?"

"At this point there probably should be. But for security and confidentiality reasons there aren't currently."

"You said you were going to have cameras installed in the labs. Has that happened yet?"

"The PSS assigned a group of Artificers to the job and last we heard they were still working on it."

Spitfire struck. "Holy shit! You know, with the nearly endless technological capabilities we have through Artificers I'm floored at how much useful technology *isn't* in that building. So much of this bullshit would be so much easier if that damn tower actually had some surveillance in it."

"I hear you and see where you're coming from, Paxton, but with more cameras and video feeds comes more opportunities for hacking and compromised security. Besides, I don't think we've ever had a need for them until now."

"Ok then, hire some more damn Duelists to patrol the place then. At least you'd have some eyewitnesses at that point!"

"That's a conversation for a different time."

I could tell Paxton was miffed by Vincent's response, but moved on. "Fine. So who do you guys think is planting these notes?" he said, directing his attention at Veronica's squad. "We still thinking the Biotects? Some other group? Someone working solo?"

Tristine cut Paxton off, "Before we get to that, I wanted to mention that we have one of the labs running an analysis on the new note right now. The security footage just outside the Presidential Suite only has the Artificers and Maya coming in and out this past week."

"Are you kidding me? We have cameras watching the elevator *outside* the suite, but we didn't bother to put any of them *inside*," Paxton muttered to himself again.

"I'm assuming you've interviewed the Artificers?" Erica asked.

Tristine nodded.

"Did you get anything useful from them?"

"Nope. No one remembers seeing a note on the podium or anything else out of the ordinary while they were working. None of them had the green ring either."

"You think Maya could have planted the note?" Paxton interjected.

"This one, maybe. But even if Maya left this one—or somehow both—why? What's the point? What do they mean?" Erica replied.

"I don't know if I necessarily believe this," Veronica took a turn, "but what if these notes *are*, somehow, from Maya and she's up to something? What if they're some type of countdown? What if she arranged to have Randy kidnapped, in hopes of getting the vice presidency like she did?"

"It's not outside the realm of possibility, but I seriously doubt Maya would do that," Vincent chimed in. "I've known her for a very long time and she's more than happy with her job at the academy. In fact, she was actually very reluctant to take the acting vice presidency role in the first place. I don't see the motive being there."

Stephen cut in. "Do they have to mean anything at all? What if they're just smoke and mirrors, something to keep us all distracted while something else is going on behind the scenes. I mean think about it. Sure, we have had a few disappearances recently, and we're working on finding those people. We've had some attacks in Brexley and Center City, but we haven't had any more since the one on the Presidential Suite. It's been quiet since you guys came here. These notes haven't led to anything and nothing's happened since they started popping up. Whoever is leaving them is probably just trying to screw with us."

The room went silent thinking about what he said for a moment. It was possible the notes meant nothing, but I didn't buy it. Everything about them, the disappearances, the attacks, it felt all too calculated to me.

"What do you think they could be a distraction from?" Vincent asked.

"I don't know. It doesn't mean they couldn't be though."

"I'm not disagreeing with you, Stephen," Vincent tried to assure him. "I just wanted to see if you had any ideas. You four have been the ones out there seeing firsthand what's going on, not us."

Out of nowhere an idea popped into my head, a very eerie one. I was almost hesitant to share it, but it made too many connections to me not to. "I think these notes do have some kind of meaning. Whoever is writing them is obviously counting down or keeping track of something. This might sound stupid, but the numbers and timing match up." I took a second to think about if I wanted to share this in front of everyone. I didn't really want to look stupid or narcissistic in front of the group, but by that point I had already led too much into my idea. "The first note read '4 of 14' and the second '7 of 14.' The Savior at the hospital told me that with the medication I was prescribed it would take my ribs two weeks to heal. On my fourth day of recovery, our fourth day here, the first note shows up. Today is our seventh day here, my seventh day of recovering, and this new note shows up. Either someone is interested in tracking my ribs, or our time here, *or* it's just a crazy coincidence."

I could see people mouthing numbers to themselves, making sure my counting was correct. My idea might have been dumb, but I was sure I counted right at least. The room was a mixed bag of facial expressions. Some were puzzled while others were excited with the possibility that we were onto something.

"It could be," Toby said, "but…why?"

"I don't know."

Vincent took a turn, the look on his face was as intense as I had ever seen. It told me that he had bought into what I had suggested. "What do you think will happen when day fourteen comes?"

"I don't know, but I feel like it can't be good, right? At this point I feel like our squad has more enemies than friends, and it seems like all of the crazy things that have been happening have revolved around us somehow." I stopped internally analyzing for once and just spoke my mind, "Maybe it's not actually Trevor, Kent, or Randy that the Biotects want. Maybe it's really been me, or Paxton, or Erica this entire time. Maybe these notes aren't from the Biotects at all. I don't know."

For one reason or another Toby was now annoyed. "But why? I mean, sure, the numbers and days add up, but the rest of it doesn't make any sense. What would the Biotects, or anyone else, want with you or your squad? And why would they need to kidnap other people to get to you? Trevor, I get, he's your leader, but some deadbeat, kid conjierum dealer and the vice president? What do those two have anything to do with you?"

Veronica jumped in before I could respond. "Relax, Toby. He already told you he doesn't know. You just said it yourself, the numbers and days add up. We just need to see if we can find anything else to support it."

Toby's eyes got huge and his jaw clenched so tightly I was surprised he didn't shatter his own teeth. He was ready to fire back at her but held his tongue.

Veronica redirected her attention from Toby to Vincent. "Here's a thought: I'll go back and talk to the Savior who treated Graham. I was there with their squad when he was admitted to the hospital. I remember her. Maybe she'll know something. She's the one who prescribed him the medication with the fourteen-day prognosis and told us that DREAM's hospitals don't typically prescribe it. If his theory is correct, then the person writing these notes would have to know about the medicine, his ribs, and the fourteen-day recovery time."

"They also would most likely know that I covered the cost of the medicine for him. That could be why we were all attacked in DREAM Tower," Vincent stated, sounding confident, like the pieces were falling into place.

"You think his Savior is personally in on this? Or someone from the hospital? You guys remember seeing a ring on her arm?" Paxton asked Erica and me.

We both shook our heads.

"I don't remember seeing it either, but her shirt had sleeves. Even if she had it, we wouldn't have noticed," Veronica added. "I don't know if his Savior has something directly to do with these notes, but I think she's worth looking into," she said almost in an asking manner towards Vincent.

"I do too," he replied. "But remember, Maya contacted your squad thinking there may be a connection between Randy and these notes. Veronica, feel free to take a day to see what his Savior knows, but remember your assignment and top priority is to keep searching for Randy. Let's all be sure to keep our eyes peeled and ears open. If Graham is right, we still have a week to figure this whole thing out. Anything else anyone would like to add for the good of the order?"

No one spoke up.

"Well then, I want to thank you four again for coming. You're more than welcome to spend the night again if you'd like. If you'll excuse me, I need to check in with the PSS. If you decide to stay, I'll see you at dinner. If not, I hope to hear from you soon," he said with a wave as he walked out of the conference room.

We all said our goodbyes to him.

"Guys, let's give them the room so they can decide what they want to do," Erica said loud enough for Veronica's squad to hear.

"Thanks Erica," Veronica said.

The three of us filed out of the room and began walking towards the staircase.

"So, what do you think Chef Hornsby's got on the menu for us tonight?" Paxton asked a few stairs away from the door to the main floor. His attitude had done a total one eighty from where it was a few minutes ago in the thick of our conversation.

"Chef Hornsby's not cooking up anything until he knows how many people he's cooking for. And it wouldn't kill you to come down and help him for once. You're no slouch in the kitchen from what I've heard," Erica came back at him.

"Vincent makes dinner every night down here?" I asked. "I thought the PSS took turns doing it."

"Nope," Paxton said, twisting the knob. "Vincent and

sometimes this one." He pointed his thumb back at Erica behind him.

"Yeah, and it wouldn't kill either of you to come down and help for once either. Well, at least Graham helps with the dishes. What's your excuse, huh?" she said, giving him a somewhat playful, backhanded smack on the arm.

"I have OFF; don't you know that?"

"OFF?"

"Yeah, Overindulgent Food Fatigue. I'm way too tired after eating to do anything," he said jokingly.

"OFF," she scoffed. "More like you need to get *OFF* your lazy ass and help out more!" She went to give him another smack but he scampered through the doorway just in time to dodge it.

The two of them decided to wait on the couch for Veronica's squad. They invited me to sit with them, but I passed. Even though my ribs were a bit upset from the steps, I wanted to get some fresh air.

I found a spot not too far into the field and just stood there. I shut my eyes, took in the breeze. The sun was only a few minutes from setting. I was trying my best to just relax, but the nagging thought of being somebody's target was utterly horrifying, especially if it was the Biotects. Just as I was starting to quiet my mind, I felt a tap on my shoulder. It was Veronica. A few butterflies began to flutter in my stomach.

I did my best not to focus on the feeling and just have an easygoing conversation with her. "Let me guess, Erica told you that you'd find me out here?"

"Paxton *and* Erica this time, as a matter of fact. I can't stay long though. My squad wants to get home and sleep in their own beds tonight. I want you to have this."

She held out her hand and materialized a cellphone. It wasn't anything fancy, just a black, rectangular touchscreen.

"If I get any information from the Savior I want you to be the first to know. Don't worry about having service; I made sure it would work out here. Also, the battery is solar powered, so when it gets low just leave it on a window sill or something. It should charge up pretty quick. I designed it to be super-efficient and low maintenance. My number is already in there, so if you need anything, I'm just a call or text away."

"Thanks, Veronica," I said as she placed it in my hand.

We could hear the front door of the cabin being pulled shut. Her squad was walking towards their two old and sun-bleached sedans. Toby and Tristine moved towards a gray one parked further away from the cabin while Stephen was just a few feet from a white one, which was caked in a thin film of light brown dust from the dirt driveway.

"Well, I should get going. I'll be in touch, Graham."

"It was good to see you again."

"You too."

She grinned and started to jog towards the car. Toby and Tristine were leaving as Veronica got into the driver's seat beside Stephen. I put the phone deep into my pocket and decided to head inside. I did all I could to suppress my excitement. The last thing I wanted was Paxton and Erica to give me a hard time about it. I felt like a little kid on Christmas morning. The only question now was, when would I hear from her again?

Chapter 24

Send in the Dogs

After two long days of silence, I finally got a text from Veronica on the morning of day nine at the cabin.

Hey Graham. I finally got a chance to talk to Savior Melling. I'll call you in a bit when I'm free.

It took me a solid ten minutes to put a simple three sentences together.

Hey Veronica, sounds good. I'm looking forward to it. Talk to you then.

After what felt like hours after I had sent that text Erica flagged me down.

"You alright? You seem pretty unsettled today."

"What do you mean?"

"You've been all over the place this morning. You're out for a walk, then you're back in. You're watching TV one minute, then turning it off the next. You're wide awake, but rolling around on the couch like you're trying to nap. And now, if I had to guess, you're heading back outside to sit on the porch swing again, aren't you?"

"What're you, some kind of behaviorist, Erica?"

"Not exactly, just observant and not half bad at reading people. Everything okay?"

I hadn't even realized that I had done all of those things. My mind was so wrapped in the call that I guess my actions were on autopilot. I figured there was no use trying to hide anything from her. Besides, Erica was my friend and I trusted her.

"Yeah, I'm fine. Veronica gave me this phone to keep me updated on Savior Melling. She texted me this morning and said she'd call me later. I'm just trying to kill time. You can see how well that's been going for me."

"Ah," she replied inquisitively while smiling suspiciously. I knew that smile. That damn squinty, cheeky, sly smile. She knew something.

"What?"

"Oh, nothing." Her smile was growing wider.

"What do you know that I don't? You're doing that weird smirk thing again."

"Well, I don't know if I *know* anything for certain," she replied, clearly enjoying herself, "but this whole situation is very interesting if you ask me."

"You really are a behaviorist. Enlighten me Savior Towson."

"Read between the lines a little bit here, Graham. A smart, beautiful, successful young woman gave you a cell phone *just* to talk with her about an investigation?"

I got what she was inferring. I sort of thought about that before, but didn't want to give myself too much credit. I wanted to see what else I could get from her, so I decided to play dumb. "What're you trying to say?"

She was on to me. Her raised eyebrows and are-you-kidding-me type of smirk told me that much. I could see her wanting to chuckle too but she held it back.

"Just let us know if she's found anything, alright?"

"Will do."

"Oh, and tell her I said hi," she added with an over exaggerated wink and a gaping smile.

I could feel myself starting to blush. "Really? The smile? The wink?"

"Oh yeah!" she playfully called out while leaving the room and heading down the hall towards the kitchen. "Don't forget. I said hi."

About an hour and a half after her initial text the phone rang. I was just as excited as I was relieved. It was her. Finally. I gave myself a second to cool off, not only from the low grade panic the sudden ring gave me, but to collect my nerves.

I exhaled then answered, "Hey, Veronica."

"Hey, Graham. I meant to call you earlier but we got back to DREAM Tower a little later than expected."

"Not a problem. How did it go? Your morning, I mean."

"It was pretty uneventful. Stephen and I went to the hospital to follow up with Savior Melling, while Tristine and Toby looked into some new leads we had gotten on Randy. Every now and then we get people thinking they've seen him at the grocery store, the bar, places like that, but it always turns out to be nothing. Toby and Tristine said it was another dead end."

"How about Savior Melling? Any luck with her?"

"No," she sounded a bit discouraged. "She claims that none of your information has been disclosed to anyone and that no one has come into the hospital asking about you."

"Do you believe her?"

She paused for a moment, "I think so. I mean, she has no reason to lie to us. We checked her arm. No mark. We also interviewed other people around the hospital: receptionists, nurses, custodial staff, anyone who was in that wing of the hospital the day you were there. No one saw or heard anything remotely suspicious. No marks on any of them either."

"If nothing else we're covering all our bases. It was a good idea to follow up with her," I said, trying to be supportive, but I was slightly disappointed too.

"I just don't get it. If your theory is true, which I think it very well could be, how would the person writing these notes know about the fourteen days?"

"I don't know, but we'll figure it out."

She paused for a moment. "I hope so." I heard a familiar voice talking to her in the background. "Hey, Graham, Toby's here and says he needs to talk to me. Sorry. I'll get back to you later, okay?"

"Yeah, no problem." I was bummed but tried my best to hide it, "Oh, and Erica wanted me to tell you she says hi."

Veronica let out a small chuckle. "Tell her and everyone else I said hi too. Talk to you later."

"Bye."

The phone clicked and just like that our conversation was over.

* * *

The next morning Paxton, Erica, and I came across a horrifying story on the news.

"Citizens are being urged to seek shelter indoors this morning as wild packs of dogs have been ravaging cities across DREAM. I repeat, at this time everyone is urged to find shelter indoors."

"Turn it up," Paxton commanded Erica who had the remote.

"We want to warn our viewers that the images you are about to see may not be appropriate for all audiences." The video cut from the news anchor to aerial coverage of a street a few blocks from DREAM Tower. CLESs and civil Duelists were fending off and shooting dogs charging down the street at alarming, borderline unnatural, speeds. A few dogs leapt and caught a hold of squad members or civilians trying to flee to safety. Some dogs began to maul at their targets while others were satisfied with just the take down and what looked like a single bite. All of the attacks ended the same way: with no one getting up.

The anchor spoke as we watched all of this unfold. "First reports of these wild dogs appearing in Center City came around the start of the morning commute. Witnesses say that all of the dogs appear to be mixes of German Shepherds and bloodhounds and desperately seem to be searching for something. Oh my—"

A dog running at full speed had just leapt and tackled a CLES member to the ground. The drone recording the footage had flown in close enough that we could hear his helmet crack against the pavement. The mic also picked up the gut-wrenching sinking and tearing sound of the dog's teeth into the man's neck. The feed cut out before the video could get too gory. I immediately pulled my phone out of my pocket and dialed Veronica.

"Hey, Graham," she answered calmly and coolly.

"Please tell me you're inside—somewhere safe."

She picked up on the seriousness and urgency in my voice. "Why, what's—" She got quiet. Then, suddenly, I could hear her running. "There's a pack of dogs running down the street. Attacking people." Her voice was breathy. "Shit!" I heard her call out. Gun shots went off. They sounded super close to her, too close.

"Veronica, what's going on?" My strained voice called out.

"I'm trying. To shoot them off," her breaths were heavier. More gun shots. "They're fast. Shit!" Another gunshot. I could hear vicious dog barks getting louder in the background.

"You've got to get inside. Now!"

She wasn't speaking. The only sounds coming through the phone were her heavy breaths, sprinting strides, and a multitude of aggressive and crescendo-ing dog barks. Paxton and Erica were hearing everything. The phone wasn't even on speaker, it was just that loud. Erica's hand was covering her mouth. She looked mortified. Paxton, on the other hand, looked angry—the angriest I had seen him in a long time.

I heard a loud thud, like a body colliding with a hard object.

"SHIT! Veronica!"

I thought the dogs had caught up to her for sure. The barks hadn't gotten much louder and she wasn't screaming or anything. What the hell was going on? Then what sounded like a door swishing up and then abruptly slamming shut came through the phone. A few seconds later there was another small clacking sound.

"Throw me the keys, now!" Veronica yelled to someone. She sounded a bit distant. She must have dropped the phone. The cries of panicked people pounded my ear drum, forcing me to pull the phone away from my ear.

"Veronica! What's going on?" I shouted.

Dogs were howling and barking like crazy. There was pounding and scratching against what I thought was some kind of glass. The distinct chime of keys smacking a hard marble or tile floor rang out. There was a bit of shuffling and then Veronica picked up the phone.

"I'm fine," she tried to reassure me while catching her breath. "I'm fine. I ran to a diner. Missed the handle the first time and crashed into the door. Just got the place locked up. There's like six or seven dogs clawing at the doors."

"Are you okay, miss?" I heard someone in the background ask. The frenzied people were starting to calm down.

"I'm fine," she replied, still sounding tense. "Thank you. Graham, are you still there?"

"Yeah." I could finally feel my heartbeat starting to slow.

"I need to check in with the rest of my squad. Make sure they're okay. We split up today following different leads around town."

"Absolutely."

The phone clicked and the call ended. The three of us all let out a collective sigh of relief. The room was silent for a minute or two while we all tried to calm ourselves down.

Paxton still looked and sounded angry. "How much you want to bet those were Biotect dogs? Damn it!"

"Veronica just texted me," I said, cutting off a Paxton rant before it could begin. "The rest of her squad is fine. They were able to find shelter like she did."

"Good," Erica responded.

Our attention shifted to the hallway. Someone was scurrying upstairs from the bunker. The door swung open and Vincent emerged. His face was stern and his body language followed suit. He looked Paxton square in the eye and said, "I'm working on it. You'll be the first to hear once I get any updates. Whatever questions or commentary you have, now's not the time." He yanked the door shut and retreated back downstairs.

We were all a bit shocked. Even when Paxton annoyed the hell out of Vincent, and we know he did even though Vincent would never admit it, he never spoke like that to any of us before. For once it seemed like Paxton was speechless.

"He's got a lot on his plate right now," Erica tried to reassure all of us. "Try not to take it personally, Paxton."

"I'm not. I get it," he stated with a tinge of annoyance in his voice. The scowl he was trying to hide from us said differently.

* * *

"Animal Control brought some blood samples from those dogs to Dr. Ryken's lab yesterday," Vincent informed us as we finished up breakfast the next morning. "He found conjierum in the blood. The dogs were in fact Biotect creations." A smirk started to grow on Paxton's face but Vincent's next statement shut it down. "That's all we know right now. We don't know where they came from or who they came from or what they were looking for—just that they came from the Biotects. I'm sorry I don't have anything else for you and I'm sorry about how I spoke to you yesterday." The second half of the sentence was directed at Paxton.

The apology fell on deaf ears. "Well, alright then. Thanks for the update," Paxton said, visibly frustrated.

"I'll keep you all posted." Vincent's tone was tired and defeated.

With his coffee cup in hand, Vincent retreated back to the control room while Paxton, Erica, and I ventured back up to the main floor. My squadmates were having a chat that sounded like it was slowly brewing into an argument about halfway up the staircase. Paxton plopped down on his usual couch once we made it into the living room while Erica stood a few feet away facing him. I did my best to keep my distance. I couldn't tell what they were saying at first. They were now in a full-on shouting match back and forth in Kai. I caught Erica's glance and she quickly switched her speech out of Kai, probably to give me an idea of what was going on.

"I get that you're frustrated," she said in a slightly elevated tone, "but that doesn't mean you have the right to be rude to him like that. He's doing the best he can, and it's not his fault that he doesn't have all the answers. He's not the one conducting tests and completing investigations. He even tried to apologize to you and didn't even acknowledge it."

Paxton sat straight up and nearly shouted, "Well, he's certainly not helping anyone by hiding in this damn bunker in the middle of nowhere! Coming here was his idea in the first place, remember? Also, if memory serves me correctly, none of us were crazy about coming here in the first place! We've been here almost two weeks. Two weeks! He told us we'd be here a few days. It's bullshit!

"Whether we're here or back in the city the Biotects can and will attack. We just saw that yesterday. So why the hell stay here and be a help to no one? What DREAM needs is for us to go back. The people need their president. We need to be helping those other squads find these missing people and figure out what the hell is going on with the Biotects. And what about this countdown? What do we have left? Tomorrow and then the day after is day fourteen? Then what?"

Erica replied calmly, "Listen Paxton, we hear your frustration, and we get it. Graham and I would love to be home just as much as you. I'm sure Vincent and the PSS would too. But if they're not telling us it's time to go home yet I'm trusting their judgement. As open as Vincent is with us, I'm sure there are plenty of things he just can't share. Maybe that's why we're still here, we don't know. I know DREAM needs us and I know DREAM needs Vincent, but maybe, right now, they really need us to just stay here."

Paxton listened to her. He didn't argue. I'm not sure if he didn't because he accepted what she said, or just didn't have the will to put up any more of a fight. My guess was the latter. His tense muscles began to relax.

I thought Erica was right about a lot of what she said. I didn't believe Vincent would want us to stay here if he didn't think we needed to. If we hadn't left this cabin yet, there had to be a reason why.

Once Paxton had cooled off, he turned on the TV. Erica, seeing that her work there was done, walked out to the porch. It was a familiar collection of sights and sounds. Paxton watching what little we got on the TV and Erica out rocking on the squeaky swing. I eased myself down onto my usual couch and tried to relax. I was happy that ribs were finally starting to feel pretty good.

"Set an alarm on your phone for five tomorrow morning," he called over to me.

"What for?"

"I'm gonna need your help with something."

"At five in the morning?"

"Yes, at five in the morning." He was getting snippy and irritable again.

"Fine," I replied unenthusiastically. It wasn't worth fighting him on it.

Chapter 25

The Day Trip

"Geez, Graham. Took you long enough to get out here."

"What could you possibly need my help with this early in the morning, Paxton?" I asked unamused. "What're we doing?"

He was a few steps off the porch while I skeptically stood on it. It was dark out but I could still make out his silhouette and a few of his features. I started turning around to go back inside and turn on the porch light.

"Where are you going?" he asked.

"Back inside for a second to turn on the light."

"No, don't." It almost sounded like he was pleading with me. "Erica might see it from upstairs."

"What's going on Paxton?"

"I was hoping you and I could go on a little day trip. Just you and me. I know everyone else would try to stop me."

"And what makes you think I won't?"

"Because I thought we could take a trip to Mylo, see where my old buddy Graham grew up. Vincent said it's not too far from here. It'll be great."

I froze. I felt my heart start to pound faster, and not in a good, excited way. I had to talk him out of this.

"It's not safe. Those dogs were there too, you know."

"*Were* there. And that was what, two days ago now. There hasn't been any signs of them since. It's fine."

"You...you don't want to go to Mylo, Paxton. There's nothing exciting there."

"It has to be better than sitting around here all day. Come on, it'll be fun. We can catch an Otters game. You know you'd love that."

"Paxton, they haven't been playing baseball, or any sport for that matter, since the dragon attack."

"What about your family? Don't you want to see them? I'm sure it's been a while. We could get a nice home cooked meal instead of the canned slop we've been eating."

Another unpleasant jolt pulsed through my body. He was making it worse without even realizing it. Going to Mylo would be bad enough, facing my family was almost unfathomable.

"Paxton, I'm not going back to Mylo," I said firmly and started towards the door again.

"Well, I'm going, and if something happens to me my blood's on your hands, buddy." He had gone from fun and playful to bitter and sharp just like that.

I thought about it for a second. He'd have to walk, and who knew what lived in these woods further out from the house. I didn't know how far he'd have to walk either. Vincent said we were a few miles away, but an extra mile here or there makes a big difference when walking, especially if you weren't familiar with the area. He didn't have any food or water if he got lost or hungry. He didn't have any way to communicate with anyone. He didn't have anything to help him navigate. He didn't have any way to protect himself if something were to happen. And if something did happen to him, I was the last person he talked to. The person who could have helped save him. I knew it wouldn't actually be my fault if something happened to him, but I wouldn't be able to live with myself if something did. I couldn't just give him the tools and supplies he needed; I felt the need to be there to make sure he stayed safe.

"Damn it, Paxton!" I barked, stepping away from the door and back down the porch stairs.

"That's what I like to hear!"

"Let me make this very clear though, I'm only doing this to make sure you get back here in one piece."

"That's great," he said, completely blowing me off. "I already left a note on the TV stand, so whip us up a ride and let's get going."

"Wait, what's the note say?"

"Just that the two of us are fine and we'll be back later, now come on, let's go."

"I don't like this," I reaffirmed. I stood next to him and materialized two mountain bikes for us.

"What're these for?" he asked.

"You told me to *whip us up a ride*, well, here you go."

"A mountain bike? Your ribs up for that?"

"My ribs don't hurt all that much anymore and this is where the conjierum caps me out in terms of vehicles. Artificer is my weakest strand, Paxton. If you want something more luxurious you can go wake up Erica."

"Alright, alright. I'm sorry. Let's get moving."

"One problem. We don't know the way."

"Well, no matter what we have to go down the driveway. That's a start," his tone was a bit too condescending for my liking. "And I'm sure your fancy phone has some kind of GPS on it."

I was slow to pull the phone out of my pocket, but did. Sure enough, to my dismay, it had a navigation app on it. Damn it.

"Nice. Put in a good spot for breakfast while you're at it. I'm sure we'll be hungry by the time we get there and you'll need to take your pills by then."

"I already ate and took them figuring that I was actually helping you *do* something this morning."

"Well, you might get hungry for some *real* food once we're there. How long does it say it'll take?"

"About an hour if we keep a good pace." My tone flattened with each failed attempt to get out of this trip.

"Let's get to it then. Lead the way Captain Garnett."

I cringed at the sound of being called captain. Images of the boat flashed in my mind and I pushed them away as quickly as I could. His captain comment only reinforced how much I hated this; how much I didn't want to go home, how much this could hurt. I flicked the flashlight on my handlebars on and started to pedal. It was going to be one hell of a ride and one hell of a day.

The ride took us almost an hour and a half. I was in no hurry to get there so I took my time pedaling, and we had to stop once for Paxton to pee. The dirt roads were pretty bare and scenic. Just big enough to fit a single car and with enough bumps and holes to make the drive miserable. Nobody was coming out here unless they had a reason to. We were surrounded by nothing but woods until we made it to the outskirts of town. That's when we finally found some riding relief on a paved, two-laned road.

"Whoa," Paxton claimed as we finally made it out of the woods and Mylo was in sight. We were on a hilltop needing to wind our way down the hill into town. It would be nice to have an easy ride down the smooth asphalt. Paxton stopped to take in the view first. As much as I didn't like this place, as much as I didn't want to be here, I had to admit the view was amazing. I had never been up here before.

There was Mylo, the place where I grew up. The place I had nightmares about returning to. I couldn't deny its beauty though. It was a town with a small city vibe made up of a bunch of little islands, like Venice or St. Petersburg when those places existed.

All of the homes and buildings had a Tudor style flair to them, even the small bridges connecting one island to the next. The streets were made from neatly arranged cobblestones. Instead of regular streetlights, Mylo had old-timey gas lamps that ran on electricity.

The sun was just starting to peer over the horizon and gave some color to the sky. Rays started to reflect off the ocean showing the patterns and ripples of the waves. I could hear the gentle, relaxing crashing of the water against the rocky shore in the distance. Many of the street lamps were still on and looked like fireflies at twilight. Smoke was trickling out of the chimneys of some of the homes across town, especially towards the coast. The breeze was laced with the scent of sea salt and felt refreshing on my hot, sweaty face. I could hear the seagulls cawing in the distance as they followed fishing boats out to sea. So peaceful and beautiful, yet haunting to me.

I looked over to Smooth Rock Stadium, the home of the Otters. It was dark and desolate. If there was one place I still felt at home in this town it was there, and being there wasn't even an option now.

Paxton snapped me out of my trance. "I could stay up here and look at this view as much as the next guy, but let's get down there and grab a bite to eat, huh?"

"Yeah."

We biked down the hill and into the city. The streets were pretty quiet. Fishermen were already out for the day and most of Mylo's other workers wouldn't be up and at it for a few more hours.

I took Paxton to a mom-and-pop diner called *Hackett's*. I never had a bad meal there and knew the owners, although I was hoping neither of them were working this morning. The place was owned by an older couple and I figured neither of them would be up at this hour.

The brown mustard-colored walls were lined with well-worn booths and were decorated with different pictures of people in the neighborhood. Photos of little kids' sporting events, weddings, concerts, you name it, were up on the walls. I was hoping Paxton wouldn't spot the picture of six- or seven-year-old me behind the helm of my parents' boat. I'd forgotten it was even here. The middle of the floor was filled with sturdy, brown plastic tables and chairs.

We seated ourselves in a booth and a waitress came to greet us. Only it wasn't a waitress, it was one of the owners: Sally Willis.

"Graham Garnett, is that you?" the older woman asked with excitement. She had to be in her sixties by now, and still had the same thin-rimmed glasses and silver, chin-length hair I remembered.

"Hey, Sally. It's been a while."

"It sure has. How have you been?"

"I'm good. I'm working in a support squad in Center City now. This is my squadmate, Paxton."

"Nice to meet you, Paxton," she said with a grin.

"Nice to meet you, too."

"I'm guessing you'll both need a minute with the menu, but how about some drinks to start?"

"Coffee would be great," I said.

"Same for me," Paxton followed.

Sally left to go get the coffee. Paxton opened up his menu and started talking to me as he flipped through the pages.

"Our waitress seems nice."

"She's the owner."

"Oh, so she's Mrs. Hackett."

I chuckled to myself. "No, actually. Her last name is Willis. Hackett is just a made-up name."

"Weird. Why not just call it Willis's then? You know her from just coming here that much?"

"That, and they're family friends, her and her husband Brian."

Sally poured us each a cup and left the pot with a hot mat on the table. "You need another minute, Paxton?" she asked. He was still thumbing through his menu while I had never even opened mine.

"You know what, I'll just have whatever Graham's having. He's been here. Whatever he gets must be good."

Both his and her gaze shifted over to me.

"You want your usual?"

"That'd be great."

"Sounds good," she said, collecting the menus. "Thank you, gentlemen."

"You have a usual? You've been here that many times?" he asked after she left.

I nodded as I raised my mug to my mouth.

"So what'd we get?"

"The Morning Mollusk Combo," I replied after my swig of coffee. "It's bacon, eggs, onions, peppers, cheddar cheese, and scallops on a croissant, with a side of seasoned home fries."

He made a face that told me he liked my choice.

"So, I know people come to Mylo to swim with the otters, but what's the real deal behind this place?"

"What do you mean?" I asked.

"Swimming with otters is a tourist trap, right? The gimmicky thing everyone does when they come here. What's this place really like? What do people really do here? What's Mylo all about?"

"That's it. I told you, there's nothing exciting here."

"Come on. There has to be more to this place than that."

I cracked a smile and snickered. "Fine. You want to know about the *real* Mylo. The real Mylo puts the E in DREAM. There's a lot of Omitteds here and people with low conjierum abilities. Take the Artificers, for example, they can materialize the materials, but then they have to manually build the buildings, the boats, whatever it is. They can't just plan them and then, poof, there they are. Uh…what else? Oh, I'm pretty sure the hospital gets a grant from DREAM Tower each year to make sure we have good enough Saviors in there taking care of people."

His eyebrows rose up. "Oh yeah," I told him. "Any case too serious gets flown into Center City. Um, what else, what else? If you're a Duelist you join a CLES here or leave town. There's really no other option for you. There's no military base anywhere near here, so that option's out. There's a handful of support squads, but it's been the same handful of squads since I was a kid. None of them seem to want to retire and I guess they perform well enough year-to-year to keep their jobs.

"The real Mylo is a fishing town like you probably guessed. It's the only thing economically keeping this place going, that and tourism with the otters. But once they finally find a way to materialize food they won't need nearly as many fish anymore and this place will be screwed. Not even the otters will be able to save them then." He was totally captivated by everything I was saying. I was a bit surprised.

"This place really does put the E in DREAM," he said.

"Yeah, they're not getting a lot of help from the conjierum down here. People really are *establishing* their lives without it."

"Ahh, I see what you did there!"

A few minutes later Sally came back with our food. Paxton shoveled his plate down like he hadn't eaten in days. As much as I didn't want to come here he was right about one thing, it was nice to have a real meal for the first time in almost two weeks.

"So, what's next?" he asked after we finished breakfast.

"This is your trip, remember? I'm your navigator, not your tour guide."

"I know I said it was a tourist trap, but I feel like I have to swim with the otters while I'm here. It has to be too early to do that though. Let's just ride around town for a bit. I'll lead the way and you point out anything we pass that's worth noting. That way you're not really playing tour guide, more like sight-seer-pointer-out-ter. That work for you, grumpy?"

"That's fine with me."

"Let's get moving then."

When we made it back outside, he threw his long leg over his bike with a big grin on his face. We took off towards the center of town. Paxton stopped on every little bridge connecting each island. He took in the rushing and babbling sounds of the water's flow and the bridge's architecture.

"They've all been different. The designs, the builds, even the heights," he commented, referring to the bridges we had seen so far.

"They all are."

"Really?"

"I'm pretty sure. I think they did it on purpose, to give the town a bit more uniqueness and personality. It also helps differentiate between all of the bridges."

He nodded to himself and then kept moving on. We eventually reached The Manor, which was the city hall building. It was a cross between a Tudor style mansion and an old medieval castle. The Manor had several high circular towers made of stone, which were worn from time and the weather. The facades kept with the Tudor theme—brown beams on a cream backdrop. They were in better shape than the stone towers, but still had a worn rustic-ness to them.

"Whoa, what's this place, Graham?"

"It's called The Manor; it's basically city hall."

"It's huge."

"It takes up a whole block."

"The Manor," Paxton repeated to himself. "I think I've heard of this place now that you mention it. Wasn't this supposed to be, like, the original DREAM Tower?"

"The town built it hoping it would impress the government and they would make Mylo DREAM's capital. There was a loose, verbal agreement that if Mylo built the government a large and grand enough building they would make Mylo the capital. So the town dumped a ton of time and money into this place. It took them *years* to build it since they actually had to build it by hand. Once they finished, the government backed out of the deal saying that building The Manor took too long. They decided on the newly built, state of the art, DREAM Tower in Center City, which had already been up and running for almost a year at that point."

"I didn't know you were such a history buff."

"I'm not really. I'm just paraphrasing the sign behind you."

He turned around and read the historical landmark sign for himself. "You ass! You had me there for a minute. I was about to be impressed."

I gave him a smirk. "I shouldn't have said anything and let you be impressed. Which way are you going next?"

We got back on our bikes and started pedaling towards the ocean, whether Paxton realized that or not. The morning sun was now in full form. I materialized a pair of sunglasses for both of us and tossed his over to him as we rode side by side.

"Are the roads always like this?" he called over.

"Cobblestone? Yes."

"No, you smartass. Are they always this quiet? There's hardly been any traffic."

"A lot of people walk or bike. Cars aren't the easiest things to own if you don't have a lot of money or conjierum skill to maintain them."

We kept on riding until we reached Ferrell Park. It was getting close to lunch so we decided to have a seat on a bench and grab a bite to eat. As I came back with our food, Paxton looked relaxed, the most relaxed I'd probably ever seen him. His eyes were closed, head tilted back, arms extended along the top of the bench, and legs spread out. It looked like he was relishing in the fresh air, the slight scent of salt, the warm sun, and the chirping of the birds.

"An everything bagel with cream cheese and bacon? What are we, brunching?" he asked as he unwrapped his food.

"Not exactly. It's kind of this park's thing. There was a woman years ago who lived to be like a hundred ten. One of the local news stations interviewed her on her birthday and asked her what her secret to living so long was. She said it was a morning walk through this park while she ate breakfast: an everything bagel with cream cheese and bacon. When she died like two or three years later, they renamed the park after her."

"I'm calling bullshit on that. There's no way that's true. You're screwing with me."

I pointed behind me and he turned to look. It was the food cart I had bought the bagels from with a headshot of Mrs. Ferrell on it. The old woman was showing off her false teeth as wide as she could through her saggy face and wrinkles. Her hair was thin and white, much like her skin. The graphic designer superimposed what was supposed to be her arm coming up from the bottom of the cart with her famous bagel in hand.

"Son of a bitch," he said, turning back to look at me. "Otter swimming, cobblestone streets, Tudor architecture, a business deal gone wrong of a city hall, and now this Ferrell lady. This town has to be one of the weirdest places I've ever been." He kept quiet after that and scarfed down the rest of his bagel, which didn't take long.

"I still don't know if I totally buy that story, but that Mrs. Ferrell does have good taste. You think this would be a good time to see about swimming with the otters?

"As good as any, I guess," I answered.

"Are you gonna make me bike around the entire town until I find where they do it?"

I thought about it for a second. I was making him lead because I didn't want to be here. I didn't want to be a tour guide. I didn't want to come back home and potentially face a part of my past that I desperately wanted to hide from. But this day wasn't turning out as bad as I thought it would, I was actually kind of enjoying myself. I decided to ease up a bit.

"No. I'll take us there."

The otter tours sailed out of a marina of privately owned fishing boats. From Ferrell Park it didn't take us more than twenty minutes or so to get there. We hopped off our bikes on the east end of the marina and walked along the boardwalk to the west end where the boat that did the tour was docked. I remembered that this was the same marina where my parents kept their boat. How could I have forgotten?

Their boat was docked near the middle of the marina and we would have to pass it to reach the otter boat. I was hoping my parents were out for the day, hoping that I wouldn't see the boat tied down and gently bobbing up and down in the mild wake. The closer we got the faster my pulse picked up. I could start to hear the pumping of blood in my ears.

I snuck a glance off to me right—down towards the end of a dock. My heart sank. It was there. I tried to walk by as calmly and casually as I could. It was vacant, though. I let out a breath I didn't even realize I was holding in. Maybe my parents didn't go out today, or maybe they came in early.

They owned a small commercial fishing boat. The windows on the cabin were foggy with baked-on salt. The hull had a greenish stain to it, showing where the algae rubbed against it and where water level normally sat. There was rust in a few places, but despite all that, the boat was in good shape and ran well. My dad bought it off some guy who was going to scrap it for parts before I was born. The guy would have gotten more money for the parts than he did from my dad, but I guess he just felt bad for him. Dad fixed up what needed fixing and the rest is history.

My hands buried themselves in my pockets as Paxton and I passed the metal memory. It didn't take long for the fingers in the left pocket to find my keys, and subsequently the key to unlock the cabin door. It was still on my keyring. My thumb and index finger ran over it, getting familiar with its ridges again. I don't even know why I kept the key after I left home. I guess it was just too hard to let go of even though I wanted nothing to do with it.

When the boat was completely out of our sight, I felt a bit of relief. With that behind us I looked forward to making a new, positive memory with Paxton. I pulled my hands out of my pockets, not wanting to think about the cabin key anymore.

"So how's this work?" Paxton asked once we had about a quarter of the boardwalk to go.

"The otters? There's a few different spots along the coast where they live. Having too many people around them at once stresses them out. So once we get far enough out to sea, they'll split us into groups and take us to one of the different locations on these motorized raft type things."

"And once we're there we get to swim with them?"

"Yup. The otters are pretty domesticated by now. They know the boats and people mean food. They'll even chase after fishing boats hoping to get a little something."

There were only a few people ahead of us in line to pay. An

older guy at the very front of the line was having a hard time counting his money or something, which held everyone else up. The people in front of us were starting to grumble and grow impatient with him.

I heard a bark in the distance. It wasn't uncommon, a lot of the fishermen brought their dogs out with them. I didn't think anything of it at first until Paxton said something.

"What the hell is *that*?" he exclaimed.

Out of nowhere a crewman came running down to the stern of the boat. He called out to the mate selling the tickets. "Get whoever's paid on board. The dogs are back. We're pushing off now!"

Crewmen started flying around on deck, casting off lines, yelling their progress up to the captain, reassuring people already on board that everything was fine. It didn't take a genius to see that it wasn't.

"Sorry folks," the mate selling the tickets said as he scrambled up the ramp to the boat. "We've, uh, reached our capacity for this trip."

I heard more dogs barking. The people in line chased him up the ramp, like they were afraid something was going to get them. He did everything he could from letting them on.

"We've reached capacity. We have to leave now," he claimed, trying to keep his cool and stop people from plowing him over.

"Graham, we need to move!" Paxton urged me with a tug on my shoulder.

His pull turned me around, and I finally saw what all the commotion was about. A pack of six or seven dogs was sprinting down Simmers Street, the main road that connected the opposite side of town to this marina. Some people called it Fisherman's Highway for that very reason. The pack looked vicious, like they had finally spotted the prey they had been hunting for weeks.

Paxton was pulling me now. "Get us out of here, Graham!"

That's when it hit me. These were the Biotect dogs that were running all across DREAM just days ago. I knew we couldn't stay and fight. We'd already seen what they could do and something told me that more dogs would be on the way now that these ones had found a target.

We bolted down the ramp, turned the corner, and sprinted across the boardwalk back towards my parents' boat. I could hear Paxton's hard-hitting footsteps not far behind me. Everything inside of me was against what we were about to do, but it was the only option I could think of.

The barking was getting louder. My heart was racing. I was scared out of my mind. Face the dogs or face my past. Neither option sounded great, but the second at least kept me alive.

We were nearly halfway down the boardwalk when Paxton yelled out, "We've gotta do something, Graham! We can't outrun them!"

The barking sounded way too close for comfort now. I couldn't help but turn around and look. They had just reached the dock where the otter boat had pushed off from. I took the next left down the dock where my parents' boat was tied down. The barking was getting deeper and more malicious. I could hear their nails digging into the wood and their powerful paws landing with each lunge. We were running out of time. I materialized a small chainsaw mid-run and dropped it on the boards for Paxton.

"Start cutting the lines!" I turned my head and yelled. "I'll get her started!"

I jumped from the dock to the stern of the boat, landing a bit awkwardly on the back deck. The boat shook as I landed. I started to scamper up to the cabin door, fumbling with my keys as I moved up the wobbling boat. My hands were shaking so badly and my mind was racing so fast that I had a hard time finding the right key.

I heard a thump and the boat shook again. A second or two later the chainsaw roared and I could hear its teeth chewing into the bow line. It was just Paxton, which was good. What wasn't so good was now I couldn't hear how close the dogs were. We both had to be quick.

The key. I finally got a hold of the key. I shoved it into the lock, twisted, and barged into the all-too-familiar cabin. Now I needed to get us out of here.

Chapter 26

Graham's Past Becomes Present

I couldn't do it. I saw her face then nothing but massive waves rising and falling. I heard her dazed and frantic voice calling out for me to save her, getting more and more desperate and faint with each passing second. I felt the boat violently swaying and the cold, torrential rain pelting down on me and making it nearly impossible to see or stand in place. This cabin was the last place I saw her alive. And I couldn't save her. Now I was going to lose myself and my friend here too. I couldn't bear the thought of that. I had to snap myself out of it.

I found a way to clear my mind and fire up the engines. The only way I knew they were running was by their rumbling through the floor. The sound of Paxton sawing through the line next to the cabin overpowered the engine's roar. I looked out the window and saw Paxton finish cutting the spring line. He darted off to cut the last one on the bow.

Luckily, it was a straight shot out to the open ocean. I squeezed the throttle like I was holding onto it for dear life. My eyes locked onto Paxton. As soon as that line dropped we were going full throttle, like a drag racer waiting for the green light.

I could feel the adrenaline pumping through every part of my body. It felt like it was taking him ages to cut the line. I fought back more intrusive thoughts of her and the dogs. There wasn't time for that now. No time for insecurity and doubt now, only action.

I didn't see the line drop but he held a thumb up. I nearly punched the throttle through the controls. The boat pushed forward. The line finally fell and Paxton stumbled backward from the force of the boat casting off, nearly falling over but managing to stay on his feet.

He started yelling something to me and pointed toward the

stern. His face was worried. I couldn't hear him, but I picked up one word off his lips: dogs.

I materialized a SRHG6 in my hand, yanked the cabin door open, and aimed for the stern. The dogs were just starting to make a hard left down the dock towards the boat. There was maybe ten yards between us and the dock, but they were closing in fast.

All of the dogs but one came to a sliding halt. They must have figured the distance between the dock and the boat was too far now. There was one that was not giving up that easily though. It kept up its speed and was ready to make a leap for it. I judged the gap with every stride it made. I didn't think I had the stomach to shoot a dog, even a Biotect one. I was hoping it would just give up like the rest of them, put on the brakes and let us sail away.

It launched itself off the end of the dock, getting more height and distance than I anticipated. My eye and hand followed its flight path. My trigger finger was waiting on edge. Everything inside me hoped I wouldn't have to shoot this dog. It started to descend. I judged its trajectory one more time and kept my finger steady. I didn't think it was going to make it. I lowered my gun.

It missed the boat entirely, crashing hard into the salt water, taking in a ton of the boat's wake. It was underwater for a few seconds, but its head eventually popped up. It coughed up some seawater as it paddled its way back to the dock with its tail probably both literally and figuratively between its legs.

"Whew! We made it!" Paxton said and started laughing in relief.

I dematerialized the gun before his lanky arms wrapped me up in a hug. It was kind of weird. He'd never hugged me before, and because he was so much taller than me it was pretty awkward. He let me go and I stepped back in the cabin to slow us down a bit now that we were safe.

"That was clutch!" he said, standing in the doorway as I pulled the throttle back a bit. "How'd you manage to get in here and get this thing started?"

252

I started feeling sick, and it wasn't seasick. How long could I really hide it from him, from Erica, from anyone else? I knew Paxton well enough that one question always led to another and they wouldn't stop coming until he got the answers he wanted.

"This is my parents' boat," I said flatly, hoping he would pick up from my tone and see that I didn't want to talk about it.

"We should've stopped by their house today and said hi. Could've saved us some money on food, that's for sure." I was surprised how quickly he was already over our potentially near-death experience.

"No, it's fine. It's better we didn't."

"Why? They busy or something? They couldn't be too busy; I mean, their boat was here, right? Besides I'm sure your parents would've loved to see their big city boy again."

"Just leave it—"

"What? Are you embarrassed of them or something?"

"JUST LEAVE IT ALONE!" I snapped at him.

He was taken aback by my outburst. His face wore a bunch of different expressions at once: confused, concerned, nervous, and then angry.

"Listen, it doesn't take a genius to see that you've got some kind of issue with something or someone here. I know you didn't want to come here but let me remind you, nobody forced you to. You can make all the excuses you want, but it was still your choice. I didn't drag you here with me.

"Now whatever all of *this* is all about," he waved his hands gesturing to my body language and attitude. "Whether it's a family thing, or a friend thing, or a Graham thing, whatever, I'd advise you get it straightened out while we're here, while you have the time and the luxury. Two days from now who knows what the hell could happen to us, any of us. This could be your last shot to make peace with it, whatever it is. Who knows?"

My eyes went from his face down to the controls. Maybe he

was right. Maybe it was time to stop suppressing it, stop trying to forget, stop trying to run and hide. I could feel a wave of intense, mournful emotion coming over me. A single tear fell onto the throttle, then another. I started choking up and then went to full scale blubbering, not wanting to hold anything back.

Paxton came back into the cabin and gave me a pat on the back. "Let's put this thing on autopilot, or drop anchor, or whatever you do with boats and have a chat outside."

We walked out onto the bow and sat on the deck after I dematerialized his chainsaw. The boat was slowly cruising itself out to nowhere. I was still really worked up, but was trying to dial it in so I could talk. I looked straight out to sea and took a deep, calming breath.

"I don't really know where to start," I said, fighting back more tears.

"Try the beginning," he joked, trying to loosen the tension. "That's typically where people start."

"I...I grew up on this boat helping my family fish. My dad's an Artificer, but his CAA scores projected his abilities to be so low that he didn't bother applying to the academy. He learned how to materialize things he needed to maintain the boat from other experienced Artificers that would come and go through town. My mom's an Omitted. So our livelihood revolved around this boat and fishing."

My eyes started to swell up again and I could feel my lip curling. A few tears escaped and hit the deck. I pushed it down as best as I could to get through the story, but it was getting harder. She was now fresh in my mind and on the tip of my tongue. I couldn't hide and hold her back anymore.

"My sister also helped on the boat." So much pain and release came from that sentence all at once. "She was four years older than me and was an Omitted like my mom." I paused, letting myself cool off, letting the heaviness of my emotions lift a bit before moving on. Talking about her was just as hard as I knew it would be.

"The day after I got my acceptance letter to the academy we

were out on the boat. I don't remember if Mom and Dad weren't feeling well that day or what, but it was just the two of us. Typically, when it was only us, my sister captained and I manned the nets.

"My parents told me I could captain that day to celebrate." I stopped again to breathe and compose myself. "Everything was fine until I was taking us back towards port. We were still pretty far out at sea and had a handful of nets to pull before we could head back in. It had been dark for almost an hour at that point. I wasn't used to running the boat and navigating the routes, so we were a few hours behind. The otters always chased our boat all the way into port looking for food, even at night. So when my sister told me she didn't see or hear any around, I knew that was a bad sign. It typically meant a storm was coming, and one did.

"It felt even darker once the storm rolled in, if that makes any sense. The waves got high and rough out of nowhere. The thunder sounded like it was right on top of us. The windows in the cabin shook with every clap. Rain was coming down so hard and fast that I could hardly see my sister on deck even with the deck's flood light shining on her. Its constant crashing onto the roof of the cabin made trying to hear her nerve-racking. Every blinding flash of lightning and bang of thunder scared the shit out of me. I thought for sure we were going to get struck and sink.

"I had never captained the boat in a storm like that before, but felt like I had something to prove. I had this thought that now that I was a Factotum, or at least going to be one, that I was different. That those test results made me some kind of better, more capable person— like I was a real man now or something. It sounds stupid, I know.

"The waves were throwing our boat around like a rag doll. My sister was doing everything she could to keep her balance and get the last few nets in as fast as she could. I just stood in the cabin and watched, hoping and praying that she could somehow move and sort faster.

"She was sorting fish starboard when the wave hit. Neither of us saw it coming. It nearly flipped us over. She lost her balance and more or less fell port side towards the crane that pulled up the nets."

I had to stop again. I wasn't sure if I could go any further. It was too painful. Too much. It was my fault. I kept picturing what happened to her over and over in my head on a constant loop.

"It's alright, Graham—"

"Her head smashed into the crane and she fell overboard. I'll never get that image out of my mind," I said pointing to it. "I ran out of the cabin and started yelling for her. I nearly fell overboard, slipping and sliding across the deck. The waves were throwing the boat around like crazy now. I heard her try to yell for me. She sounded like she was in pain, like she was on the verge of losing consciousness. I ran back to the cabin hoping I could position the boat to get one of its lights on her. I hung my head out of the cabin door and then ran back to the helm once I heard her voice, trying to get her in my sights. The problem was her voice came from a different direction and got weaker and weaker each time she called out for me.

"I kept looking and screaming until my throat was on fire. I felt helpless. After a few minutes I couldn't hear her anymore and had to make a choice: keep looking and potentially capsize or try to save myself. I…I left. She drowned because of me. Because I captained that day. Because I couldn't find her. Because I decided to save myself."

"Don't be so hard on your, Gra—"

"That was it, the last time I ever saw her. They sent out search boats once the storm died down but they never found her body. My parents were devastated. They never blamed me, even though they easily could have. They always tried to reassure me that it was a freak accident—that I did everything I could have done. It's never felt that way to me though. I feel guilty. A few weeks later I left for the academy and never came back…until today."

"What was her name?"

"Huh?"

"Your sister, what was her name?"

"Kira."

"Well, I know you don't need me to tell you what happened to Kira wasn't your fault, but it wasn't."

"It doesn't feel that way. If I would've just—"

"You can't live your life in what-ifs, Graham."

"I know but—"

"Do you think Kira would want you living this way? Isolating yourself from your—"

"No!" I felt myself getting angry. "I know where you're going with this. I know I need to ease up on myself and try to heal, but it's not that easy! I'm constantly afraid. Constantly unsure and second guessing everything I do because I can't fail like that again! Getting through the academy and into a support squad was supposed to be my way of redeeming myself. I couldn't save Kira but maybe, just maybe, I could help save DREAM if the time and need came. But now that it's here, now that DREAM needs us, I can't do it. Every time our backs are against the wall I relive this nightmare in my head over and over again. I'm terrified of letting more people down, or worse, losing you or Erica."

It was silent between us for a second. "There's a lot to unpack there." I could tell he didn't really know what else to say.

"Sorry, I didn't mean to—"

"Don't apologize. I'm no shrink, but I can tell you've been holding on to all that for a long time. It's good you got it out. That's a start. How're you feeling?"

I exhaled. "Okay, I guess. A little relieved, maybe."

"You've got a lot of good people in your corner, Graham; don't forget that. Me, Erica, Vincent, Veronica, Trevor—wherever the hell he is— we're all there for you. It sounds like your parents are too, so let them be there for you."

"You're right. I'll try," I said, finally starting to relax. The reality of our situation finally came back to me. "Shit. How are we getting back to the house? We have to tell Vincent the dogs are still out there, and how they found us."

"Does that fancy phone of yours get service out here?"

Veronica. Thank God for Veronica. I pulled the phone out of my pocket. It did have service. She really was a Savior. I called her and explained everything. She said she would see if she could get in touch with a local CLES to covertly escort us back to the safe house.

"I'm sorry you didn't get a chance to swim with the otters," I said to Paxton as we both walked back into the cabin.

"It's fine. Once we get the Biotects in order you can bring me back here and make it up to me," he stated with a smirk.

"Sounds fair enough."

I turned the boat around and set our sights on the marina. It didn't take long for the sea otters to realize what direction we were going and start chasing after us, thinking we had a nice haul. They barked and jumped up and through the water like little dolphins. Paxton was in awe of them, excitedly scampering out of the cabin once he heard them. He watched them over the starboard side the entire ride in and even tried a few times to bend over and touch them.

Once we docked, I materialized new lines and tied the boat down for my parents. It didn't feel like that was enough, so I conjured up a paper and pen and left them a note:

> Mom and Dad,
>
> I was in town today and needed to borrow the boat. My friend and I were in a bit of a pinch and had to cut the lines, but don't worry, we're both fine. I got you these new ones. I'm sorry I didn't get a chance to stop by and see you, and I'm sorry it's been so long since I've been home. We had to leave town a bit unexpectedly, but we're hoping to be back soon. I'll be sure to visit you both then.
>
> Love,
>
> Graham

Two CLES officers met us on the dock. They were wearing regular street clothes and we wouldn't have known them from Adam until they ID'd themselves to us. The two men led us to a navy four-door sedan and drove us back to the safe house, cautiously watching that we weren't being followed.

As we pulled up to the safe house we were met by a visibly angry Erica on the porch standing next to a disappointed looking Vincent.

Before we could even close the car doors and thank the squad members Erica was giving it to us. "What the hell did you two think you were doing sneaking off to Mylo like that? We've been trying to figure out where the hell you've been all day! You couldn't even bother to leave the number for that damn phone of yours on the note, could you? Do you know how worried we all were?"

We started our walk of shame towards the house as she kept firing at us.

"Erica, please," Vincent said as we stepped onto the porch. "First of all, are you two alright?"

"Yeah, we're fine," Paxton responded for us.

"Good. Good. Now, I have to ask you this. Did you come across a pack of those Biotect dogs in Mylo?"

"Yes," Paxton answered sheepishly, "How did you—"

"Mylo Animal Control reported seeing a pack of dogs similar to the ones a few days ago to Maya. I hate to break it to you guys, but your little trip could potentially have us all at risk now."

"What do you mean?" Paxton asked a bit defensively.

"How many dogs were in that pack you saw?" He sounded a bit annoyed now.

"I don't know. They were moving fast; it was hard to tell. Six, maybe seven."

"Did they come after you or were they after someone or something else?"

Paxton made the kind of face one makes when they know they've been caught red-handed. "They came after us."

"You're sure there were more than four?"

"Definitely more than four. Why?"

"Well Animal Control only spotted four and luckily was able to round them up before they could harm anybody. They thought they had them all, but based on what you're saying there's at least two more out there still."

"So? What's the big deal?" Paxton was getting even more defensive.

Vincent ran his hand down his face. "If dogs tracked you down in Mylo, what's stopping them from tracking you back here?"

Chapter 27

One Comes, One Goes

The next morning Paxton was as livid as I'd ever seen him. "You can't stop me, Erica!" He was nearly yelling at her at the top of his lungs. "This is exactly why we just can't keep hiding here. DREAM needs us. Sterling needs us. I thought you more than anyone would understand that!" He then spat out some other things in Kai that didn't sound pleasant.

"You don't even know what's really going on there," she tried to reason with him. "What if it's nothing, or what if it's just a misunderstanding?"

"A misunderstanding? You know that's bullshit!"

"Okay then. You want to play it that way? What if it's worse...what if they occupy Sterling? What if they arrest you? What they shove the barrel of one of their rifles in your face? Huh? What are you going to do then?"

They went back and forth at each in Kai. Paxton was near the front door and Erica was behind the two couches, almost in the hallway. I was sitting awkwardly stiff and silent on my usual couch, hoping that if I kept quiet and didn't move they wouldn't realize I was there and drag me into it.

Paxton reached for the door knob ready to fling the door off its hinges. "It beats the hell out of being here another damn day! This whole thing of laying low in this house is cowardly, selfish bullshit, Erica, and you know it! You've always known it! Those people need us. Our friends, our families, our people need us, even if it's just to stand there and tell them everything is going to be okay. But, if that's not the case, if everything isn't going to be alright, we'll fight. We have to. We can't just take this lying down, Erica. We can't let them take our city. We've gone through so much shit as it is! I won't let them take Sterling, our home, and I won't let our people die, not if I can help it. Now if you don't mind, I could use some help with a weapon and a ride."

"You don't know if any of that is going to happen, Paxton!"

The room got uncomfortably quiet. Paxton angrily stared Erica down, but she couldn't look him in the eyes. Her face was worried, too scared to give him what he wanted.

I caught his eye. "Graham, a little help." His tone was still tense and firm, but he dialed it back a bit for me.

I thought about it for a moment. It was the second time in as many days that Paxton had backed me into a really irritating position. I couldn't let him go on his own to Mylo yesterday. And if he was that dead set on going to Sterling today, I had to at least give him something to defend himself with. I wasn't going with him this time. I doubted he'd even want me to. A SRHG6 appeared in my right hand and a box of ammunition in my left. I handed them over to him.

"You're just going to let him go?" Her voice was shaky and her eyes started to gloss over with tears.

"I mean, he's right. I couldn't stop him yesterday and can't stop him today. Like you said, we're not even sure what's going on up there. It might be nothing."

"Why would they be there if it were nothing?" she cried out on the verge of tears. "Of course something is going on! I just…I just don't want to see you get hurt, Paxton. Even though I haven't really known either of you that long, you guys are like family to me, after all we've been through. And I can't bear to lose any more family!"

Her last statement hit both of us pretty hard, and it looked, for a split second, like Paxton reconsidered leaving. He was too strong-willed, though, too fixed on the mission he set out for himself.

"You should be worried about them, not me," he replied confidently as he loaded the SRHG6 with a bit of a smug grin on his face. "Nothing's going to happen to me. Promise." I could tell he was trying to lighten the mood, but it wasn't really working.

Erica hesitated again as she wiped a few tears from her cheek.

She wasn't relaxing; she was giving up. "Okay. Okay. Just come back as soon as you can. In one piece."

He told her that he would. The three of us went outside where Erica materialized an on-off motorcycle for him. Paxton hopped on and noticed the key wasn't already in the ignition as it usually was.

Erica held it in her outstretched hand, dangling it so he could see it. "Promise me that you'll stay safe, and that you'll be back as soon as you can."

"I promise," he said as his fingers clamped for the key.

She tossed it to him and he wasted no time firing up the engine and driving off. A large cloud of dust flew in our direction. Erica stood there like a mother watching her child leave home, like she had lost something really dear to her, like he was never coming back.

"He'll be fine," I tried to reassure her. "He's smart, he's armed, and he's a Savior. The near perfect combination for safety."

She gave me a weak smile, but it didn't beat out the sadness. As she turned and started to go back inside, she said, "I hope you're right. Maybe you should've sent him with two boxes of ammo though. He might be all those things but he's a terrible shot."

Vincent came bursting out the front door before either of us could even make it back to the porch. "We need to talk, now!"

"If it's about the troops preparing to occupy Sterling we've already heard. It's all over the news," Erica said stoically. "Paxton just left," her sentence trailed off.

"I didn't authorize this, neither did Maya, and we can't get in contact with the commanding Duelists outside of the Sterling."

"Well, someone had to. What about Randy? He's in charge of Militaristic Operations, isn't he?" Erica quietly questioned.

"Yes, but, if he's missing...how?"

"Maybe the Biotects, or whoever has him, are forcing his hand," I suggested.

Vincent's face became serious as a thought entered his head. "I need to talk with the PSS; we need to put a stop to this even if it means going Sterling ourselves."

He dashed back through the doorway and down into the bunker. Erica and I felt helpless. We came back inside the house and couldn't help but just pace around, waiting to hear something, anything, from Vincent. We kept the TV on hoping for some good news, but there was nothing we could do but sit and wait.

Our excitement for the day was far from over. As the sun had just finished setting there was a knock on the door. Erica and I were the only ones in the room. We both looked at each other confused at first and then worried. Vincent didn't tell us to be expecting anyone.

"Maybe it's Paxton?" I whispered to her.

Her face became even more nervous. "Paxton wouldn't knock."

She gestured for us to slowly get up from the couch. I materialized a SRHG6 for each of us.

"You man the door and I'll cover you from along the wall," she ordered as I handed her the gun.

The knocking on the door continued and became more urgent as we carefully got into formation. Erica stood in the front left corner of the room, completely still with her gun raised and ready to fire. The door didn't have a peep hole which made my job here even more nerve-racking. I thought about putting my ear to the door, but didn't want to risk losing it if our visitor was armed and impatient. As I got closer to the door our visitor banged on it again, startling me.

"I know you're all in there," a woman's voice called out impatiently. "Hornsby and you other three from Trevor's squad. It's Natalia. You need to let me in, we need to talk. I have some business to discuss with you."

Erica and I gave each other puzzled looks. What *business* did we have with Natalia?

Erica came and stood next to me. "What's this about, Natalia?"

"Trevor."

264

We both looked at each other at the sound of his name. A thousand different questions started swirling around in my mind. The first being, was Trevor still alive or dead at this point?

"Dune wants this done as quickly as possible, can you just let me in so we can get this over with?"

Erica whispered to me, "You let her in, but stay on your guard. I'll go get the others." She quietly scurried towards the bunker.

Dune's name specifically caught my attention. I slowly opened the door, keeping one hand on the knob and the other pointing the gun.

"Oh please, put that thing away," she said as she barged her way into the room, and nearly slapped the gun out of my hand. "I'm here to make a deal not start a shoot-out."

Erica, Vincent, and Emmett had just made it to the top of the bunker's steps as she started snooping around the room. She looked behind the couches like someone would be stupid enough to hide there. I kept my gun close to my side. Natalia wasn't armed, and since she was an Omitted there was no way for her to quickly arm herself. Something about this still wasn't sitting with me quite right.

"Where is he?" Natalia asked, trying to look past the group of three who had just made their way into the room. Emmett, with his own gun drawn, covered Vincent.

"Who?"

"Don't play dumb with me, Hornsby," she barked. "Trevor. Where the hell is he?"

"We haven't seen him since the night you two met in the park. No one has," I said, trying to ease the tension.

Erica spoke next. "What do you want with him anyway?"

She ignored Erica's question and pulled back her hair pressing what must have been some kind of communicator in her ear. "Send in the dogs."

Within a matter of seconds, a pack of dogs came charging through the front door. The same ones that nearly mauled Veronica in

Center City and Paxton and me in Mylo yesterday. These ones didn't look vicious though. They were on a mission. Each nose was a vacuum on the floor sniffing up any trace of a scent that could lead to Trevor.

Vincent advised us to stay in place and keep calm. Natalia's dogs wouldn't find anything and she would be out of here in a matter of minutes. The problem now was that Natalia and the Biotects had found us.

I really tried wrapping my head around what was going on. Biotect dogs were sniffing out our safe house looking for Trevor. Trevor, not us. Maybe it was Trevor they wanted this whole time? It made sense to me at first. Natalia worked for Dune. Trevor and Natalia were not exactly on the best of terms. But what would either of them want with him? Revenge? If so, then why would Dune be involved? What would be in it for her?

The house remained quiet, which was not what Natalia wanted. After a few minutes she was getting frustrated. Her body was stiff and she looked uncomfortable and displeased. A vein in her forehead started to bulge a bit. Her hands clenched into fists. Dog after dog exited the house with nothing to show for its efforts. After the last one had left Vincent asked me to shut the front door.

"So, ma'am. Why don't we have a talk about *your* business with Trevor?" he asked, trying to put on his diplomatic charm.

She focused on her communicator again, blowing off Vincent like she did Erica earlier.

"Ma'am?" Vincent prodded.

"Dune is willing to make a deal with you, Mr. President," she regained the serious and confident demeanor we first saw from her in Brexley. "She is willing to spare the lives of everyone in this house in exchange for Trevor. Dead or alive."

Whoa. It was a bold and unexpected statement. A surge of panic hit me like a ton of bricks. Dune. The Biotects. They weren't screwing around. And as far as I knew they were right outside ready to kill us all. "We already told you we haven't seen him!" I chirped nervously.

Vincent gave me a look and a nod telling me to relax and then spoke. "Ma'am, *you are* Mrs. Donaldson, correct?"

She became even more uptight and flustered by the sound of that name, "Yes, but that has nothing to do with why I'm here!"

"But you can see how it appears that way though?"

"Stop!" she yelled at him starting to shake.

"An angry wife now on a hunt for retribution since she's made some powerful friends. What else could you possibly want from him?"

"STOP IT!" she screamed with nearly everything she had. "You have no idea what you are talking about!"

I had no clue what the hell Vincent was doing. Why would he egg her on and piss her off like that? That wasn't like him and it didn't seem smart. Natalia made that clear. Did all this time cooped up in the cabin give him some kind of death wish or something?

"Last we heard he was with you and now *you* don't even know where he is. Why can't you just leave an innocent man be?"

Oh shit! My hand ran through my hair on its own and my eyes widened more than I ever thought they could. I was in total disbelief at what I had heard. I turned my dumbfounded face in Erica's direction. The man had lost his marbles. He wanted us all to die. He had to.

Natalia's face contorted in disbelief at what he had said. "An innocent man, huh?" she said in a low tone. "Would an *innocent man* do this to his wife?"

She pulled back her bangs revealing a scar on the left side of her head near her hairline running down close to her eyebrow. It was old but pretty sizable. Erica's hands covered her mouth in awe. Vincent's demeanor changed from the antagonistic interrogator to the one I was more familiar and comfortable with: the sympathizer.

"Trevor did that to you?"

Tears rolled down her face as she nodded at Vincent and replied, "Yes."

Erica spoke as Natalia let her bangs fall back over her scar.

"Trevor said you left him because he was working too much, that he didn't spend enough time with you. He told us one night you guys had an argument, he threw a stool at your balcony door, and that was it. You left."

She was doing her best to hold back a floodgate of tears and wiped away a few that managed to escape.

"That's what he told you, huh?" she asked, letting out an emotionally charged chuckle of disbelief. "He just happened to leave out the part where he hit me with that stool first before throwing it at the door."

The room went still. We all knew Trevor was a tough guy. He was a Duelist after all. But I don't think Erica, or anyone else in the room for that matter, ever pinned him as the abusive type, especially after his sob story about how heartbroken he was when she left him.

"I'm sorry," Vincent said softly. "I shouldn't have—"

She cut him off, "No. No, it's alright. It feels good to finally get it off my chest."

"You haven't told anyone?" Erica asked, surprised.

"No. I was too afraid. Too afraid of what he might do to me if he found out I did. Too afraid of what it might do to him if other people knew. He was already in pretty hot water after one of his students lost sight in one eye. I loved him, I really did, but after he hit me with that stool, I…I just couldn't take it anymore.

"That night…that night when I got home from the studio, I found Trevor lying down on the couch with the TV on. Half watching it, half asleep, but completely drunk, which wasn't uncommon for him by that point. He loved and hated his job all at the same time.

"When he noticed I was home he sat up to greet me. I asked him about his day and he did his best to hold a conversation. His speech was really slurred, and he couldn't form a coherent sentence to save his life. For a month he had been working fourteen-to-eighteen-hour days during the week and teaching a few courses at the academy on the weekends.

"I asked Trevor again that night to leave the support squad and come join me in my studio. He lost it. He started screaming about how he was doing this job for me. To give me the life I wanted, even though he really didn't need to.

"I was terrified. I had seen Trevor angry and drunk before but never like this. Our living room opened up to the kitchen so I went in there to avoid him. I was crying into the sink, doing some leftover dishes to keep my hands busy. I could hear him stirring, but was too upset to look.

"I heard him shuffling on the tile floor and turned around to look at him. He was irate and had one of the stools from our eat-in counter in his hands, ready to swing. Before I could react, he bashed me with it. I fell to the floor. Blood started pouring from my head and onto the tile. I was scared out of my mind. I thought I was going to bleed out and die. I managed to grab the kitchen towel from the oven handle and pressed it as hard as I could against my head.

"Once Trevor realized what he had done to me, he stumbled out of the kitchen and threw the stool at the balcony door. He started sobbing and apologizing to me, and the door, after the glass shattered.

"He eventually stumbled back towards the couch, probably not even realizing where he was going, or what he had done, and fell over the armrest face first onto the cushions. I guess he blacked out, because after a few minutes I didn't hear him anymore. When I was sure he was out cold, I got to my feet and ran.

"I told the Saviors at the hospital that I tripped up the stairs and hit my head on one of the steps. I know they didn't believe me for a second, but they never questioned me any further about it. I never went back to that condo. Nothing there was worth going back for. After being released from the hospital, I went and closed down my shop for good. I knew that Trevor would be looking for me, so I hid with friends and family who covered for me until my missing person's case went cold."

It was silent for a moment while we all took in Natalia's story, while my squadmates and I came to terms with what kind of man our squad leader really was. There was one thing that didn't quite make sense to me, though. "So, if you've spent all of this time running and hiding from him, why are you here looking for him now?" I cautiously asked.

"Justice. I made a deal with Dune. I bring her Trevor and once she gets what information she wants from him, she not only protects me from him, but helps me cover the cost of a divorce and a lawsuit. With Dune by my side, I'm not afraid to act anymore. The problem is, he escaped before she got whatever it was she wanted. I need him back."

"Why did you think he would be here?" Erica asked.

"Either to gain your support or get you out of his way," she answered. "Dune's gotten word that he and Randy McGregor are plotting something together, something that could potentially end life as we know it in DREAM."

"How did you find us? How would Trevor know where to find us?"

She gave a small smirk and said, "Two of our dogs from Mylo led us here. We know that Trevor and Randy have been watching and following our dogs too. I'm willing to bet he'll be here soon enough, and if he already knows I'm here, he won't be coming alone."

"Damn it!" I mumbled to myself. "Damn, Paxton. Damn those dogs." I knew going to Mylo would somehow come back to bite me in the ass.

"He'll know that I've exposed him and Randy to you, and he'll have a small army down here to kill us all," Natalia added.

"Well, what do we think?" Vincent aimed his question at Emmett.

"It is our job to take any threat towards you seriously."

"In that case we need to prepare to evacuate. The PSS and I will inform Maya of our situation and we'll leave promptly after. If you'll excuse us," he said as he and Emmett hurried down the hall towards the bunker.

"Natalia," Erica began, "I truly am sorry for everything you've been through."

She shrugged off Erica's remark as she started walking towards the front door.

"You said you don't think Trevor would be coming alo—"

Before she could finish the back window shattered, causing all of three of us to jump. Down the hall gas from a smoke grenade silently filled the kitchen and dining room and was now creeping towards us. It moved lazily but swiftly. We didn't have much time before it reached the living room.

"We need to leave now!" Natalia demanded.

"What about the others?" Erica countered.

"There's no time!"

"We'll have to go out the front. Graham, riot shields and handguns, now!"

I did as Erica commanded. Once I handed over what I had conjured, she hastily led us to the door. Natalia followed and I brought up the rear.

Bracing herself for the unknown, she flung the door open. The porch light came on, which normally wasn't a problem until it illuminated us as easy targets. Erica was being bombarded by gunshots. She carefully pushed her way through the fire with her shield, flinching and twitching with each bullet that connected with the only thing keeping her from an instant death. Natalia followed next, but even more panicked and fidgety, squealing with each bullet that hit her shield.

By the time I made it outside the porch light had been shot out. It didn't matter. The rounds were being fired so fast and frequently it made a strobe light effect. I managed to use the small amount of light coming from each barrel to count out how many were firing at us. Five, all pretty equally spaced around the front of the house. They timed their shots well—as someone was always unloading rounds while another one was reloading them. We were pinned against the siding of the house, sitting ducks.

"Graham!" Erica yelled waving her gun at me. "We need something else! There's no way we can get shots off like this!"

I had to think fast. I looked at the two of them in defensive stances behind their riot shields. The front of the house was becoming holier than a slice of Swiss. Splintered siding started raining down on our heads. I felt chips of wood fall on my hair and sawdust settle on my scalp. One long, annoyingly high-pitched note from the shots rang through my ears. Gas from inside the house was just starting to creep its way through the open doorway and onto the porch. Erica's shield was beginning to crack in a handful of different places and chip away around the edges. Natalia kept screaming as some of the rounds were now lodging themselves into the shield's clear material.

I had nothing. No idea of what to materialize or how to get us out of this. We were screwed. This time, we had to be dead. I didn't see a way that the three of us were getting out of this.

In the distance I heard a loud roar coming from behind the firing squad. The shooters heard it too, which caused a brief ceasefire. Everyone stood there stupefied, terrified of what made that noise, of what was out there in the dark. I hadn't heard anything like it in the two weeks we had been here. It sounded big and menacing, like a lion, tiger, or some other kind of big cat.

I was losing it. My body started trembling. My mind hurtled into overdrive with panic, with memories, with regrets, with questions of how to escape, with thoughts of what would kill me first. I was angry, anxious, depressed, and defeated all at once.

I started giving up. I started to accept my fate. I kept telling myself that this is where it all ended. Where my story, our story, maybe even DREAM's story as we knew it, ended. This is where I would die. On the porch of a cabin out in the sticks a few miles from Mylo. At the hands of a five-man firing squad, or whatever the hell was howling out there past them.

Erica hadn't quit though; she saw the ceasefire as an opportunity. Leave it to her to be the one not going down without a fight. She took a shot in the dark at where she believed one of the gunmen to be. A man's dying voice cried out in the dark and we heard the thump of his lifeless body hit the ground. It was one hell of a shot.

That only pissed off the other four, who started firing again. Not more than a minute later we heard gut-wrenching sounds out in the distance. Growls, shrills, shrieks, what sounded like flesh tearing, and bones crunching. I could start to smell the distinct, nauseating, metallic scent of blood wafting through the air towards us.

I caught myself dry heaving once or twice. The gas was about to close in on us now. I tried to get a final few gulps of clean air after my heaving. This was all too much for me to take. All I could picture was the three of us getting mauled next. Our limbs being thrown around the porch. Giant fangs or claws ripping through us like tissue paper. Drowning in a pool of my own blood. Maybe the gas would put us out of our misery first.

"This is our chance," Natalia urged us. "Flashlights, now, someone!" The gas hadn't reached her yet.

I conjured up the flashlights for us and passed them down, not even registering that I did it. The gas was starting to caress the skin on my arm. I had one thing to be thankful for—it didn't burn on contact. I kept trying to keep myself calm and not think about how long I had been holding my breath.

Natalia took off towards the field.

"Have you lost your mind?" Erica called out to her.

"They're with me. Come on!"

I could tell Erica was skeptical, but Natalia didn't have to tell me twice. I took off after her, leaping off the porch and swallowing as much clean air as I could fit in my lungs. I flashed my light forward and saw the creatures that had taken the men down, and the carnage of what was left.

The creatures looked like a cross between saber-toothed tigers and leopards. They were built like tigers with huge protruding fangs and paws, but decorated like leopards with unique spots running up and down their bodies. The cats had a forked tail that split into two which moved independently of each other. Both tail ends had tufts of darker fur at the tips like a lion's. Eight or nine of Natalia's killer cats were gathered in one spot. When she reached where they were standing they started jogging alongside her like they were her own personal escort.

So much was still going through my mind, but I kept running. My breathing was picking up and my chest was starting to feel heavy, but I had to keep running. That's all I could tell myself—keep running. We probably made it about halfway across the field when the unimaginable happened. A huge explosion from behind me pounded my ears and lit up the landscape around us. A strong wave of hot wind plowed into my back, almost knocking me face first into the dried soil and what was left of the dead crops.

I looked over my shoulder as I ran, not really wanting to, but feeling compelled to, like when you pass an accident on the road. In my mind I knew what I'd see but for some reason I felt like I had to see it to believe it. The safe house was engulfed in flames, shining like a lighthouse in a sea of trees.

Damn it! We didn't see Vincent or the PSS escape. I desperately hoped they made it out in time, but something inside me was telling me otherwise. My survival instinct pulled me back to reality. I was as good as dead too if I didn't keep moving. The torch that was once the safe house illuminated a military style chopper at the end of the field. Its rotor was starting to pick up speed. That had to be what Natalia was leading us to.

My eyes fixed on it as I ran even harder. Focused on that and only that. I felt like a horse with blinders on trying to win the race for my life. My breathing became even heavier. My muscles were begging me to stop. My legs started to feel like weights had been strapped onto them. My lungs and chest burned. Two weeks of sitting around the house was catching up to me at the worst time. The gap between me and Natalia had grown, and I could see Erica passing me on the left out of the corner of my eye. Damn her long legs!

More adrenaline pumped through me. Shots started coming from behind me. Patches of dirt and shards of dead shrubbery were kicking up to my left and right. I was terrified to turn around and look, but felt like I had too again. Seven silhouettes stood in front of the blaze. Backup. Probably coming from different sides of the house.

Natalia reached the chopper and directed her band of tigers to turn around. I wasn't sure what for. To go back and attack the shooters? That would be suicide for them. She had to be protecting us. She'd rather have our attackers focused on what was coming towards them instead of what was running away.

Shots kept whizzing by me. They were getting louder and clearer. Their aim was getting better with each shot too. They must have been charging towards us. Clumps of dirt from the missed shots were starting to pelt my calves and ankles. Each one stung pretty badly, but I couldn't slow down. I had to keep moving.

More reinforcements must have come. Rounds were being fired at a faster pace. That damn helicopter still felt miles away. Erica was beginning to feel miles away, too.

The tigers were close to me now. They uprooted huge chunks of earth with each powerful stride. With teeth bared and fury in their eyes, each let out deafening roars that scared the shit out of me.

As the pack began to pass me, one of them took a bullet. It shrieked in torment. Its legs gave out and its momentum carried its body across the ground, rolling and tumbling for way longer than I would have expected. It was like watching a train trying to come to a stop before crashing something stuck on its tracks. The pack got even louder, even more angry, even more powerful and destructive with each step, which didn't seem possible. I could feel the ground tremble as the rest of them flew past me.

Erica was now in the helicopter. I was close enough to hear her and Natalia screaming their lungs out for me to hurry. The horrifying sounds of guns firing, manic tigers fighting, and the safe house burning behind me was more horrifying than ever. My heart and lungs were pounding so hard it felt like they were going to burst. I just had to push myself a little further. I was almost there, almost out of this hellish nightmare.

I could see Natalia telling the pilot to pull up, giving him the thumbs-up motion. She and Erica laid belly-down on the chopper floor, each reaching out a hand to pull me in. The helicopter was pulling up fast, maybe a bit too fast. I jumped, reaching with everything I had for their outstretched arms. They caught me, but my sudden additional weight tipped the chopper. They gave everything they had to pull me in. I rolled to the middle of the floor and sprawled out on my back, trying to catch my breath.

Natalia handed us one of the helicopter's pre-existing headsets to communicate over the noise of the rotor. Erica slid the headphones over my ears and adjusted the microphone for me. I thanked her in between huge huffs and puffs of breath and she replied back with a smile. Natalia handed us each a water bottle. I sat up, immediately downed half of it, and flopped back down on the cool, metal floor.

"Who was that?" Erica asked after taking a large swig.

"I told you Trevor wouldn't come alone."

"I heard you the first time, but *who were they?* Trevor's one man, not an army. What's going on, Natalia?"

Erica took another large gulp as she replied.

"I already told you what I know, but as you can see, he had no problem trying to kill his own squad, and the President, for whatever he and Randy are planning."

Silence settled in. We all took a minute to cool off and digest what had just happened. Erica wasn't calming down though, if anything she was heating up.

"This is your fault!" she yelled, aching my already worn-down and sensitive ears. "If you didn't come to the house. If you didn't drag us into this vendetta with Trevor. If you, and Dune, and the Biotects didn't attack DREAM. The president and the PSS could very well be dead now because of you!"

"Honey, I might not have all the details about what's going on, but I wasn't the one who burned down that house. I wasn't the one who opened fire on you as you ran to safety," she said as she started to make her way to the vacant seat next to the pilot. Once she got herself situated she turned back to look at Erica and continued. "What happened here tonight, what's been happening across DREAM, it's much bigger than some hard feelings between me and my husband, believe me."

Chapter 28

Bargaining and Revelations

I woke up to a low humming and high-pitched beeping. I opened my eyes and saw that I was in a hospital bed. The room was dark except for the flashing lights of medical equipment. The noises were coming from the machines monitoring my vitals. There was a window to the right of the room's door on the wall in front of me. It looked out into the hallway, which was as dark as the room I was in.

I removed the oximeter from my finger, noticing that the lights in the hallway had now flickered on. I heard someone walking down the hall towards my room. The steps were loud, like a woman's heels clacking against the tile floor. It was Natalia. She passed by the window and came into the room.

"Good news," she said in a dress similar to the one she wore in Brexley. "Your ribs are completely healed. Right on schedule."

"Where am I? Where's Erica?" A different question then came to mind. "How do you know about my ribs?"

"You're at Biotect headquarters, and don't worry, Erica is safe and sound next door." She slowly started to pace the room, obnoxiously clacking with each step. "The Biotects have friends in many places, Graham, especially in the pharmaceutical field. Dune has had her contacts digging up information about you and Erica since I brought you here. I didn't take long for her to get wind of the prescription information for your ribs."

Damn. There was nothing I could do about that now. My mind started to wonder about how we got here. Even in my deepest sleep, I felt like I would have woken up and realized someone was carrying me off a helicopter and into a hospital room.

"You drugged us. How? Why?"

"I had one of the Saviors here at the facility make me some

special water bottles in the event we might have to bring you back here."

I could hear new footsteps in the hallway. They weren't nearly as loud as Natalia's were. In fact, they sounded like they were dragging their feet. Passing by the window was a very groggy looking Erica. She managed to shuffle into the room and rested her forearm on the wall to keep herself steady.

"Hello, Erica," Natalia greeted her. "I was just about to come check up on you."

"Why are we here?" I asked keeping an eye on Erica as she was slowly becoming more coherent.

"You're here because Dune wants to speak with the two of you."

"Why?"

"I couldn't tell you. Dune's business is her own. She asked me to bring you both to her once you woke up."

I looked at Erica skeptically. She seemed defeated which caught me by surprise. Maybe it was just the drugs, or maybe she had finally reached the end of her rope.

"We might as well just go with her, Graham. She could just spike another drink and take us to Dune that way if she really wanted to. I'd rather do it on our own terms."

"Fine," I said, giving Natalia an untrusting glare. "Let's go."

"Follow me." She started to make her exit.

Erica ducked through the doorway and followed. I pushed myself off the bed and tailed the two. We fell into step on either side of Natalia's as we proceeded down the hallway—me on her left and Erica on her right.

Judging by the sheer number of different corridors we passed, I got the sense that this place was massive. Strangely, there weren't any windows letting in outside light. I didn't know if we were underground or if there were just no windows here to hide its location? We took all sorts of twists and turns down different halls. They all had the same light gray paint on the walls. I noticed all kinds of people passing by.

Some wore lab coats; others were in suits and business clothes. Most people were dressed in regular street clothes though. How many different people were actually involved with the Biotects? I always imagined their operation, clan, cult, whatever it actually was, being a smaller collection of close-knit people. What were all these people, Biotect or not, doing here?

Natalia stopped us in front of an unmarked room. A sand-colored door against another light gray wall. She knocked and turned to tell us that this was Dune's office. It felt weird to me that Dune had an office. I still couldn't get over the idea that the Biotects weren't just a wild group of crazies scattered across DREAM living in the shadows. This facility, their manpower, their infrastructure—these people were the real deal. If everyone in here even had a basic command of the strand there was no doubt they could easily overtake DREAM. So why hadn't they? It came back to the question of all questions: what did they want? Natalia opened the door and motioned for us to enter before I could think about it anymore.

The room was darker than I expected, like the inside of a five-star restaurant during prime evening hours. We walked down a short, narrow entryway with what I guessed to be long closets with sliding, mirrored doors on each side of us. Having my reflection on either side of me felt unnerving for some reason.

When we emerged from the mini hall of mirrors, we got our first glimpse at her space. Dune kept four lavish armchairs facing her beautifully crafted wooden desk. Its deep, brown finish made the room seem even darker than it already was.

"You must be Graham and Erica," she greeted us. "I'm Dune. Please have a seat."

She was just like Trevor described, but not nearly as intimidating as I thought she would be. She had a collected and professional aura about her. I wouldn't have pegged this woman to be the leader of a group like the Biotects in a million years. So far, Dune just seemed like a regular person with a really nice desk. She wore a sleeveless, pale-yellow blouse that put her two trademarks on full display. The green ring was around her right bicep and her left shoulder had the tattoo: a side profile of a roaring tiger head. She caught me staring.

"I see you've noticed the ring around my arm, Graham. I'm sure you both already know this by now, but it's the mark of a Biotect. It separates us from the numerous other strands of conjierum. We're one of two strands currently known to have a physical marker like this, you know. I personally like to think of it as a badge of honor."

"Whoa, whoa, whoa," I blurted out. "What do you mean 'numerous other strands'? There's only five including *yours*." The thought of there being more than that instantly overwhelmed me.

"The Duelist, Artificer, Savior, and Factotum strands are the only ones recognized by the academy and government. They're the easiest to regulate and master, but I can assure you there's more. Hopefully our strand will soon get the recognition and respect it deserves alongside the other four. That's not why you're here though. I wanted to talk to you about the Kaisiust boy who was living in one of our homes in Brexley: Kent."

Some sort of switch flipped in Erica. She squirmed in her seat as her face grew stone cold and disgusted. She crossed her legs trying to look relaxed, but she wasn't fooling anybody. It looked like all of the raw emotion she had been holding on to was ready to burst through her skin, but she was doing everything in her power to keep it in.

"We are very concerned about his safe arrival back home to us."

"Back home to *you*? Who the hell do you think you're kidding?" Erica finally erupted. "The only home Kent is going back to is his parents' in Sterling. And we know what you've been forcing him and those other poor kids in your *homes* to do for you, you conniving piece of shit!"

I had never seen Erica so fired up.

Dune's temperament stayed the same, totally unaffected by

Erica's outburst. "Natalia did say he spent some time with your squad before he went missing. He must have shared more with you than we thought. Regardless, I need your help getting him back."

Before Erica could lash back at her again, she was cut off by a muffled ringtone. Dune pulled a phone out of her pocket. It was almost identical to the one Veronica made for me. "Excuse me for a moment," she said before taking the call.

"Hello," she began. "Randy McGregor? How did you get this number?" She listened. "It looks like we both have some disloyal followers on our sides then." There was a long pause while he spoke again. "Funny you mention them…I only have Graham and Erica…you know what I want."

Randy, or whoever it was, was now doing the bulk of the talking. I casually strained to hear what was being said, but couldn't make out any of his words. Erica and I shared alternating glances between ourselves and Dune. She brought the phone down from her ear, held it out towards us, and put it on speaker.

"Graham and Erica," she said loud enough for him to hear, "say hello to Vice President McGregor."

We found this a bit odd but did what she asked. Dune took the phone off speaker and brought it back up to her ear.

"What the hell's going on?" I whispered over to Erica.

"I don't know," she whispered back, "but I'm already not liking it."

"Well, I'm in a bit of a tough spot now," Dune began as she returned the phone to her pocket. "It turns out Randy was the one who kidnapped Kent from DREAM Tower, as I suspected. He was also the one who ordered your former squad leader and a group of his lackeys to kill you all last night. It seems like he's had a hard time deciding what he wants with you. He wanted you alive, then yesterday he wanted you dead, and now he wants you all alive again. Trevor reported seeing you two get away in one of our helicopters and figured we'd bring you back here. He wants to make a deal with me. You two for Kent."

I tried to process everything she said. It was a lot of information to unpack. I played it back through my mind, step by step. So many of the questions we had no answers to over the past few weeks were answered for us in a matter of seconds. I still didn't have all the pieces, but the puzzle was finally starting to come together. What about Paxton? Did Randy already have him? What about Vincent and the PSS? Were they alive or did Randy have Trevor kill them?

"What do you mean you're in a tough spot?" Erica asked with a tinge of attitude. "We're nothing to you. You just told us you wanted Kent back."

The idea of being a bargaining chip for Dune boiled my blood. There was no way in hell I was going to sit back and let her hand us over to Randy. I shot up from my seat, materialized Sunshine, and deployed the top blade an inch or two from her throat. My eyes anchored onto her. In my other hand was a handgun for Erica. She took it from my outstretched arm. Then I gripped Sunshine with my other hand for more stability and power. I was done playing games. I was done being kept in the dark and speculating what was really going on. I was done with Randy. I was done with Dune and her Biotects and their nightmare, death beasts. I was done getting hurt and seeing people die. All that bullshit ended now.

"Give me one good reason why I shouldn't slit your throat right now."

The door behind us burst open. Erica turned and aimed at whoever had come in. My grip on Sunshine tightened. I could feel the cushioning in the handle squeezing through my fingers. My eyes didn't stray from Dune.

I didn't know what had come over me, but I didn't care. Part of me felt powerless to stop it, like someone else had taken control of my body. This was the Graham from the boardwalk that wasn't taking shit from anyone. This Graham was done going along for the ride. He was taking control and driving the damn car for once. A Graham I barely recognized and hardly believed I could actually be. I felt Erica shift behind me so we stood back-to-back.

"You haven't even heard my proposal yet," Dune said to me calmly, not displaying an ounce of fear. She didn't even flinch at the threat of death being only a fingertip's length from her throat. It pissed me off even more.

"There's two in front of me, Graham. They're both armed," Erica informed me.

"You two have me all wrong," Dune continued before Erica could say any more. "I have no intention of giving you over to Randy. I do, however, intend on getting Kent back. That's the only use I have for you. You get him back for me and you're free to go. Now, if you'd put the weapons away, I'd like to discuss the details of that arrangement."

As much as I wanted to impale that bitch, I needed to be rational. The odds were stacked against us now and I didn't feel like I could make a decision alone. "Erica, what do you want to do?"

"Why would we help you get Kent back?" she called out to Dune.

"Put the weapons away, and I'll explain everything. You don't know it yet, but we need each. There are a lot of moving parts at play and since much of it revolves around your squad, I believe you have the right to know."

"You buying it?" I asked my squadmate, still locked on to Dune.

She thought for a moment but then reluctantly replied, "Let's hear her out."

The weapons vanished. I turned and saw the large gentleman who came to Dune's aid walk out of the room. Erica and I retook our seats. A slight smirk came over Dune's face: this must have been a small victory for her.

"Let me explain a few things to you two. I hope that once I'm finished you'll see things for how they really are and will be willing to help us. I know there's been nothing but bad press about me and the Biotects over the past few weeks. I want to start by saying we aren't by any means perfect, but we aren't as bad as everyone's made us out to be either. The real, underlying problem DREAM is now having with us is very old, nearly forgotten history.

"Randy told the media that our strand was just recently discovered. That's not true. The Biotect strand was discovered not long after the infamous reactor accident that subsequently created the Kaisiust race. After the accident, the government was *extremely* afraid of the Kaisiusts. DREAM had never seen anything like them before. A handful of Kaisiusts soon found that they were born with a genetic strand of conjierum, which then really sent DREAM in a panic. They named the strand Teleconcealist—"

"What does this have to do with anything?" Erica interjected.

"You'll see. Please be patient with me." Dune continued on, "The Teleconcealists had three distinct abilities through their conjierum: teleportation, shape-shifting, and invisibility. You can see how this combination of abilities could scare a lot of people, especially a government who had never seen anything like this before. A new strand of conjierum specific to an entire new race of people created a lot of anxiety across DREAM. The four strands gave its users more and more power as time went on, but besides that DREAM hadn't been changing that much over time.

"Teleconcealists became the topic of focus and study in the conjierum world. However, a new strand of conjierum was discovered a few years later: the Biotect strand. Ours proved to be much pickier of its users than the 'core four.' It also proved a lot harder to learn and master too, which meant there were a lot of Biotect related accidents across DREAM.

"People were too unskilled to materialize the wild and deadly creatures that they were. Cobras were popular with young Biotect boys. Fairly easy to materialize, but difficult to control. These boys would play 'snake charmer' and would unintentionally end up getting their friends or themselves lethally bitten. Early Biotect horticulturists didn't fare much better either. Their flora either killed whatever else was growing around it or never grew healthily at all. And I know you're probably thinking it so I'll answer it now. We couldn't materialize food bearing trees, bushes, or crops then and we still can't now.

"Once users started figuring out how to conjure hybrid plants and animals is when things really started getting out of hand. Those new concoctions were even harder to control, which led to even more tragic accidents. It wasn't entirely their fault. It was just the growing pains of our strand.

"So, between the sneaky abilities of the Teleconcealists and unpredictability and dangers of the Biotects, a huge portion of the population called for government action. They wanted anything that would restrain these two precarious strands and make themselves feel safer. The government eventually came out and officially proclaimed that these two news strands were unnatural, which is funny considering that the abilities we have through any strand of conjierum aren't exactly natural.

"Anyway, when the fear of the Teleconcealists and Biotects was at its highest, Penelope Hu, a distant relative of mine, made a plea to the president. She wanted a place in the academy for the two new strands to be able to learn and hone their abilities. Phineas Douglass, the president at the time, was on record as being anti-Teleconcealist and -Biotect unsurprisingly denied her request.

"Not long after Douglass claimed that Biotects and Teleconcealists were too dangerous to be intermingled within the general population, he decreed that all Kaisiusts, Teleconcealist or not, and Biotects be moved to the northwest region of the DREAM, present-day Sterling. As you probably know this was the area of DREAM where the reactor that started the Kaisiust race originally stood. Kaisiusts, as well as a large number of non-Kaisiusts, were outraged. Douglass stuck to his guns and kept reiterating that his decision was in the best interest of public safety. In actuality, Douglass was an Omitted who feared not being able to control the Teleconcealist and Biotect users.

"That's all bullshit!" Erica spat, nearly launching out of her chair. "I've never even heard of a Phineas Douglass. And Hornsby was the first, and only, Omitted president."

"You may not have heard of Douglass but I'm sure you've heard of Chaz Almanson. Almanson was Douglass' vice president who eventually took over for him and went on record as the elected president of that time. You've never heard of Phineas Douglass because he's a dark stain on DREAM's past. He's been erased from almost all of our historical records purposefully. Same with the Teleconcealists and Biotects, until now that is. You'll see why in a moment. And don't worry, I'm almost done. I know you're anxious to see how any of this relates to you.

"There was one Kaisiust in particular who rose up and took a stand for the two groups: Percival Agton."

"Agton. That's Paxton's last name," Erica interjected.

"They're related, distantly, but still related," Dune informed us. "One of the ways this story ties to the two of you. Percival fought for the rights of both Kaisiusts and Biotects. He led nonviolent demonstrations and service projects all across DREAM. Penelope saw what he was doing and joined forces with him while still fighting for their places in the academy.

"Despite their efforts, Kaisiusts and Biotects were still being forcefully relocated to what is now Sterling. The government started dedicating an absurd amount of money and resources to try to contain them. Support and civil Artificers were commissioned to build walls in a particular section of the developing town, making them their own little prison. Once the walls were built civil Duelists were assigned to guard the walls full-time to keep everyone who was supposed to be in, in.

"Support squads were specifically assigned to round up Kaisiusts, Biotects, and eventually their supporters. With each day

DREAM was becoming more and more divided. Many people believed the quarantined 'city' to be the best and safest thing for DREAM while others saw it for what it really was: ignorant, prejudiced, and inhumane discrimination.

"Penelope Hu was eventually captured and sent to the town. Percival Agton was too. He and Penelope continued their work inside the walls, trying to find ways to escape and continue their fight for freedom and equality. The captives living in this new town named it Huagton after Penelope and Percival."

"But the Teleconcealists had all the tools they needed to escape—" Erica began to say.

"Yes, they did. But any Teleconcealist caught outside of Huagton was shot and killed on the spot. They had the means to escape Huagton, but many chose not to. They didn't want to risk almost certain death outside the walls. Those who had become extremely skilled at shape-shifting did leave Huagton and tried to resume a normal life posing as someone or something else, but many of them didn't want to live their lives that way.

"It eventually got to the point where Huagton wasn't enough for Douglass though. He knew Teleconcealists were able to come and go as they pleased, like you said, and he was afraid that Biotects would eventually get skilled enough in their abilities to materialize creatures to help them fight back and escape. He decided to send more civil Duelists into Huagton to kill all the known Teleconcealists and Biotects."

"What?" Erica exclaimed.

"That's awful!" I blurted out in unison with her. After a second of somber silence I asked, "How could they tell who was a Teleconcealist and who wasn't?"

"Great question," she said with a smile out of the corner of her mouth. "Their blood. Like the Biotects, Teleconcealists also have a physical marker: black blood. They're the only other strand known to have a physical marker, as I mentioned before. Groups of fifty or so at a time were lined up in the center of Huagton to check for either strand's marker. Kaisiusts were cut to reveal the color of their blood. Red-blooded Kaisiusts were spared, for the time being. Black-blooded ones were shot on the spot. Biotects tried to cover up their marks with dirt, clay, or whatever they had that would match their skin tone, but it didn't work. They were also shot as soon as the physical marker had been discovered."

"Oh my god!" Erica said, covering her mouth.

"Some Teleconcealists and Biotects managed to escape, but the majority of them were eventually found and killed, in or out of Huagton. The Duelists assigned there *hated* Percival and were desperately hoping he had black blood so they could bring him down once and for all. But he didn't. They checked Penelope for a Biotect ring, hoping she could be their consolation prize for not being able to kill Percival. She didn't have a marker either.

"It went against their orders but they took it upon themselves to make a statement. After everyone in Huagton was tested, the remaining Kaisiusts and supporters were brought into the center of town. They were forced to watch as a large group of Duelists tied Percival and Penelope to separate posts and unloaded an ungodly number of rounds into the two of them.

"Douglass wasn't pleased that his Duelists had done it at first, but he hoped that the death of two leaders would quiet Huagton and their outside supporters down. It didn't work. A group of Teleconcealists and Biotects that had managed to escape before their blood testing shared what was happening in Huagton with a local news station in Center City. The story spread like wildfire and the people of DREAM had now reached their limit. Demonstrators, both pro- and anti-Huagton, were no longer peaceful. Homes and businesses were torched and vandalized. Mobs of people broke out into fights all across DREAM. Support squads were now assigned to help the civil squads, which are now CLESs, control the chaos all across DREAM. Even with the help of the support squads they were still far too short-handed. DREAM was on the brink of civil war.

"All eyes were on Douglass. And when everyone needed him to step up and publicly right his wrongs, he vanished. Chaz Almanson assumed the role of president and demanded that the remaining citizens of Huagton be freed, the walls be torn down, and any remnants of its existence be destroyed. He also passed a law requiring any conjierum user be registered with the government. That's why, to this day, you have your conjierum strand printed on your ID, granted you've been chosen by one. He hoped everyone would have some peace of mind that the government was aware of what conjierum users were out there and were able to identify them."

"Life didn't get any easier for the Kaisiusts and the few Biotects that remained however. They were still ridiculed and resented by a large portion of DREAM. Almost all of them gave up practicing their strand and stopped testing new, potential users. Teleconcealists and Biotects nearly went extinct. As far as the government is concerned, they never existed, and neither did Douglass's presidency, or Huagton, for that matter. So do either of you see what implications this story has on you?"

"Besides learning a piece of your and Paxton's family tree, no. Not really," I replied a bit annoyed.

"As interesting of a story as it was, remind us again how it relates to anything that's going on with us now?" Erica questioned. There was a bit of snark in her tone too.

"First, I wanted you to know the truth, to know how our strand has been persecuted over the course of DREAM's history. Randy and I have a bit of rivaling family history. I'm a descendant of Penelope Hu as Randy McGregor is Phineas Douglass. Hatred of Kaisiusts and Biotects runs deep in his family as does being Omitted. Randy is one of the few in his family that isn't. Like many Omitteds, I'm sure his lineage has felt powerless among conjierum users over time. Phineas, Randy, and a few other of their relatives have gone into politics in their time. They all did it for the same reason: a need for control."

"That's a bit of a bold claim don't you think?" I challenged her.

"Well, my informants working on his staff have relayed to me that he's been secretly researching and testing a newly discovered strand of conjierum for the last six months with the help of Dr. Ryken. A legitimately new strand of conjierum. My sources also believe that even with limited knowledge and understanding of the conjierum, Randy could easily manipulate its users into eliminating the Kaisiusts and Biotects for him. They speculate that Trevor was one of his first test subjects, as he seems to be behaving very out of character as of late. Rumors have been swirling that Randy can, and plans to, somehow use this conjierum to forcefully bend all the Omitteds to his will. I don't know what this conjierum can actually do, but if what I've been told is true, I can't let that happen. I believe Randy is trying finish the genocide Phineas couldn't, and take it even a step further."

"How do we know you didn't just make all that shit up?" I snapped. I was frustrated not knowing what was right or wrong at this point. Not knowing who to believe or not believe. Not knowing who was truly good or bad here.

"I don't think she's lying, Graham, about Percival at least," Erica said softly. "I remember my parents telling me stories of a man named Percy and all these crazy, amazing things he did for the Kaisiusts when I was young. I thought they were just made up, like old wives' tales or folk stories. We used to take turns playing as Percy in our neighborhood. One of my favorite stories was when Percy went out to fight a huge bear that had been terrorizing Sterling and attacking people's homes. The bear lived in one of the old abandoned silver mines. Not only did Percy beat the bear, but he brought back a huge silver ore he found hiding in the bear's den. He sold the ore and split the money between everyone whose homes had been damaged and the struggling miners. Our Percival was a hero, not an activist. All the Kaisiusts kids in Sterling heard stories about him growing up, I just didn't know there was a real person behind them."

"Percival Agton was absolutely a real person. Records of him are hard to find, but if you know the right Kaisiusts in the part of Sterling that used to be Huagton, it can be done."

"Even so, that doesn't prove anything she's saying about Randy is true," I argued.

"Right," Erica said, taking charge. "So what does Randy want with us? What do you want with Kent? And why have the Biotects been attacking the DREAM?"

"All fair questions, especially if I'm going to convince you that what I'm saying is true and gain your trust," Dune acknowledged. "Let me work through them backwards. The attacks on the DREAM by our creations were not meant to be *attacks on DREAM*. Once I got wind of Randy's plan with this new conjierum, we started off small Brexley, having small creatures run around and cause superficial destruction, hoping to draw him out that way. When he more or less bribed them to keep quiet I knew we had to go after a greater target. That's when I had one of my better Biotects materialize that black dragon your squad fought a few weeks ago. With Randy being the exceptional Duelist he is, as well as being a glutton for praise and accolades, I hoped that he and his PSS would take the dragon on themselves.

"Thanks to your squad, he never got that chance. After your squad managed to take down our dragon, Randy must have gotten savvy to our plan and assigned you four to investigate our 'attack.' Investigate us for him essentially. Your squad foiled all of our attempts to draw him out."

"So you were after Randy this whole time and anyone or anything else was just collateral damage?" Erica asked with a surprised look on her face.

"I told you we aren't perfect—"

"But you 'aren't as bad as everyone's made you out to be,'" I said sarcastically, completing her line from before.

"Exactly. I'm not necessarily proud of the destruction and pandemonium we've caused, but it's for the greater good of us all. If

Randy were to become president, or get a good grip on this new conjierum, we would all have a lot more to worry about than a few damaged buildings and casualties along the way."

Erica and I looked at each other in astonishment. She was crazy, but her actions did make some twisted sort of sense. The bigger picture started coming into focus for me. Both sides, Randy's and Dune's, were in the wrong, but it was looking like Dune was actually the lesser of the two evils. It was hard to digest. It had become so ingrained in my mind that we needed to stop the Biotects, but in reality, that was only partially true. They were only part of a bigger problem.

"What about Kent?" Erica pushed the conversation along.

"You haven't figured that out by now?" Dune asked with a smirk. "Why else would I go through so much trouble to get him back.

It was quiet for a moment.

"Oh my god…he's a Teleconcealist," Erica answered her.

"Very good," Dune replied with a nod. "He *is* a Teleconcealist, but he didn't know it until Randy got a hold of him. I was planning on telling him and getting him training once he was a little older. With his abilities, distributing Biotect conjierum would be so much quicker and easier. Think of all the people we could test. It would exponentially help our numbers grow and strengthen our forces against Randy. It appears that Kent is also a Biotect. It's very rare for a person to be chosen by two strands of conjierum like that."

That was an understatement. I didn't even know it was possible. "How do you figure that?" I skeptically asked.

"Well, I didn't authorize any of those flying apes. Anyone chosen by our strand is offered to come back here for training, free of charge to them. There may be a handful of rogue Biotects running amok out on the streets, but the chances of that are slim. Most of our new users are more than happy to come here, learn the strand, and live off of us.

"Apes are also an easy conjure for young, relatively

inexperienced Biotects. The fact that Kent's were a hybrid and were so advanced shows me he has natural talent, even with little knowledge or experience. I wonder if he's Prime.

"That first set of apes came from DREAM Tower. Kent was staying in one of those rooms up there on the top floor at the time. I wouldn't be surprised if at some point Randy injected him with the conjierum in his sleep. He probably forced Kent to materialize those apes to find you three after your squad landed him in hot water with that recording. I know Randy's not the Biotect because my informant has confirmed multiple times that he doesn't have the mark—and neither does Ryken or anyone in his PSS. The only other person that's had close contact with Randy is Kent. He's become Randy's pawn and Randy must have enough knowledge of our strand to at least guide Kent on how to materialize."

Things began to click for Erica. "That would explain why the apes never actually tried to kill us, only carry us away. Oh my god! The notes. Randy's probably been having Kent leave those notes."

"But why would Kent do all of that for him? If he's a Teleconcealist he could just teleport somewhere safe and not come back, or shape-shift and hide," I questioned.

"Randy must have some kind of leverage over him," Dune stated. "Kent also probably doesn't know about, or have full control over, all of his abilities yet. What notes are you talking about?"

Erica took a few minutes to explain the notes that had been found and our theories behind them.

"I wouldn't say it's a coincidence that he called today looking to make a deal for you two, especially now that Graham is healthy. It's clear to me that he wants you all alive and well for something." Dune thought for a second. "I also wouldn't say it's a coincidence that he had troops occupy Sterling early this morning."

"Oh my god!" Erica blurted out. "They didn't!"

"They did. Sterling is under occupation."

"Why haven't you stopped them then? Why did you let them

invade Sterling?"

"My target is Randy, not his troops. Getting involved in Sterling right now would just escalate the problem. Trust me, I hate the fact they're there just as much as you do, but I can't win the battle only to lose the war."

"Why are they there?" I joined in, before Erica could continue.

"They claim to be looking for Kent. They say that his alleged captor was hiding out in Sterling making terroristic threats."

"But Randy has Kent, so it's a ruse," Erica reasoned aloud to herself. "What if she's right, Graham? What if he really is trying to finish what Phineas started?"

"There's no doubt in my mind that's what's happening," Dune stated.

"I still don't see what he would want with us though." I said to no one in particular.

"I don't know. You've tarnished his reputation and now know too much of what he's planning. He might just want to kill the three of you himself," Dune shared. "Let you get healthy first so you at least have a fighting chance. He is a Duelist after all. Fighting an already injured man would go against their code. Then he would have his own little revenge on you. Or. He might try to force you to work for him like I believe he's doing with Kent and Trevor."

The room fell silent.

"I understand that Randy seems to be the greater evil here, but why should we help you? You haven't exactly been a saint yourself," I remarked.

"Like I said, I have no intention of bargaining with Randy. He won't get anything from me that will help his twisted plans along. If you won't help me merely for the greater good of DREAM, maybe you'll do it to save Veronica Tavares," her eyes fell directly on me. "It didn't take my team long to search your phone and find her."

"YOU BITCH!" I yelled, flying out of my seat, knocking it backwards onto the floor. Sunshine was in my hand again with its blade now nearly touching the skin on her neck.

"It looks like I've struck a nerve. Do what I say or she dies," her voice was serious now. Dune was done trying to reason with us. She had the leverage she needed.

My heart was in overdrive. My grip was so tight on Sunshine's handle that I thought it might snap from the pressure. Randy was DREAM's bigger issue here, but I was one swift jab away from taking out the second biggest one. And in that moment, I really considered it.

Erica stood up from her seat and put a hand on my shoulder. "What do we have to do?"

Chapter 29

Where DREAM Fades to Nightmare

I picked my chair up from the floor and listened to Dune talk about her plan. As she gave her spiel, I couldn't help but think of Veronica. I hoped she was somewhere safe and not already here at their headquarters. As much as I hated giving in to Dune, I had to protect Veronica. I couldn't get past the nagging guilt that she was only ever involved in this because I dragged her into it.

Dune's goal for us was simple enough on paper: retrieve Kent and bring him back to Biotect headquarters. Easier said than done. From there, Erica and I would have to devise our own plan to get him out of here once and for all. Randy was holding a press conference right outside of DREAM Tower today to announce his safe return and also to reveal that Trevor and the "missing Kaisiust boy" had been found. This is where the "trade off" would take place.

After the press conference ended Randy, Kent, Erica, me, and a Biotect sent solely to help retrieve Kent, would meet in DREAM Tower's lobby. Kent would go with the Biotect and we would stay with Randy. That was what Dune negotiated with Randy at least. Her actual plan was for her Biotect to ambush Randy while Kent teleported the three of us to the house he led us to in Brexley. From there a van would be waiting to transport us back here to headquarters.

Erica and I weren't fans of the plan. It was too vague, had too many loopholes and "what ifs" in it. Randy was a smart man and great Duelist surrounded by four PSS members who were also extremely skilled in their strands. It didn't feel like she took any of that into account. An average Factotum, a skilled Artificer, a random Biotect, and an inexperienced, half-Biotect-half-Teleconcealist boy, against five of DREAM's finest conjierum users. Dune was confident though. Unless there was more to her plan that we didn't know about, I couldn't see how or why she felt that way. Whether we liked her plan or not though, we really didn't have a choice. We had to go through with it.

Dune told us the press conference was being held in two hours, which meant nothing to me or Erica. We had no clue what time it was or where we were in relation to DREAM Tower. She wanted us to get moving though, like time was of the essence or something.

Once she was satisfied that we were clear on the plan, which didn't take a genius to understand, she had Natalia show us to two unoccupied apartments so we could freshen up. I walked down the space's small hallway into the main living area which housed a small desk, armchair, and bed. To the right there was an entryway to a small kitchen and a bit further along the same wall was the bathroom.

After checking out the three main spaces, I went back and opened the closet in the hallway. Inside was a Speedy Wash 'N Dry, a machine that both washed and dried clothing in a "speedy" fashion. That's how it was advertised at least. There were a few of these at the academy, but I had never used one before. I decided I'd shower and wash my clothes while I waited. By the time I had finished my clothes were clean and waiting for me. I looked, and felt, much better than I had before. After that I went next door to check on Erica.

I knocked on her door. She opened it, letting me in while tying a towel around her head. Her clothes looked fresh; she must have done the same thing I did. She greeted me and then retreated back to her bathroom.

"I see you also found the Speedy Wash 'N Dry," I called out to her.

"And I'm glad I did," she said, elevating her voice over the bathroom fan. "I was grungy after our fun at the cabin last night."

"I had never used one before. It did a really nice job. I was impressed. The name is bad though. Speedy Wash 'N Dry sounds like a really sketchy car wash. You Artificers are great at creating these machines. Not so great at naming them though," I said teasingly.

I heard her laugh over the bathroom fan and then reply, "I won't argue with that."

I sat on the edge of the bed and didn't speak to her again until she finished in the bathroom. When she was finally done, she let out a huge sigh while plopping down the bed.

"I don't feel good about this, Graham," she said, staring at the ceiling. "I don't really trust Randy *or* Dune. There's no way this plan of hers is going to work, unless she has something else up her sleeve and isn't telling us."

"I wouldn't put it past her."

"I just need to keep reminding myself that we're doing this for Veronica and Kent," she replied, now starting to sit up, "Do you really think this will work?"

"Honestly? Maybe. Hopefully. I don't know."

She lied back down again, letting out another, even louder sigh. "I just wish there was a more surefire way."

We kept to ourselves for a minute or two until we heard a knock on the door. "Let's go." It was Natalia's voice. "We need to get moving."

I left the apartment first while Erica hung her towel back up. Once we were both ready we followed Natalia through the maze of hallways and people again. We eventually reached the end of a hall that opened up to what appeared to be a parking garage.

A single black van sat in the lot, eerily similar to the one Vincent's PSS drove us to DREAM Tower in a few weeks ago. It's two back doors were held open by two well-built and scruffy men. No windows and benches along the perimeter of the walls, just like the van from before. I couldn't help but think of Vincent and his PSS.

"Good luck. We'll see you soon," Natalia said, herding us in.

Neither of us answered or even acknowledged what she said. I stepped into the van first and took a seat on the bench along the left wall. Erica took a seat on the right. The two men also filed in, pulling the doors shut behind them, and took a seat next to each of us. It was dark until the van started up and a small singular light on the ceiling lit up. We started to move. Erica, from what I could make out in the dim light, looked uneasy. Not car sick or anything, but even more unsure than she did the apartment.

"How long will it take us to get there?" she turned and asked the man next to her.

"We get there when we get there," he said, keeping his view fixed upon the wall across from him.

It was a decent attempt to try to gauge where we were. I didn't blame her for trying. Seeing that talking to them wouldn't get us anywhere, we didn't from then on out. We hardly spoke to each other. I could tell all sorts of thoughts were running through Erica's mind. As she stared at the floor, her face cycled between looking nervous, relaxed, and confident. It was tiring just watching her.

"It's going to be fine," I eventually said to her, hoping to settle her down. "We've got this."

She looked up at me and with a small smirk said, "Thanks, Graham."

I rested my head against the wall of the van and shut my eyes. Somehow, I nearly dozed off a few times despite being whacked back awake with every bump in the road we hit. We drove for what felt like an hour, but I couldn't really tell. Dune had my phone and no one was wearing a watch. The van eventually came to a stop and shut off. My heart pounded a little bit faster. We had arrived. This was it. The beginning of the end, at least if everything went according to plan.

The two men got up from their seats and opened the doors, letting the bright afternoon sunlight in. Erica and I both squinted as our eyes adjusted. I looked over at her and found that she was already looking at me. The expression on her face was one I was used to seeing. Her fears and anxieties were gone. She was determined.

"Let's do this," she said, stepping out of the van.

Once I hopped down onto the street I realized we were a few blocks from DREAM Tower.

"Follow us," one of the men instructed.

His counterpart trailed behind us, I guess to make sure we wouldn't run off. Within a block of the building, we could see a stage set up. Sitting on it was an upscale folding table covered by an expensive-looking blue table cloth and a slew of microphones from different news outlets. Pristine white carpet covered the stage as well. Randy must have been trying to make this look way fancier than it actually was. The stage's backdrop was the front of DREAM Tower. Barricade fencing surrounded the area with several armed CLES members standing between it and the stage.

The turnout was better than I would have expected. Nearby streets were closed off to accommodate the crowd. There had to be several hundred people packed together waiting to hear what Randy had to say.

We were led behind the stage where a white, canopy-style tent was set up. It was hidden to the public by the height of the stage. One of the CLES members on duty let us through a gate in the fencing. Dune's men didn't enter but directed us to make our way to the tent.

"We'll see you inside," one of them said as we passed through the gate.

I realized these two were the Biotects that Dune promised us. She originally said there would only be one. I wondered if she decided to add a second one after we left her office. I wasn't complaining. Two was better than one, and we needed all the help we could get. In the center of the tent we saw a man sitting in a chair getting his makeup done. I recognized his bad blonde bowl cut. It was Randy.

"Erica, Graham, so good to see you again," he said too smugly for my liking. We kept quiet. If everything Dune said was true, he wasn't exactly the kind of man I wanted to shoot the breeze with. Lucky for us, he didn't wait for any small talk.

"Diane!" A short, older woman hurried to his side. Her glasses were hanging on for dear life on the tip of her nose and she clutched a clipboard against her chest like it was something incredibly precious to her. She was dressed professionally: a white shirt with a black skirt and blazer. The bun in the back of her head was starting to loosen and get messy. She had probably been running around since they started setting all of this up, who knows how long ago. "This is Diane. She'll show you to your places on stage."

I was confused. Places on stage? I thought we were just sitting back while he did his little press conference. No one told us we were going to be participants.

Not wasting any time, Diane nudged us along from the middle of the tent, up a set of stairs, and onto the stage. We stopped on a blue piece of tape, which stood out pretty easily on the white carpet.

Diane searched for information on her clipboard and found what she needed. "Mr. Garnett, you stand here on this first blue marker." I had to really strain to hear her over the buzz of the crowd. They started getting excited and cheering thinking that me and Erica were actually important.

Her voice was nasally and borderline shrill. I had to stop myself from cringing after hearing her speak. She moved incredibly fast, like the world around her was on fire. No wonder her bun was falling out. Before I could even get a good look at my spot, we were moving across the stage. All I noticed was that my marker was to the table's left.

"Ms. Towson, this is your mark." Her's was about the same distance away from the table on the opposite side.

"GRAHAM!" I knew that voice. That familiar mix of excitement and nervousness started bubbling up in me.

Veronica was jumping and waving to get my attention. My eyes met hers and I forced a smile. I was happy and super relieved to see her, but something wasn't sitting right with me. Before I could say anything Diane grabbed me by the arm and started pulling me off the stage. She was surprisingly strong for a woman her age and size.

"What the hell was that about?"

"Five minutes until we go on. Let's move people!" she said not even acknowledging me. It wasn't worth fighting her on it; besides, my ears couldn't take any more of that voice.

"Don't worry, Graham," Erica whispered to me. "I gave her *the look*."

"What do you mean, you gave her *the look*? What *look*?"

"You know, the look you give someone when you think something bad is about to happen. She caught on right away and pulled out her phone. I bet she's calling in backup."

"You think we're going to need it?"

"I hope not, but better safe than sorry."

I started hoping this was all for show. That Dune was going to send a small army of Biotects flying in on majestic, bulletproof griffins or something to save us.

"Randy and Kent will proceed first. Followed by Towson and escort. Then Garnett and escort. You'll all go on my signal." Diane spoke so fast I could hardly make out what she said.

From the edge of the tent I could see Kent being led out the front doors of DREAM Tower by Randy. He looked like shit. Hardly recognizable. His eyes were bruised and had nasty bags beneath them. The clothes he wore were dirty, torn up, and covered with sweat stains. The right side of his face was swollen. The rest of his body was lined with cuts and bruises. Some asshole had been beating the shit out of him, and I had a wild guess who that asshole was. He was on the verge of tears as he and Randy made their way to the tent, but I could tell he was trying to be strong and hold them back. Randy whispered something in his ear as they walked the steps up to the stage.

"OH MY GOD! KENT! WHAT THE HELL DID HE DO TO YOU?" Erica nearly screamed as she made a break for him after getting a good look at his condition.

Her "escort" instantly grabbed her arm from behind and pulled her away from Kent and Randy. She struggled to reach the two but her escort was too strong. Erica started screaming at Randy, but I couldn't make out anything she was saying. I was too shocked at his appearance.

The vice president grabbed a fist full of the boy's shirt and pulled him up the stairs onto the stage. He was too worn down, too beaten, too damaged to even look at us. Not to mention how ashamed he probably felt.

"Don't try anything stupid," Erica's escort warned her while materializing a handgun in his other hand and pressing it against her back.

The crowd began to roar. Diane ushered Erica along next, then me. I felt the barrel of a gun pressed against my back as we walked to my mark. My escort led me in such a way that the crowd wouldn't be able to see it, but I was now getting the same hostile treatment as Erica. My eyes were bombarded by flashing lights from photographers and recording equipment as we walked to my mark.

"Same goes for you. Don't even think of trying anything," he said to me before leaving the stage, dematerializing the handgun so no one would see it. He rematerialized the gun once he made it to the top of the steps and watched me like a hawk, just waiting for me to move the wrong way so he could pop a cap in me. I looked to my right and saw Erica's escort doing the same as mine.

She was sobbing, covering her nose and mouth with her hands. She went to kneel down but her escort yelled for her to keep standing. The crowd might not have heard him, but she certainly did. I didn't know what to do, so I searched for Veronica. She was in the middle of the sea of people on Erica's side of the stage. Her hands were covering her mouth and nose, like Erica's, as if she were expecting something tragic to happen. She knew something was up, but no one else in the audience had caught on yet.

I looked over at my escort again. He was trading in his handgun for some type of rifle that someone on the ground level handed him. I recognized the gun; it was a type of rifle that was normally loaded with tranquilizer darts. I found that slightly reassuring. If anyone decided to act out today at least they wouldn't be taking a real bullet. I looked to my right and saw that Erica's escort now had one too.

Randy and Kent, who had been standing up until this point, now took their seats at the table causing the cheering crowd to quiet down.

"Ladies and gentlemen of DREAM, before we begin today, I would like to introduce you to our special guests on stage. Sitting to my left is a young, Kaisiust boy named Kent. You may remember him as the boy who went missing from DREAM Tower a few weeks ago. After an extensive search across this DREAM, we found him in Sterling early this morning safe and sound."

The crowd erupted with applause and cheers.

He continued as the crowd died down. "To my left is Mr. Graham Garnett, and to my right, Ms. Erica Towson. Both are members of the support squad that has been working tirelessly to fight off the Biotect monstrosities and end their reign of terror over us."

The crowd got even louder and more animated.

"I have two final guests for you that I would now like to invite up with us on stage. Please welcome President Hornsby accompanied by Mr. Trevor Donaldson, the leader of Mr. Garnett's and Ms. Towson's squad."

Vincent and Trevor entered the stage by Erica. It really was Vincent! He made it out of the bunker alive. The PSS was nowhere to be found. Maybe they weren't as lucky. He didn't look as bad as Kent, but was a bit roughed up himself. He had a very alarming look on his face, like focused and determined frustration. Like he knew he was in a bad spot, but was going to do everything he could to get out of it.

"Yesterday we performed a raid on a building here in Center City that we suspected of being used to store and distribute Biotect conjierum. Not only were we able to confiscate hundreds of vials of the conjierum and arrest the dealers on site, but we had the added bonus of rescuing Mr. Donaldson who had been held hostage there for several weeks. I'm sure many of you remember hearing of his mugging and capture."

The crowd broke out into a roar again. I began to feel sick. If only these people knew how badly they were being lied to.

Trevor escorted Vincent between me and Erica, right behind where Randy and Kent were sitting. Trevor had changed. His face was cold, harsh, and empty, almost robotic. So were his movements and mannerisms. Something else was different about him too. It was his eyes. They were a royal purple color now.

Erica and I somehow caught each other's attention. I mouthed over to her, "*What's going on?*"

She had calmed down a little, but only enough to give me a confused look and shrug of her shoulders.

"Over the past few weeks many bizarre things have been happening across DREAM. It has caused much stress upon everyone in some form or another. As you all know I was placed on administrative leave by President Hornsby after my own stress got the better of me. In my absence, Maya Varma was appointed as acting vice president until I was deemed fit to return to work. I am pleased to announce that as of today, I have been reinstated and will be back in office, effective immediately."

There was applause which quickly died down as Randy looked to continue.

"During my absence Kent here was abducted from DREAM Tower by the Biotects: the menacing group that has been terrorizing you and your families with their savage, reckless, wretched creations. He became an invaluable resource in our investigation against these abhorrent people and I am proud to say we now have him back. Alive and well. Ready to continue our work in bringing the Biotects to justice!"

The crowd broke out in excitement again.

"Stand with me, Kent," he said. "Your return is one small victory in our ongoing fight against these miscreants."

The two stood together. Randy raised Kent's right arm into the air, like he was a boxer who had just won his match. The cheers grew louder. Something was wrong though. Kent didn't look like he had just won anything. He picked up his head and yelled something in Kai at the top of his lungs, which blared through the speakers. It sounded like it took him nearly everything he had to get his message out loud and clear.

Randy let go of Kent's arm, materialized a handgun in his same hand, and swiftly raised it to Kent's temple. *POP.* Blood and brain matter splattered across the stage. Kent's limp body fell to the floor. His dark, black blood started soaking into the white carpet.

Everyone in the crowd started freaking out. Screams of fear pounded my ears. People scratched and clawed their way through one another to escape. The CLES members lining the fence raised their weapons. More had arrived to surround the crowd. They were stuck. A captive, terrified audience. I was frozen. Stunned. My mind couldn't process what it was seeing let alone any emotion to tie to it.

"WHAT THE HELL ARE YOU DOING?" Vincent yelled as Trevor yanked his arm to shut him up.

I heard Erica letting out a bloodcurdling wail. She had fallen to her knees. "HOW COULD YOU?" Her voice was hoarse, full of rage and despair. "You know what he said? HE SAID YOU'RE THE *TRUE* MISCREANT! GO TO HELL YOU TYRANNICAL PRICK!"

He turned and looked her in the eye without any sort of emotion or feeling, just a wry smirk. It seemed so effortless to him, to gun down a childlike that with all of DREAM watching.

"Yes, ladies and gentlemen, Kent's return was one small victory in our ongoing fight against the Biotects. Because now that he is gone, there is one less traitor in our midst. When we found Kent and his Biotect captors in Sterling we realized he was just as diabolical as the men who abducted him from DREAM Tower. Kent was working with them to distribute Biotect conjierum in Sterling and was teaching people basic materializing methods and techniques. He was never a victim at all, nothing more than a wolf in sheep's clothing.

"I additionally learned that Kent was no ordinary Kaisiust boy. He was a Biotect himself. You can see his Biotect marker with your very own eyes: a green ring of pigmentation around his left bicep. As if that didn't make him dangerous enough, Kent was also a Teleconcealist. The Teleconcealist strand is genetically exclusive to Kaisiusts and grants its users the powers of teleportation, shape-shifting, and invisibility.

"In fact, many Kaisiusts are secretly Teleconcealists, using their abilities for their own advantage at our expense. The person next to you could be a Kaisiust in disguise. Your pet could be a Kaisiust covertly stealing from you. There could be a person standing behind you right now, and you might not even be able to see them. These people are dangerous and need to be identified and monitored. Like the Biotects, Teleconcealists have a physical marker of their own. One way we can indeed identify them: black blood," he stated gesturing to the dark stains in the carpet.

Chaotic chatter broke out. People didn't know what to think, what to feel, or what to do.

"Some of you might still be wondering how and why Kent came into our custody in the first place. As a Teleconcealist he had great value to the Biotect leader: a woman named Dune. Kent was a known distributor of Biotect conjierum in Brexley, helping Dune grow her horde of misfits. As a Teleconcealist, despite his young age and limited knowledge and experience with his abilities, he was able to do his job with great success and efficiency. He was captured from DREAM Tower to continue this work in Sterling.

"My friends, these two groups, the Biotects and Kaisiusts, are planning to join forces to overthrow and destroy us all. Joining forces to take everything you have and rule DREAM through fear and brutality. I've seen their work with my own eyes. While on my leave, I dedicated my time to getting to the bottom of this, to figuring out their hidden agenda. This is it. And I promise you all, I will not stand for it!"

People were believing the bullshit he was feeding them—whistling and cheering for him.

Erica had had enough. "YOU LIAR!" Erica shrieked, rushing at him. She didn't get very far. A dart from her escort's rifle lodged into her neck. Her lanky frame fell to the ground instantly, stirring up even more pandemonium. Her escort stepped out on stage and dragged her body off. I felt powerless. Scared shitless. Kent was dead. Erica might have been too, who knew what was actually in that dart at this point. Any help from Dune was nowhere to be found.

"She's right! YOU'RE A LIAR AND A FEARMONGER!" Trevor yanked Vincent's arm again for his remark.

Randy continued on like he never heard Vincent. "My fellow citizens, more traitors and enemy sympathizers stand among us, Ms. Towson being one of them. But I regret to inform you that the president is one as well. President Hornsby claims that he and Mr. Donaldson's squad had left Center City for their own safety. This was not entirely true. They were secretly wheeling and dealing with the Biotects and Kaisiusts in a remote location outside of your eye. Not only did they abandon you, but they betrayed you.

"They were hiding from *you*! They were plotting against *you*! The president sent me away not to better myself or atone for my sins, but because I was growing wise to him and his plans. Instead of standing up to the enemy, he has been making deals with both parties behind our backs to ensure his own safety once they inevitably overran and dominated DREAM. You all know Vincent Hornsby is an Omitted. He has no power to stop or control these people. I am telling you that he is willing to let the Biotects and Kaisiusts have full reign of DREAM if it means his own self-preservation. You've already seen him do this once! While President Hornsby was safely tucked away, Biotect dogs ran wildly through our cities' streets all over DREAM."

"I WOULD NEV—"

"I will not stand around any longer and watch the president let these terrorists roam freely! He's a fraud, a coward. *He's* the liar. He's one of them! He's putting all of our lives at risk by not keeping these people in check. Mr. Donaldson, if you would."

In the same fashion as Randy, Trevor raised a handgun to Vincent's head and pulled the trigger. Vincent didn't even have time to react. As his lifeless body fell to the ground, I lost it. The stage's white carpet now had a large stain of red to go with the black. It was too much for me to take. Everything was crumbling before my eyes. Hot, ugly tears started running down my face. Without thinking I started to break towards Vincent's body until I was met by Trevor's gun inches from my face. His empty, purple eyes stared right through me.

About half of the crowd was in a frenzy, doing anything they could to escape past the CLES members. Terrified that they might be the next ones gunned down. The other half had fallen for Randy's propaganda hook, line, and sinker, and were as loud and rowdy as ever.

"That leaves our final guest."

Chapter 30

The Start of a Lucid Dream

"GRAHAM, RUN!" I somehow managed to hear Veronica shout at the top of her lungs.

My eyes frantically bounced through the crazed crowd trying to find her. I couldn't. Damn it, I couldn't find her!

POP!

Someone had fired a gun, but I didn't see who. I collapsed on stage and covered my head. I fell over into the fetal position. The man that used to be Trevor left me to try to find the gunman in the crowd. The shrieks and howls from beyond the stage were louder and more desperate than ever before.

"GODDAMMIT!" I heard Randy yell.

He'd been shot. He was clutching his left shoulder with his right hand. Blood started to seep through his fingers.

Something came over me. I sat up, conjured a gun of my own, and aimed for his head. This was my shot. My opportunity to end everything Randy was beginning. Right here. Right now.

POP!

I had been shot. My neck started stinging. I could feel something stuck in my skin. I immediately felt woozy and weak. A burning sensation started jolting down my body. The gun fell out of my hand. I reached up to feel what had hit me. It was a dart, just like the one that brought down Erica. Large men from off stage rushed to whisk Randy away.

"GRAHAM!" Veronica's faint voice called me. I couldn't tell where or how close she was. My vision was fading. Everything around me was slowly turning white. My muscles were shutting down, giving way to gravity. The panicked noises around me started dying down until I couldn't hear them at all. I couldn't hear anything anymore. I couldn't see anything either.

Randy, the stage, the people, they were all gone. White. Just an endless, white, silent void. Everything that existed only seconds ago was now completely gone. Erica, Veronica, Paxton, my family, would I ever see them again? I thought I was dead. I kept asking myself if this was all there was after you died. Silent, lonely, white nothingness.

Out of nowhere a blurry figure appeared a few yards away from me. I tried to get to my feet. My body began to feel strong again. My vision sharpened up a bit. It felt like I was being recharged.

I heard footsteps coming towards me. I made it to my feet and rubbed my eyes. I couldn't believe what I was seeing. Standing in front of me, was me. A purple-eyed version of me. Identical in every other way besides the eyes. The same purple eyes Trevor now had. I was beyond freaked out.

"Who...who are you?" I asked.

"I'm you. Now let's get moving, we've got a lot to do if we're going to get you out of here."

AFTERWORD/ACKNOWLEDGEMENTS

It's always been a dream of mine to write and publish a novel. As a child I loved to write short stories and share them with my family. Growing up I wanted to be an author but was afraid of the financial instability it would bring. I also never felt confident in having an idea for a story that people would actually want to read.

During the spring of 2015 I put the first words of this story on a Google Doc. Writing was an occasional hobby I had when I felt inspired at that point. I didn't plan on it becoming anything more than that. It wasn't until about three years later when I started my current teaching position that I put serious time and energy into this book. I was initially motivated by my students who had no fear of chasing their dreams, despite how difficult those dreams may be to achieve. If they weren't afraid to pursue their passions and put stock in themselves why shouldn't I do the same? Why couldn't this story be more than just something I wrote for fun on a Google Doc?

Getting to this point was truly a team effort and I want to thank a handful of people for their work and support.

I want to start off by thanking my local library for giving me a place to write in peace. I'll always have fond memories of sitting at a table in the corner, throwing on some background music via YouTube, and typing away for hours on Saturday mornings during the summer.

Thank you to the many iterations of my creative writing class for reading portions of this story at its sloppiest, giving me the constructive criticism I needed to get to this point, and always being a motivating and inspiring presence for me.

I also want to give a special shout out to Beth Barlet and Matt LaPalomento for their constant support and genuine interest in how this book was progressing over the years. Your check-ins always gave me a smile and helped me validate my time and effort in this project.

Hats off to Ryan Bunting for doing an amazing job on the cover art. Thank you for all of your patience, stylistic ideas, insight on the self-publishing process, and overall positive energy. Working with you to get this all-important, and potentially very stressful, part of the book complete was enjoyable and fun.

A huge thanks goes to Chad Meadows for being an awesome friend and mentor. Thank you for reading through a very long draft of this story as well as all of your insight and advice on the writing and publishing process.

Lastly, I can't thank my wife, Sonia, enough for all of her dedication and support. Thank you for your countless hours of line editing and discussing the details of this story with me. There's no way I could have done this without you!

Where DREAM Fades to Nightmare is the first book in this series, and I hope you stick around to see what happens next. Thank you for the time you spent reading this book and making my dream of becoming a published author come true.

Made in the USA
Middletown, DE
19 September 2021